Kiss
of the
King Brown

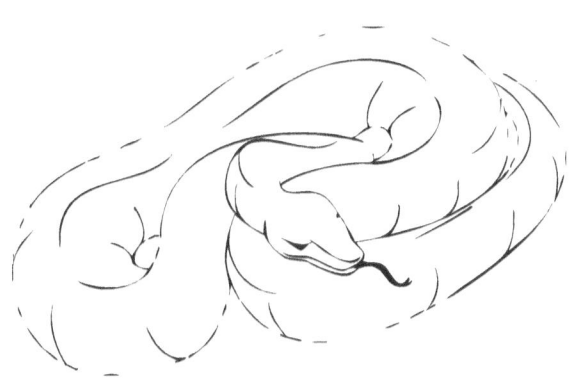

John Condliffe

ISBN 978-0-9872214-0-7

www.kissofthekingbrown.com.au

Dedicated to:

Those who were here before.
Those who came.
Those who are here.
Those who are to come.
Thank you to my beautiful girls:
Maureen.
Alison, Janice, Angela and Katherine.

The Race

Sean Buttenberg cuffed his mate on the shoulder. 'Righto, carrot head, race you to school.'

'You're on, ya Abo-loving bastard!' The freckles on Johnny McCarthy's face danced.

'Shit,' Sean cursed as Johnny made a quick start. His Malvern Star was flying before Sean had mounted his pedals, but Sean soon gained. They built up good speed. The pregnant-looking old Austin school bus was the first obstacle to navigate. Johnny launched himself around it, the bike swerving and just missing the rear bumper bar. Tearing along beside it, the kids on board cheered and clapped them on, their hands and scarves hanging out the windows. They sped by the open windows.

'Silly bastards!' the driver cried out.

Sean waved as he hurtled past.

Johnny went to the side of the road and nearly lost control as he hit a pothole. Sean avoided it and shot past. He had the open road in front of him until a Ford, Sid Filo's, from the co-op, came out of the last street on the left and nearly cleaned them up. Sean swerved, Sid Filo gunned the big car away from them. Sean stuck to his lead and even Frank Symon's veggie cart didn't slow him. The big wheels of the wagon turned slowly, and it hugged the roadside verge. The huge sides of the wagon dwarfed the boys. The old grey horse seemed nearly dead in its traces, but it whinnied in fright as they raced past. The old man, face as brown and cracked as a leather boot, whooped and hollered.

'Go for it, boys!'

Sean took off his school cap and waved it madly.

Sean was now on the slow sweep and rise that led up to the bridge. On his right was the impenetrable thickets and the blackened stump of the Dingarra tree, on his left the co-op. He swept past trucks, drays and train bogeys that were being loaded and unloaded from raised bays. The place swarmed with workers. Sean saw that Mr Filo had arrived and was talking to a group of workers near the gate, day labourers looking for work. They looked up as the boys swung past.

Sean realised now that it was not such a good idea to be out front. The long, slow climb and sweeping bend meant he was cutting the way for his competitor. He also knew that Johnny was stalking him, and could take him at any time. He slowed down to save his energy. Johnny slowed with him. Sean looked behind. Johnny's face was red. Sean felt the sweat dripping from his forehead, and the dampness under his school cap, back and armpits. He was breathing heavily.

The bridge was big but it was not wide. It only had space for one vehicle at a time, and cars, carriages or bikes stopped at a white line on the entrance verge and waited until it was clear and safe to cross. Sean realised he did not have that luxury. He passed Mr Willis in his chemist's delivery van. The river sparkled far below. He stood up on his pedals and gunned the bike forward. This was his chance. Mr Willis's cigarette glowed red. Sean sped past. He could hear Johnny close behind. Sean was intent on a head long rush across the bridge but the looming carriage of Jim Owen's big Blitz truck with a fully loaded timber jinker was swaggering its way across the carriageway. Three large red-gum logs strained at their chains on the tray. The clearance on either side was less than two feet and the truck and jinker were over forty feet long. The big V-eight of the army surplus truck was in full throttle.

This is going to be close, thought Sean, but it was just another hurdle to get by. The pedestrian walkway on the right side of the bridge was busy with kids on their way to school and people going to work. Sean was aware of the squeal of breaks as he sped into the gap on the left side, between the truck and the railing of the bridge. The big wheels of the monster truck blurred past, but Sean focused only on the outlet at the jinker's end. He felt the hot air as the truck shuddered past. The noise was so loud it hurt his ears. He crouched down low over his bike to minimise his profile and shot out of the moving tunnel like a rabbit out of a hole. He nearly went down as his front wheel caught a large gap in the timber lattice that was the road way of the bridge, but he stayed up and regained balance. Johnny was right on his tail. Sean was ahead but still in trouble. Johnny would jump him on the downhill run over the bridge and onto the school.

Sean's ears seemed to explode with an enormous bang now that he was out of the wind tunnel and away from the bridge and truck. His heart thumped. He had to get to the bike rack at Saint Joseph's before Johnny. He crested the downward slope. His bike was flying. Sean was desperate. He knew Johnny would make his move now. He saw the big gates of the school in the distance. In desperation he went into the gravel and put his bike into a forty-five degree skid. Dust, stone, gravel and bike skidded along the ground. Johnny, following closely, followed him into the gravel. The sudden skid threw him off and he over corrected. He rode straight into the deep gutter that ran along the side of the road. Sean pushed up, corrected and headed off again towards the prize. Johnny took longer to recover. Sean knew he had him. He looked back as Johnny manfully tried to make up the distance, but it was no good. Sean stopped just before the school gate and waited for his mate. Johnny came up to him.

'Why haven't you finished?'

Sean wiped the sweat from his face and removed his cap. 'You're my mate. Only a trick saved me. We were running even.' They gave each other the clenched fist salute and then instinctively looked behind them at the road and the bridge rising in the distance. There was a cloud of dust and a crowd of people. A line of cars and conveyances lined up, reaching into High Street. They looked at each other.

'Oh, shit.'

Rumour and Punishment

Sean made his way into the school ground. It was quieter than usual. The eerie silence was backgrounded by the sound of police sirens in the distance and the town fire alarm. They were in for it, Sean thought, really in for it.

His mouth was dry and he could feel his stomach knotting. 'Look, Johnny, if anyone asks, it was my idea. You stayed at my place. It was my idea, right. If anyone was killed...' The thought shook him.

'No way, we are in this together.' They faced off.

Berty White raced up, his pudgy face flushed with excitement. 'Have you heard? Some kids were racing and...' His voice trailed off. He circled them. 'It was you, wasn't it?'

Sean turned on him.

Berty quickly changed the subject. 'Did you hear Mr Campbell has bought the Koonarook Mill from old Hughsey and wants the council to give him the swamp for a camping ground?'

Sean grabbed Berty's shirtfront. Berty stumbled back.

Johnny put a hand on Sean's shoulder. 'Easy mate, take it easy.'

Sean released the small boy. 'Sorry, Berty, just a bit agro today.'

Berty giggled nervously. 'Yeh, no worries, Sean.'

'Where d'ya hear the news about the mill?'

'My dad says Campbell made an offer he couldn't refuse.'

Sean shook his head. It was hurting. He would have to ask his dad about this. He looked to Johnny for encouragement.

'Old man White is normally on the money,' Johnny said.

'Yeh,' Sean heard himself saying. The events of the last week or so crowded into his mind. He put his hand to his forehead and rubbed. It didn't make his headache any better.

His thoughts were interrupted by the strident voice of the Head Sister. 'Mr Buttenberg, Mr McCarthy! A word if you please.'

Sean looked at Johnny.

Berty backed off. 'Good luck,' he whispered. His face was even more splotched and discoloured than usual. Sean scuffed his hair.

This wasn't going to be good. The Sister's face, framed by the nun's headpiece, was scarlet. Her thin mouth was curved in a tight grimace, her eyes were mere slits. Her hands were on hips, the right one crooked a little so she could play with the rosary beads. The cross was angrily poking out from the large black belt. Sean looked steadily at the ground. His shoulders drooped. His shoes scraped along the blue metal.

'Hurry on now, you two.'

A group of grade fours were watching the proceedings off to one side. They scurried away like a mob of sheep.

Sean took off his school cap as he climbed the verandah stairs to the Head Sister's fury. Johnny followed suit. Sean noticed that a band of sweat had formed white shadows along the rim of his cap. He hid it behind his back as he approached the nun. He wished he had his Bora Bora penny with him now to protect him. The Sister's quick, angry steps, her back, stiff and rigid, led them to her office door.

'Mr Buttenberg, please stand and wait outside my office. Mr McCarthy, accompany me.'

Sean started to speak. 'Sister, it was my...'

She turned on him. 'Mr Buttenberg, please do not add to your woes with bad manners.'

He put his back to the wall and looked out over the playground. Students had formed into groups and were looking up to where he stood, chatting and talking excitedly. One pointed at him. He saw Mary Addison. She stood slightly apart from the others, with her head down. He saw that most of the Koonarook kids had not made it to school yet. He looked along the verandah. The nuns were gathered in a group. Even Mrs Newcomb, the school clerk, was there. Their excited voices floated in the air like arrows before they descended to strike. He looked over to the shelter shed. The resident sparrows were waiting impatiently for the kids to go in. The magpies, similarly, were waiting on the back fence. He looked up into the sky. A tiny speck indicated the sea eagle on patrol, its giant white wings with black after-feathers giving him the identification. He felt awkward and sweaty even though the morning was chilly. The nuns moved into the school yard and organised the children into playgroups.

The door opened. Johnny came out. He looked chastened and cowed, like a yard dog. He seemed smaller than before and his complexion had faded, even his freckles were paler. Then Johnny looked at him and the familiar cheeky larrikin face reappeared. He winked. Sean returned his gesture and cocked his head in their secret salute.

'Come in, Mr Buttenberg.' The Head Sister's voice boomed like a cannon enfilading a row of soldiers. Her office was all too familiar. The green light of the cobra lamp glowed in the dark space. The Head Sister was sitting behind the desk. Her hand held a big black fountain pen with gold inlay. She was writing furiously.

'Sit down, Mr Buttenberg.' She placed the pen on her writing pad. 'What do you have to say for yourself?'

Sean felt uncomfortable. He had been here before. There was an empty feeling in his stomach, his hands were clammy. 'Johnny stayed at my place yesterday...'

The nun interrupted him irritably. 'Mr Buttenberg, I am well aware of what happened yesterday. What happened this morning?'

Sean regathered himself and looked directly at the Sister. Her eyes flashed. 'I talked Johnny into having a race.' He paused.

The Sister shook her head. 'Is that all you have to say?'

'We came a draw, Sister.'

Sister Hildegard shook her head. Then she exploded. 'How dare you insult me with that cock and bull answer!' Her voice cut through him. 'Most of our Victorian school children are stuck on the other side of the river, as well as many business people. Mr Filo from the co-op phoned to ask if you had made it to school and not been killed on the bridge. He said he had nearly killed you in Koonarook. He had Mr Willis there with him. They have set up the co-op as an evacuation point for all those stranded on the other side of the river. Mr Willis is in a state of nervous shock and they have had to lay him down. He thought you two were going to die. The bridge is not expected to be open for two to three hours. Mr Owen's truck and load are blocking it. You may remember there was a truck on the bridge you rode at like kamikaze pilots? Apparently, Mr Owen had to break so hard he lost his load. It is lucky for him that he did not end up in the river. On top of that, we have the police and fire services on both sides of the river called out to try and clear up this mess. ' She took a deep breath. She looked directly at him.

Sean fidgeted in his seat. The sweat popped out on his back and forehead. He felt sick. The ache in his head became worse. His stomach ached. He looked at her green cobra lamp. 'Mr Buttenberg, will you please look at me and try to explain to me what happened.'

'I challenged Johnny to the race. It was my fault.'

Sister Hildegard stood up very quickly. Sean thought she might take off like a V2 rocket. Her hands slammed down on her desk. The big telephone moved sideways a couple of inches, but the green cobra stoically held its ground. 'Mr Buttenberg, you sit there smugly, while all around you is chaos and destruction. You have not only endangered your own life but have put many other law-abiding and peaceful people into much danger, and terror. Why, even the inconvenience you have caused has bought many people to despair. You may thank the Lord that no one was killed. This school has been terribly embarrassed by you and your friend's foolish actions.'

From his position where he hung at Sister Hildegard's neck, Jesus on the cross looked straight at Sean, a look of pain on his face, he looked at Sean accusingly. Jesus moved erratically in time with the nun's breathing. Sean slumped in the chair. He knew how that bloke on the cross felt. His mind swam with guilt, defiance, fear. This road was going to be a bloody hard and long.

The Sister's tirade continued. 'Well may you sigh, Mr Buttenberg. The repercussions...' She was cut off by the ringing of the telephone. She picked up the receiver and pressed a silver button. 'Sister Hildegard,' she hissed. There was a long pause as she listened. 'Will you please hold?' she whispered into the mouthpiece. She put her hand over it and looked angrily at Sean. 'Mr Buttenberg, wait outside with Mr McCarthy. No talking.'

Sean slinked outside and took up his station beside his friend, giving him the bravado look that he did not feel.

He waited in silence. The playground was active. Impromptu games were still going on. There were games of cricket, and the grade fours were playing kick to kick. The younger kids made line drawings with sticks in the playground, others were playing hopscotch. Sister Rose had hitched up the skirts on her habit and was batting in the cricket game with her class. Her face was full of the joy and the freedom which only sport could provide. Sean watched as the flowing habit moved with grace through the strokes of an accomplished cricketer.

'Mr Buttenberg, Mr McCarthy.' The Sister's voice was calm and controlled, but cold. She was again seated behind the desk. 'Take a seat, and do not say a word.' She looked at them both in turn. Her face was stern and granite-like. The lines on her face seemed etched as with a chisel, and her scaly hands, resting flat on the table, were maleficent and menacing. Sean involuntarily shuddered. The head-ache started to get worse and the pit of his stomach did another revolution. 'It may be very commendable of you to stand up for each other, but it is not what I was looking for.' Her eyes narrowed. 'And what was I looking for?' She looked at Sean and then flicked her gaze to Johnny. 'What I was looking for, boys, was some remorse, contrition and empathy for those you have endangered, inconven-ienced and embarrassed. I think this morning I have seen very little evidence of any of that in your stories.'

Sean felt his scar burn his chest. 'But Sister...'

The big desk rocked again. The Head Sister's face was scarlet. Her eyes were luminescent. 'Mr Buttenberg, the time for stories is over!'

Sean was stung by her ferocity. He slumped in the chair. 'Please sit up, the both of you. At least sit like educated boys, not like louts.' Sean shuffled upright. 'You are both banned from riding to school for two weeks. That means this last week before the holidays and the week commencing after it. You will be on yard duty for two weeks. You will have extra homework. You will each receive six strokes of the strap across both hands, which will be administered in front of the school assembly after we have finished here. You are barred from any communication with each other during the course of your punishment. Any failure will result in further extension of your punishment. Do I make myself clear?'

'Yes, Sister.' Sean chorused with Johnny. He was sweating pro-fusely now. He felt a void appearing before him. Sean had seen boys go into Sister Hildegard's office for the strap and come back with tears streaming down their faces, and that was after only a couple of cuts. The ultimate humiliation would be to cry out or cry in front of the school. He shivered again. He glanced at Johnny, whose jaw was set and clenched in a profile of defiance.

The nun had not finished. 'I will be contacting your parents today. I will be strongly suggesting that they impose further punishments. The police will interview you. I hope you will not disgrace yourself, your families or this school any further. Wait outside my office.'

Sean lifted himself from the big chair. He did not feel that well. He felt his mouth was dry, and his body was aching with the pain of it all. He stepped out with Johnny into the brightness of the verandah. The morning sun was breaking through the branches of the big oak. Silhouetted in the middle of the playground, Sean noted the buds of new growth on its outstretched limbs. It was preparing for the spring. How in the hell did this happen, he thought. He looked over at Johnny. His mate gave him a wink and a smile again. The freckles were vivid on his Celtic skin.

'Don't let that old snake get the best of us,' Johnny whispered. 'Don't make a sound or flinch when we get the cuts. Don't give her the pleasure of seeing us beaten.'

Sean nodded. He didn't feel confident.

The bell announced the late assembly. The grade sixer ringing it was standing outside the main entrance on the verandah. Only trusted grade sixers were allowed to ring the assembly bell. Willie Fitzpatrick rang it too vigorously, Sean thought, as if he expected a good show to come. The boy grinned. Sean thought he was taking far too much satisfaction. He stiffened and tried to look confident. The school assembly was taking shape from those that were here. The assembled children gradually melded and moulded into almost straight lines. The grade one and two children were prodded and cajoled into order by their teachers, but their lines still moved like a ragged wave breaking on unseen rocks, an invisible but irresistible force making them unable to be still. The older classes waited, still and muted. Their heads were uniformly uplifted towards the verandah.

The hum was constant. Sean saw Berty, his face white, shoulders slumped even more than usual. Sean nodded in his direction. Berty gave a muted thumbs up. Mary Addison stood at the head of the grade sixes. She was the tallest girl in the class and nearly the tallest kid in the school. Her face was expressionless. She looked through the school building into the beyond, her eyes fixed and staring.

The Head Sister's door opened and the throng hushed. All eyes looked up, fixed on Sister Hildegard as she walked purposely to the verandah rail and clutched it vigorously with one hand. In the other was a long, black, stiff barber's belt, shiny and dark in its malice, threatening even as it hung there, limp, over the rail. She drew herself up. She seemed to stand there for an eternity. Sean shuffled nervously. He saw Johnny drop his head. The Head Sister narrowed her eyes. She scanned her audience, her school. Not one person dared to move.

'It is very disappointing for me, boys and girls, to be standing here before you this morning.' Sister Hildegard paused for effect. She seemed to be basking in the timid warmth of the morning's late winter sun. 'I am here to mete out punishment to two of our students.' Sean looked over the assemblage. There was not a murmur. She continued. 'These two,' and she gestured in turn to Sean and Johnny, 'have shown a complete disregard for the law, other people, this school and themselves by riding to school dangerously and unlawfully. They caused many near accidents, the closure of the bridge, shock and apprehension to many people, and the complete disruption of this community.' She paused again and her eyes scanned her charges. 'Then when questioned about this, to my great disappointment, they showed no remorse or sorrow.' She again looked at Sean and Johnny. 'They are to be severely punished, starting with the strap. They are a disgrace to this school, to their families and to this community.' She retrieved the barber's belt from the railing. 'Mr McCarthy, please come forward, and put your hands out in front of you.'

She edged back as Johnny stepped before her. He slowly raised his hands, palms up. They were shaking and very white. His face was tense. His eyes were closed, but his jaw was firm. The sister's face was very stern and very pale. She explained harshly, 'Mr McCarthy, if you draw your hand away from the strap two more strikes will be forthcoming. Do you understand?'

'Yes, Sister,' Johnny mumbled. His voice was barely audible. Clare Fitzgerald, Johnny's cousin in grade one, began to cry. Other children joined her. The air was filled by a canopy of muffled whimpering and moans. Sister Hildegard turned and faced Johnny at right angles. She adjusted Jesus on the cross and her rosary beads, she placed her feet wide. Her face was deathly white now. She swung the belt slowly a few times, backwards and forwards, in her right hand, seeming to get its balance, then suddenly, like a python uncoiling, it was in full flight, coming back quickly past Johnny's outstretched hands, and then pausing momentarily before descending in a blur.

The striking of the hard glistening leather on Johnny's palms was like a pistol shot, clean, sharp and short. Johnny's hands were involuntarily flung downwards by the force and his whole body lurched forward. He stumbled slightly. The sharp sound of the strap was followed by the long whispering purr of the school assembly. Some of the students looked away. More children cried. Johnny's palms were now bright red. He raised his arms again. His hands were outstretched and trembling. A tear glistened out of the corner of each eye. But he didn't make a sound. He did not open his eyes or change his stance but stood there squarely, gamely waiting for the next stroke.

Sean watched with fascination. It was like a dream, as though he was watching from somewhere else. His ears felt as if they were blocked. The hiss of the strap came from a distance. Again and again the strap hissed. Each time Johnny put his hands up for more. The tears rolled freely down his face and pooled on the verandah. His hands shook more with each beating and he started to bend at the knees. But not once did he open his eyes or whimper. After the last stroke he put his shaking hands up for more.

'Mr McCarthy, you may resume your position,' Sister Hildegard said with effort. Johnny opened his eyes, red rimmed and swollen by the continuous flow of tears. He stumbled back and stood rigidly at his former post. He did not whine or murmur. The crowd was silent, except for the muffled moaning and crying of the younger grades.

'Mrs Newcomb, would you kindly bring me a glass of water?' the Head Sister muttered wearily. She took some deep breaths. Johnny looked straight ahead., his eyes still streaming. The school clerk hurried back with a glass of water in a gold embossed glass with an etching of Saint Joseph on it. Sister Hildegard took the drink and slowly sipped. The crowd shifted collectively, nervously. The whimpering continued.

Sister Hildegard finally put the glass aside and whispered quietly to Sean, 'Mr Buttenberg, please step forward and raise your hands.'

'Yes, Sister,' Sean heard himself replying, but it was a strange voice that spoke. He closed his eyes. The lightning Dingarra flashed through his head, his scar stung him, and then he was watching from above. He did not feel that he was on the verandah. The Sister went through the same motions but he saw them only from above. He saw her preparing the strap, swinging it slowly backwards and forwards. He saw his outstretched hands waiting for the impact. Then the sharp crack of the strap and the searing pain of the impact cascaded on his hands and burned up his arms and into his brain. It fused with that Dingarra fella and was still. He raised his hands for more. No tears. No sound. Again and again the strap fell, and again and again Dingarra was there, stronger with each blow. The lightning raging in his head controlled him, the pain merged and rolled into him, into Dingarra. He did not cry. He did not whimper. His hands came up strong and steady.

'You may go back to your position, Mr Buttenberg,' the Sister quietly said.

He opened his eyes. He was surprised it was over. He looked straight at Sister Hildegard. She was looking at him intently. He walked back to his place and nodded to Johnny. The crowd was still and looking at him. His hands were numb and stinging but his mind was incredibly clear. For the first time since the race, his headache was gone.

The Fight

Sean and Johnny had not always been friends. If fact, Sean had a run in with Johnny and the leader of his gang on his first day at Saint Joseph's...

Saint Joseph's School loomed large as Sean pedalled his way up Church Street. He could see Sister Hildegard's small frame in its habit of white, on the wide verandah. She was surveying the main entrance and her charges as they straggled in through the rusty iron gates. They came in dribs and drabs which fanned out as they passed through and then came together again in the playground into little groups which ebbed and flowed. One group of boys became a cricket game, another a marbles contest. A girl's group was skipping, but mostly they were talking. The boys were dressed in grey shorts, shirt, cap and short socks with brown and orange facings – Saint Joseph's colours. The girls were attired in simple cotton shifts of grey, brown, orange check, with the same socks as the boys, and a simple straw bonnet with the Saint Joseph's ribbon. All wore black shoes or sandals and, being Monday, were reasonably well presented. Sean headed towards the bike racks and felt the Sister's gaze upon him.

He lined up with the grade sixers. Sister Rose indicated for them to follow her into the classroom and she directed Sean to sit in a back desk.

She announced in a strong voice, 'Students, we have a new student – Sean Buttenberg – please make him welcome.'

The first class was on maths and he found it easy. At playtime he wandered over to the shelter shed in the big blue metal playground. A group of grade six kids he recognised from the classroom sauntered over, led by Harry Smythe. They surrounded him. They started a play on his name, their arms raised in a Nazi salute. Harry yelled:

> 'Buttenberg's a German dog,
> Sitting on a log,
> Eating Jewish frogs,
> He ain't got no cods.'

'Heil Hitler!' they all joined in.

Sean was of average height and weight, but was a much lighter build then Harry. His anger rose as the mob's chant engulfed him.

> 'Buttenberg's a German dog,
> Sitting on a log,
> Eating Jewish frogs,
> He ain't got no cods,
> Heil Hitler!'

Without warning he lunged forward at the bulk of Harry, his right fist leading, hitting him below the midriff. He felt his fist go into Harry's soft abdomen. A look of surprise and pain, then blankness, come over Harry's face, there was a grunt of pain and rush of air as his lungs emptied. Sean stepped back as Harry collapsed towards him, and automatically he drove his left fist into Harry's face. Harry wavered for a moment, then buckled, hitting the ground with a thud, his head jerked backwards. He lay completely still. Sean took a couple of steps back; as he had seen boxes do on the Cine News. When Sean looked up the crowd had moved back nervously. It parted like a wave as Sister Hildegard moved through it and towards him. He could see her small oval face, framed in the stiff white collar and veil, the thin mouth bent in a faint grimace.

Her words came in a flurry of excitement, a tinge of Irish giving it a softness that curtailed the harsh Australian twang.

'Mr Buttenberg, you have been here two hours and have distinguished yourself by assaulting another student into unconsciousness. Well done, my laddie. Please wait for me outside my office.'

She bent over Smythe's prone figure, rolling him onto his back. She tilted his eye lid open and the pupil rolled upwards. Harry started groaning and the eye lids flickered.

Sean was bewildered for two reasons. He did not know the whereabouts of the Head Sister's office, and he did not know how he had knocked out Smythe.

He had seen fights on the news reels at the pictures, and once Uncle Jack knocked a bloke out in the ladies lounge of the British Arms in Brunswick. A big foundry worker had drunkenly laid his hand over his mother's shoulder. Uncle Jack hadn't said a word, but hit him with a right and left. They had to leave then, spoiling the drinks in celebration of his mother's birthday. He had quickly gulped down the raspberry lemonade and walked out with the rest of the family.

Sean walked up the steps onto the wide verandah. Looking back he could see Smythe wobbling to his feet, supported by the head sister, and a couple of grade sixers. Sean reasoned that he had acted like his Uncle Jack - just instinct, a word he had heard his father use to describe Uncle Jack's actions that day.

A sign boldly proclaimed 'Head Sister's Office', with a large arrow pointing to the right. His footsteps sounded out a hollow clomp on the polished boards. He kept his eyes down but was aware of the stares of the kids hanging around the front of the school. He already knew that the veranda's surrounding the school were out of bounds during lunch and play times. You were in trouble if you were sent to wait on the verandah. He waited beside the closed door.

Sean didn't know why he had hit the Smythe kid. He had been called a German before but that really did not worry him. He had heard his father talk about Germans and the war, usually over a few beers with his mates or Uncle Jack, and his voice would take on a hard edge and the lines in his face would stand out. As for Jews, he didn't really know much about them. One Saturday, driving to see Auntie Irene in Oakleigh, they had passed some men dressed in long black coats and broad black hats.

'Who are they?', Sean had asked his dad.

'Their Jews on their way to Synagogue.'

'What's a Synagogue? Why are they dressed like that?'

'Well, the Synagogue is their church and they wear those clothes as a sign of respect for God.'

Sean's mum had said, 'They crucified Jesus so they should wear black, and fancy going to church on Saturday. It's queer.'

Sean saw his father's face go red and tight in a way that made his features hard.

'Mary, it's statements like those that led to the last war. If you must be prejudiced I would prefer it if you kept it to yourself and not inflict it on me or anyone else for that matter.'

'But that's what Father Jo...'

'Don't quote that opinionated little ball of Catholicism to me, Mary. He's back in the dark ages.'

Sean always remembered that trip and conversation. His mother had not spoken again for the rest of the journey.

He didn't mind being called a frog. Frogs were wonderful animals. OB, his best mate at St Ambrose, Brunswick, and he had caught some little yellow ones down by the big drain that ran at the back of the school. They had a jumping competition in the quadrangle by sticking their compass points into the frogs' backsides. His frog, Yellow Flash, had won all the time. But then the Ryan gang had come over and all the frogs were squashed, except Yellow Flash, which he had scrambled to save and then hidden in the top pouch of his school bag.

At home he had nicked one of mum's preserving jars from the laundry and put some grass and water in it and had kept him for two weeks. He had been playing with the Flash in his bedroom when his mum had come in as the frog was making a gigantic leap for the door. The frog landed on her exposed skin below her neck. She screamed, like when his dad had run over the cat's tail. She ran into the kitchen, the ironing flung in all directions. Sean quickly ventured out after her, putting Yellow Flash into his jar on the way. Mum was being comforted by dad, sobbing on his shoulder. He was stroking her hair and saying, 'what is it, Mary?' Katy, his young sister, started to howl. After things had settled down, dad had ordered him to get rid of the frog. He had taken the Flash back to the school drain and had coaxed him out of the jar and into a bed of reeds. On his return home he was ordered into the bath and checked all over for warts, and scolded and threatened with dire consequences if he ever brought another live animal home. His bedroom was scrubbed and the sheets and blankets changed.

No, it wasn't the names that had upset him, it was the way Smythe and his mob had taunted him. He heard the Head Sister's voice through the door.

'Please come in Mr Buttenberg.'

Sister Hildegard was seated behind a large polished desk. A photo of a peasant couple standing outside a thatched roof cottage and a holy picture of Saint Monica stood beside a black phone with silver buttons. A small electric light held in the mouth of a coiling green cobra acting as its base. Its shade looked as though it was made out of snake skin. It looked strangely out of place. It was dark and cool. The walls were fully enclosed by glassed-in book shelves, a large brass and wood fan hung from the ceiling, and there was a door opposite to the one Sean had entered. Sister was leafing through a brown folder. She did not look up, just muttered.

'Sit down, Mr Buttenberg.'

Sean slumped into a chair. The silence was painful. At the same time he felt a surge of defiance – after all, he had not done anything wrong, only defended himself. The bell marking the end of playtime sounded, which seemed to be the signal for the Sister to look at him. Her little brown eyes bored through him. He looked directly back, feeling a tingle of fear. There was a lump in his throat and he started to feel pain in his hands. He looked down and noticed for the first time that his left hand was bleeding and skinned across the knuckles. He looked at it intently.

'Well, Mr Buttenberg, what do you have to say for yourself?'

'Sister, I was in the playground and Harry Smythe and some grade sixers started calling me names...'

'Being called a name, Mr Buttenberg, is no excuse for knocking another laddie out.'

Sean shrugged.

'Mr Buttenberg, I spoke to your mother at some length when she enrolled you. She seems a lovely lady. Your father is a war veteran and I understand has taken a position at the Forestry Commission. I know this is a difficult time for you all, moving from Brunswick. However, taking your frustration out on the local laddies on your first day of school will certainly make it very difficult for you, and won't gain you many friends. If this episode is any indication of how you are going to conduct yourself, laddie, than you will certainly not go far in life, or at this school. Do you understand, Mr Buttenberg?'

'Yes, Sister.'

He felt a surge of anger and frustration. To say anything would be useless. She looked at the folder again.

'I notice, Mr Buttenberg, that you were considered a good student at St Ambrose's, and will put this episode down as an aberration on your part, a sign of your unsettled last few weeks. But let me remind you, Mr Buttenberg, we do things differently here in the country. You may go back to your class. I will be writing a letter to your parents and will expect a reply by tomorrow.'

'Yes, Sister.'

Sean moved silently out of the chair and back through the door he had come in. The playground was empty. A flock of sparrows had moved in and were busily pecking up the crumbs and scraps, a mob of magpies were gathering around the rubbish bin warbling. A tree martin was catching grasshoppers, riding the heat waves, and the faint echo of kookaburras laughing echoed up from the river. What in the hell was an aberration? He knocked on the classroom door and went in.

Any Friends Here?

His mother was in shock. Sean had handed her the letter in a heavy brown envelope embroidered with orange facings and a little brown image featuring St Joseph's face, with 'Sisters of Mary' stamped under it in blue. Sean stood silently. He watched her pretty face contort into a shape that foretold of punishment and banishment from her affections, and possibly presence, for a long period.

'Sean, how could you? Go to your room.'

Sean slowly walked down the passageway to the back of the house, his feet scraping on the worn, yellow linoleum. His room was small, just enough space for a wardrobe, a shelf for his books and an iron bed. A large window opened onto the backyard and a faint afternoon light filtered through. He lounged on his bed and looked out at the wood heap and the big iron shed. A welcome swallow was darting and diving under its eaves, catching insects, the patch of red under its neck standing out against the greyness of the surroundings. His mind wandered back to Brunswick and his friends: Johnny O'Brien – OB – Benny Marsh and Bluey Riley. They would probably be wading up Back Creek catching leeches or building forts on its banks. Why did we have to move into this strange, faraway town? Even going to and from school was an adventure in Brunswick. It took him through the local shopping district and past the factories and homes of people he knew and trusted. People like old Mister Smith the greengrocer who gave him an apple or cobber if he delivered a parcel or box of fruit. The gang meetings in their secret fort on Back Creek, the fights with the state school kids – 'State school fools, sitting on their tools, eating gruel'.

He was interrupted by the appearance of his father's black Buick. The peculiar chump, chump of the big engine reminded him of the busy streets of Brunswick, the tyres crunching on the dry, grey, packed earth. The welcome swallow flew away nervously in the direction of the river as the car parked in the shed. His father stepped and stretched his thin frame skywards, drawing in the cool air of the evening. His movements were slow, deliberate, his back slightly bent. He wore grey trousers and a green shirt under a sleeveless pullover, and his brown elastic-sided boots had a never ending shine. The dark black hair was slightly receding with faint streaks of grey, the blue eyes slightly watery and transparent when they looked straight through you. The creases in the brown face never went away but deepened depending on his mood. He carried the brown Gladstone bag easily. An Akubra was parked at an angle on his long head, the top of which was five feet, eleven and one-half inches from the ground, a height his father said was tall enough to see over the top of most people but shorter then would make you stand out.

Sean heard the back flywire door bang and saw Katy run out, her blond curly hair streaming behind, the short dress drawn up high.

'Daddy, Daddy!' She flung herself into the air with the sure knowledge that she would be caught.

'How's my little Katy?'

He swung her around and kissed and cuddled her. It was a scene Sean had seen many times. It was different for fathers and sons.

'Where's Sean?'

Katy excitedly answered. 'He's in trouble with mum. He killed someone at school and, and...and Sister sent a letter.'

His father looked at the window. Sean's face felt warm and he ducked down onto the bed. He heard his father's footsteps, slow and measured, down the hallway. He heard him greet his mum.

'G'day, Mary. How's your day been?'

And the pause, which Sean knew would be his father giving his mother a gentle hug and a kiss.

His mother's soft answer, 'It was a good day until Sean came home,' and then silence as the kitchen door closed.

Sean wondered what his mum was telling dad. He thought about the welcome swallow and where he had gone. In Brunswick, on Back Creek, the swallows had made little mud nests under the bridges. His gang had caught the Carter gang throwing rocks at them. That was another time he had felt sudden anger. They had charged down on the Carters, and he had caught Puddings Carter full on in a beautiful hip and shoulder. Sean's lot had easily won - they had the element of surprise, and a cause. After that, they called themselves the Fighting Swallows.

There was a knock on the door. His father came in.

'Sean, I need a hand with the wood.'

They walked silently to the wood heap. His father started splitting blocks. Sean split kindling, stacking it against the side of the shed. They worked for about fifteen minutes.

'Time for a break.'

Taking out his pipe, his dad sat on the chopping block. Sean sat next to him.

'What happened today?'

Sean went through his story. His father nodded, grunting an occasional hmmm or ahhh.

His dad looked at the sky. The face creases deepened.

'Hmmm.'

Sean fidgeted. His father looked pretty good with that pipe. Tomorrow he would find a hollow peppercorn at school and make a pipe, just like they used to do in Brunswick. Where could he get some tobacco?

His dad said quietly, 'I met Harry's father, in the pub last week. Nasty piece of work. I think they are made of the same stuff. It pays to be careful around people like them. They do not respect themselves or anyone else. That was a deadly left hook, where did you learn that?'

'It was instinctive.'

'That's a big word for a eleven year old.'

'Remember when Uncle Jack knocked that bloke out in the pub? You said it was instinctive.'

His father laughed. 'It might be good to keep your hands in your pockets for a bit. This will not be the end of it. Oh, and if you feel angry again, just wait a minute. Sometimes rushing in does not always help your cause. In the army we had a bloke called Jack Higgs, a real hero. He joined my section. Us young blokes really looked up to him and thought he was the ants pants, being as he had been in the first war. We tried to copy him in everything, until one night at Puckapunyal we had an air raid drill. Jack Higgs jumped off the cot with just his jocks on and darted out of the tent and ran fifty yards, but not into the slit trench – into the latrine pit. The rest of us blindly followed and were covered in shit and piss from one end to the other. Our section was known from then on as the shitty second and Jack Higgs as Shitty Higgs. He never lived it down. If only he had taken a minute. Poor bastard was killed in Crete.'

His father's face twisted into a hard shape. 'Let's go and see what kind of a job mum has done on them snags and mash.'

'Dad, what's an aberration?'

'I think it means something you don't usually do or maybe only once in a lifetime. Let's hope you only have to belt up a school bully once, eh?'

After tea his father wrote a brief note in his bold script with the large black fountain pen. He sat at the secretaire pulling out the heavy yellow paper that looked old but was new. Sean sorted through his marbles, counting and grading them. His mother darned a pair of school socks and hummed along to Mario Lanza on the big gramophone in the corner. Katy played with her favourite doll, Nelly. His dad switched on the seven o'clock news, and the small His Master's Voice sitting on the mantelpiece vibrated with the familiar ABC theme music. This was the signal for Katy's bedtime and for Sean to get changed into pyjamas.

Sean changed, cleaned his teeth, washed his face and put a comb through his hair a couple of times. He went back to the lounge room, retrieving one of his dads National Geographics and a Ginger Megs comic. He knew his mother would examine him to make sure he had completed his tasks to her satisfaction.

'Sean, please go and put your slippers on. Do you have your singlet on?'

He went and completed the required tasks. Venturing again into the lounge room, he pulled a volume of John Gould's *Birds of Australia* carefully from the bookshelf and sat in front of the boarded-up fireplace. His dad was talking, leaning forward out of the big green chesterfield, his hands moving animatedly, something about the anti-Communist Labor Party and a bloke called Stan Keon from Richmond, who he knew.

'Those right-wing conservative do-gooders Bishop Mannix and his mate Santamaria will be the ruin of the working man, and Labor. Menzies and his crew must be laughing all the way to Canberra and back, the big Bastard Anglophile!'

His mother looked up from her sewing. 'James! It is bad enough defaming good Bishop Mannix, but please do not use that type of language in front of the children, or me. It is not Friday night and you are not in Kelly's pub, thank you.'

His father's hands dropped to his side. He sat back in the big chair, looking to the ceiling.

'You're right, Mary,' he said in a low voice. 'I shouldn't swear. Sorry, I just get so agitated, the futility and stupidity of it all.'

His mother went back to darning, his father to reading the Forest Report.

There was a long pause.

'Dad?'

'Yes, Sean?'

'What is an Anglophile?'

His parents looked at each other and smiled. His dad's hands started moving again.

'Well, it's someone who really likes the English and everything they do and copies how they talk and act, sometimes they are more English then the English. Understand?'

Sean had met some English kids in Brunswick. They spoke funny, like they had a marble in their mouth.

'Does Mr Menzies try to talk like an Englishman, dad?'

Sean's dad reached for his pipe. 'Not only him, Sean, but a few of his mates also.'

'Dad, my mates at St Ambrose's said the poms were all whingers. Why would Mr Menzies and his friends want to act like that?'

'Don't make the mistake, Sean, of underestimating any people. I worked with the English in the war - some good, some not. They do have that reputation, which is sad. But they stick at it, which is their strength. They don't call them bulldogs for nothing. Ah, but Mr Menzies and his like grew up when England was the most powerful country in the world. They think English culture is the greatest gift to mankind since Adam found Eve. But we don't have to copy them slavishly. Australia can be great in its own right. We don't have to be transplanted Englishmen. A couple of years ago King George died. Mr Menzies came into the Parliament with tears in his eyes as if his own father had died. It's a pity he did not have the same feelings during the Great War when he handed his commission in rather than fight to protect the England he loves so much. I am sure it is one of the reasons he did not intervene when the poms sent us into the muddle of Greece and Crete during the last show.' His father paused. The lines on his face became deeper, his eyes sombre. 'Soon we will be all copying the Yanks. It's the way of things – everyone wants to copy the most successful, the most powerful. The main thing is never try to be someone else, you are an Australian. Be proud of that. Be your own man, follow your own dreams, not others'. Learn from the good and bad in all people – don't just mindlessly copy them… Bloody hell, now I'm sounding like a politician!'

'James!'

Uncle Jack said his dad was a Labor man. When he grew up, that's what he would be, a Labor man.

'Thanks, dad. I think I've got it. Can I light your pipe?'

'Sean, bed time.'

Sean closed his books and got up slowly. He kissed his mother's cheek and hugged his dad. 'Can I read for a bit?'

'Ten minutes and then lights out.'

Sean made his way outside to the toilet, to the left of the back door, over by the fence. It was a good toilet with an electric light on the outside and inside. The one in Brunswick was right down the end of the yard with no light in or outside. You had to take a pressure lamp or torch. Often in Brunswick he had not bothered at night, going to the lemon tree against the back wall, until his mother had found him one night. Her torch light had caught him in its field.

'Jim, come out here, please! Sean will you please stop that!'

Sean had tried but in the effort had lost his grip. The stream soaked him. His father had come outside and burst into laughter.

'I wondered why that lemon tree was growing so well! The lemons are delicious.'

'James, this is not the time or the place for your humour. This is a serious matter, a health hazard!' Then she had burst into soft giggles, her body shaking.

A routine set in for Sean. Each morning he woke as the light filtered in. He waited and listened, snuggling into the bed. Old crabby Mrs Bloomington's rooster next door crowed, and sometimes the laugh of the kookaburras echoed up from the river, a dog barked or a car went past on Kane's Way. The whistle of the six o'clock train crossing the Mitchell Highway sounded. A little later the quiet sounds and scrapings of his father in the bathroom. This was the signal he waited for. Quickly he was up, putting on his school uniform, making his bed and then out to the shed collecting kindling and firewood. He relit the combustion stove.

'Grey box to start it, red gum to keep it going,' his dad always said.

Then to the bathroom where he splashed some water over his face, and slashed the comb through his wavy hair. Mum called it 'a gift from God'; Sean often wished he had kept the bloody gift. The routine was the same as in Brunswick, except for the red gum and grey box. In Brunswick they had mainly coal.

By this time his parents would be in the kitchen, mum cooking dad's breakfast, normally porridge and toast or sometimes mash and toast, eggs and bacon on the weekend. Always the irresistible smell of coffee. His dad said he picked up the coffee habit from the Yanks in the war. Every month his mum made a trip to Echuca to shop and she would pick up her husband's special coffee beans at the Beehive Store. Mum often said, 'that coffee is so expensive, James, can't we just have tea like everyone else?' but his dad would say, 'the morning is not right without proper coffee, Mary'. Sean loved this time with his dad, who would be reading the paper.

'That silly bugger, Everitt. Essendon has a chance for the flag this year. The price of wool is rising again.'

Sean did not know what a lot of his dad's comments meant, except the bits about Essendon.

'If you don't follow Essendon in his family, you don't get fed. The Buttenbergs have followed Essendon from the time they had first set foot in Melbourne.'

Grandfather had been run over by a tram outside the Essendon Pub celebrating a win. It was a matter of blood. Sean normally had porridge and toast.

After his dad had gone to work, Sean cleaned his teeth. His mother inspected him, noting and correcting any shortcomings. Then he was on his bike down Kane's Way and onto the Mitchell Highway, which led to the big retractable bridge over the river. Sean loved crossing it in the mornings. He would slow down and sometimes even walk across the walkway, often stopping to take in the brown swirling water below. The water flowed and circled in different patterns and shades, leaves and sticks, whole trees and branches sometimes, floated past. One morning a cow floated right under him, its sides blown up like a party balloon. The stink had nearly made him vomit. Always the rumble and jumble of morning traffic vibrated and made the bridge creak and groan. Horse and drays carrying goods for the produce shops, trucks of all descriptions from green war surplus big wheelers to little Austins, shiny new Bedfords and Fords, some carrying oranges or tomatoes to the co-op on the Koonarook side of the river. The old Austin school bus would rattle past. Its dirty cream and yellow sides seemed to breath in and out as it clanked along, the clamour and noise of children engulfing him, body parts sticking out of its sliding windows or back door. Mr Smith, the bus driver, a fag stuck to his lower lip but never alight, slumped over the wheel, staring ahead, oblivious to all going on behind.

Sean was always amazed by the changing patterns, colour and movement. As he looked up the river, he would often see Mr Elliot, the professional fisherman, and his son Jimmy, who had a gummy foot, unloading their nights catch at the floating wharf. Their boat had a tiny steam engine; a chimney blew out odd balls of white smoke. The boat would rock in the swirling currents with the exertions of the two men on board. The fish were in wicker baskets covered with old hessian or orange sacks or in battered kerosene tins. Sean wondered why someone with something wrong with them was always named with a 'y' after their name. Like Jacky, the polio cripple he had known in Brunswick, or Franky, the idiot son of the local publican.

On the Caladonian side of the river, ten foot high cliffs rose up, their dirty grey sides interrupted and broken by masses of roots from the towering red gums. Long, gentle river paddocks sloped upwards towards town until they gave way to the confused jumble of the shops and buildings facing north onto High Street. Further upriver the cliffs ran into the manicured lawns and exotic trees of Caladonia Park, a large estate his father said was owned by the richest man in the district, Lachlan Campbell. A small jetty jutted out into the river there. On the Koonarook side, steam would be rising from the saw mill, the mill men like ants moving on and about the big piles of red gum. Sometimes the 8.05 Swan Hill train would go past on the Victorian side, puffing and whining as it made its way on the other side of the co-op factory. Closer to the bridge the fuselage of a broken B17 lay broken and crumpled on its belly with the cockpit glass gone and weeds and small trees growing through it. It had no wings but the huge tail pointed defiantly up at the sky with a faded '5' on it. His dad said the mill had bought it as war surplus and scavenged all the parts off it. A large stand of underbrush, weeds and towering red gums swept up from the plane, seeming to form an impenetrable mass. Often smoke would be swirling in irregular circles from a campfire or chimney in its midst. Searn wondered where that came from. The bush pushed back for half a mile into the natural hollow and bend formed by the river on one side and the highway on the other He had heard some of the boys saying it was haunted and full of blood-sucking bats. The Abos sacrificed their young maidens there in the old days, and their spirits would get you if you went in there. Everyone referred to it as 'The Swamp'

Just below and to the right of the bridge was the graveyard; skeletons of old barges and steamers stuck up through the mud of the shore line and further back were rusty iron boilers and pieces of pipe. One Sunday after Mass he stood around and waited as his mum and dad made polite conversation.

'That place is haunted by crews who died. If you go there at night you can hear them stoking the boilers and loading the logs,' Paul O'Dwyer told him. 'They get you if they can and you never come back.'

Sean thought that was bloody bullshit and told him so.

'How would you know? You're just a city bastard.'

Sean's anger rose. 'Well, I might be from the city but I sure know a furphy when I hear one.'

Paul went to high school in Morang. He walked over and stood toe to toe with Sean. 'Look, Buttenwog, if you don't believe me I dare you to go in there one night by yourself and see how you go. You've only been here five bloody minutes and you know everything!'

'My dad says ghosts are a figment of people's imaginations.'

The bigger boy laughed and backed off. 'Daddy's boy, are we? Can't think for ourselves, can we?' He pranced around as he made fun of Sean's blunder.

Sean's fists clenched. He began to advance on Paul just as their parents approached with Father Riley.

'Good on ya, Paul,' the little priest darted out in his quick way of talking. 'Well done for making the new boy welcome.'

There were smiles all around. His father gave him a funny look as if to say, 'well, what's going on?'

Sean thought now as he looked at the jumbled wreckage that he would never have any friends in this town - not like Brunswick, where he had his own gang, things to do and adventures to follow. For one last moment he took in the mighty river, and then headed over the bridge and up the hill to school.

Smythe's Intentions

Harry and his gang let him be, but the sullen glares and the not-so-gentle shove and push signalled their intentions and his isolation. Often after school his tyres were flat or a valve was missing. One day the bell cup had been screwed off. His school bag, hung on a peg at the back of the classroom, was often undone, with his lunch missing or on the floor, pencils and books scattered. Smythe and gang watched and sniggered at him from a distance. Harry had been away for two days after the fight, the first day in the big white hospital three blocks from the school. On the second day Harry's parents had come to the school during lunchtime to speak to Sister Hildegard. Harry's dad was a big round man with a red face and a few whisks of hair, who breathed and sweated heavily. Mrs Smythe was a small woman whose flower print dress gave no indication of shape. She carried along in his wake. They had been in the head sister's office for a long time. Sean was playing marbles and saw Mr Smythe storm out with his wife straggling behind. Sister came and leaned against the railing of the verandah, her pink knuckles showing white as she gripped the rails, her feet apart and her eyes staring straight ahead. A faint smile crossed her lips. Her gaze dropped and she saw him. Quickly she stepped back into her office, the long white robes and big black rosary beads making her seem as though she was floating above the boards.

'Had a visit from that Smythe fellow, Henry, Harry's dad,' his father said that night at tea. 'He came into the office and threatened and blustered something to the effect that "you city people are no good and your son is a menace and should be kicked out of the school". I told him to wake up to himself and to let things settle, but he would have none of it. So I suggested that we settle now. When I came from behind the desk, he'd run out the front door and down the steps at such a rate Phar Lap would not have caught him. He crashed into the fire hydrant crunching his you know what's. He was bawling out and cursing me for everything under the sun.' Dad had looked around to make sure mum was okay.

'Thank you, James.'

'It was embarrassing. Everyone around about came to find out what the din was about. Anyway, the last I saw of him he was headed up toward Market Street and his produce store. I don't think it's the last time we will hear of the Smythes.'

Sean told them about the Smythes visit to the school that day and how they had stormed out of Sister Hildegard's office.

'I think Sister Hildegard is a good judge of character.'

'Yeh, I suppose,' Sean answered quietly.

Mary Addison

Class was arranged alphabetically, he sat with a girl named Mary Addison. As Sean and Mary went in first, they sat at the back of the first row next to the windows, built so as kids like him, when seated, could not see out. If the weather was hot, Sister would order the big blinds to be drawn down and the windows hinged outwards.

Mary Addison was a mystery to Sean. She was tall and thin, forever sniffling and rubbing her nose. Her hair was tied back in a ponytail and she wore shoes that were too big. Her dress was always clean and pressed but was so old; the grey, the brown and orange check had almost disappeared. The hem was creased and lined from being taken down over the years, and the hand-knitted jumper she wore was worn and patched. If Sister Rose asked her a question, she answered shyly, quietly. But she was very good at writing and English, and always had these completed on the slate ahead of Sean, although her maths skills were ordinary. If he said anything to her, she nodded, blushed and sometimes giggled.

At the tea table one night he asked why girls giggled, blushed and talked silly.

Mum said, 'That's not true always. Some little girls are just shy.'

'I'm not silly,' Katy yelled. She catapulted a glob of potato mash at him from her fork.

'Sean never said you were,' his mother scolded her, smacking her fingers. 'Young lady, if you ever throw anything across the table again... ! Sean, go and clean your face.'

'Why did you ask that about girls, Sean?' his mother said when he came back.

He told them about lining up and how Sister Rose liked girls and boys to sit together as it created less 'cross conversation', whatever that meant, and so he was stuck with Mary Addison.

'I'm sure Mary is a lovely little girl and, of course, Sister Rose knows what's best for young children. The CWL are very concerned for the Addisons and have organised some food and help for Molly Addison, Mary's mother. I have not been to their place but am on the roster with Flo Mahoney for a couple of week's time. With nine children, it is hard.'

His dad cut in. 'When he isn't drunk, Paddy Addison is a really wonderful blacksmith and iron monger. But as soon as he's paid, that's it - down to Johnson's and into it. Then at six o'clock closing he's out back of Kelly's drinking himself silly. He's a good drunk, though, never violent, but he does have a habit of laying down in High Street or out front of the clock tower in Caladonia. Then the cops have to take him home or lock him up for the night.'

As mum was putting Katy to bed that night, his dad said, 'Great shot by Katy at tea, Sean. Do you think she might get in the cricket team when she's older?' They both laughed. His father's face turned serious.

'As for women, Sean, you will never understand them. No man ever has. Just appreciate them for what they are - beautiful creatures, wonderful partners, better in most ways, people we definitely cannot live without. Although, a break every now and then for both sides is good, I think, especially if they start throwing things at you.'

His Mum came in. 'Now what are you two up to?'

'I've just been telling Sean about the virtues of women.'

'James, I hope you are being nice.'

'Of course.' His dad rose and gave her a kiss on the cheek, at which she blushed and giggled, a bit like Mary Addison.

Berty White

At lunchtime Sean was playing marbles under the peppercorn trees. Berty White wandered over.

'Betcha I can beat ya,' he blurted.

Sean had been playing the Big Ring. Berty was good at this game. Sean discovered he was very good at marbles, full stop, as the games went about three to one in Berty's favour. Berty showed him his problem. He was not holding his marble right in his firing finger. He needed to flick it out at a faster speed and to hold it further back. Berty's fingers, especially his thumbs, were made for marbles.

'You're like a Roman catapult, Berty.'

The grade fiver smiled, his big mouth open wide. 'Do they play marbles too? Where can I play them? Are they in Melbourne where you come from?'

'No they lived a long time ago and conquered half the world with soldiers and war machines which fired big rocks. They probably played marbles too, but I don't know if they had glass. But I know they did play jacks with bone knuckles.'

Berty understood jacks. 'Sean, I have the best set of jacks in the whole school, the whole world. Wanna see them?'

'Yeh. How come they call you "Berty", Berty?'

'My real name is Albert. I hate it. It was either Al or Bert, so I chose Bert. That's what the kids call me. The only ones who don't are the Sisters and my mum.'

Berty fished deep into his pockets. Out came string, rocks, a dirty hanky, an apricot kernel and a little blue cotton bag with a string tie opening. Berty looked around carefully. 'These are the best, Sean.' He spilled out the jacks. 'No one else has these.' A series of bright coloured knuckles, red, blues, yellows, greens, orange, glossy and bright, rolled onto the ground. 'My big brother works at Myer in the city. He got them for me at Christmas. Aren't they bonza?'

Sean looked at the treasure. All the knuckles he had seen were old and yellow. 'Can I have a throw with them, Berty?'

Sean had a couple of throws. 'Berty, they're fantastic.'

'Yeh, let me show you how they go.' Berty went through a routine so fast. The number of jacks on the ground reached ten, then Berty started throwing up multiples and catching them on the back of his hand, two and three in the air at once. Then he put the knuckles carefully back in their cotton bag. 'Swear that you will tell know one I have them, or hope to die.'

'I swear, Berty, or hope to die.'

'I really had to show you, after I won so many marbles. Do you want to swap some of your ordinaries for your shot marble? It must be worth at least five green or red eyes?'

The two boys spent the rest of lunchtime trading and comparing marbles. They were so engrossed they did not notice the Smythe gang watching from the back fence.

That afternoon was a writing afternoon. Sean was never any good at this. He wrote scrawly and fast across the page but this was not how it was meant to be according to Sister Rose.

'An orderly script shows an orderly mind,' she said.

Sean's mind was unorderly. His game with Berty had got him thinking of Romans, catapults and Brunswick. Mum had gone crook at him for dragging a sheet off the line and using it for a cloak for Julius Caesar, even though he had put it back. He set up a sandcastle in the front garden with one of dad's beer cans on top and was bombing it with his catapult just as Beryl Fletcher walked through the front gate. He had let fly with a beauty. It hit the can, ricocheted and hit Beryl on her bosom – as mum called girl's tits. She screamed and sank to her knees, clutching them. His dad had given his backside a work over, mum had not spoken to him for a week and his catapult was taken away.

'That was a bloody good catapult, Sean,' his dad had advised, 'but Caesar would have had the good sense to use it in the backyard away from everybody, specially your mum's best friend.'

Sean looked across the desk. Mary Addison's letter book was like a textbook.

'Not playing today, Berty?' Sean sauntered over the next morning to a group playing marbles. 'Did you win enough off me yesterd'y?'

Berty turned around on the words. His left eye and face were different shades of black, blue and purple.

'Berty! Did ya get kicked by a horse or somethin'?'

The grade fivers moved away. Berty's voice quavered. 'Last night I was goin' down to the barber shop like normal. I cut down Butchers Lane, but Smythe's gang came at me blocking my way. "You hang around with that fucker Buttenberg," they said, "and we'll cut of ya balls"! They knocked me off my bike, took my bag and emptied my pockets. They took my marbles and knuckles!' Berty's began to shake, the tears and sobs uncontrollable.

Sean looked around in embarrassment but no one seemed to be paying any attention. Then he caught sight of Harry Smythe lounging on the back fence. Sean's hands became sweaty, the hairs on the back of his neck stood up, his breathing came in short deep bursts.

Sean took a couple of steps in their direction.

'Sean!' Berty grabbed his arm. 'Johnny McCarthy has my knuckles and they split up the marbles between them. Don't go down there. They'll bloody kill you. They had it planned. "This will get that shit-head riled," they said.'

Sean looked at the little bloke and his hard white knuckles digging into his arm.

'What did your mum and dad say about your black eye and lost things?'

'Them blokes said if I told my Mum and Dad, they would get me again. I told them I fell of my bike. They don't know about my marbles and knuckles.'

'I'll get your knuckles and marbles back for you. I promise'

'Sean, you'll always be my pal even if I can't play with you. The gang are telling everyone this is what will happen if they hang around with you.'

The Battle of Waterloo

After school Sean turned his bike up the slight slope off the highway. He pulled in behind the Caladonia Oval grandstand. The place was quiet. He hoped Mary Addison had been right.

'Mary, I have to drop something off at the McCarthy's place. Do you know where they live?'

Mary had looked to where Johnny McCarthy was heading out the door with Harry Smythe and a few of his mates. 'Sean, why don't you ask Johnny?' She nodded in the parting boy's direction. 'He lives up past the Caladonia oval on Waterloo Street in a white weatherboard house. 'Thanks for helping me with maths today.'

Sister Rose was looking at them.

'Good afternoon, Sister.'

She nodded in reply. Sean noticed that even the flowing habit could not completely hide Sister Rose's woman's outline. He wondered if nuns were capable of 'it'. Did they have 'all of the equipment', as his mate Roger used to say? They must have. He knew they had toilets like everyone else. He had seen the night cart going up the alley behind the convent. He wondered if it was a sin thinking about nuns that way.

Sean left school quickly and hid behind the Caladonia grandstand just off the highway. He saw Johnny McCarthy coming up the highway. His bike looked new. It was blue with twirls of red. Must be a Malvern Star. The bell was shiny. It even had hand grips and a carry rack on the back.

Sean looked down at the silver hand-painted handle bars, the red painted frame and bare wheels of his own contraption. His dad had bought it at the market in Melbourne over a year ago, and done it up for him. He cleaned and oiled it every weekend. It was not full sized, but it was fast.

Johnny was almost level. Sean gunned his bike through the front gate. Johnny was sucking on an all-day sucker. His mouth opened wide when he saw him and the sucker fell onto the tar. Johnny was quick, though, and reacted instantly to Sean's charge, standing up on the bike and giving it a mighty push forward. Sean had to make a wide circle not to lay his bike over. Johnny was in full flight as Sean regained his balance. Around the corner of the oval and into Wellington Street they went. He gained on Johnny, the houses flashed past, the oval on the left had given way to paddocks and factory sheds. Suddenly Johnny turned right. The street sign flashed by – Waterloo Street. He was on Johnny's wheel now, he could hear the other boy's laboured breathing. He wobbled as he tired. Sean could not push the bike any faster, his legs were hurting, Sean's front wheel caught the gravel. The bike swerved and swayed, nearly throwing him, he lost five yards, he was not going to catch him. Sean started to gain again. He could see a big white weatherboard place coming up on the left

'Bugger it,' he yelled. He wasn't going to stop him.

Suddenly, Johnny swerved off the road towards the white house, aiming to cross over a small bridge that covered the deep gutter. But Johnny misjudged the crossing. His front wheel missed the leading edge of the bridge and he crashed into the gutter at full speed. Sean heard a muffled 'whoomph' and Johnny's cry. There was a cloud of dust and Johnny was propelled onto the wide hard gravel walkway beyond the gutter. The bike stayed in the gutter, the front wheel bent at an odd angle. Johnny was lying on his stomach upon the pathway groaning. The leather school bag strapped to his back had one strap torn away. His knees were bleeding and one of his shoes was lying in the gutter.

Sean hit the brakes and skidded to a halt. He ran over the bridge to the prostrate figure and turned him over, grabbing his shirt. Johnny put his hands up to his face, the elbows were grazed and bleeding, his nose was bloodied.

'You gonna get me!' Johnny cried out.

'Listen, you shithead. I'll make bloody mincemeat of you if you don't shut up!' Sean grabbed his collar. Johnny's eyes were nearly opaque now. His hair had gravel and sticks through it.

Sean lowered his face to within an inch of Johnny's. 'Where's Berty's marbles?'

'I haven't got them. We split them up.'

Sean looked up and down the street. There was no one in sight, which seemed unusual for this time of day.

'You bastard! Berty had thirty marbles and his set of jacks. I want them back.' Sean raised his right fist while holding the limp figure by the collar. He felt the sweat trickling down his back. 'Don't hit me, don't hit!' Johnny cried. 'In the bag, in the bag.'

'Get it off then, you arsehole.'

Johnny stiffly removed the bag from his back. Every movement he made he winced. Sean grabbed the bag and roughly undid the straps. Flicking it open, he piled out pencils, books and war comics, and threw them in the gutter. He stood up over the cowering figure, pressing his right foot onto Johnny's chest.

'Don't move, you shit,' he growled as Johnny tried to sit up. Sean pushed the injured boy down roughly. He groaned in pain. Sean found Johnny's marble bag at the bottom of the bag, and beside it the little blue cotton bag. 'How come you have Berty's jacks, Johnny?'

'They gave 'em to me 'cause they're a set and I didn't get as many marbles.'

'Alright. Berty had thirty marbles in his pouch. How many have you got in yours?'

Johnny glared at Sean.

Sean quickly did a count. There were about thirty-five marbles. 'I'll just take about thirty for Berty.'

Sean put the marbles in his shorts pocket. He placed the little blue jack bag down his shirt front. He picked up his bike and straddled it. Looking back at the crumpled figure, he yelled, 'leave me and my friends alone or I'll get you again, Johnny!'

Johnny looked up, the blood on his face a dirty brown. 'You don't have any friends, Buttenberg, and you won't! We'll get you, city bastard!'

Sean faked to get off his bike again. Johnny shrank into the path.

Sean rode off at a leisurely pace as a group of small school kids turned the corner into Waterloo Street chatting and giggling. Sean felt a stab inside, like bees floating in his gut, as he remembered the many times in Brunswick he had walked home with his mates. He looked back at the now distant figure on the footpath. Johnny was up, bent over picking up things.

I'm in for it again, thought Sean. He smiled. At least Johnny had met his Waterloo.

He turned onto the highway. It was easy riding downhill towards the river. Instead of going up the small incline onto the bridge verge, he turned left past the two pubs that marked the start of High Street in Caladonia. His dad had given him a brief description of the pubs and who used them. The one on his left was called Kelly's. The name stood out in big green letters on its large facade. Dad said it was the Catholic pub. He had a drink in it every Friday night on his way home from work. The one on the right was The Thistle but everyone called it the River pub. It was the Prodo pub. At the end of High Street was another pub, The Caladonian, it was called the top pub. Sean could see its grand columns and imperial facade as he looked down through the busy after-school traffic. It was the posh pub in town and behind its grand entrance, fake marble columns and polished timbers resided the squattocracy, landed gentry, visiting businessmen, senior public servants and politicians. Koonarook had two pubs. The Pig and Whistle, called the mill pub, stood opposite the timber mill and was where the mill workers drank. There was also the Shammy, or Shamrock, in High Street. Dad said it didn't worry him where he drank it was all bullshit anyway. But it was nice to catch up with the blokes from the church and St Mary's tennis club on Fridays. The river pub was a really solid pub, but he liked the friendlier atmosphere of Kelly's. On hot nights the drinkers would spill out onto the street and they would often mix and have a friendly beer. All the pubs except the Caladonian had dart and hooky teams which travelled around and played each other. The River pub was where the Masons drank. Sean meant to ask his dad how come all the masons were Prodos and did builders ban all Catholics from being brickies? Dad's boss, Mr Caruthers, had taken him to the top pub the first day on the job. He said the dining room was as big as Myers, the silverware was heavy and chunky, and they even had pineapples and mangoes on the sweets table, things he hadn't seen since the war. The bar was built on the English style with lots of stained wood and big oak tables and the manager even spoke like a pom. He put on airs like a queen dick. His dad had said he was mighty glad Mr Caruthers was paying for the meal. Five shillings for a main course seemed a lot, good as it was. Every time Mr Caruthers came to town they would have lunch there but otherwise dad said he was happy to stay out of the place.

Sean passed the shops and businesses in High Street, heading towards the little shop with the red and white striped pole and the big 'Craven A' sign out the front. The shop sign read 'Smithy the Barber' although it was Mr White's shop. Sean leaned his bike against the verandah post and went inside. The floor was bright yellow linoleum and one wall was all mirrors. Mr White was standing over a bald head and a white face with a cut-throat razor in his hand. The steam was rising from a big cream mug on the red-gum counter. The bald head glistened under a bare electric bulb suspended from the pressed metal ceiling. Mr White looked up as Sean entered the shop.

'G'day, Mr White. I'm Sean Butts, a friend of Berty's. Alright to see him?'

Mr White pointed to the back of the shop through some cane hangers hiding the back door. 'Through there, young fella.'

Sean went through the back door to another room with a chair and table supporting stained and chipped tea cups and a tin of bikkies. Another door led to the backyard of the shop. Berty was sweeping the back steps, a Ginger Megs comic poking out of his back pocket. His face looked worse than yesterday. His eye was blood red and half closed.

'G'day, Berty.'

'G'day, Sean.'

Sean squatted on the back step. 'I've got your marbles back. Probably not the same ones. Better, I think.'

'Jiminy Cricket, Sean, where did you get them from??'

'Johnny McCarthy and I had a bit of a talk.' Sean pulled out the little blue bag. 'He also wanted to give these back.'

Berty's face went white, the bruised cheek went a deeper shade of purple, the red eye squeezed out a tear. 'Oh, Sean, you're the best!'

The next morning the gang surrounded him at the bike rack. Johnny's arm and legs were covered in bandaids and mercurochrome.

Harry Smythe blustered and bellowed. 'We're gonna get you, Buttenwog, you German Kraut bastard!'

They started to push and shove. Hands were on his back, someone was pulling at his bag, and his cap was knocked off. He grabbed Harry's throat. Suddenly the booming voice of Sister Hildegard sounded out.

'What's going on over there ladies? Do ye have a problem over there?'

Sean felt the pressure relax around him, suddenly there was space. The bag on his back fell back into position. Sean's arms fell to his side. He looked up to see the Sister on the verandah. Berty and a group of grade fivers were standing just below her. Sean knew Berty had saved him.

'Laddies, what is going on?'

Harry Smythe said, 'We're just helpin' Sean with his bike, Sister.'

'I'm sure Mr Buttenberg is quite able to take care of that by himself, Mr Smythe.'

'Yes, Sister.'

'Well, I'm thinking you all better be away with you. Mr Smythe, may I see you for a minute in my office? And also you, Mr McCarthy. Have you been mauled by a dog?'

'No, Sister. I fell off my bike on the way home from school.'

'Well, you must be more careful, laddie. Come and we will have a little talk about it.'

Smythe and McCarthy slowly made their way towards the verandah. Their feet dragging in the blue metal, little swirls of dust followed the marks they made. The rest of the gang slowly dispersed. Mary Addison and a group of girls were looking at him curiously from across the playground. Sean thought the Sister's eyes were looking straight through him. He turned and straightened up his bag and set his bike in the rack. When he turned again, it was as if nothing had happened. The playground was the usual activity of marbles and skipping, running and jumping, laughter and chatter. McCarthy and Smythe were waiting at the Head Sister's door. The apostle birds waited patiently in the trees.

The sniping and low-grade attacks continued, but that was all. Only Berty was a friend. No other kid was game to come near him. Except for Mary Addison, but she was only a girl.

The Swamp

One day he diverted off the highway into the swamp. He had noticed a track barely passable just down from the bridge on the Koonarook side. He rode no more than a few yards, before it petered out and became muddy. The bikes wheels stuck in the gooey grey mud. He left it against an old burned out red gum, which poked its long dead trunk up through the underbrush. Through the saplings, reeds and grass beds he pushed. There were birds here: swallows, pelicans, ducks, and darters. Ibis flew around, lots of them, all white with long black bare necks, black heads and wing tips, long curved beaks like Turkish swords. They walked like kings. In groups and pairs they strutted making hoarse croaking noises. The young ones were white with puffy black feathers around their necks. Sean knew they were Sacred Ibis. He had checked out his father's bird book after seeing them circling around the swamp on his way to and from school. A goanna darted away into the scrub, its long tail waving, the tongue flicking in and out, its short legs carrying it along at a quick pace. He chased it up into a tree and it quickly blended into the foliage. A bush wallaby, frightened at his noisy approach, bounded off, its grey coat making it almost invisible in the dappled light beneath the trees. He passed ducks and waterhen feeding off the many pools and reed beds spaced between the trees. It was like another planet. Bats hung in the trees in dark recesses. They had little dog faces and folded skin wings with strange back legs which gripped the trees. Sean knew they did not suck blood like the boys thought, but ate fruit and nectar from the trees. He walked along the track slowly, seeking the prize that waited for him at its end.

The bomber lay on its belly, its body open at the middle around the gun bays. The wings were sheared off. The tail pointed defiantly at the clouds, and the big number '5' in faded red stood out with the red, white and blue circular tricolour just visible underneath. Red-gum saplings grew up through it. Sean made his way in and climbed up through the body and into the pilot's seat. There was no covering on it, just bare metal and springs. Not much was left of the instruments but gaping holes and wires. The joy stick was still in place on the pilot's side. It moved backwards and forwards, and the half-round wheel on its end still moved. Sean could look down through a hole in the floor and see where the bombardier and navigator front gunners had sat. His mind filled with pictures of aeroplanes, he could hear the drone of the planes taking off and cruising above the clouds. He saw the Nazi Messerschmitt 109s coming in with red corkscrew noses, guns blazing, and his gunners blazing away, shooting them out of the sky. He was over his target and gave the command, 'Bombs away!', and banked the plane sideways as shells burst all around. He frantically adjusted the throttle levers and turned the joy stick to keep control. He gave instructions to his crew – fighters at twelve o'clock, feather the starboard engine, radio base, check tail gunner. He raced to the mid-section and blasted away at the Nazi foe with his red-gum machine gun. 'HN hn hn hn hn hn.' He shot the Krauts out of the sky.

After a time he dragged himself away, time to go home.

More and more often after school he wandered off down that nothing track into the secret world of the swamp. There was always something to do; killing Nazis, watching the birds, trying to spear a goanna. Sometimes he would go down to the river just beyond the aeroplane. Here the banks sloped at a gentle incline into the river. The last foot or so before the water was grey, sticky, soft oozy mud. Sean guessed that this side flooded. It was on the inside of the wide curve that made up the course of the Murray between the two towns. The swamp was indented every twenty feet or so with rivulets that were most often dry. Sean would see the holes of the yabbies and shrimps in the soft mud and, above them, the cormorants and darters sitting in the trees drying their wings or waiting for a meal to present itself. Little swallows in the evening shadows darted up and down chasing the millions of insects on the water. Every now and then a fish would jump and there was a flash of silver. Little minnows darted among the shallows. Sometimes they would rush across the surface skipping and weaving, chased by something. Often it was quiet, the sun sparkled on the brown waters. It was as if the whole world was taking a breather. Sean would sit quietly too. Then, bang!, something would happen and the world was suddenly awake. Once, while sitting in the afternoon shadows, all had gone quiet, the ducks had headed inshore, the constant chatter of waterhens, snipes and sand pipers had gone. Looking up, Sean could just make out the white under-belly of the sea eagle as it patrolled for the fish, bird or marsupial that would be its next meal. How did they know? What was the signal?

Sometimes, Sean would make his way along the bank to the grave-yard. The skeletons of the barges lay broken and scattered over a wide area of muddy foreshore. This was a place where there were many water rats and field mice. If he looked carefully he could make out the little enclosures the field mice had made in the grass and often the water rats could be seen hurrying along the water's edge, their long black bodies shimmering. He had to be very still to see them. One time he had seen a swamp harrier with a water rat in its mouth, circling above. Looking up from the graveyard he could see the underside of the bridge, its four massive cylindrical columns jutting, brown and rusty, down into the water, the rivets standing out like pawns in a chess set. The huge retractable part thrust upwards into the sky like the spiers at St Patrick's Cathedral.

He had gone to St Pat's once when his uncle became a priest; it was as boring as hell. The bridge was much more interesting, the traffic going over making the bump de bump noise as the timber decking under the bitumen surface moved. Sometimes the muffled voices of the co-op workers walking home could be heard, mainly women. Sometimes he would hear a faint giggle or high-pitched laugh. At times a bottle or an apple core would sail over the walkway and plonk into the river. As the sun sank lower in the sky, long shadows thrown by the pylons would move up river, falling over the graveyard. He would sit there, very still, as the shadows slowly moved over him. The water rats became active and the harrier hawks and kookaburras took up their positions. After a while the birds, sent hurrying by his intrusion, would come back, the animals would start scurrying and the noises of the swamp would become louder. It was as though he didn't exist. He had been swallowed by a dinosaur and the columns of the bridge were its ribs. He was invisible.

There was a freedom in the swamp. He was not the new kid, outsider, city bastard, unwelcome. He wondered why he never saw anyone else.

Sean had not been able to penetrate right into the heart of the swamp. He was always blocked by water, mud and dense undergrowth. Still, he would do it sometime. It looked as though there was an island of taller trees there, he could just see them in the distance above the shrubs and trees. They looked big. On his way to school in the mornings, looking over from the bridge, he could make out a distinct circle of trees.

The sniping and jostling continued at school but Sean thought Sister Hildegard's power kept the gang off him. He often sensed someone was watching him as he left for home. And sometimes a kid on a bike would be not far behind as he rode towards the bridge. So far he had not been challenged but he knew it must come.

Sometimes Sean would look at Mary Addison, her pretty face, the dimple on her cheek which deepened the more she concentrated, the wavy black hair protesting at the bands which kept it locked in, the little chest bumps pushing against the fabric of her dress.

The Storm

His mother was frustrated by his late comings and goings. As autumn came on it was nearly dark by the time he came home sometimes. At the weekends and in the afternoons when his dad went off to play cricket he would head off to the swamp, coming home just before night fall. One evening his mother confronted him.

'Where have you been. Sean?'

'Mucking around with some friends.'

'Well, I want you to come right home from school. It's a worry. I hope you're not hanging around by that dreadful river. There's snakes, goannas, all sorts of nasty things. If you fell in the river, you would never be found.'

'The animals in the bush won't hurt you.'

'I will speak to your father. We will have to see about some more chores around the house to keep you busy.' Mrs Paver at the mother's club said to Mrs Johnson, 'These city kids never seem to fit in. They just cause trouble in the class.' She looked at me as she said it. 'Is it true, Sean? Are you a troublemaker?'

'Mum, I just want to be left alone. Can you understand that?'

'Don't speak to me like that. You're not in the school yard now!' She retreated into the kitchen. He followed her.

'I won't, you're a bitch, always nagging me. I hate you!'

His mother's back arched. She turned on him, her face reddening. 'How dare you! Go to your room.'

'I won't. I'm never coming back here. I hate you!' He ran out through the back door, slamming it. The little swallow on the wood heap flew off in a panic as he rushed past. He headed to the river.

In the graveyard watching the sugar ants fight off an invasion of bull ants, Sean was trying to forget what had just happened. He felt compelled to help the little ants by killing a few of the bigger bull ants. As they struggled for supremacy, his anger made him cruel. Suddenly explosions of dust erupted around the battlefield. Who was using artillery? One explosion knocked a bull ant off its feet. The black sugar ants swarmed over him. Sean looked up at the sky that had been clear and blue. It was now black, purple and forbidding, the air was still and close, thunder and lightning filled the northern sky. Suddenly the visibility that had been so bright was gone. He looked down at the ants, they had all disappeared. Must be headed for home, and he better do the same. He was up and away along the bank and past the B17, the night was gathering, the raindrops were falling heavier and more constantly. He ran into the bush following the usual trail. He could hardly see. Suddenly, he sprawled onto the ground, his grey school jumper tore at the sleeve, his foot caught around a dead branch. He picked himself up. All around him was shadow and grey, all unfamiliar. He had never been in the swamp at night. The rain was coming down much harder now. He struggled forward, but his feet gave way, he was in mud and slush. One of his shoes came off. He struggled forward. He crashed into trees and branches. They grabbed at his clothes, arms and legs. He kept going. Would he ever find his way out? The sky was completely black. He heard the roll of thunder and saw the lightning. This was real trouble.

Slow down. He stopped. The rain was like a waterfall on his head, his clothes stuck to him, the ground was soft and slippery, his shoe-less foot was numb. He took the other shoe off and placed it in his pocket. He took some deep breaths and concentrated hard. The lightning came again and he saw it, the track, he was going in the right direction and not far away was his bike. He followed the memory of where he had seen the track. Another thunderclap, a bolt of lightning, and there was his bike against the burned out red gum. He had made it, he was nearly there, nearly at the road. He felt his way over to the bike, the handle bars felt heavy. He started up the rise that led onto the highway, the track becoming clearer as he went. The lightning kept coming, showing him the way, he made the highway. The bridge in the distance was illuminated against the black sky as the lightning tore the blackness in half. He looked back towards the blackness of the swamp.

Suddenly all was light. A hot blast struck him, exploding, his ear drums seemed to be bursting, thunder vibrated his very being, he was blown off his feet and propelled through the air. He landed in a jumble of confusion on all fours in the middle of the highway. His eyes hurt. He felt the salt of tears mingling with the rain on his face. He saw that the lightning had exploded the old gum tree into pieces. Burning ingots of wood lay all around him and the stump was flaming like a Chinese lantern. Lucky, thought Sean. As he stood up, he felt blood trickling from his knees. His face was dry and parched despite the rain, and he noticed his shirt had been torn open. An ugly red welt burned across his chest. It was hard to breathe.

Suddenly there was light again, but this time along the road, coming directly at him, it was blinding and urgent, getting larger and larger. Sean could not see anything except the light, which seemed to overpower him. It contained him and held him. Suddenly Sean knew and reacted, throwing himself into the culvert beside the road as the big truck sped past. He felt the air from its passing wash his face as he dived, the wave of water and spray enveloped him, he felt the impact on his nose as he gouged a path into the gutter, his shoulder gave way as his body ricocheted into the stonework. He saw the sparks fly as his bike was hit and dragged along under the truck, the screech of metal was like the cry of a night owl.

When Sean awoke the rain had eased and the thunder was rolling drums in the distance. Occasionally there was a distant sideshow as the lightning played in concert with the storm. He got up shakily. His head ached, and the blood on his knees and face had dried, making his skin feel tight. His left shoulder was stabbing with pain, he could not move his left arm, his chest felt like it was on fire. He felt a sickness rising up and vomited into the gutter. The liquid splashed his bare feet. The swamp and all around was quiet and still, the rain now a fine mist. The red gum stump stood jagged and diminished, and glowed red from its inside.

He started to walk towards home along the side of the highway. His feet did not want to go, he couldn't feel them. Every step jarred his head, his chest, his shoulder. He crashed into something, toppled and fell. A searing pain punched into his stomach. He had fallen over what was left of his bike. Sobs racked his body. He dry reached onto the bitumen. He saw the light of another truck coming around the bend from the bridge. He pulled a piece of jagged pipe from his stomach crying out in pain. He pushed the remains of the bike into the gutter. In the light of the oncoming truck it was a twisted pile of junk. He saw the seat in the middle of the road as the truck sped past. He stumbled onto the road and groped for it. He fell down. With his good hand he felt for his stomach. There was moisture. He felt for the seat again, and found it, the little oil skin tool bundle still in place under the seat, everything was not quite lost. He began the impossible trudge towards home.

The houses were strangely dark. The powerlines had been hit. Here and there through the windows he saw the flicker of a lamp or candle. He was struggling to breathe and kept falling and stumbling. He staggered along in a daze, sometimes on all fours, but he kept moving. His house loomed in the distance. The back gate was open. He stumbled into the gate post and clung to it. He could see his father in the light of a pressure lamp talking to a circle of men, a khaki shirt clung to his body, his felt hat oozed water, his face was creased, the eyes hooded and heavy, his shoulders were stooped more than normal. The faces of the men were sharp with intent and concentration. They were for the most part dressed in an assortment of working clothes and Driza-Bones, their hats a uniform dirty brown, blackened with water. Sean staggered, crawled into the circle of light, the dozen or so men looked as one at him as he came into view.

The look on his father's face was something new. He passed the lamp to the fellow standing beside him. His lips quavered. His hands went to his forehead.

'Sean!'

Then he was in his father's arms. He felt his father sigh. Now he was inside, pressure lamps everywhere, and women and kids, some he had never seen before. His mother was in the kitchen, tea cups and bikkies on the table. Her face was tear streaked, her makeup had run. Her hair wet and tangled, she gasped as his dad brought him into the room.

'He's home, Mary. He's home.'

Wounded

Sean woke. He was in a bed, the sheets tight around him. It was not his bed. He could hear female voices. There was a strange smell. A hospital.

When Katy was born, dad had taken him to the hospital. They looked at the baby through a glass partition. Dad had said, 'Isn't she beautiful?' How did she get out of Mum?, Sean had thought. Annie, their cat, had holed up in the laundry once, on one of dad's work jumpers. Sean had found her because he had stored his swallow eggs in mum's preserving jars. As he watched her, a little kitten had started coming out of her. Annie had started to lick it and then bit through the cord coming out of its stomach. It had wriggled and meowed and moved up to Annie's tits, then another had come out and another. That was how his mother had probably done it. She had the help of some nurses, though she must have a sore bum. Sean grimaced. He knew a bit better now, but that smell was the same.

He moved ever so slightly. A stabbing pain caught him in the left shoulder and the strapping around it pulled. His body felt heavy and lifeless, his right knee was stuck to the top sheet, his head was going to explode. There were strapping and dressings all over him. He tried to open his eyes. Sean brought his good hand up to feel them. Why wouldn't they open? They were oozing a thick sticky substance. His face was dry and sore. He could feel the skin come off against his hand. All was black. He felt a surge of panic. He'd been blinded by the lightning. He squirmed in the bed, and the pain like a wave hit him again, the sheets hemmed him in. He felt a surge in his stomach. A burning sensation came up his throat and into his mouth. He spat it out, and felt it trickle across his throat.

He cried out. 'Mum! Dad!'

He heard the female voices come together. Something clattered on the floor. A metal dish? A door opened and he heard his mother's voice.

'Sean, Sean, your awake?'

He felt his mother beside him. The sweet smell of her perfume filled his senses, the softness of her hands were on his brow.

'Mum, I'm blind and I'm dying and...' he blurted.

'Shush, shush, Sean, you'll be alright. You've just been asleep for a while. You'll be fine.'

He felt her lips brush his forehead and the softness of her hair against his parched face.

Another voice. 'Thank you, Mrs Buttenberg. We will look after him now.'

He felt the bed grow lighter as his mother move away.

'Now, Sean, laddie, let us have a look at you,' the female voice said, and there was a swish of linen. She was Irish, like Sister Hildegard. 'I'm Sister Louise, Sean. I have been looking after you. You have been asleep for a couple of days and you're in the hospital. We'll give you a bit of a cleanup and see how you're going, eh.'

Sean felt big strong hands on his forehead. The palms were coarse and rough but strangely gentle.

'Mrs Buttenberg, can you go and fetch Nurse Harradine?'

Sean heard his mother's footsteps move away. 'Now, laddie, relax, lay back we'll see what to do, eh.'

Sean felt comforted by the confident voice. He felt the sheets slowly pulled back, and winced as they came away from him.

Nurse Harradine made herself known by a 'yes, Sister, what do you want me to do?' He had not heard her enter the room.

'Nurse, I need a warm, mild soap solution, some eye wash dressings and creams, over on that trolley there. Also some gloves, aprons and scissors.'

He winced in pain as the dressings were replaced. Nurse Harradine's hands were small, smooth and gentle. She smelled of lavender; the big sister smelled of hospital and soap.

'Tell me where you are hurting,' Sister Louise kept saying as she probed and prodded. All over his body she went feeling and pushing. Sean felt every move, but he gritted his teeth and told her exactly where it was hurting.

'Nurse, keep washing. I will give Sean something for the pain.' Sister Louise moved away.

'Am I going to be blind?'

'We'll ask Sister when she comes back. I think you will be all right.'

The sister's presence was again announced by the swish of linen and a rush of air. 'Sean, we are just going to give you a little needle. We need to change your main dressings.'

'Sister, Sean wants to know if he will be blind.'

There was a pause.

'No, laddie, you won't be blind. Dr O'Loughlin thinks you have sunburned eyes caused by the lightning strike and will be alright in a few days. Now, laddie, just a small prick in the backside.'

Sean felt the needle go in. He didn't care.

'We'll clean your eyes, stomach and knee dressings, all right, then?'

Sean felt her hands on his eyes and warm liquid slowly caressing them. He felt he was floating, his body was lifting off the bed. He heard his father's voice faraway, then his mother's. Nurse Harradine's small hands were cleaning his parched face and then the blackness came again.

Sean woke and squirmed in the bed. The pain was not as intense now. His left arm was strapped to his body, his lips cracked and dry. His stomach felt stretched, he could feel the dressings on it and his chest pulling against his skin. His muscles were tired but he felt alright, even hungry. He tried to open his eyes. There was still some goo in them but they opened. They felt a bit sandy but the pain had gone. The room was semi-dark with white walls. A ceiling fan directly above him was not going. There was a slight chill and he struggled further into the bed. The cast metal bed head loomed up large and black behind him. It had a plaque with some writing on it. There was a door into the room and, opposite the door, a large window. In the evening twilight he could just make out the posts of a verandah and some creepers crawling along cast-iron facings. At the end of the bed was a trolley with bowls and dressings. He closed his eyes. They were starting to hurt again.

Sean felt the presence of someone in the room. There was a gentle breathing and over the hospital smell he could trace the perfume of his mother. His dad said that was the best thing to ever come out of the war. He had bought it from a Yank. Now, whenever he went to Melbourne, he shopped at Georges. It was expensive, he said, but it lasted for ages and, besides, it made Mary feel like a real lady.

Sean opened his eyes. His mother was slumped in a cane easy chair. Her dress was creased and partly covered by her favourite blue cardigan. Her shoes were partly off, hanging on her outstretched feet, and her head had fallen to one side. Her hair hung loose down to her shoulders. Her hands were clasped lightly in her lap, and at the foot of the chair her black go-everywhere bag was laying open with a copy of the *Women's Weekly* sticking out. Her ivory rosary beads dangled over the lip of the bag, and she was breathing quietly.

He looked at her until his eyes started to hurt again. He didn't really get on with his mother. He knew she found him difficult. But, just now, he understood he was looking at one of the few people who really cared for him and he thought her the most beautiful person in the world. Her eyes opened and she looked at him. She sat up and stretched.

'Sean! You're awake at last, thank God.' She came over to him and put her arms gently around him. The warmth of her body made him dreamy, the wetness of her tears stung his face, her body was rent by deep sobs. They stayed that way for a long time.

'Thanks mum,' he whispered.

'Sean, that's alright, as long as you get better. Can you see?'

'Yes, but they hurt a bit.'

'Good, good, good, they will get better.' She moved back, the moment of closeness gone. Sean could see that her eyes were red. 'Sean, you also have a broken arm, up near the shoulder, and a stomach puncture wound. They had to operate on that. They were hoping you didn't get an infection. There's a deep burn across your chest, which will scar, and cuts and bruises all over your body and you probably broke your nose as well.' She slumped back into the chair again. 'What happened, Sean? Did you get run over by a car? Dad found your bike just up the highway. It was mangled to bits.' Sean noticed black rings under her eyes, but before he could say anything she was off again. 'Katy is at the Herds. They have been wonderful neighbours. Sally has been making meals and cleaning the house. The whole town has just been wonderful. The St Vincent de Paul fellows dropped around some goodies, and the cricket and football clubs have been calling, and ran a raffle to pay for the hospital. The CWL ladies have been baking cakes and Father Riley came in and blessed you. They said prayers for you in Church and Sister Hildegard phoned and passed on her regards and said the school and nuns have been praying for you. Dad has been dropping in here all the time before and after work. He should be here soon. Sean, you are a very lucky boy. You could have been killed.' Now she was getting up. 'Sister Louise said I was to get her if you woke again.' She started to leave.

'Mum, how long have I been here?'

'Why, Sean, nearly a week.'

'Mum, I love you!'

She stopped, stood still, and looked at him intently. 'I love you too, Sean.' Then she was out of the room, the door creaking as it opened and closed.

Sister Louise was a big robust lady about five foot ten and broad across the shoulders. Her face was creased in amused lines and continually held a smile or look of expectation. Her manner was brisk, though not hurried, and she talked as she worked. Over the next couple of days, Sean got to know her well. She was the head nurse at the Caladonia Hospital. All the workers seemed to like her and called her Sister, rarely Sister Louise. She was a religious sister who had come to the hospital more than thirty years ago because the government could not staff the hospital. Four sisters had come and she was the only one left. The order wanted her to leave but she said this was her home and she was happy to do the Lord's work here. She said she had told them that more than a few times. She seemed to know most of the town and district people and all of their family histories. She had even delivered some of the nurses. She told him something new each day as she inspected his wounds, bathed and dressed him. She wore a plain brown dress of starched linen and a funny kind of stiff board on her head. She said her order wanted her to wear the habit, but she told them to move over into the twentieth century. It was impractical up here, especially in the summer.

'Anyway', she said, 'they probably don't make habits big enough for my size anymore,' and she laughed and laughed.

As they talked and she worked, Sean felt drawn to the good-natured Sister and he told her about the swamp and school, even about the Smythe gang and his troubles with them. She listened and hummed and hahhed, and she never once asked how he had injured himself or passed a bad word about anyone to him. She just said, 'Oh, yeh, I know the Smythes, delivered all of them. I don't know how she does it, poor little thing.' When Sean told her how he had been injured, she just said, 'Well, Sean, God must have you in mind for something pretty special, if he saved you that way. But then Sean's Irish for John, you know, and St John was always a special person for Jesus.'

Sister Louise wasn't Irish at all, but her parents were. They had immigrated before she was born, settling in Collingwood near St Vincent's Hospital. That is where she got her interest in nursing, seeing the sisters go about their work. Her father had been a boiler man at the hospital and she used to follow him around at work during the holidays and weekends. She knew everything about steam boilers and wished she could have been a boiler man like her dad, but, of course, she was not allowed to. That was men's work.

Dr O'Loughlin was a small, tidy man in a dark waistcoat and white lab coat, and did his rounds with Sister Louise every morning. They chatted as they examined the patients. The doctor seemed to be taking orders as much as giving them. Sean could hear them before seeing them. They would talk to him about his condition as though they had rehearsed it. The doctor confirmed his mother's report and repeated that he was lucky to be alive. If the lightning hadn't killed him, the puncture wound to his stomach should have.

Nurse Harradine

Nurse Harradine was very young and had just started her training. She wore a blue dress with white pin stripes and a little nurse's head piece. Her face was small, her hair pulled up and back accentuating her prettiness. She gradually took over more of the duties from Sister Louise as he got better. She would flit around and Sean noticed that even under the severe nursing uniform she had a nice shape. She babbled away about her home in Deniliquin, or Denny as she called it, her family's farm up there and how she hoped to travel onto Melbourne and Sydney as she got older. She would bathe him, and massage his back and tell him 'this is to keep your circulation going'. Sometimes he could feel the softness of her as she leaned across him to do her work. A couple of days after he woke, Sean knew he was getting better by his reaction to her massage. He could feel 'it' tighten as she rubbed his back. He hid his face in the pillow, biting into it. He hoped she did not notice.

'Roll over, Sean. I'll tuck you in.'

Sweat was breaking out on his forehead and he trembled. 'Nurse, can I just stay on my tummy for a little while.'

She considered this. Finally, 'Oh, alright then, but only for a little while. I don't want you breaking those stitches. I'll be back soon to finish,' and she was gone.

His stomach wound felt sore and non cooperative, his chest painful from the heavy breathing, but thankfully the other subsidence was going away. The sweat dried on his face. He relaxed and started to doze.

Just before they had left Brunswick, he and his mate OB were inside their fort on Back Creek. Bluey Riley had burst in, his red freckled face redder than usual. Sean and OB were planning their next raid on the Carter gang.

'Leave that. This is more important,' Bluey had said excitedly. He pulled a curled, yellow, rolled-up magazine from under his school jumper.

'Yeh,' said OB, 'what can be more important than knocking over the Carter gang again, especially Puddings Carter.'

Bluey cut him off. 'Knockin' off a sheila, that's what.'

Sean and OB looked at each other, shifting nervously. They wondered what Bluey was up to.

Bluey moved in between them. He was breathing heavily as he opened the well-turned pages, his eyes wide and moist, his voice cobbled with excitement. 'Get a look at this!' He thrust a page at them. 'Have you ever seen tits like that before? You'd get lost in 'em!'

The pictures continued page after page. Sean's hard-on was so strong it hurt. He looked at OB and Bluey. 'Bloody thank God the Carters aren't here now. We'd all trip over!'

'I wonder what it's like sticking it up a girl?' OB said.

Bluey was serious. 'Frank and that Sheila McGloshin are going out. Well, he said she lets him finger her after the Saturday night dance at the Town Hall. They go down the lane right beside it. He said it's like putting your finger into a warm orange. But, you know what, she goes down and sucks him off. It's amazing.'

'Why doesn't he put it in her?' Sean said.

'She won't let him. She doesn't want to end up the duff like her mum. Frank said her knockers are so big and smooth, he can't hold them all in one hand. He sucks her nipples and she squirms and comes and becomes all moist.'

'God, I'd have to stick it in her,' OB exclaimed.

'No, he tried it once and she hit him over the head. She said if you try that again, Frankie, we are through and you won't get to do anything.'

'Bloody hell,' said OB.

'Whow,' said Sean, thinking of the McGloshin girl. He would see her on her way to the knitting mill in the morning and at Mass with her family. He would take more interest in her next time. She was not that pretty, with short, mousy hair and a kind of dumpy figure, but she was well dressed and fairly quiet, always standing in the background. She did have big tits, though. The boys had all gone quiet, each lost in their own thoughts. Sean broke the silence.

'Well, better get home. How come Frank tells you all that stuff, Bluey? Is he fair dinkum?'

'Yeh, him and I always get on. You know, Frank takes care of me when the old man comes home drunk on Friday nights lookin' for a fight. Frank always said he wished he had an older brother to teach him things about girls, seeing we don't have any sisters. He said he's giving me a head start.'

'Yeh, he's a good bloke, is Frank,' said OB.

'Yeh, I reckon,' said Sean. Standing up awkwardly, he turned quickly. 'See you blokes later.'

Later at tea Sean had looked at his mother and Kate and pictured the magazine. He played with the food on his plate.

'Sean, are you all right?'

'Yeh, mum, I'm just not hungry, that's all.'

'That's all? It's your favourite, pot roast and mash.'

That night, in bed, he couldn't keep his hands off it. Pictures of

Bluey's magazine, girls and the McGloshin sheila flashed through his mind. He hardly touched it in his hand and it came all over him, warm and lots of it. He awoke in the morning exhausted, his pyjamas clung to him. He made the bed and got on with the day. No one had noticed. But then, a few days later, walking to the footy, his dad had spoken to him about men and women, love and sex. He had said it was all natural and described the act as though he was discussing the footy scores.

'The most important thing is don't get love and sex mixed up. They are two different things. You can have one without the other, but if you have them both, it's a bonus.'

Sean's dreams continued, on and off, but never as intense as that first night. Sean smiled. OB and Bluey, they had probably done the same as him, the wankers.

Hospital

'I wasn't knocked off my bike by the truck, the lightning blew me away, and then I tripped over the bike on the way back home.' Sean's words tumbled out quickly.

'Slow down, Sean, and start at the beginning.'

Sean's dad had come in soon after he had woken that second time. Sean told his Dad the whole story.

'That's the damndest escape story I've heard since the war. If you told that to anybody in the pub, they wouldn't believe you. Oh, the *Courier* ran a story on you with pictures of the burned out tree and all. I'll bring it in tomorrow.'

'Thanks, dad.'

'And Shorty Malone wants a statement from you. I'll go and see him. It'll be right.'

Sean's days at the hospital started at six when the night nurses came in to wake and bathe him, then breakfast arrived soon after. The doctor's round was at nine and his mother's visit at about ten. She brought books and comics for him to read, and stayed for a couple of hours. Lunch, normally sandwiches and milk, was at twelve. He read for a while and then slept. Tea was at five, mostly hot meat and vegies, then visitors from six to eight. Nights went really quick. He dreamed of Nurse Harradine and sometimes the lightning would come and he would wake, sit up and feel the darkness. After a few days he was allowed up in the afternoons to sit on the verandah.

The first day Sean was allowed out on the verandah, he was sitting quietly, soaking up the sun. A man dressed in the brown bib overalls of the tradesman, old army boots and a battered felt hat came over.

'Warm enough, Sean?' The man's face was as brown and battered as the hat. Its lines were deep and friendly.

'Yes,' Sean said. 'Thank you.'

'That's good. Bill Heanen's my name. Gardener and handyman. Your father in the army during the war?'

'Yes.'

'Do you know what unit?'

'My dad doesn't say much about the war. I think he was in the Second Seventh and then on special service with the Americans.'

'Ah,' Bill reached for a rolly. A cloud of blue smoke enveloped him as it ignited. He blew out and spoke at the same time. 'Second Seventh mud on blood, bad deal in Crete, some of them abandoned on the beaches after acting as the rearguard, what was left of them. Ceylon, home, then New Guinea and the Islands, great bunch of blokes.' He drew deeply on his cigarette. 'I'll catch up with your dad at the RSL. He's in Koonarook, eh? See you around, then.' He shuffled off, one boot leaving a drag mark in the soft gravel of the pathway.

Abos

As Bill left, a group of people in the centre of the hospital grounds caught his eye. Aboriginals. There was a bench there but they were not using it, preferring to squat and sit in a circle on the sparse grass under a tree. The group consisted of men and women. The women were in colourful cotton dresses and their hair hung long behind them. The men were in blue jeans and western shirts, with wide belts and wider brimmed hats. They were listening to a tall man who gesticulated and occasionally answered some question. He was thin, wiry, his face large and generous with a full flowing beard. His white hair contrasted sharply with the deep shiny blackness of his skin.

Even from where he was sitting, Sean could see the man had the others entranced. Charisma, his dad had said once after they had read a book on Sitting Bull, the Sioux warrior. His dad said some people just had it, other people thought they had it, and some people worked hard to get it. It was something you felt rather then saw, he explained. It normally meant that you felt persuaded to follow that person or his views.

As Sean watched, the man looked over and smiled. Sean nodded and smiled back. The man went back to his talking, and Sean saw Sister Louise joining the group.

The next day Sean asked the big sister about the group.

'Oh, Sean, they were poor Billy Mullet's family and Joseph Wirrinum come to see about burying him. Billie is in the mortuary waiting for Dr Simpson to do an autopsy. They found him in the river down by Taylors Lagoon. Probably fell in and drowned. He'd been missing about three or four days before anyone noticed. Last person to see him was old Ben Herbert, the butcher. He saw him swigging sherry at Gunpowder Island, dead drunk he was, swearing and yelling at Ben, who was trying to do some fishing. He was a nuisance, but harmless. His mother was an angel. Didn't complain one bit when I delivered him. She had six kids to that man Jacobs. The seventh killed her.'

Sean knew the big sister didn't approve of Jacobs because she called him by his last name. All people she approved of were either given a title or a first name. Sean had noticed that Nurse Harradine had become Harradine one time when she had not changed Sean's dressing to her satisfaction. But then Sean had never heard the nun really say anything bad about anyone. She continued.

'Jacobs blew his brains out with old man Shelton's twenty-two. Sometimes I wonder if those half-caste people ever know where they belong. They always seem to be in Limbo to me. Neither black nor white. Those poor people have enough to worry about what with all their land gone and drink and disease and all that, without knowing who they are thrown in as well. Anyway, Sean, you don't have to worry about that, you'll experience enough of it, by and by, as you grow up without me gabbing on about it. Now, to answer your question about the Mullets, they are a big Abo family who live out at Five Mile Creek, downriver from here. Good people mostly. They come and go. Old Malachi Mullet is the leader of the mob. They come from around Barmah way originally. They want to bury Billy in the town cemetery. The shire has a blacks section there, where they bury the destitute and those who can't pay. It's just one step down from the Catholics,' she laughed. 'Joseph Wirrinum, the blackfella doing all the talking, is a local, a mighty good fella. He's been here or coming back here for longer than I can remember. He's a holy man, you know, like a witch doctor. He knows all the old ways. After Tom Reaper buries Billy in the Methodist way, Joseph will bury him in the Abo way. You know, Sean, that Joseph must be closer to God then the whole of us Christians put together. He has a way about him that's special, so humble and quiet. He lives down in the swamp, you know, that bit of rubbish land where you nearly got yourself killed.'

'I've never seen him there.'

'Well, he's down along near the mill, a little bark and tin hut among the trees. I went there once when he broke his leg and he was having it treated. Said he'd walk up to the hospital, but no I said, no it's too far. I'll come and see you. He made me billy tea and damper. By God, that tea was some of the nicest I've ever tasted. Out under the gum trees with the river flowing past, makes you wonder why we ever work inside. That was about twenty years ago now, and him and I have had a bit to do with each other ever since. Births, deaths, sickness, family disputes. If I have a problem, I send for him. The blackfellas are all scared of him or something. He's a Gooweera man, I think. He has all kinds of powers. If one of them Abos is sick, he brings them in some herbs or special powders. Dr O'Loughlin doesn't like it but I tell him it's all natural and they are God's people out of the wild and so wild things work for them. And, you know, Sean, I think some of Joseph's medicines are better than the stuff we give them. Roll over, young man, we'll see how those scratches on your back are going.'

Home

Sean's return home was uneventful. He was checked out by Dr O'Loughlin, but would have to make regular visits for a few weeks. Sister Louise gave him a big hug.

'You've been a good and brave laddie, Sean. Make sure I don't see you in here again.' She pressed him against her bosom.

'Thank you, Sister, for everything,' Sean stammered.

'Nice to meet you, Sean,' Nurse Harradine said. She curtsied to his mother.

As they walked out to the car his mother said, 'Well, she certainly is a lovely lady, that Sister Louise. I must invite her to the CWL. Now, Sean, Dr O'Loughlin said you will be home for about three weeks and then if all is well you can go back to school. I've arranged with Sister Rose for homework to be sent home. She said you won't have any trouble. You were ahead of the class anyway, and you're a good student.'

Sean was surprised at this revelation. He thought he was just going along, neither out front or behind.

'Sister Hildegard said to tell you she hopes you are well and that you will be back soon.'

'Thanks, mum,' Sean said without much conviction.

At home there was a red bike leaning against the back wall of the house. It was a Malvern Star.

'Jiminy Cricket!'

His mother smiled. 'Dad bought it off Kenny White, the green grocer. He said you can pay it off by doing some extra chores.'

When they were inside his mother sat him at the kitchen table. She put SAOs, Anzacs and a glass of milk down before him. 'I have been talking to your father and he said that you are an outside boy, you need to do that sort of thing, and he thinks we should encourage you and that I may have been a bit harsh on you, before you had the accident. At the same time he went and saw Sister Hildegard and she informed him of the troubles you are having at school with that awful Smythe boy and his friends. Dad thinks you should resolve this yourself over time and the less we get involved the better.'

Sean watched the routine of her tea making, which had seemed so mundane before but now made him feel secure. She placed the shiny silver pot on the stove to warm, then the Irish breakfast tea was recovered from the pantry and two generous spoonfuls placed in the pot. The boiling water was poured into the teapot. She retrieved the china cup and saucer with the little pink ribbons and blue swallows on them from their place on the large sideboard. The milk in the jug with the embroidered cloth and glass beads over it was placed next to them, and the strainer in its silver holder next to it. A small biscuit plate, a tea cosy with bees knitted into its thick side, and a red-gum teapot stand completed the assembly. Dad had bought the teapot stand for mum when they had first moved here. It was a deep, lustrous red and had little flowers and swans engraved into it. It looked out of place with all the other things but mum liked it because it had come from dad. The milk was poured into the cup with a flourish and the strainer placed on the cup with care. The teapot was then picked up and a little bit offered to the sink – his mother said that first part was never any good. And then the pot was put down on the pot stand and the cosy placed over it with care, the creases and lines pulled out. His mother would then turn the teapot three times on the stand and only then would she pour the tea in short bursts until she filled the cup. The strainer was then returned to its holder.

'I have drawn up a list of jobs you have to do every day and through the week, and if you do them you are allowed out. The only thing is that you must tell us where you are going and promise not to swim in the river. Mrs Andrews from the CWL was telling me her cousin Bill died when he was about your age, in the river.'

'Mum,' he said as he finished an Anzac. 'I'm really sorry for everything. I don't have any friends here except Berty White and he's in grade five. It is a bit lonely but I really like playing in the swamp.'

'Thank you, Sean. I think this matter has been an education for both of us. You better go and have a rest. I have to get Katy from the Herds.'

Sean was unable to ride, run, climb or do anything much. His mother had restricted him to bed and the lounge room. On the third day they went to the doctor, who told them he was doing nicely and that the district nurse would take over. Gradually his mother relaxed and the routine at home became almost normal, except he didn't go to school. He built a model Lancaster bomber his father had given him, read library books and did the homework sent by Sister Rose.

He was soon walking around and taking his arm out of the sling. His eyes were fine. About five days after his return home he wandered along the highway towards the swamp. Sean was surprised to see there was nothing there to indicate his near-death experience. No blood on the roadway. No black tyre marks with deep gorges and broken bitumen. It looked just like another piece of highway. The gutter he had fallen into looked like any other gutter, not the jagged painful pit that occupied his mind.

The dead gum that had once pointed its grey limbs towards the sky was now a burned out stump no more than four foot high and hollow through its middle and down into the ground. Sean walked over and looked into it. He saw the blinding flash and fireball again. He wandered down into the swamp along the obscure track. All was the same as he remembered it. The birds were still there, the little lizards still basked in the sun. This must be like when you die, he thought, life just keeps moving on. The big bomber almost seemed to be waiting for him. Sean looked up at the big tail. It was so peaceful here after the last few weeks.

He sat on a large red-gum stump and watched the river gurgling and churning past. The swallows were just starting to make their runs in the mid-afternoon sun, diving and darting above the water. The eddies and whirls were in constant movement, the brown water alive as it traced patterns that were always different but always similar. The sun reflected along the ripples and made the water light and reflective. Leaves and sticks floated along, mixing and swirling. Sean drifted into that state of mind his mother called daydreaming.

'Sean,' she would say, 'you are always daydreaming. Wake up, lad. Wake up and get on with it.'

His dad would say, 'the world has to have daydreamers like Edison and Einstein'. As long as you had some action to go with it, it didn't hurt to dream a little bit now and again.

Joseph

Sean's thoughts came and went - home, school, Nurse Harradine, his marble collection, the lightning strike, the darter diving out towards the other side of the river. Then he felt something. Someone was watching him. In a small clearing at his rear was the tall Aboriginal man he had seen at the hospital. He was squatting against a small sapling, the whites of his eyes stood out like beacons. He was dressed in dark trousers and shirt, and red braces. His face was shaded by a pale grey hat with a wide leather band. He was watching Sean intently and sucking on a pipe. The sweetness of it aroma caught his nose.

Sean felt a twinge of fear - and a sense of disappointment that his private place had been invaded.

The man stood and walked towards him. His legs were bowed and Sean recognised that he was a horseman.

'Sean, I didn't mean to make you afraid. I seen you sitting there and I thought maybe I might say hello to you, eh. But I bin wait in here so you could finish your dreaming.'

'How do you know my name?

'That man, Bill Heanen, from the hospital. He a friend of mine.'

'You live around here?'

'My camp just up a little bit. I bin seeing you here often. You play in the old bomber and down in the graveyard. I kept away from you.

No one else bin comes here. They think it is has a ghost. Maybe afraid of the snakes, lots of snakes here. But you different. You enjoy it here, ah.'

Sean had never spoken to an Abo before. The one's he had seen were either drunk in the street on Friday night or hanging around the edge of town in little groups or on the backs of utes. One day after school in his father's office he had seen a black man speaking in broken syllables and expressions.

'That bloke speaks funny,' he had said to his dad later.

'No. He didn't have much education but he sure was smart enough. Great talkers in their own lingo, great memories.'

Dingarra Dreaming

'You got time to sit down with an old fella?' He gestured to a fallen log.

'Yeh, some.' They sat on the log looking out at the river.

'My name is Joseph. From the Tamba Tamba clan of the Bindaree people. I gonna tell you a Koori story, that bin explain something about the lightning that nearly killed you. It old time long time ago story, alright.' He spoke in a soft, even way. 'Nooralie, the god father of all and creator, said my world must have light otherwise the plants and animals I have created will grow twisted and sick. He called one of his wives, Yhi, to him. She a favourite of this fella Nooralie, and very beautiful, energetic and playful. "Yhi, my world is coloured grey. It must have light. You are the brightest of my wives. You will travel above my world half the time and stay with me the other half. You will do this till the end of time and make the world of the Koori warm and light." Yhi was sad to leave Nooralie because he was kind and good but she was obedient to his wishes. She travelled across the skies lighting the day and making the earth warm and nice. Nooralie would sleep with Yhi at night and the whole world would go dark. The animals and man became afraid of the darkness. You see, Sean,' he said, 'the evil Marmoo dwelt in the darkness and preyed upon the men and animals.'

Sean hunched over in concentration. Joseph animated his story, every part accompanied by hand and arm movements.

'Nooralie heard the cries of his people and animals. Dingo made a din that woke Nooralie up. Nooralie said, "You have no respect dingo, you will cry every night". Poor dingo dog, he still cries until this day.'

Sean laughed.

'Nooralie thought what can I do, I cannot let Yhi be above them all times. She has to rest and I need her beside me. She will make it too bright for them to sleep. Nooralie went off alone into the blackest part of the sky to think and think about this problem. Ah, then he had a solution. I will make another light to brighten the night sky but it will be a gentle light to sooth men and animal and keep the evil Marmoo away. Nooralie looked about the earth for a suitable light. He came upon Bahloo, a Kobi man holy and wise. Nooralie appeared to Bahloo in a dream and said, "I will give you eternal life and great holiness until the end of the world. You will not die but see all and brighten up the night sky." Bahloo said in his dream, "Great and Holy Father, I will do your command".' Joseph looked up briefly at the sun passing behind high cloud.

'The next day Bahloo's clan found him gone and only a little shining stone where his body had been. Nooralie transferred him to the sky and that night for the first time the moon shone over the earth. Man and the animals were no longer afraid and the Marmoo stayed away. For many years Bahloo was happy in the night sky and he would rest in his wirraway during the day. But often he would see Yhi rise just over the horizon as he was going to bed and he wondered what this wonderfully beautiful and bright lady was like. He lingered and began to hunger for her as men hunger after women. Yhi would see Bahloo also and she too would wonder what Bahloo was like. He was a very handsome, tall man. Gentle, strong, wise looking. She too lingered at the sunset and would thirst for the sight and thought of Bahloo. But Nooralie's spirit was everywhere and the two lights could never meet. Am I going too long for you?' Joseph asked.

'No, go on. I've never heard a story like this before.'

'The evil Marmoo were stalking and stomping around in the blackness of the far sky. They said, "We must change this, otherwise we will never have power with these men and animal creatures". They saw how Bahloo and Yhi craved for each other. They bin make an awful plan and trap. The Marmoo held a great feast and invited the rain and wind spirits, men and animals. The Marmoo gave them much food and fermented brew and they all danced until they were like in a trance. There was much singing, dancing and boasting. The Marmoo drew those fellas the wind and rain to one side and said, "We are very powerful and can make the men and animals afraid. What can you do?" Burando the wind said, "I can make it blow until the sand will sting their eyes and they cannot see," and he did. Wainbaroo the rain said, "I can bring the clouds together and make it as dark as night and the rain thick so you can't see". So he did. The earth was covered in darkness, rain and cloud, with much wind. The men and animals ran away in fright, jabbering and speaking strangely as they went. The Marmoo snuck up to Bahloo's wirraway and whispered in his ear. "Wake up, wake up. It is dark and you have slept too long." Bahloo woke up with a fright and saw it was dark and raced into the sky. He was soon above the clouds where Yhi was still shining brightly. He saw her and loved her instantly. He had to have her for his woman. Yhi saw the handsome Bahloo and said, "Come over. You are a handsome and wise man. I will lay with you." And so Yhi and Bahloo came together.'

The old man looked at Sean and smiled. 'You understand what that mean, young fella?'

He continued. 'The Marmoo did all types of harm on earth. The dark became even darker as Bahloo lay with Yhi. I will have to tell you those stories about the dark time another day, Sean. The animals and men were afraid and they called out in fright and anger to Nooralie. "Why have you abandoned us to the evil Marmoo and the wind and rain?" Nooralie who had been far away heard their cries and he came to see what was happening. There was much crying out and the wind and rain made much noise. Nooralie saw it all in an instant and at the same time saw Yhi and Bahloo lying together. Nooralie's anger knew no bounds. He was so angry his words came out as fire, and so lightning Dingarra was born. He spoke harshly to wind and rain and told them to stop. The Dingarra made them much afraid and they ran and hid in the great cave far to the north. Nooralie said, "You have broken my trust. You will stay in the cave until I summon you. And only are you to blow strong when I send the Dingarra that will smite you if you are evil." The Marmoo ran in all directions from the wrath of Nooralie. The Dingarra lightning chased them and killed many, also trees and animals, even men were killed by the wrath of Nooralie.'

The old man paused. The effort of the story had transformed him. His skin glistened and his eyes were bright.

Sean said, 'What happened to Bahloo and Yhi?'

'I bin just coming to that, Sean, and to the part that concerns you also. Nooralie was storming around the sky cursing and chasing the Marmoo. He approached Bahloo and Yhi who were cowering in each other's arms afraid of what was to happen. "You have been unfaithful to me, Yhi. No more will you come to me, but always you will shine in the sky, you will be alone." Yhi went weeping away into the sky, her tears falling to earth and making them salty lakes in the middle of the desert Pintinjarra lands and some around here. Sometime you will feel her tears on you, even though she is still shining. "Bahloo, you will now die as you have lain with my woman, breaking my law and trust." Bahloo was sad because he knew he had done wrong. He went into the sky and started to fade away.

'Nooralie went into the twilight of the sky and brooded. The man and animals were afraid as the world was filled with half light. What you call twilight. They held a great meeting. In them days the animals and man were equal, all could speak to each other. How man became the master is another story, eh, Sean? The animals said, "We will all wither and die away if we do not have the light of Yhi and the Marmoo will come to rule us if Bahloo is to die". They sent Nompie the eagle to speak with him. Nompie flew up and up and glided around Nooralie and said to him, "Nooralie, hear me, the evil Marmoo have done all this and they will be back to plague us and scare us and turn us one upon the other. If you kill Bahloo, and send Yhi away forever, the animals and men will always be in pain and fear." Nooralie thundered, "They have done great wrong and have broken my law". Nompie kept pleading for the men and animals. He not afraid that big bird fella. "But they have been weak for just a little moment, and they do love you, and they love each other and we need them." Nooralie's anger was cooling. There was a chill in the air as he thought and brooded.

'Then he said, "Bahloo will come back to the night but he will always be dying and reborn. No longer will he stay a full man for longer than a night." And so Bahloo has been reborn and lived and died ever since. "Yhi will never come to me again but will spend her days apart from any other bright stars. They will be sent far away," and the stars have been distant ever since. Nompie said, "They so love each other, Nooralie. Can't they spend some time together?" Nooralie felt sorrow at these words of the great bird and said, "Every life of a man they may come together and lie with each other that they will not be always entirely alone". And so Bahloo and Yhi lie with each other and the earth goes grey as it was before they were made. "And let it be known that men will be scattered and not able to understand each other from this day as they scattered from the feast of the Marmoo. And to remind man and animals of my power I will send Dingarra with the wind and rain. Any man or animal that is marked by Dingarra has my spirit in him and belongs to me.'" Joseph looked directly at Sean. 'You have been marked with the spirit of Nooralie. Always the great father spirit will be with you and you will walk among man and the animals as one who is blessed.'

'Jiminy Cricket!'

The old man began to laugh a deep belly laugh and he rolled and rocked so much he had to stand up, and Sean also began to laugh from deep inside. And far on the other side of the river the kooka-burra laughed with them, and high above the eagle flew.

At the tea table that night Sean recounted the meeting with Joseph.

His mother's hand came immediately to her mouth. 'He didn't touch you. Sean? He wasn't drunk?'

'Mary,' she was cut short by his dad. 'Joseph Wirrinum is an elder and a respected person in his community. Last month he came and spoke to some blackfellas camped along the Edward's and they stopped drinking and moved on. They were causing all kinds of trouble with the local group at Ryan's creek. They were bad mouthing my crew out there. Bad news they were, but one talk with him and they moved back to their own country. He spoke to me not long after. Told me they were bad fellas from up north, drinking and causing trouble. He said I wouldn't have any further trouble from them. They were gone quick smart, I can tell you. I don't know what he said, but it didn't take much. He's a good, clean living fella, Mary, as honest as the day is long. They say he was a champion rider and horse tamer up Denny way and he lives along the river somewhere. This is his country.'

'He lives in the swamp in a little hut,' Sean said. 'He said I can go there any time.'

His mother sighed.

His dad said, 'Yeh, that's alright by me but don't make a nuisance of yourself.'

'Is that wise, James? There won't be drunks and other ill sorts hanging around?'

'Mary, for Pete's sake! Joseph is a holy man. Sister Louise thinks he's a saint. We could do a lot worse than to listen to some of these fellows. They have knowledge we've not even touched on.'

'The Aboriginals I have seen, James, have been in the gutter or asleep at the side of the road. I don't think they are fit company for anybody. People will ...'

'I don't care what people think! He's a good bloke. We could learn a lot from men like Joseph!'

His parents glared at each other down the table. Finally his mother said, 'Sean, as long as you tell me where you are going. And you take care of your injuries.'

Julungul and the Billa

Every day the Ibis returned in wide sweeps to the middle of the swamp. Sean played around the bomber and the graveyard, and tried to find his way to where they were landing, but the tangled underbrush stopped him and thick oozing mud sucked him down. One day he heard the quiet voice of Joseph.

'You bin lost.' The old man leaning against a tree.

'I'm trying to get to the middle of the swamp where the Ibis land.'

'Like a cuppa?'

After a short walk they were in a small clearing with a bark hut featuring a rusty corrugated iron roof and a short kerosene-can chimney. Sean saw a small garden at one end of the hut fenced in by cut branches and bird wire. Onions, cabbages, lettuce and carrots grew in neat rows. In front of the hut was a pit fire with smoke meandering out of a large coal bed. Staked into the fire was a thick, blackened iron pole from which iron grills and rods with hooks swivelled. From one of these hung a large, blackened billy. Steam was coming out of it and twisting in the cold afternoon air. Arranged around the fire were red-gum logs. They were old and grey and scored with burns and carvings. Joseph indicated to Sean to take a seat while he went inside. He emerged with two battered enamel cups, a green tin and a glass sugar jar.

Sean could feel the warmth of the fire pit even though there were no flames. The old man placed his load on a red-gum log. He threw a few small pieces of saplings onto the coals and stirred them with a long, twisted poker. The aroma of burning red gum mingled with the freshness of the bush. The old man worked silently. He produced a smaller billy from the other side of the fire where it had been warm-ing. Picking it up with a forked, green stick, he threw in a handful of tea leaves from the green tin, then using the stick he tilted the large billy until water came tumbling out and into the small billy. It splashed in with a hissing, steaming gush. The old man put a lid over the small billy and sat back on his haunches.

'You have milk and sugar Sean?'

He nodded. 'Two thanks.' He wondered how it would taste. His mother said he was too young for tea or coffee. At home he was restricted to milk and water and sometimes, if he had been good or it was a special occasion, cordial from the big, long-necked bottle she kept in the pantry.

The old man poured condensed milk straight from the can. With a brassy battered teaspoon he put two sugars in each cup. Then he tapped on the lid of the billy with the spoon, flicked the lid off and poured out the tea, stirring in the milk and sugar as he went. He handed a cup to Sean. 'You are a real curious fella searching around the swamp tryin to find that place where the ibis go. What do you reckon ya will find there?'

Sean smelled the pungency of the tea. It smelled of mum and home.

'From the bridge I can see a raised area and a group of large trees all close together. Every night the ibis come and nest around it, so it must be like an island.'

The old man sat and sipped his tea and stared into the fire. 'Mmm, you clever bloke. You know my people the Tamba Tamba, they bin camping here long, long, years. This a holy place for us.'

'It's a great place to play.'

Joseph nodded. 'Ah, like when I was a boy, we used to camp just down from here on the Gunpowder Island. Big mobs of us. We would wander in the bush all day playing and swimming in the river, catchin bush tucker and havin lots of fun.'

'Can you show me how to catch bush tucker?'

'Yeh. Have some of your tea before it gets too cold.'

Sean looked at the liquid in the cup. He closed his eyes and sipped. It tasted sweet and bitter at the same time. It was hot. Sean opened his eyes.

'You drinkin that one as if it you're first cup of tea ever.'

'It is.'

Joseph laughed and laughed. 'Well, I not gonna tell anyone.' And he laughed again.

'How long have you been here, Joseph?'

'I was born down Gunpowder Island, but I bin here in this place long time now. I worked on the stations up in Danny for most time as a stockman but every year in the off season I come back around here. Not many of us left now. They bin scattered all over, some down at Five Mile Creek, some other mob at Tyler's Lake Mission, some in Mathoura settlement, some in the cities, all over the place now Tamba Tamba are.'

'Sister Louise said you're a holy man.'

'That sister Louise is a good women. She bin helpin' all the people a lot of the time. She help me when I broke my leg. She not caring if you black or white fella, she help you anyway. She help our people a lot. Sometime she asked me to help her explain things so it make it easier on her so she can help them better. She a good woman. Maybe she a holy woman.' He poured another measure of tea from the billy.

Over the next two weeks Sean went nearly every day to the old man's campsite. Most times Joseph was there. If he wasn't, Sean went and hung around the bomber and graveyard. Joseph told him stories about the old times, which he called the Dreaming. He taught him the words of his lingo pronouncing them out carefully and explaining their meaning to him. Sean told him stories about the city, his gang and family. At home Sean made sure all his chores and schoolwork were done and he was home on time.

'This river here, he bin here for long longem time,' Joseph told him as they looked at the river one day. 'He old fella. We call him Billa, which means in Tamba Tamba lingo river, but we also call him Warde Yallock, which means big fella river.' He laughed. 'He brings us life. Long time away when men were only small and not many around, Julungul or Rainbow Snake was making camp in the mountains near where that Snowy River bin start. He did not look like a snake then, Sean, but was in the disguise of a medicine or Kobi man. He could draw bones out of the people's bodies and mix potions and make them well. He could talk to Nooralie and bring the rain and wind and Dingarra. The people were afraid of him but they needed him for his help in the bad times.'

'He sounds like you,' said Sean.

The old man looked at him for a while. 'This rainbow serpent is not man like me. He a Dreaming spirit who never dies but lives on. Anyway, the people in their gratitude for Julungul's help sent him some young lubras, girls, to make his nights warm, tend his fire and dig his herbs and roots for him. Their names were Kamballa and Yarterwee. They were young and very pretty. Julungul was very happy with them.'

'Did he root them, Joseph?'

Joseph's mouth dropped open. He rubbed his chin through its curly white matt. 'Mmm, no one bin ever ask me that one before. But if he didn't, he would have been a fool, hey, and Julungul is no fool.'

He laughed. 'Why you ask me that for?'

'Nurse Harradine, who looked after me, well, she was so nice with soft hands and everything. When she took care of me and touched me, I, well, I just felt, you know...'

'Yeh, well that why some women girls have the power over the man or boy, they be soft so that you may be hard, eh. It be natural that the soft be good for the hard. They make a good thing together as it was planned by Nooralie, eh? But then sometime Taldrees – that mean boy, Sean – sometime their head ahead of their body, or they have much expectation without them much chance of achievement.' Joseph laughed, and laughed. Sean moved uncomfortably on his seat. The old man quickly said, 'Well, I bin doing the same thing when I was em young fella. It the natural thing to do, eh.'

They watched the river for a while.

'Anyway, Julungul was happy at his camp in the mountains, where the nights were cool and the stars close, and his young women kept him warm.' He looked over at Sean as he said this and Sean smiled. 'But Wornkarra the crow was jealous of Julungul because he had power with the people and also pretty lubra. He said, "I will kill this Julungul and take his women and I will be powerful also". Wornkarra waited until a very dark morning before first light, when Bahloo had died and the clouds and fog was swirling about. He crept up on the camp and watched and waited for Julungul to come home from his dawn hunting. He knew Julungul would be tired and at ease in his own camp. Wornkarra sharpened his spear and fitted it to his woomera. The young girls were up and busy at first light, pounding seeds, making seed cakes. They did not notice the crow waiting in the trees, ready to strike. Julungul came wandering into the camp. He looked around. All was quiet and peaceful and his beautiful lubra were preparing his favourite cakes. Julungul's heart was happy. The young women saw him coming and ran out to greet him and to help him carry in the Marlo, the kangaroo. Julungul was carrying his hunting spears and was tired from his long hunt. He gave his spears to one of the women and the kangaroo to the other, and walked up to the fire. At this time when Julungul was not watching Wornkarra struck. He threw his spear with all his might at Julungul just as the holy spirit man bent down to eat one of the seed cakes sitting on the rocks by the fire. The spear went whistling straight at his head and gave him a glancing blow. It made great wound, lots of blood spurted out. Julungul staggered over to a gum tree and fell against it, his blood splashing the trunk. Ever since these trees have red gum blood of Julungul. White fella calls them red gums. We call them Yarrah Yarrah. The young women went screaming and hid in the dardur, in the bark hut that Julungul had made for them. Wornkarra strode into the camp and seeing the Serpent man collapsed agin the tree, thought him dead. He went into the dardur and took them women and said, "You bin coming with me, you my woman now". They cried and wailed. "I will take you far away otherwise the men might kill me for doing this to Julungul." Men were coming running up the hill because the women's cries could be heard. If you are in the mountains today, Sean, and quiet, you can still hear their cries. Wornkarra tied the two together with his grass rope and he ran off down the hills draggin the women behind him. They screamed all the way. He saw that men were few and very weak. They could not catch him this Crow man who flew over the ground, even dragging two screaming women they could not catch him. Wornkarra went far away and made the two young women look after him and tend for him. He was a lazy fella.

'Julungul woke up with a big pool of blood around him. He dragged himself up and the tree bent and twisted under his weight. They still all the same today in that Banool country, some day you go and see them, Sean, eh. Julungul was a hopping mad fella with that Wornkarra, but happy with the people who were trying to help him. But, even they were scared as they felt Julungul's anger. The snake man in his fury was terrible to look at and his body grew bigger and bigger, all green and black and throbbing with power and life. The people ran away at the sight of him. He started to follow on the drag marks of his women. Julungul's body was so large that wherever he crawled he left a mighty bed where the Billa or this Warde Yallock now flows to this day. Wherever he stopped to rest, it became a depression which filled up with water like that Barmah place up the river a bit, eh, Sean. The longer he stopped, the larger the hollow. He even stopped here just for a little while, where we are camped here and that why this little swamp is here and the bend where he changed direction. The Tamba came to help him here because Julungul was tired and the women's drag marks were getting faint.'

'That's your tribe,' said Sean.

'Yeh, you smart fella. That Tamba, the ibis, they helped Julungul when he was getting tired. Pranggiwatyeri that King Brown fella he related to Julungul, but that another story. He our totem and brother. We do not kill or eat this fella. The snake and Ibis brought him food and plants to eat and feast on so he could keep his strength. They our mob, how you say, dreamtime father blokes.'

'Like descendants.'

'Yeh, kinda like that. Anyway, Julungul was gaining his strength back and he said to the Tamba, "You will always have this place. It is special to you and to your people. While you are here, this Billa which is following me will always be a good place and not die. If you go away from here, this place will die as I might have if you had not fed me. Not like other Tamba, you fellas will be all white, to say you are holy fellas, but so you don't be proud your neck and wing tips be black, for nothing under Nooralie's sky is perfect." He tells them, "You Tamba, take care of the Billa fella here and he will always be good".' Joseph scratched a line in the ground with his stick. 'This like Julungul do.'

Sean nodded.

'The Tamba flew up high and a long way away they found Wornkarra in what you fellas call South Australia in the Kakuri mob's land. The crow fella was very happy. He thought Julungul was dead and the two young women did everything for him, even catch his food. But the Tamba saw his camp and came back and told Julungul, who raced toward it. He sent up big clouds of dust, sometimes in that Mallee part there you can still see the red dust like when Julungul sped along. He had many other adventures and I could tell you lots of tales, Sean, about the trek of Julungul the snake but the day not long enough. Anyway, Wornkarra in his camp saw the clouds of red dust and he felt fear because he knew only one being could cause that. Wornkarra said, "I will flee to the sea and build a bark boat and sail across. Even Julungul cannot catch me there." Wornkarra tied them women up again and off he went toward the sea. Julungul was not far behind when he reached Wornkarra's old camp. He saw the drag marks on the ground though and changed direction and headed off after that crow man. You can still see that place today where the serpent changed direction, the Billa makes a mighty turn toward the sea. You fella call it Morgan. We call it Thuckara Julungul or place where Julungul made the bend. Wornkarra reached the sea and started in a big hurry to make the Korong.'

'What's a korong?'

'Ah, that bin a canoe, you know, like made out of the bark of the canoe tree. Some around here from old time. I will show you sometime, but tin boat much better. Maybe Wornkarra may have got away if he had tin boat.' Joseph laughed and spilled his tea.

The afternoon shadows crept long across the campsite and the scent of the gums was powerful. Blue wisps of smoke hung in the air. It was cold. Sean could feel a chill in his backbone, but there was some other thing here, something he could not define. The blue of the day had turned to the purple of late afternoon and the quiet of the surroundings matched the quiet he felt inside. The story was the only thing with a place at the moment. The old man, looking at him, nodded.

'Ah, Sean, you have the spirit in you. This place Julungul place, holy place, he here when I tell his story, eh.'

'Yeh.' Sean edged closer to the fire.

'When you quiet here and inside you is quiet, you can feel the presence of Julungul from long ago.' The old man smiled. 'You want more tea eh. I bin think you like it lots.'

Sean watched as Joseph went through the ritual. When all was settled, even the bush seemed quiet, expectant- the old man went on.

'Wornkarra stripped the trees and it came off in threads like paper because the Banya had seen what he wanted to do. They hated this crow fella and wanted to help Julungul.'

'Banya?'

'I bin not so clever using this blackfella lingo, sorry Sean. Banya is possum fella. Try as he might Wornkarra could not find a tree to make the canoe. Today if you go to that Banya country you still cannot find a tree to make a canoe. Wornkarra was lazy and evil but he was not a coward, he went back to his camp to face Julungul. Julungul came on. Wornkarra rose up to shoot him through the body, but the young women started wailing. Crying out to Julungul just as the crow threw his spear, Julungul heard the cries of his women and ducked. The spear hit a rock and flew high into the heavens. It landed way out long way away flattening all the trees. They no grow there ever again. The snake and the crow they grabbed at each other and wrestled all over the place sending up big mounds of dirt and rocks as they went. It was a fearsome time because they rolled and crashed over the earth, throwing each other here and there. You go to that country now, Sean, you see the marks where they fought. The blood of Julungul and crow was everywhere, all that country now is red and they dug out deep gorges and plains rolling and throwing, fighting and clawing at each other. Eventually, Julungul coiled Wornkarra in a death grip, and the crow was unable to breathe. Julungul was going to kill him. He gripped him hard, so hard the entire colour drained out of him and he went black. As he was about to kill the crow man, Nooralie came to Julungul through the wind, whispering. Your job is to teach, instruct and punish, not kill if possible. Julungul said to the crow, "If I don't kill you, treacherous crow, will you not harm me and my people again?" Wornkarra said, "I will never obey you". Julungul squeezed harder and the crow man went blacker. At last he gasped "Alright, I will obey you." Julungul let him go. He fluttered on the ground, trying to get his breath. Julungul untied his women. They rushed up on the crow and beat him with their sticks and threw rocks at him. Ever since the lubra have never liked the crow and always they throw stones and sticks at him. Julungul said, "For your punishment you will be forever black and no colour will you show. Your cry will be hard on the ears of the people so they will be reminded of the evil you have done to me. You will be shunned by all the other bird clans and you will make your nest high above in the trees out of dead sticks, the same as my women hit you with. You will be the enemy of the snakes forever you and them will forever be fighting your young ones never be safe. You will cry out for peace but peace you will not have." Wornkarra slunk away and all that Julungul said was done.

'Julungul and his women returned quietly to their home in the mountains along the Billa. Many are the stories of Julungul and his wives. Where they stopped the places are holy, sacred and beautiful. Julungul gave Kamballa, the younger of his women, to the Tamba because they helped him. Then he went on with Yarterwee up home into the mountains. Kamballa is mother of the Tamba Tamba. Not many of her children left around here lately.'

'Did Kamballa like to stay with the Tamba birds?'

'Ah, yes. It bin a different time then when men and animals were not separated like now, they just different forms of Nooralie's goodness. Only later they become different when they stray from Nooralie's law, but that a different story.'

'I betta go.'

'You say hello to your dad, Sean. He a good fella to us blackfella blokes in the bush. He let us travel to our special places, not like some others.'

'Yeh, no worries,' said Sean. He got up to go.

'You like to go fishing?'

'With spears?'

'No, this blackfella bit smarter than that. We bin gunna do some trappin and netting. Maybe not so exciting but then we bin gunna get a feed, eh.'

Back to School

At school the Smythe gang kept up the constant niggling and abuse, but Johnny McCarthy was no longer part of it. Sometimes he gave Sean a nod of recognition and a mumbled 'G'day'. Mary Addison was more open, not as giggly. They mostly talked about schoolwork.

'Wow! Look at that mistletoe bird,' Sean spontaneously exclaimed one afternoon as they were packing up. A male had landed on the shrub outside their window. 'Isn't he beautiful? They must have a nest here somewhere?'

'No,' she said, 'they nest later on in the year, around October or November.'

'Yeh, how do you know?' He was surprised she even knew what a mistletoe bird was, let alone the nesting dates.

'On the farm there's lots of fruit trees and some mistletoe trees. The mistletoe birds fly in and make their nests out of cobwebs and sticks. They make a racket getting food for their young and then in about three or four months they fly off to somewhere else.'

'How do you know what type of nest they have? They always hide them.'

'Because me and my brother Ben climbed up and had a look last year. That's why'! She jutted her jaw out.

'Mmm,' murmured Sean.

'Yeh, you hear them before you see them, and they spend all day chasing insects and eating berries. Their nests are decorated with insects and bits of weed. They're shaped like a pear.'

'Yeh, really? I've only seen one in books. You're lucky,' said Sean.

'Alright, you two can go home now. No need to stare out the window all afternoon.'

Sean looked around, the classroom was empty. Sister Rose was standing up the front. 'We were just looking at a bird out in the tree, Sister,' he stuttered.

At home, over biscuits and milk, he asked his mother, 'Mum, did you ever climb trees and look at birds when you were a kid?'

'Once, with your Uncle Alfred when he was your age and I was six. We climbed up the old mulberry tree at the back of our place, and stole some little finch's eggs. Alfred wanted them for his collection.'

'Your brother who was killed by the Japanese in Singapore or something?'

His mother turned back to the bench.

Fishing

Sean asked his dad that evening at pipe time about the fishing trip.

'Sounds okay. Where you going?'

'The other side of Gunpowder Island, to do some netting and trapping.'

'Ah, cunning old bugger. I bet you'll come back with a bag full.'

'Do you think it's alright, James?' His mother said, anxiety quavering her voice. 'I mean, going down to the river.'

'Sean is eleven plus now, and old Joseph won't let him get into trouble, I'm sure of that.'

'I am not so sure,' she said in a soft tone. 'Six o'clock on Saturday morning is early.'

'Well, if Sean brings home a feed of cod, it'll be worth it,' his dad said.

'I'll make you some sandwiches,' she said, but she was not convincing.

His dad's old alarm clock rang out at five. Sean put on his work boots, shorts and woollen jumper and the old beanie that had belonged to one of his uncles. He was surprised to see his dad in the kitchen.

'Eggs and mash, Sean? Best time of day by far. Great day for fishing.

I made up a rod and some tackle for you in case you get a chance to throw a line in. Take care of it. It was my father's.'

Sean ate hurriedly, and grabbed his lunch bag and a flask, pushing them into the brown canvas bag. He grabbed the old cane rod and bag of tackle on the way out.

Joseph was waiting for him outside his hut. A wisp of smoke from the fire hung lazily in the air, and the smell of the river, red gums, smoke and tea welcomed him like an old friend. But above all a smell like his mum's scones washed over him and made his mouth water despite his just completed breakfast. The greyness of the new day made everything seem larger, the colour of the bush muted.

'You bin have some tucker yet?' the old man greeted him. He gestured to the fire, where a blackened camp oven lay half-submerged in the coals.

Joseph opened the oven and with a pair of tongs and handled out the big damper, brown all over and smelling like a baker's shop. He sliced and buttered the steaming damper, holding the pieces with a cloth. He opened a jam tin and added huge dollops of apricot.

'Have some, Sean. You need it to stick inside for this little walk we do.'

The damper was wonderful, washed down sweetened tea.

'You look like you like that.' A kookaburra laughed nearby. 'He a noisy bloke, that fella. One time Nooralie spirit fella he said those Koori people becoming lazy, we need have some fella bin wake them up in the mornin, so he call Kookaburra to him. "Hey, you fella have big voice and giving me cheek all the time, you bin now have a job, you wake up the world every day." You white fella have that rooster bloke who does the same job, when them two get going no one damn sleep, all have to get up,' he laughed.

'You have a story for everything.'

Joseph pondered a moment. 'Nooralie, that Great Spirit, he in all things, animals, plants, trees, rocks, land, river and men, everything. He joins us all together and so we all related. Those stories tell of his creation and why it happen. They help us Koori fella to understand what's going on.' He picked up a gunny sack and khaki army bag and threw them over his shoulders. 'Enough talkin. Let's get along and get some nice Kooya fish fella. You bringum that rod along too. He bin catchin some fish today maybe. We go up to Gunpowder Creek side of that Gunpowder Island.'

He strode off down the track leading away from the camp towards the mill. At the mill the big logs lay in gigantic piles. The smell of red gum and smoke from the incinerator washed over them and made Sean's nose tingle. The old man loped along. Soon the smell of tobacco joined that of the red gum. The early sounds of work drifted towards them, the distant rumble of the timber lorries sounding off as they skirted the yard, the pulleys and jacks lifting and moving the logs. On their left, the glimmer of the river occasionally glinted through the trees. Soon they broke into Manning Street, the main thoroughfare of Koonarook. The early morning train to Morang was being turned around on the turntable. Its diesel puffed out black smoke and passengers huddled on the station platform waiting for it to pull up. Mr Corrigan, the station master, waved to them. Joseph doffed his hat.

'That fella Corrigan, he good fella, he let me travel to Morang for free when I wanna go there sometime. I drop him in a fish now and then, he like fish that fella.'

They crossed the street in front of the Shamrock Hotel, the smell of fried bacon from its kitchens and the stench of stale beer greeted them. Then they turned down an unnamed dirt track. Horse pad-docks on either side gave way to the bush in the close distance. Grey mobs of kangaroos bounded away, startled by the crunch of their feet on the gravel. They were soon in the bush and skirting between a billabong and the river, the flat, glassy water of the billabong steaming in the morning light. They woke up the resident ducks, which scurried away, struggling to get into the air. Water hens hurriedly hid in the reeds and bulrushes, the reeds still dripping with the perspiration of the night.

The loping, steady pace of the man ahead never altered. The road gave way to a track.

'This Gunpowder Island fella road. We go down this over that bridge to the island.'

They approached a rickety wooden bridge over a creek that had a lazy swirl of water about twenty feet wide. Across it, they turned along a barely distinct path. The trees here were bigger and wider apart. Joseph stopped by a big, straight red gum marked with a yellow slash. He ran his hand over its rough bark.

'This fella he bin here long time. Them white fella, they soon bin come and chop him down, take him to the mill, make him into houses and chairs, sometimes just burn it. They keep choppin and cutting no place for Mingga to live, the spirit of the tree's he gone. Who gonna keep the Marmoo away?' He sighed and squatted under the tree. The sky was turning blue.

Joseph lit his pipe again and the smoke rose around him. 'Maybe Tamba Tamba time is gone and the Marmoo will rule in this place.' He bent down and scraped away the fallen undergrowth and top layer of grey dirt. 'Ah, Naruoo! Naruoo, he here,' he laughed. 'We bin have some grub for your fishing pole Sean, you lucky fella.' He retrieved a short length of wire and a cotton wad from the gunny sack, and poked it down a hole the size of his thumb. When he withdrew it, a long grub, all white and segmented with a tan end, wriggled on the end of the wire. 'Naruoo, you little good fella for fish. These fella good to eat, white fella call them Bardi grubs, but better to fish with than eat I'm thinkin.' Soon Joseph had a dozen grubs, which he placed in an empty tobacco tin. 'Sean fella, you bin gonna catch that Kooya,' he grinned and went to the tree and stroked it tenderly. 'Where all these Naruoo gonna go and Mingga, when you gone?' He shook his head, and walked silently on.

The smell of eucalypt and damp earth was refreshing, and the distant sound of the town could just be heard. A small mob of black-tailed wallabies crashed through the bush ahead of them.

'Barraberri fella!' exclaimed Joseph.

The ground began to dip down to the right. 'We at Gunpowder Island, Kallakkire place. When river up this place here covered in water, that why these trees so big, but now most of the big fellas gone by that whitefella saws.' Joseph stopped by a big gum tree with a huge scar in it. 'This fella here he canoe tree Korong fella, long time away blackfella make canoe or boat from the bark. They take off in one piece and heat and bend over low fire then seal with mud and tie up, make good boat. This one here he take three or four fella, but not as good as tinny,' he laughed. They turned through thick saplings and underbrush. Suddenly they were on a long, sandy beach about fifty yards long.

'This place special, fishin good here, good camp place when river not so high, old people's spirit here. Tamba Tamba bin here long time, they eat and drink, plenty Kooya here, and collect heap lot of Lokure, that whitefella bin call fresh water mussel. See here there heap of those shells.' He pointed to the rise of the beach behind which were heaps of bleached mussel shells. Here and there black-ened fireplaces could be seen. 'Those fellas have lots of good time, no need the beer drinks, no beer drink those times. We go fish just near the Bora Bora trees, up at the end, long here.'

They walked along the beach. On a small raised area grew three grey boxes, old and gnarled, many of their branches fused together and marked and scarred. The man and boy climbed the steep shaly bank and squatted on the ground under the trees. Sean looked out over the river and noted that it was disturbed as it travelled over a rocky escarpment. On the other side of the river there was a similar rise with the same sort of grey box trees on them. Joseph bowed his head in silence for some time. Sean followed his example.

'This place here long time use for boy to man ceremony, here the boy long time Tamba Tamba he become a man, he also get scar like on tree. This place around here he never flood even when all around he bin under water. It Bora Bora place, long time strong spirit he bin here. Long time here if woman come here these spirits they kill her, no woman come here, they have other place for them.'

'Does the boy get a needle before they mark him?' Sean said.

Joseph laughed. 'No, he bin on fast and staying up thinkin about it, like a trance or dream. When time come lots of dancin, singun, and noise, he not feel much. He gets cut and then we rub special grass and mud in the cut. If fella don't have man scar, can't stay Tamba Tamba, he have to leave. He bin gonna die, if he leave he then bin killed by other blackfella down the track. If boy don't become a man then he no good, old time he Wundee Wundee, no good fella to people, that old time law. You, Sean fella marked already by Dingarra, you Dingarra fella, he bin mark you himself, he no need us blackfella, you man now first step, you can gonna come here.' Joseph looked at him with piercing eyes.

For a time they continued squatting in silence, looking at the Bora Bora trees. Sean thought of the scar on his chest, and wondered if the old man had scars on him.

The silence was broken as Joseph said, 'Even Dingarra fella must eat'.

They walked over the rise and down to where the beach continued. They followed it up a short way to where a creek left the river. The water flowing down the creek was deep, green and clear.

'Sean, you bin get em that rod, I bin gotta fetch that trap around here, you bin wait here.'

The old man walked off into the bush. Sean set up his rod. Willy wagtails fluttered nearby and a dart flew low over the water. Looking up, Sean saw an eagle circling high in the pale blue and wintry sky. There was a splash in the creek and Sean looked to see the tail of a platypus disappearing under the water. He heard Joseph coming back, and saw him dragging a wire barrel about the same size as a beer keg with small openings on each end. The wire tapered back inwards and there was a coil of black rope attached to it.

'This here bin gill net great whitefella idea good if you know where fish is, eh.' He walked to the edge of the creek. 'We throw here, there a big hole just out a bit, fish wait there for food to come along, first though we tie in some bait.' He reached into his gunny bag and pulled out a parcel wrapped in newspaper and tied with string. 'This bin little brim I catch the other day.' The silver fish had opaque eyes and flaky scales. Joseph reached into the gill net and wired it into the centre. He stood on the edge of the river and threw it straight out, the black rope uncurling behind. The net hit the water and quickly settled, and Joseph tied the rope to a sapling. 'Sean, you throw your line in downriver of where I put that net, not too far out now, just little bit right on edge of that hole out there. Them fish love those Naruoo, just bin hook him through the tail there so to keep him alive little bit, eh. I bin go and get a couple of crab net, I bin got hidden over here.'

Sean baited the hook with the unlucky grub and threw it out. He sat down to wait.

Joseph returned with two large, round flat nets. 'We bin tie some dead meat here in the middle, and then throw out down this river a bit.' Joseph dived into his bag again and pulled out another newspaper parcel. 'Ah, this bin rabbit bin killed on the road but still he good for crays.' He retrieved a large pearl handled knife and cut the skinned rabbit in half. The sweet sickly odour of fouled meat filled the air. Joseph wired the one half of the rabbit onto each net. He walked along the beach and threw each in turn into the river, again tying the ropes to saplings. He yelled, 'These fellows gotta be just off the current in nearly still water'.

Sean looked over at the far bank. The sun was coming up, sending shining, broken shafts of light onto the river and creating a patch-work of patterns on the swirling water. He looked up. There were more bird sounds now. In the stillness he heard the crashing of a limb falling to ground. His dad called them widow makers and said a lot of fellows over the years had been killed or injured by the sudden fall of a red-gum branch or tree. Sean dozed while Joseph gathered twigs for a fire.

'We bin have a brew, eh, this fishing hard, he be hard work.'

Kooya

The rod in Sean's hand jumped. Awake suddenly, he grabbed hold tightly. The line spun quickly off the Bakelite reel. Sean jumped to his feet.

'I got one, I got one!'

'You bin hang onto that fella, he bin take you into the river.'

The rod bent almost double. Sean was on the water's edge. His arms started to ache from the strain. Occasionally he could wind in some line but mostly he just held on, and hoped the fish did not snag or break the line.

'Keep that rod up!' Joseph stood beside him giving instructions.

Slowly Sean was able to bring more line in. Sweat stood on his brow. The sun was now nearly level with the tops of the trees on the far bank. The line went up and down the river. Slowly the tension on the line eased, the movement became less agitated. It felt like a dead weight, it was as though Sean was hauling in a sack of potatoes.

'You bin don't take that fella out of the water, he bin break your line, I gonna have to bring him in by the gills.'

The fin and back of the fish broke the water. Every now and then it gave a last effort. Joseph walked into the water and hooked the fish with his hands through its gills.

'This mighty Kooya for young fella to catch.'

The fish lay half out of the water, its gigantic head the size of a football, the mouth opening and closing in quick starts. The large shiny black eyes were the size of pennies. The back of the mighty fish rose sharply away from its head, where a large jutting fin ran, the dorsal fin, nearly rectangular, then the back continued to the small tail. Its belly was even larger than its head and Sean doubted whether he could get his arms around it. The skin was motley green and yellow with a pattern like the German Tiger tanks that Sean had seen in war comics.

'He's so beautiful,' Sean panted.

'He make up some good tucker for us hungry fellas.' Joseph looked at him intently. 'You wanna eat this fella fish?'

Sean stroked the back of the fish. 'He's so beautiful. He fought so well, he's a champion, a bonzer fish. I'll never catch anything so big and beautiful again, ever.'

Joseph laughed. 'A cod what we call Ponde fella -Kooya, he your totem, maybe your brother, he bin sent here by Nooralie to teach you. We put him back. Nooralie will send you more Kooya, this one your brother.'

Sean ran his hands over the fish. He noticed a deep scar on the right side. 'What's that there, Joseph?'

'Ah, when this one young fella, kookaburra or maybe a cormorant try to have him for tea but only graze him, left mark on him, maybe like you, he bin marked. Nooralie he bin send you a message.'

'Let's get him back.'

They pushed the fish back into the river. The big tail waved slowly from side to side, and the pectoral fins moved.

'He as big as you,' Joseph mumbled.

They held the fish in deeper water up past Sean's knees. It was getting stronger. Sean could feel his power as they held him steady in the water, and then he slowly moved off.

Joseph grunted. 'I bin holdin out for that tea.'

They squatted near the small fire. They sipped their tea in silence. Sean thought about the fish. Why had he let it go? Perhaps he would never understand, but he knew he could not have killed that fish or eaten it for all the tea in China.

'Special time, when you bin see your totem,' Joseph said.

'Do you have a totem?'

'When I bin born longem time ago, not too far where we are here now, my dad saw the Tamba bein born, from the egg, then he comin home sometime see me just bin born also. Later when I become a man and go through that markin dance, I have a dream bout that Tamba fella. I tell my father uncle and he say that be your totem, you and Tamba be brother. This bin special in our people cause that bin our name and people's totem, all time through my dreamin time I think about my brother Tamba, my uncle father say that why I must be so tall, cause I like my brother totem. All time I look and care for my brother Tamba, and he bin carin for me. I think this be your path to know that cod Ponde fellow be your totem. You now his brother all time he bin in your dreamin and in your time, he take care of you and protect you as he can. You do the same for him. You not do this, then Nooralie he bin angry with you and his law be broke. When law broken, then all this place become wrong, you become wrong, cause you hurt your brother, you bin hurt yourself. Not many um white fella or even blackfella knows this.' He gestured all round him to the trees and sky. 'Maybe you cod fella dreamin boy.'

'So you think I will be like a cod, like a fish?'

'Ah, he bin not just a fish fella, he the top fish, the king of the fish. He strong and make this river special.'

'The king?'

'You bin bound now to care for him and his place. Here have some damper and jam. We starving after all this fishin and talkin.'

The sun was coming over the trees as they began fishing again. A goanna run up a tree on the other side of the river and a bird called out in alarm. Joseph hauled in the gill net. Sean propped his rod on a tree branch and went over to help him.

'Bin plenty fish in here.' The drum was full of fish. 'Kooya fella, yella and cod, brim and red fin.' He laid them out on the beach quickly, and killed each one with a quick blow to the head. 'We havin couple for lunch and take the rest home.' He started to gut them. The two redfin he put aside. 'They be lunch, young fella, you bin look at that rod, he bin have another Kooya there.' The rod was bending and straining against the prop. Sean ran over and started a new fight.

Over the next two hours Sean caught seven fish. All but two were yellow bellies. The two cod he let go. Joseph showed him how to kill and gut the fish. It was very similar to how his dad did it. For lunch Joseph wrapped the red fin in bark from a stringy bark tree and laid them in the coals. He carefully removed the blackened bark parcels from the coals and opened them, revealing the steaming fish.

'These red fin fish here, in old times not here, they come with that whitefella, but they good to eat, have to eat with hands. Have some salt here.' He pulled a salt jar from the gunny bag, and sprinkled salt onto his fish and pulled it apart with his fingers. Sean copied him. It was the most delicious fish he had ever tasted. The bark had given it an earthy, bushy flavour. They ate in silence.

'Maybe you quiet and strong like that cod fella. Come on, let's see um how many there Meaukes, that my lingo for crays. Bring them in quick. When you start pulling, do not stop.'

The old man dragged the nets up the beach. 'We bin lucky fella this day.' Large crays were entangled in the nets. 'Keep draggin up, young fella, we check em, only need two, one for me, one for you. Make sure them not female we take.'

Joseph picked up one of the monsters behind its claws. It was as big as three hands and as thick as a man's arm. 'Ahhh, see um young fella, this one woman. Cray eggs under tail, see.' He put it by the water's edge. It backed into the water and squirted away. 'You do the same, do not bin loose a finger to those fella, they like fingers and toes.'

Two of Sean's crays were female. He kept the other. Joseph had two males so he kept the biggest and they put the two keepers in a potato sack.

'We bin take em home and cook them. They be fresh that way. You bin take home some fish too for your family, Sean. I salt the rest and keep for other day, when no fish about. Maybe now time to go home. It bin a good fishin day.'

'It's been the best day of my life,' Sean whispered.

'Maybe you have some better ones comin up,' Joseph laughed. I bin have good time too, you bin like me having a son.'I call you Mai-yarare now. That mean grandson.'

Sean looked into the old man's dark eyes. He felt a swelling in his chest. 'And what should I call you, Joseph?'

'Ulwai, you can call me Ulwai. That mean grandfather.'

They cleaned up the fire, scattering the coals and damping them down with the billy water. The fish were carefully wrapped in news-paper and put in the gunny sack. Sean's fish went in his haversack. They packed up the rods and put away the nets and started on the walk home. Sean looked back to the beach. The sand was scarred where the cod had been, his cod. They retraced their steps. The day was turning cold but Sean felt no chill.

His father was 'at the football' his mother said when he got home. 'He has taken Katy along for an outing. How did you go?'

Sean undid the brown canvas bag and reached in. The green cray came out with claws going wild.

'Get that thing out of here,' his mother screamed. 'Leave it in the shed till your father gets home! Go and have a bath.'

His dad was soon home, and Sean, now dressed in pyjamas, slippers and dressing gown on his mother's orders, ran out to meet him. Katy danced inside.

'Dad, I caught the biggest cod in the whole world and red fins and, yella bellies and bream and...'

'Hey, slow down.'

Sean took a deep breath and told his story. He fetched the canvas bag and took out the Cray carefully.

'What a beauty! That's the biggest cray I've ever seen.' He reached over and took it from Sean. 'He'd take your finger off if he got hold of you.'

'That's what Joseph said.'

'Well, put him back in and we'll cook him up tomorrow.'

Sean then showed him the fish.

'Beautiful, just beautiful,' his father mused. 'No cod?'

'No. Joseph said they're my totem.'

'Mmm. That Joseph knows how to catch a fish. Not quite sure about this totem business, but he sure can catch fish. We'll have these for lunch tomorrow, instead of the Sunday roast. Let's put them in the ice box, and later I'll put that cray in a nice cold place so he goes to sleep.'

The cray was boiled, cut in half his dad had one side his mother the other, Sean had one claw and Katy the other. They ate the fish with chips.

'We'll have to send you out with Joseph more often,' his dad said.

The Bora Bora Penny

The mornings were cold, often the puddles on the side of the road and the water in the bottom of the drinking troughs at school were frozen. The free milk quart bottles were icy until lunch time. Sean wore coat, scarf and gloves, but was down to jumper or shirt by lunch. The long planks of red gum on the bridge were too slippery to ride across in the mornings, so Sean would walk his bike across. Most days were like this, with the odd day or so of rainy, stormy weather.

Berty White played marbles with him and nearly always beat him, but Berty never took Sean's marbles. He said 'he owed him.' Knuckles were always on too. Berty never bought his special set now, but a cheaper version. However, Sean was often alone at lunch or play, and found a quiet place to read a comic. Sean talked with Mary Addison during breaks in class, but never outside of class. She sure knew a lot about birds and animals, which was amazing.

Sometimes on his way home he felt that he was being watched or followed. A Smythe gang member would be hanging around as he left the school, or he would see a bike following in the distance. He told Joseph.

The old man listened, nodding occasionally with quiet concentration, puffing on his pipe, swigging his tea. After a long while he ventured, 'Yeh, some fella they bin dunna like any other bloke different to them, they bin thinkin all have to be the same, if not they feel afraid and frightened. They have no contact with their dreamin, they bin gonna act in fearing, I bin keep a look out down here for them now, you be ready but not afraid. Dingarra takem care of you, you have his mark, he a mighty warrior fightin spirit.'

'Thanks. I hope Dingarra can stop a rock to the back of the head.'

Sean did as much of his chores as possible in the morning. After school he did any jobs his mother wanted. After that headed down to the swamp, to spend an hour or so fishing, playing in the bomber, talking to Joseph, sitting by the river daydreaming or bombing rocks into the water. The river was down from its summer flows. His dad said it was because they did not need the water for irrigation.

'In olden time river not flow like that,' Joseph said. 'Often it rain in winter and spring then have big flow, then dry in summer so it be low. But, now it bin made different, maybe I bin thinkin long time this bin why those Kooya and Otayaba, ah, that mean bird, not so many now. But Tamba Tamba he still come, while he here we bin be good.'

Sometimes his mother asked him to go into Koonarook to pick up groceries. He walked down Kane's Way a couple of blocks and then turned into Manning Street. Manning Street was the widest street that Sean had ever seen. A railway track ran down its middle. The station consisted of a raised platform with a sheltered waiting area, a station master's office, a corrugated iron goods shed and a toilet. Directly opposite the station was the redbrick council chambers and, adjoining it, the war memorial dance hall, the RSL hall and the coffee palace. In front of the council chambers, mounted on a high roman column, was a life-sized statue of a World War One digger in full combat pose thrusting his .303 rifle at an imaginary enemy. It dominated the street. Underneath the column and facing off in each direction were large black marble slabs bearing long lists of names in gold lettering. Many had a cross next to them. The non-descript RSL hall consisted of a brick-fronted timber building. The coffee palace was a standalone building with large verandahs that jutted out onto the footpath. Just down from there were the three shops grouped together in the Hammond building – the general store, which was called Hammond's but was run by the Walshes, the butcher's shop run by the Joneses, and the dress and millinery shop run by Mrs Smith. The baker shop stood further down the street and was run by the Boromeos. The milk bar and petrol station situated on the opposite side of the road, just behind the station, was run by the Kennedys. The Shammy was the last commercial building and stood another fifty yards on from the garage, surrounded by old gnarled and weathered peppercorn trees. Large timber slab stables stood out the back and a line of water troughs and hitching rails were in front. An expansive beer garden with pergola and garden seating was situated on a vivid green lawn and spilled out onto the side laneway. There were various small timber workers cottages, and larger Victorian and federation-styled houses between the shops. Most of the larger houses had horse paddocks and stables behind them.

Both pubs were always full of workers. Often they spilled out onto the street, drinking hard to beat the six o'clock closing.

Sean hated going into the general store. Mrs Walsh, who every one called Aunt Bessie, served everyone from behind the big red counter running the length of the shop. She never stopped talking. She was big and fat and always wore dresses with flowers on them. Her husband, Tom, never said a word. He was always putting things on shelves and stacking, and never served anyone. When he went in, Aunt Bessie yabbered about his mum, his dad and his sister Kate, how beautiful they were and what his mother was wearing the other day. Sean could feel his eyes glazing over and his jaw going slack. She held him there by only filling the flour or biscuit bag half way. Relief only came in the form of another customer. Sean felt like he was escaping from prison, but going to Boromeo's Bakery was another thing altogether.

The bakery stood alone in a paddock surrounded by fruit trees. The paddock went all the way back onto Johnson Street, behind Manning Street. The Boromeo's house faced this street and was a little timber cottage with an iron verandah and a back sleepout covered in fly wire. Just behind the house were a mud brick meat house and a little stone dairy, where the Boromeos made their cream and milk from the two house cows that wandered around the bakery paddock. The stable housed the bakery cart and horse, which Mr Boromeo's son Juliarno rode. The bakery proper was a big redbrick building with numerous chimneys sticking through its rusty corrugated iron roof. A covered walkway connected the bakery to the little timber shop. The shop had a large verandah, which covered the pedestrian walk, and a big sign at its front boldly proclaimed 'Boromeo's Bakery' in red. But the thing that picked you up and drew you to it was the wonderful aroma. It made you hungry at its first embrace, and instantly coloured Sean's mind with pictures of bread, cakes, pies and tarts. His mouth watered at its urging. To Sean, it was like a piece of heaven on earth. The front of the shop was nearly all glass and inside he could see into the glass display cabinets and the big black pie warmer behind the large red-gum counter. Old man Boromeo sat out the front in a cane chair at a little round table smoking, reading Italian newspapers, drinking coffee in little cups and talking to people. Sean saw him and his wife Sophia at mass on Sundays. They and their family of six children, husbands and wives, grandchildren and assorted friends sat on the left-hand side, starting six from the front. Sean did not know Mr Boromeo's first name.

As he went into the bakery, Mr Boromeo would say, 'Buongiorno, Sean,' and give him a big smile. The smoke from the cigarette curled round his head.

'G'day, Mr Boromeo,' Sean would say and take off his cap.

Then Mr Boromeo would say, 'You try our jam tart today, Sean. You ask my daughter in there, she will give you one.'

He always did that for children and then he would start reading his paper again or start talking in his lingo to an Italian mill worker, farmer or co-op worker who happened to be sharing his coffee and company that day.

Behind the counter one of Mr Boromeo's daughters or daughter-in-laws waited, dressed in a white blouse and a long blue skirt with a little white doyley pinned onto the top of her head. They always smiled and knew everyone's name.

'Good afternoon, Sean, and what does your mama want today?'

Sean made his order and they wrapped it in the white paper.

'Would you like a tart, Sean? Papa made them today.'

'Yes, thank you!'

The routine never varied. Those tarts were the best in the world.

One evening as he sipped tea around Joseph's campfire, the old man paused in his storytelling.

'There bin young Amerjig about your age hanging round here yesterday. I think they gonna be planning something.'

'I'll be careful.'

'Ah, Sean, Maiyarare, before you go I give you this.' He handed Sean a shiny copper penny attached to a thin leather thong.

Sean took the penny. 'Joseph, I... '

The old man interrupted him. 'My father he bin give it to me, he say it to protect me, and when I wear it, he with me. He bin good at etching and carvin, I give it to you now, you need protection me thinkin.'

Sean rubbed the smooth penny. It was shiny with circular lines etched into each side like the Bora Bora trees. 'Joseph, it's beautiful. Did it protect you?'

'Ah, I bin in a few stoushes over time, now me old, so maybe,' he laughed.

Sean placed the leather thong over his head. The medallion snuggled onto his chest. He reached out and grasped the man's hand.

'Thank you, grandfather,' Sean whispered.

'You best be getting home, young fella. Them parents of yours be getting worried.'

Sean did not tell his parents about the Smythe gang coming down to the swamp. He thought they may stop him from going there. But he did show them the penny after Katy had gone to bed.

'Very old,' his dad said. 'An interesting pattern. The old timers say they're ceremonial trees.'

'Bora Bora trees,' said Sean.

'Is that what they are? Bora Bora,' his dad nodded in appreciation.

'That's where they held some of their initiation ceremonies. Those places are sacred, like a church.'

'James,' his mother interjected. 'Do you think Sean should be wearing a heathen medallion? It's not Christian.'

'It can't be any worse than wearing a Saint Christopher's medal. He's only a legend, not really a saint.'

'But what would Father Riley think?'

'Does it matter what he thinks, Mary?'

'Yes, it does, James. He is our guide and adviser here on earth.'

'That may be so, but this penny has no graven image or mark. It's just circles in circles.'

'But look where it comes from!'

'Probably came from the royal mint in London.'

'James, you know what I mean.'

'Yes, Mary, unfortunately I do know what you mean.'

His mother's face flushed pink, silence prevailed. His father gave the penny back to Sean. It felt cold against his chest.

Attack

A couple of weeks later Sean headed to the swamp at the usual time. His knapsack swung on his back. It contained worms in a battered pipe tobacco tin. The cane rod was in his hand. He passed the Dingarra tree, its hollow trunk holding a pool of water from recent rain. The air was cold and damp, the winter sun behind him low in the sky. He was thinking about the reds or yellas he was going to catch and take home for tea. The old bomber came into view. The river was dirty and dark. The dim skies made the place sombre. It was still and quiet. He slowed his step. Must be a storm coming. He looked around warily and carefully made his way forward. It did not feel right.

As he came level with the bomber, a hard thump on his back propelled him forward, knocking the air out of him, and felling him to his knees.

'Get him! Get him!'

Sean rolled onto and over a gnarled old red-gum root just as a volley of rocks and clods slapped into the plane, through the space where he had just been. From out of the bush about a dozen kids from Sean's school converged on him, throwing rocks. They were led by Smythe.

'Get the bastard! You're dead, Buttenberg. We've got ya, you bloody dick!'

A stone grazed his forehead. Others hit his arms and legs. Sean threw his rod under the plane. He swung his knapsack from his back and to his front to protect his body. He started to advance towards his attackers. He had nowhere else to go. Sean felt sweat on his brow and under his shirt. His cap flew off as a clod collected it and grazed his skull. He swung the knapsack wildly, trying to keep them at bay. They were like a pack of wild dogs. He managed to keep them off him but he couldn't last much longer. They closed in.

'You're dead, Buttenwog! Buttenwog! Buttenwog's dead.'

Some had sticks and clubs. Others threw stones. A stick hit his left arm, stinging it. He dodged a rock. He ducked and weaved, and tried to fend them off. Then he heard it.

'Hetra akameri Dingarra worlba Itterra Yelga,
Hetra akameri Dingarra worlba Itterra Yelga,
Hetra akameri Dingarra worlba Itterra Yelga.'

The voice was Joseph's strong and booming, like Sean had never heard it. Suddenly, time stood still. The boys around him were like statues. Their arms dropped to their sides. Mouths fell open but no sound came. Their eyes were large, wide and shining. They turned as one towards the sound, forgetting their prey.

Sean saw Joseph through a gap in their circle. He was bare footed, bare chested, his head had a red band tied around it, his face marked with streaks of yellow, the red fireman's braces holding up his pants bright against his black skin. Scars ran horizontally across his chest from above his nipples to his belly button. Circular scars ran down his arms like the Bora Bora trees, and two red-painted lightning stripes stood out on each side of his chest. In his right hand was a nulla nulla, long and wicked with a large knobbly end. He was swirling it around in great arcs, and all the while he chanted.

'*Hetra akameri Dingarra worlba Itterra Yelga,*
Hetra akameri Dingarra worlba Itterra Yelga,
Hetra akameri Dingarra worlba Itterra Yelga.'

The boys gave out a collective scream, broke and ran.

'*Hetra akameri Dingarra worlba Itterra Yelga*
Hetra akameri Dingarra worlba Itterra Yelga.
Hetra akameri Dingarra worlba Itterra Yelga.'

Searn chanted along with Joseph.

Sean picked up some stones and threw them hard, hitting two of them as they fled. He moved forward punching one of the slower kids in the stomach. He buckled and fell. He shouldered another, who crashed to the ground, crying out in fear and pain. Picking up a long stake left by one of his attackers, he speared it into a boys back. He screamed and fell over, his eyes wide in terror. Sean was looking for another target when he saw Smythe heading towards the graveyard. He raced after him. He was fast for a fat kid. He caught up with him as he reached the river side. Sean lunged but fell short, clipping him on the ankle. Smythe tripped, slipping on the wet mud of the bank. He fell into the muddy verge of the river, wallowing in the mud, spluttering and coughing. He tried to get up, but fell back with a splash. He was crying and blubbering. Sean picked up a big clod of hardened mud and threw it with full force into his back. He struggled in the muddy water, his face going under. Sean picked up a large stake. He raised it above his head and hit Smythe with all his might across his legs. The boy cried out. He hit him again, across his back. Smythe cried out and went under again. Sean raised the stake for another strike but paused.

He looked around. There was no one. All was quiet. It was only him and Smythe. He could beat him to a pulp. He spat out at him.

'Hetra akameri Dingarra worlba Itterra Yelga.'

He stood back and watched as Smythe stumbled, fell, squirmed, coughed and wriggled. Sean watched. He felt nothing. Smythe's face was bleeding. He was black and grey from the clinging mud. Finally, he was able to stand. His shoes and socks were missing, his eyes thin slits of red. His hair stood up, transfixed by the mud. He stared at Sean, then dropped his head. His shoulders slumped. He wiped his forehead and whimpered. Then he limped off, up past the old bomber and out of the swamp.

Sean retrieved his gear from the under the bomber and wandered up to Joseph's camp. The old man was sitting by his fire as though nothing had happened. He wore his grey flannel and black coat, the Akubra perched securely on his head. The billy was boiling on its stand. Sean sat beside him. He looked at the fire. The old man gave him a towel.

'Them fella they bin sneak down here after school I bin see them but they not see me. They hide in the bushes all round where you normally come. I know they gonna get you. I think I might scare them a bit, they all gone now, heh?'

Sean nodded. 'Yeh, they're gone. You scared the hell out of them. They'll never come back here again.'

'You bin want some tea?'

They sucked on their tea, pondering for a while.

'What did you yell, Joseph?'

Joseph smiled. 'Ah, scary thing, something like come on get going, Dingarra get you, you dogs, it nothing really but sound scary, heh.'

'It bloody scared me! But I think the thing that scared them most was the paint and the scars on your chest.'

The man thought about this for some time. 'That bin how we paint up in olden days when I bin a boy, or at a Korobra.'

'Where did all the scars come from?'

Joseph looked at Sean intently. Finally, he said, 'They bin given to me by old fellas long time go, initiation and ceremony they show where I be in my manhood. I a Dingarra man in Tamba Tamba. That means I am a man of the lightning, special to Dingarra. You also Dingarra, you special. Me only marked by men, you marked by Dingarra fella.'

Sean thought for a while. 'I could have really hurt that Smythe kid. I could have killed him, but something stopped me.'

'Ah, Dingarra not only give you mark, he give you wisdom. It easy to kill man when he down, but far better to have control and use your strength for good things. If you have power over yourself, you have power over weak fellas like that Smythe, then only have to use force when all else not bin workin.'

Sean got up to go, suddenly feeling very tired. The old man restrained him and Sean sat down again.

'Maiyarare, maybe those fellas tell cop fella. You stay out of it, no need to get into trouble for me.'

'No fish, Sean?' his mum said.

'No, but I nearly got a big one in the mud.'

'What's that cut on your forehead? Sean, you're all dirty,' she tut tutted and shook her head. 'Go and clean up before your dad gets home.'

Sean went into the bathroom, noting the scar on his chest from Dingarra and thinking of Joseph and his scars.

Next day, school was different. Johnny McCarthy came up to him in the bike shed.

'Heard about last night,' he stammered. 'Some black devil comin' and helping you beat up the gang down at the swamp. Some of the fellas said they were lucky to get away alive. Scared shitless, they were. Smythe's not here. Bluey and Hughsey have gone missing. What happened?'

Sean looked at Johnny. The freckles stood out on the pale skin. His red hair was tussled and blown, his shirt hanging out, shoes scuffed and marked.

'Johnny, sorry, dunno what your talkin' about. Must be someone else. See ya later.'

Johnny grabbed him as he walked off and spun him round to face him. Sean clenched his fist, ready to fight.

'Sean, I know I had it comin' to me, the thing with Berty's marbles, and Smythy bad mouthin' you and everything. But I wasn't there last night because I told them to go easy on you. I think you're all right, Sean.'

'See you around,' Sean muttered as he turned again and crossed the playground. There was an eerie silence. The only kids moving were him and the kindergarten kids, who never knew anything about nothing. All of the rest were looking at him. It was like walking through a sea of statues. Then the silence was broken.

'Sean, Sean! You killed them, you beauty!' Berty White was running around like a wild Indian, jumping up and down. 'Yah hoo, yah hoo.'

'Berty, settle!' Sean yelled. He grabbed him by the arms and pulled him close and whispered into his wild face. 'I'm trying to keep it quiet.'

'Oh.'

At playtime Sean leaned against the brick chimney of the old assembly hall, which nestled in beside the main school building. He was against the wall to protect his back, but the Smythe gang was nowhere to be seen. He saw individuals but they weren't in their usual group on the back fence. Sean looked at the apostle birds in the trees, drab and serious like the day, their harsh cries indicating impatience for the end of playtime.

'Mr Buttenberg, can I please have you come into my office?'

Sean looked and saw the Head Sister on the verandah.

'Thank you, Sean. Please come in and have a seat.'

Again he sat in the chair across from the Sister. The cobra lamp's light making the room yellow. The Head Sister was reading from a brown manila folder. She closed it and looked up at him.

'Sister Rose tells me you are doing well in your studies, Sean.'

He nodded, waiting for the punch line.

'Young Smythe is not in today. I have just had a visit from his mother with some fantastic story about him being attacked by a black ghost and that you were involved. It was down on the river, a place called the Swamp. Do you know anything about this story, laddie?'

Sean noted friendship, not hostility.

'I can't say anything, Sister.'

She nodded. 'Sister Louise tells me that you are friendly with Joseph Wirrinum. Is that right, Sean?'

'Yes.'

'Do you often play down there after school?' Her gaze hadn't lifted from his face. He felt clammy.

'Yes, I play down there a lot.'

'Umm.' She looked up towards the ceiling. There was silence for a period. Then her gaze returned to him. 'Laddie, go back to class now.'

Sean rose and reached towards the door. As he opened it, she said, 'Say hello to Joseph for me, Sean. A fine man, a good man, indeed.'

Sean looked around. 'Yes, Sister,' he blurted out.

'And, Sean, please be careful down near that river.'

'Yes, Sister.'

Lunch time was a blur of marble games with Berty and Johnny McCarthy and some grade fives and sixes, even some of Smythe's gang. Some of these kids had never spoken to him before. Afternoon playtime was like in Brunswick. He was part of the crowd, playing knuckles, and surrounded by kids. Sean almost felt uncomfortable. He rode home that afternoon in a daze. What had happened? It was as though he was a hero.

Sean did extra chores at home that night and waited for his dad. They sat out in the cool gloom of the early evening at the wood heap. His dad looked at him intently, he sloped his hat back.

'Dad? If you were involved in a fight and someone came to help you when you were fighting off a mob, and then you and him whipped them, what would you expect to happen?'

His father smiled. 'How do you mean Sean?'

'Well, would you expect people to treat you really well the next day? Even some of the people who had tried to beat you up the day before?'

'Well, people always love a winner. Most people are followers.'

'Yeh, they would be pretty scared, I suppose.'

'Another thing,' his father added. 'People respect you if you stand up against the odds. It's a powerful attraction. Is this anything to do with the fight down at the swamp last night, Sean?'

Sean was stunned. 'How did you know?'

'Had a haircut today at Smithy's. Whitey said there was a commotion down there yesterd'y afternoon. Told me all about it. Berty said you beat the lot of them.' His dad waited.

'I promised not to say what happened, Dad.'

'Mum said you came home muddy with cuts and bruises last night.'

'They attacked me! Now they're treating me like I am a hero or something.'

'Yeh, life's like that. The real friends are those who are with you when you're losing. Things change quickly. Take it all with a grain of salt. Tell Joseph if he needs a hand with anything I will help.'

'Okay, dad.'

'Those Smythes, they'll cause trouble. I'll have a word with Shorty Malone. He'll look out for Joseph.'

Tamba Tamba

The next day Harry Smythe was not at school again. Johnny McCarthy hung out with Sean. Johnny was an excitable sort of a bloke, but solid, no bullshit.

Sean asked, 'Did you get your bike fixed up after the crash that day?'

'Yeh, no problem. My dad's pretty handy. It was a great race. I was scared shitless. You were going like a bat out of hell. You looked like you wanted to kill me.'

'I did.'

'Oh, well. Shit happens.' Johnny smiled.

'Yeh, shit happens.'

'Double you up next game?'

'No worries.'

That afternoon Sean rode home quickly, did his chores and went to the swamp. He rested in the B17 cockpit, looking out over this special place, feeling the quiet, letting it seep into him. He thought about the river, his totem, the Bindaree people, Joseph... He felt himself being lifted up. He was above, looking down on the river and the towns of Koonarook and Caladonia. The river, long and winding, the bridge, little and grey, this old bomber where he sat, a mere dot in the swamp. Nompie the eagle circled, and the Tamba Tamba were returning to their nests of sticks. The sun was a big ball of red in the west and the haze and mist of the winter evening was settling over the land. He came out of his daydreaming, left the bomber and made his way up to Joseph's camp. It was, as always, neat and tidy. The campfire coals were glowing and a fluff of smoke hung in the heavy winter air. The old man in grey flannel, moleskins, stockman's boots and hat was sitting on the fire stump carving.

'G'day, Sean,' he said without looking up. 'You bin dreamin about this place here?'

Sean was not surprised by the old man's intuition. 'I was thinking about this place from high on, like Nompie.'

'That Dingarra spirit fella he take you for a look at this place, they mark you, maybe you gonna help them.'

'I'm only a boy.'

'But you not always gonna be, Maiyarare. These spirit fellas, they not gunna think like me, you or other fella. They no have any time. They live in all time, in what has happened and what is maybe gonna happen. They mysterious fella, hard to understand, but Dingarra, he has job for you, he come to you often I bin thinkin. The spirit fella they have no hate or what they say preduce.'

'Prejudice.'

'That right. No white or black fella for them, they all the same.' The old man put his carving down. 'You want to have a brew, young un, before you go?' The old man stiffly bent over the old billy and went through the familiar routine. Soon Sean was drinking a hot mug of sweet, delicious tea. 'It time I show you Tamba Tamba sacred place, Bullima place. You can come this place tomorrow in the morning, Sean?'

'I'm going to the footy in the afternoon with dad. Koonarook plays Caladonia. It's gonna be a bloodbath he reckons. Koonarook is third on the ladder and Cal is tops. Should be a great game.'

'My cousin Noah Midjeeri he bin playing for Koonarook.'

'He's one of their best players my dad reckons.'

'Yep,' the old man laughed. 'They all good runners, those Midjeeri. Their name mean stick. They good people.'

'If I finish my chores early, I'll get here mid-morning.'

'That be good. Them Tamba Tamba be out for the day by then, we no disturb them.'

'Oh, you know Sister Hildegard, the Head Sister at my school? She said to pass on her regards to you.'

The old man smiled. 'Yeh, long time I know that lady. When she young she bin teaching up at that place called Denny, in mission school, she bin goin to take a sick porle, a kid, to Denny. Their horse break a leg on way. They stuck there for five days. Them fella could not find them, they maybe gonna die. I bin lucky that time and find them, that little porle all right. That Sister give her all her water and food. She bin sick for a few days but she a tough lady that one. She come find me after a while and give me a present, this buckle on my belt here.' Sean looked at the battered and tarnished silver of the bucking stallion at Joseph's middle. 'I wear this one since that time, when she comes that day I ask her if she learn me to write this white fella lingo. She give me a book and slate, and when I am going near this mission place she or other nun teach me and learn me, so I write and read. A Father there, Brother John, he writes down my story some time too, and since then we bin know each other.'

That night around the tea table Sean told his family the story about Sister Hildegard and Joseph.

'Some of the fellas, including Shorty Malone, say that old Joseph is one of the best trackers in the state. He can track across rock. In his young days they say he could track up the middle of the Murray River.'

'James, do not exaggerate!'

'Just trying to make a point, Mary. He was a bloody good tracker.'

'James, please do not profane in front of the family. You're not at the pub now.'

'Sorry, Mary. Much better to see your pretty face across the table than them ugly blokes.'

Sean's mother blushed. His parents looked at each other, and they smiled. Sean's dad had to work in the morning, so he arranged to meet Sean at the entrance to the footy ground at one o'clock. His mother was going to a hospital fundraiser with Katy for the afternoon.

'Say hello to Joseph for me today, Sean.'

Sean told his father about the Tamba and what they meant to Joseph's people while he ate his eggs and bacon and drank his Milo.

'Hmm,' his father murmured over his coffee. 'There's some talk that that area down there is going to be bulldozed and turned into a caravan camping ground and some of it given to the mill.'

'But they can't! Joseph lives there. It's his place.'

'It's council-managed public land and they can do whatever they want. There are all these cars on the roads now and tourism, fishing, caravan parks and river parks are all the go.'

'But the Tamba, the graveyard, the trees. It's a holy place, dad.'

'Holy or not, Lachlan Campbell is pushing to have the place developed. He normally gets his way. Sean, don't tell the old man about this. It's only a rumour. He'll get upset.'

'But it's his home.'

'Promise, Sean?'

'Oh, alright,' Sean said angrily.

'Right. I'll see you at the footy, hope the tigers belt the daylights out of those blue buggers, hey Sean?' His dad cupped him over the ears, messed his hair and was gone into the cold grey of the early dawn.

Sean got to work with the firewood, chooks and his room. By the time his mother and Katy were up he was finished, and he had a piece of toast and warm milk with them. He minded Katy for a while as his mum got dressed, then his mother said he could go. She gave him a hug and two bob.

'Be careful, Sean, and go straight to the football after you have your play down at the river.'

'Yeh, thanks, mum.'

Sean tied the two bob in the corner of his hanky. He made his way to Joseph's camp. This was such a beautiful place – how could they destroy it?

At the campsite the old man was where he was the night before, carving and drinking tea. Sean hunched down beside Joseph and sipped his tea and watched the man whittle. The thing was about eight inches long, two inches wide and maybe three-sixteenth of an inch thick. Carved on both sides were intricate circles and lines. A lightning flash was central to one side, and on the other was a fish. Gouged out in one end was a small hole.

'This here be a Churinga, what you call a bullroarer. I have string here.' He tied the string through the hole and stood up. 'You stay where you are, Sean.'

Joseph swung the Churinga around, letting string out as it turned. Starting down low, the Churinga made a noise like a roaring bull, the air vibrated, birds cried in alarm and flew away. The old man laughed and sang.

'Illa booker mer ley urrie urrie, illa booker mer ley urrie urrie, doongurra, doongurra.'

Over and over, on and on he went, the bullroarer making its roaring, the old man chanting his song. He was in a trance.

'Illa booker mer ley urrie urrie, doongurra, doongurra.'

Sean saw only the whirl of the bullroarer, all else was lost. The noise was mesmerising, his thoughts came of lightning, and the Ponde Ponde, the world only existed in this space, this holy place...

Then it was over, the spell was broken. Joseph sat down and poured himself another mug of tea. The world came into focus again, and Joseph handed the bullroarer to him.

'This bin your Churinga, it holy thing, it have your totem Ponde Ponde and Dingarra. Always when you need guidance and peace this Churinga will connect you to them, they always with you. You use it later on, always it be special dreamin thing for you.'

'I can't take what you've taken so long to make.'

'Take it, Maiyarare.' The gnarled, scaly, strong hands pressed the Churinga into his. Then Joseph passed him a piece of oil cloth to wrap it in. 'I make you a kangaroo pouch, for you to put it in and keep it safe. You oil it every now and then, it last long time you see.'

'Thank you, thank you.' The old man laughed and put his arm around his shoulders. They peered into the blue smoke of the fire.

'Well, let's go and have a look at this Tamba Tamba place. Every day the Tamba Tamba comes back here to nest in the evening and every morning they leave. When I young porle the Bindaree fella go out every day hunt, fish and gather then come back in evening to their home. Tamba Tamba same.' Joseph got up.

Sean put the Churinga in his pocket carefully and they walked out of the camp site and down a track towards the mill. A short way down they stopped and turned towards what seemed an impenetrable layer of small trees and bushes. Joseph stepped through them and around them. Sean followed closely along a faint path. In no time they were in an area about the size of a small football field, the ground inter-spaced with old trees. Their trunks were straight for about twenty feet, then they became interwoven and meshed together, forming a dense canopy about thirty or forty feet high. On top of this Sean could just make out nests, multitudes of them jutting out, jagged, ragged and majestic. Sean and the old man walked beneath them. It was like being in a cathedral. The sun was blocked out and nothing grew. For five or ten minutes they walked around. It was eerily quiet. Most of the trees were marked with Bora Bora carving.

'My people come here for long, long time, since the dreamin. They mark the trees and give thanks for Tamba Tamba and remember Nooralie's promise. While they here this Billa place be good place for the people. If they go it die. Is quiet now but when them Tamba come back at day's end, this place be noisy, noisy place. They all talkin and dancing and singin. If good season they lay their egg here and raise their porle until he strong enough to fly. The same as Bindaree. Maybe Tamba not take as long to be fully grown like Bindaree, but otherwise the same.'

Joseph drew out his pocket knife and began to carve into one of the trees. 'We mark our visit and make special mark for Tamba and Nooralie.' He was soon finished. He had carved three concentric circles, one inside the other. 'Now your turn, young fella.'

Sean hesitated. 'Is it okay? I'm not Bindaree.'

Joseph looked at him. 'You marked by Dingarra, you his special son by Bindaree law.'

Sean nodded and carved a circle into the tree below Joseph's mark.

'You only young fella, not yet old enough or powerful enough for full circles, you only draw one, eh.'

Sean was soon finished. They pulled back to look at their work.

'When you Taldree you come back and carve second circle. Then when you reach Thalera you do third. We have big Korobra eat and drink, dance and sing. Now you are joined to this Bullima Tamba dreamin place for long time, maybe all life.'

Sean felt a great pride and happiness, but also sadness for what could happen to this place if his father was right. They sat for a long time enjoying the quiet.

'We go back have some damper, and tea. All this dreamin make me hungry. You gonna be mighty big fella I think maybe, by the size of that Bora Bora circle you carved,' he laughed and laughed.

'What were you dreamin of, Joseph, back in the Tamba ground?' Sean asked as they sat and ate slices of damper, smothered in butter and jam.

Joseph gulped his tea and thought for a minute. 'I bin thinkin about the old days of my family, when we lived here, you know before that big war not this last one. Those times we bin fishin, and huntin, Korobra and living like old ways, we have some white fella stuff too, but we bin happy. Then they make us move, say we can't stay next to town, they move us out to that Barmah place with all other people. It too sad for my mother, father, they soon die, maybe their heart broken. These first white fellas who come here in olden days, this Caladonia fella, we fight him, then make treaty paper. They say we can stay here this Tamba place forever, but they no listen to us, they move us. They give my grandfather treaty plate to wear. I have in my hut. It says King Joseph. They name him Joseph too, but they no listen to us.' He took a gulp of tea. 'Enough sad times, you bin dreamin too in there.'

'Yep, I was dreamin about my family also and how lucky I am, and to have you as a special friend, like another father.'

'Ah, this Tamba Tamba place, it always seems to make you dreamin about family and country, that sort of stuff. Nooralie make it so, I think. Tamba is family.'

The old man leaned back and stretched. 'The peeler feller Sergeant Malone and another fella come this morning before you come, asking if I was all right, if I had any kids coming down and annoying me. I said no one has annoyed me. They said that fella Smythe made a complaint to the New South Wales blue bellies about me attacking his kid. They have to investigate and make a report. They say your father had a word to the Sergeant, told him about your troubles with that mob. The peeler bloke says this Smythe fella is a nuisance, but they have to make a report. Be careful, he said, and that was all. He had some tea and left. He a nice fella that Sergeant.'

'Yeh, my dad and him are friends. They're war veterans, in the RSL.'

Football

Sean made his way out of the swamp, across the highway and towards the oval. The streets here were filled with workers cottages; timber, single fronted, chicken wire fences, small verandahs and squat red-brick chimneys. Some had sleepouts, all had outhouses, many had young children playing around them. Sean slowly merged into a stream of people. They were mostly family groups decorated with hand-knitted yellow and black scarfs and beanies. They were talking excitedly; some kids had footballs and were kicking to each other between the few cars that passed along the street. Sean knew a lot of them from church, school or both. He passed the Catholic Church, St Gerard's – patron saint of mothers, his mother had told him. It was a large timber structure, one of the largest in Koonarook. The double doors were open and a steady stream of people went in and out. The presbytery sitting beside it was an imposing redbrick building. Magnificent date palms grew around it, and an ironwork lattice verandah protected it from the weather.

Sean reached the arched rusty iron entrance to the oval. His father was in deep conversation with another man. Sean waited at his side. His dad looked at him and winked, He was dressed in elastic-sided boots and bone-coloured moleskins, held up by a thick kangaroo hide belt. His shirt was dark green, heavy duty corduroy, with large pockets. The jacket he wore was deep brown and waisted. A light grey Akubra with a green feather sat at a cocky angle atop his head. After the man had gone his dad turned to him.

'G'day, Sean. Dougy Black, old mud on blood mate. When this is finished we'll have a few at the RSL. Oh, mum said to give you this.' He pulled out a yellow and black beanie and scarf.

'Fantastic!'

His dad laughed. 'Let's go in and beat these toffs.'

They passed through the gates where committee men in sports coats and ties were selling tickets. The ground was filling fast, the whole district seemed to be there.

'You had something to eat, Sean?'

'I could go a pie.'

'No worries. Me too.'

They walked to the canteen at the foot of the grandstand. Sean looked into the stand directly above. Attendants were ushering people to their seats. There were a lot of navy blue and white cockades, scarves and badges in this crowd. In a roped-off section directly above them were men and women dressed in suits and matching outfits.

'Dad, who are the toffs?'

'The presidents of the clubs, and the mayors of the towns. Also Mr Hughes, who owns the mill and sponsors Koonarook. And Mr Campbell, who owns most of everything else. He's the major sponsor for Caladonia. I hope Campbell has a bad day. I'd like to see that arrogant bastard get rolled. He's brought players from Melbourne and Bendigo. We'll have to sell a lot of bloody pies to come anywhere near his payroll.'

Sean looked at the trim man his father had indicated. He sat bolt upright in his seat. His hair was jet black with streaks of grey and the tie he wore had a tartan pattern.

They eventually got their pies and moved off to the bar, behind the grandstand. The line up here was equally impressive, the long-necks and glasses clinking above the noise of the crowd. Other men asked his dad how he was going, about the game and work. His dad joked and told a few yarns and joined in the general banter. Soon enough they had a longneck and glass to add to their pies, and Sean had a real treat, a bottle of Caladonia Preserving Company raspberry drink. They went down to the fence near the player's shelter, sat on the bench that ran around the ground, and got stuck into the pies and drinks. Everyone was there. Local church ministers, shopkeepers, farmers, teenage netballers who played their games in the corner of the oval reserve before the footy, cockies in their corduroys and tweed coats, labourers in their overalls and beanies, shopkeepers in soft shoes and muted clothes, mothers with babies in prams and pushers, Aboriginals with barefoot children, the men in western shirts and hats.

The umpires, all in white except for black long stretch socks, appeared on the oval. The centre umpire held the ball in the air, the timekeepers sounded the siren, the crowd cheered. The goal umpires swung their flags in practice. The field umpires ran around warming up, backwards and forwards. Then the Blues ran onto the field in a tight group, and the Caladonian fans waved their flags and cheered. The Blues ran to the river end of the oval and started warm up kicks and hand passes. They looked big, professional and mean. Then the Koonarook team came onto the field. The crowd erupted into a sea of yellow and black, standing, waving, cheering, and yelling. Some were crying. Sean recognised quite a few of the Koonarook players. He watched Joseph's cousin Noah Midjeeri go through his warm-up procedures. He was a small wiry fellow running around energetically. As far as Sean could see, there were five Aboriginal players playing for Koonarook, none for Caladonia. The teams warmed up for five minutes, the siren blasted again and the teams went into a huddle as their captains walked to the centre and shook hands. The umpire tossed the coin. Koonarook won the toss and the captain Skinny Fitzpatrick indicated by a wave of his hand that they would kick to the river end. The captains ran back to their teams, said a few words, and the players ran to their positions. As the players paired off, Sean felt a feeling of apprehensive.

The umpire bounced the ball and the teams went at it. From the start the Caladonia side was more skilful and stronger. They hit the ball and their opponents hard. The Koonarook lads sprawled on the ground. They were shoved aside. The Caladonia scored three goals before Koonarook had scored. Each time the Caladonia side scored, the crowd groaned. When Koonarook scored, the crowd went wild. Noah Midjeeri was starring, roving and weaving like magic up and down the field. He and a few of the smaller Koonarook players were keeping them in it, but by quarter time Koonarook was behind by twenty-one points.

'Wanna hear the quarter time address?' his dad asked.

It seemed to Sean that half the crowd, boys and men, vaulted the fence and went over to the Koonarook huddle. The Caladonia huddle was much smaller. The Koonarook players were in the middle of a quiet thoughtful crowd. The players were drinking out of jugs and were draped in black and yellow dressing gowns. Their faces were red. Their knees, arms, boots and playing gear covered in mud. All waited expectantly for Jock O'Day, the coach, to address them. Jock was a small man dressed neatly in corduroy trousers and shirt, with a black committee coat laced by the yellow facings and pocket emblem of the roaring tiger.

Jock quietly called his players in closely. 'Well, fellas, well done on a great quarter. You're doing the club proud.' The crowd applauded and cheered. 'Now,' he said, 'stick with your man this quarter. Treat your opponent like he's your sheila on a Friday night. Like you're not gonna see her for six bloody months!' There was general laughter and sniggering. 'Stick with 'em!' he said more strongly now. 'If we can hold these toffs this quarter, on this heavy ground and with the people here behind us, we'll run over the top of them in the last half. Now go to it. Nothin' fancy, just go to it!'

They all cheered and the boys slapped each other on the back and broke for their positions. The crowd hastened to their seats.

The Koonarook players shadowed their opponents closely. It was a grinding affair, the Caladonia side skilful and flamboyant, the Koonarook side gritty and determined, holding on like grim death. The Koonarook men spoiling and chasing, scragging and tackling. By the second half of the quarter, the Caladonia side was frustrated and there were niggling incidents, heavy bumps and side swipes, with heated words exchanged. The barracking was deafening. Just before the end of the quarter Noah Midjeeri marked the ball off a beautiful low pass from up field. Immediately he sprinted and bounced it down the ground, weaving and turning, mesmerising the crowd and opponents alike. With a beautiful drop kick, he planted it on the chest of Sammy Black in the goal square. But a big Caladonia player kept coming and charged into the lithe Aboriginal full on. The little man flew backwards with the impact and landed with a thickening thud. Knocked out cold. The Koonarook players rushed the offender. It was an ugly brawl. The siren sounded. The umpires and coaches tried to quell the players. Peeler men rushed onto the ground. The noise of the crowd reached a crescendo. The player who had knocked Noah out was king hit and fell beside Noah.

His dad shook his head in amusement. 'This is the greatest barney since the war. What a rumble. Let's get another drink before the crowd gets to the bar.'

They ambled to the deserted bar. His dad helped himself to a longneck and a bottle of raspberry and left the money on the counter.

By the time they got back to their seats the field was clearing. Players were separated by a line of umpires and officials. The Koonarook side had kicked a goal after being awarded a free kick right in front. They were only sixteen points behind.

During half time they discussed the game, the determination of Koonarook and the skills of Caladonia.

'I think Jock is right,' his father said. 'If we can keep going, those other fellas will tire and we'll have them.'

Sean felt eyes on him. He looked around and there was Mary Addison. She was dressed in a cotton dress, faded cardigan and plastic sandals. Three smaller children were with her.

'G'day, Sean,' she said in her quiet voice.

'G'day,' he said and felt embarrassed. He hoped none of the blokes from school saw him. He turned away as his father turned towards her.

'Hello,' he heard his father say. 'I'm Sean's dad, Jim.'

'Hello, Mr Buttenberg.'

'You sit next to Sean in class, right?'

Sean squirmed on his seat and took a swig of raspberry. He looked at the sky. His father continued.

'We must thank you for helping Sean with his writing.'

'Sean helps me a lot, Mr Buttenberg.'

'You out for the day?'

'Yes. Mr Jones, our neighbour, gave me and the three smaller ones here a ride in on the back of his ute.'

'Enjoying it?'

'Yes, I really am, but I didn't enjoy the fight.'

'No, but that's boys for you.'

'Well, I must be off. The younger ones want to play on the playground.'

'See you later.'

Sean muttered, 'see ya later,' without looking at her.

'That girl has a quality about her that's priceless.'

'I have to go to the loo,' said Sean. He raced off and caught up with Mary.

'Wait! I have something for you.' He reached into his pocket, found the knotted handkerchief and unknotted the two-bob piece. He offered it to her.

'I can't take your money, Sean.'

'It's for the kids. Buy them a lolly or pie. I owe you for helping me at school.' He pushed the money into her hand, and she clutched it reluctantly.

Sean returned to his father. The third quarter was about to start. The umpires and four police, including Sergeant Malone, emerged from the grandstand. The crowd emitted a low murmur. The Koonarook side emerged first with Noah Midjeeri back on his feet, but a bit unsteady. The Koonarook side ran around, looking refreshed and sprightly. The Caledonians' emerged. The umpires went to their posts, the police to separate points around the boundary. The players of both sides grouped, gave a cheer and took their positions.

The third quarter was a bloodbath. There were hits after play and more than one player went down. Players sported streaming cuts and some were limping. Koonarook lost another player to a head high tackle. They were now out of reserves. A Caladonian player had to go off. It was gruelling stuff, with tough play up and down the ground. Slowly, the Koonarook side was getting on top. The gap in the score closed as Koonarook pushed forward again and again. At the final break, it was anyone's game. Koonarook was down seven points.

Sean and his dad went to the huddle again. The players were eating orange quarters, some were inhaling smelling salts. The trainers were busy bandaging, strapping, massaging. Jock stood in the middle.

The siren sounded the resumption of play.

'Huddle round, huddle round, in close, in close, in close!' Jock cried. The players closed in, arms around each other. The coach slowly looked at each player in turn. He drew a deep breath.

'Boys, I don't have to tell you what to do. You know. We've talked about it often enough. This is it. We are tired, but they are bug-gered. We're going to roll right over them. We're going straight down the middle. We're going to keep moving. Move forward at all costs. We are going to handpass, protect the ball carrier and we are going to win, win, win! We're going to walk off this ground, this sacred ground, as winners. For three generations our fathers, brothers, grandfathers and mates have battled and bled for the black and gold! We'll hold our heads high. They will say this was the greatest team that ever played for the Tiger, the most courageous team that ever was. They fought for this town, we fight for this town! Your wives, your mothers, your families, your girlfriends and your mates are all watching you! This is not a game, boys. No, this is a matter of blood! Can you feel it, boys?'

'Yeh!' they yelled.

'Can you taste it, boys?'

'Yeh, yeh!'

The crowd broke into cheers and applause. The players huddled and embraced and with one great 'hurrah' they ran off to their posi-tions.

The play started and immediately the Caledonians' made a quick break and goaled. There was a collective groan from the crowd and the Caladonian supporters found their voice. The Koonarook play-ers scrambled forward. The play was tough and relentless but the Koonarook players went straight down the centre, moving the ball forward. They scored and the play was back to seven points. A Koon-arook player went down, and was dragged off. Koonarook was down to seventeen men. The runner was exhorting and pleading. The ball was pushed forward again. The sky was heavy, the air damp, the light dim, the play unrelenting. A Caladonian went down with cramp, and another. The trainers ran out, stretching them and pushing them back into play. Koonarook kicked a point. The difference was one straight goal. The crowd was hysterical. Sean had butterflies in his stomach. His father's face was like granite. They rode every bump, every kick, and every mark. Another Koonarook player went down with a high tackle. Noah Midjeeri ran into the centre, putting himself on the ball. Time was running out. Koonarook pushed forward again, but Caladonia was stacking the back line. Sean could hardly bear to watch. A high kick went forward, and Noah floated over the pack like an angel. He seemed to hang in the air forever, clutching and juggling the ball. The pack had cleared and he pulled himself to his feet, still holding the ball.

'No-ah! No-ah! No-ah!' the crowd chanted.

He slowly made his way back and then casually planted a drop punt right through the goal posts.

'Noah Midjeeri, you beauty!'

The crowd went wild. The scores were level. The ball was back in the centre. It was a free for all. A score, any score, would do. Again the Koonarook players pushed it forward, again it was a scrum. Then somehow Noah broke free from the pack, the ball clutched in his hand. One bounce. He dodged a lunge from a Caladonian. Another bounce. Another tackle. He feigned a hand pass. Then he kicked. The ball sailed through the air, high and long. The siren sounded. The ball curved left, then came back right. It seemed to hold in the air. Then through it went for a point. Koonarook had won! The crowd were on their feet, stamping, yelling, hugging, kissing. The players embraced. Sean and his dad hugged and shook hands. The crowd was on the field. Noah was on their shoulders. There were tears and hugs. Scarves and hats waved in the air. The crowd converged on the ground.

'We're from Tiger land!' echoed across the ground and into the town as the crowd joined the players in the team song.

Sean felt he was part of something big, bigger than anything he had felt before. Whatever it was, it was in the air, in the people's faces. Sean looked up at the grandstand. It was subdued. Mr Campbell was scowling at the man next to him.

After long exaltation, numerous renditions of the team song, back slapping and cheering, the crowd started to disperse. The gaggle of people were animated and excited as they walked along, strangers and chums spoke, farmer and labourer, Aboriginal and white, squatter and storeman. Sean saw Johnny McCarthy up ahead, the blue Caladonia scarf around his neck. He straggled along slowly by his father's side. Sean raced up to him.

'G'day, Johnny. Great game. Hello, Mr McCarthy.'

'Hello, young fella. You one of Johnny's friends from school?'

'Yes, sir.'

'You were lucky today. Hope you aren't as lucky come finals time.'

Sean's dad caught up to them and introduced himself.

'Great game. Pity one side had to lose.'

'There's always next time.'

They ambled along talking animatedly and laughing as though they had known each other for years.

As they neared home Sean's dad said, 'Dick's coming for a few beers. You and Johnny tell mum we'll be home soon. Dick will pick Johnny up later.'

Sean's mother listened to all the details about the game. 'Better serve you up some tea, Johnny. Once those men start gabbing, they may not be home for some time.'

Katy was in the lounge playing with her dolls but on seeing Johnny she ran into the kitchen. The boys sat by the record player and talked about marbles and yonnies. Johnny showed him a brand new marble that he had bought over at Hayes' merchants and hardware in Caladonia. It was a beautiful thing to behold, agreed Sean, multicoloured with metallic spots streaked though it.

'Trade you five of your cat's-eyes for it.'

Johnny picked out five cats-eyes. Sean went into his room and reached under the mattress where he stored his secret things and favourite comics. He found the oilskin. Sitting beside Johnny in the glow of the fire, he unwrapped it carefully. The bullroarer's oily surface shone in the firelight. It seemed to absorb the warmth and give it back. Sean handed it to Johnny. The skeleton fish swam in the shimmering light. As Johnny turned it over, the lightning strike of Dingarra leapt up at him.

'Wow, this is bonzer.'

Sean explained how it worked.

'Where did you get it from?'

'A mate.'

'The old Abo who lives down by the river?'

'His name is Joseph. He's a member of the Bindaree, the Tamba Tamba people.'

'This is some nice bullroarer.'

Sean wrapped it and returned it to its hiding place.

The Campbells

At school, Sean felt part of the place at last. Harry Smythe had lost his swagger and most of his gang, and was a brooding, sullen figure.

The nights and early mornings were very cold, and the days cool but mostly fine. The rain, when it came, was brief and intermittent. Most mornings Johnny McCarthy met him at the Caladonia side of the bridge and they walked or rode together to school. Sean visited the swamp after school most days and on the weekends, and listened to Joseph's stories. Tales of his time as a drover, of the Dreaming and his youth flowed out of him like the river flowing nearby.

One night at tea his dad said, 'I'm meeting with Mr Campbell at Caladonia Park on Saturday morning. He wants to see me on some forest and milling issues. Want to come for a ride and have a look at the place, Sean?'

'What's there to see?'

'One of the best gardens in the whole of Victoria. Baron von Mueller planned it. He visited here on his trip down the Murray in the eighteen fifties. Not many people get to see it. Mr Campbell's a stickler for punctuality. We'll leave at nine thirty.'

His mother joined in. 'Maybe you will see Mrs Campbell's high tea. I'm told they are spectacular, invitation only.'

'Mary, the last thing I want to be going to is a bloody hobnobs' morning tea. This bloke Campbell will want more concessions on access to the state forests for his mills, that's all. He will try and smooth talk me and then when that doesn't work he'll go over the top and get what he wants from his mates in Spring Street.'

'James, no need to raise your voice.'

His father shook his head. 'Ah, what a pickle we're in. It's bloody frustrating, that's all. I tell you, Mary, the country is gonna pay for having these conservatives entrenched. Mark my words, John Cain is in trouble with all these anti-communist Labor fellows running around.'

Saturday came. Sean's dad cleaned the Buick. Sean did his usual chores. His mum fired up the copper, washing the sheets and heavy work clothes.

'Sean, comb your hair and change your shirt before you go please,' his mother called.

Sean sat in the front of the Buick beside his dad. It was hard to see over the front bonnet. The clock on the glovebox said nine thirty. The timber dashboard was polished to brightness. The radio in the middle of the dash was tuned to the ABC. The speedo in front of the large steering wheel vibrated slightly as his father gave the big V-eight a little choke.

'Okay, Sean. Let's go see what this bloke Campbell is up to.'

Soon they were out the other side of Caladonia. They turned into Campbell Street. On the right side park and bush swept down to the river. To the left, house after house of grand proportions – Victorian, Federation and Edwardian styles – with sweeping gardens, established trees and picket fences.

'Welcome to Toffsville,' his father said. 'A lot of these places are holiday or town houses for the squats. This whole area, indeed, the whole town, was excised or given to the Caladonia Shire from the

Campbell's original holdings. I believe they still own a fair chunk of the town.'

The street ended at a large, closed gate. A huge crest of two snarling white lions with crossed swords adorned it. Behind the gate, to the right, was a squat cottage in the English tradition with red bricks and an overhanging verandah, up which ivy climbed. Sean's dad got out of the car and rang a large bell. He waited. The front door of the cottage opened and a man in green trousers and overcoat came out and spoke to him. Sean noted the same lions crest on his coat. He went back in and the gates swung open. The Buick crept up a curving white gravelled road bordered with small English shrubs. The place was like pictures of England Sean had seen in books: elms, fir, chestnut and spruce. The grass was vivid green, like carpet. There were fountains and statues. Away on the right Sean could see the river's grey sheen through the trees.

'Strewth,' Sean whispered.

'Sure is impressive,' admitted his father.

They passed workers in green trousers and coats digging a trench along the side of the road. Sprinklers played in the distance. The road swept around a sweeping bend and suddenly they were in view of a massive mansion.

It was a pile of sandstone with huge arches and a central tower featuring a flagpole. Large windows faced out across a manicured lawn where a fountain with lions and gargoyles sprayed water into a pond. Even though it was midwinter, masses of flowers adorned the paths. A gardener in the green uniform was tending a flowerbed. A sign proclaimed tradesman and travellers entrance left. Sean's dad turned the big Buick down the side drive, which was shielded from view by trees and a tall hawthorn hedge. Another sign proclaimed parking, and they pulled into a car park beside a workers cottage similar to the one at the gate. The sandstone building was completely hidden from view except for its upper turrets and central tower. Another sign indicated to them if the cottage was unattended to press the buzzer at the front for service.

'Well, I'll be buggered! I knew it was grand but never this grand. Sean, you wait here. Don't leave the car park. I shouldn't be more than half an hour.'

His father got out and walked to the front of the cottage and pressed the button. He waited. In a few moments a very tall man in a white shirt, green and blue tartan tie, black trousers, highly polished shoes and matching black vest sporting the crest came down a white stone path meandering between the trees. Sean's dad turned and extended his hand. The man ignored it.

He said in a clipped pommy accent, 'Mr Buttenberg, I will take you up to the side office. Mr Campbell will meet you there. He will be ten minutes.' He turned and walked briskly back up the path. Sean's dad looked over at Sean, smiled, shook his head and followed the man up the path.

Sean got out of the car. He had spotted a tree he had only seen once before. A cork tree. He walked up to it and felt it, running his hands gently over the soft spongy texture. He looked at the old gnarled limbs. He put his nose against the bark and smelled it.

'Eh, you there, what are you doing?' called a clipped nasally voice.

Startled, Sean stepped back too quickly, tripping over a root, and sprawled on the ground. In front of him was the man he had seen in the grandstand the day Koonarook had beaten Caladonia. Slightly behind him and holding his hand was a thin girl about his age with dazzling blond hair. She was dressed in a sailors outfit and was giggling.

Sean got up shaking off the twigs, dirt and grit. 'Apologies, sir, I was looking at the cork tree,' he stuttered.

'Who are you and why are you here?' the man demanded.

'Sir, I am Jim Buttenberg's son. Sean. He has come for an appointment at ten o'clock, and I came along for the ride. I was told to wait here, sir.'

'And the tree, do you know anything about it, or were you going to take some of that cork?'

'Oh, no, sir! I would never hurt the tree, it's beautiful.'

The girl sniggered.

'Young man, my great grandfather planted that tree. It has been known over the years for young fellows like you to take pieces out of it, and even carve initials into it,' he said accusingly.

'Oh, no, sir, I would never do that.'

'What do you know about trees anyway?'

Sean stood to his full height. 'Excuse me, sir, but this is *Quercus suber*, a Cork Oak. It is an evergreen medium-sized tree. They harvest it for cork, mainly in Spain and Portugal. It can live for up to two hundred and fifty years. This one is full size, sir.'

'Mmm, very impressive. How old are you, boy?'

'Eleven sir'

'Well, I hope your father has as much knowledge about trees as you.' The man turned on his heels, pulling the girl around behind him. He looked back at Sean as he strode off. 'Do not touch anything else while you are here.'

'Yes, sir.'

The girl looked behind her as she followed the man up the path. She giggled again. Sean sat in the car.

'I'm in for it now,' he mumbled.

Sean waited for what seemed an eternity. He saw no one else. A cold south wind stirred the trees and a group of regent honeyeaters flashed in and out among the low foliage, cleaning up the insects. Finally his dad came back.

'That wasn't so bad' he muttered. 'Just as I thought, the bastard wants an increase in his quota, what I look after. He wanted my opinion. I told him I did not think it was viable, and then it went from there, maps, stands, terrain, rainfall, the whole lot. He knows his stuff. He'll get his way, too, the bastard. Oh, he said he met you down here hugging his cork tree. He thought you might be carving your initials in it, as he did at your age. His dad gave him a belting for it, he said. He said you know more about that tree then his head groundsman does.'

'I was just feeling the bark, and smelling it. He came up behind me and scared me to death. Remember that one in the Botanic gardens in Melbourne?'

'Oh, yeh? He's offered you a job here in the gardens on Saturday mornings.'

'He what!' Sean felt himself flush.

'He offered you a job,' his dad repeated, and slapped him on the knee. 'I don't know what you told him but he was impressed. He obviously wasn't expecting a snotty nosed kid like you to know things like that. Let's go and see how that pie mum was working on is going.'

If he wanted the job he was to report to Mr McCarthy, the head groundsman, at seven o'clock on Saturday. He would work to eleven and be paid at the junior gardener's rate.

'That's about two bob an hour,' his dad said.

'You think I should do it, dad?' Sean was looking out the window but not seeing anything.

'Well, Sean, it's your choice, but you will be working in one of the best gardens outside Melbourne'.

'What about my chores at home?'

'We'll talk to mum about your chores when we get home. Sam at the newsagency was asking me the other day about you doing a paper run. I told him I'd get back to him. This job would pay as much in four hours as a paper run would for five days starting at six every morning.'

Sean's dad took another piece of pie and chewed on it appreciatively. 'I betcha in spite of all his fancy cooks and what not over there, Campbell doesn't eat half as good as I do, and that's a fact Mary.'

'Jim, don't embarrass me. Are you going to give Mr Campbell the extra timber?'

'Not my decision, Mary. I only pass the recommendation up the line. But I know for a fact we can't take any more timber from these forests. I will most probably recommend against it. I told him that.'

'Oh, Jim, you didn't!'

'I did.'

'But Mr Campbell has so many connections and friends, he can make it very hard for you.' His father looked exasperated,

'Maybe so, Mary, but facts are facts. I'm not gonna bend them for any man. Besides, men like him are surrounded by so much bullsh-hhh.' He pulled the word and grinned at his wife. 'By so many yes men. They like to hear the truth occasionally.'

'Oh, Jim, I hope your right. I really do,' she sighed.

'Can't be too bad. Campbell offered Sean a job. He caught him loving his cork tree to death,' his father laughed, Katy started giggling. Sean went red.

Sean's father told her about the morning events. His mother was very enthusiastic and readily agreed to a rescheduling of chores.

'The girls at the CWL will be so interested to hear about your job, Sean. What a clever boy you are.'

Next day, after mass, was painful as Sean's mother told everyone who would listen about his job at Caladonia Park. During Sunday roast she was in good spirits.

'You know, he's retiring soon,' his father said. He had been reflecting on the life of Winston Churchill. 'One of the greatest minds and politicians of the century, even if he was a conservative. He's not well.'

'He's the man who led the poms during the war?' Sean asked.

'Yes, and the Gallipoli fiasco in the first show and the Greece-Crete disaster in the last one. A real goer and thinker, unlike that conservative nong we have as Prime Minister.'

Sean mother's eyebrows arched. His father ignored the look.

'"Courage is what it takes to stand up and speak, courage is also what it takes to sit down and listen",' he quoted. 'Yep, led those poms through the war and in gratitude got kicked out of office at the end of it. It's hard to read the voters' mind sometimes.'

Beewee

Sean made his way down to Joseph's camp. The old man listened with interest to Sean's story.

'That Campbell mob, when they first bin come into Bindaree country, they bring big mobs of sheep with them. My Ulwai, that my grandfather fella, he say they bin friendly to this Campbell and his family and workers. But then they start chasing off the Bindaree from our places. Them shepherd boys and men they bin steal our women, they foul up the waterholes and billabong, then they cut down our Bora Bora trees. When some young Bindaree Wundara go to talk with them they get shot. Big mob of white fella chase them with horses and gun, they kill them big. Bindaree hold talk, old fellas they talk a lot. Then they say no more of this Amerjig, we kill them all. They go round kill the sheep, kill them shepherd fellows, kill the horse, burn them yards too. Then they surround that place where that big house now stand, and let no one out or in. They stuck in there, all them white fella. We fight them long time, lot of them get sick and die. We kill everything they own. Then them trooper fella and black police fella they come up and we run away and hide. They search for us long time. We fight them, kill some, but they kill lot of Bindaree. After some time government fella come to Bindaree and say enough fighting, we tired we no longer want to fight also. We make agreement. They give us this sacred place here and reserves of land around here and they pay us with food and blankets. That when they give my grandfather that neck shield to wear. They call him King Joseph. That Campbell fella, he gets fat on our place, we get skinny. Then the lumpy sickness come and take big mobs of the Bindaree away. Now only few Bindaree, Tamba Tamba people round here. The sacred places no longer hear our voices. All this place change, lot of the brother, sister animals they bin gone like the Bindaree. Our dreamin places disappearing, young fella he no longer know the law. Nooralie maybe he bin think time for the Bindaree to go from this place. Maybe Tamba Tamba goes from this country, all this Billa Billa place here he bin die.'

The old man sighed and bowed his head. He relit his pipe and looked at the fire, staring deep into the coals. Sean poked at the fire with a stick.

After a while the old man said, 'Maiyarare, it bin good that I know you and that you been picked out by Nooralie and marked by Dingarra. You bin learnin good about Bindaree country and show good manners and respect for this place. You be a smart fella, you learn easy. It maybe bin good for you to learn some from that Campbell fella. If it be true that Nooralie let Bindaree disappear from this place maybe you bin take care of it for him.'

'Me?' Sean whispered. What did Joseph think he could do? Did he know about Mr Campbell's plans?

'We all have to be little before we can be big,' the old man laughed and slapped him gently on the back. 'Let us make some of that damper and tea. Enough talkin. Maybe after we go and look for them goanna fella egg.'

After the damper they walked towards Gunpowder Island. The old man carried a gunny sack, a small shovel and a long piece of fencing wire. He loped along. Sean walked easily beside him.

'This Beewee fella he special for Bindaree old time. He a male totem big time. Lot of them fella they not bin able to eat him or them eggs, but me, my family, he never bin in my family totem. In the dreamin he bin speak for the other fella animals to Nooralie and when the man split away from the animals. He have no fear this fella, he bin bite you he cause some serious injury. When I boy like you there be a lot more of these Beewee fella around and they grow lot bigger. When stand up, they tall as a man, now not so many around here, maybe they get no chance to grow.'

'They lay eggs, right?'

'Yep, they bin lay in burrow or hole filled with leaves and vegetation to keep warm. In the Marangani, that mean autumn, they lay eggs, and then hatch out in spring if lucky no fella like us get them.' He laughed and relit his pipe. 'They smart them fella Beewee, they like no other lizard or snake around here. When we see them lay their egg it bin time to get ready for the Kilpanie, winter time. If lay a lot it mean hard winter. Not many it gonna bin mild. If there bin many boy hatching more than girls it mean not good spring.'

'Bloody hell, Joseph. How do you know all that stuff?'

'Them Beewee fella, they our cousin. If you live sharing the same place you know them and what they do, they know what we do. In old time all this law and story about the animal pass on from old fella or women Bindaree to young ones. All time tellin story and remembering story, every day we bin talkin about this place and the story and animals of it. After a while it sticks to you, like damper on your fingers.'

They walked over the bridge and onto the island. The damp winter soil muffled their steps, the trees bowed to a brisk cold southerly and the weak sun threw pale shadows off the trees. They branched off the track where a small creek cut across it.

'This Beewee, she smart girl, she make plenty of burrows but she leave some not covered, others she cover up before she go, these one she put her egg in. These Beewee like humans, both male and female they build the nest and for a little while protect it. Then they go away north for the winter time. When they come back it bin spring time. Bindaree then get ready for summer.'

They followed the creek down towards the river. The trees here were all red gums, big and twisted. Wide stumps left in the ground showed where the loggers had been. The old man turned off and climbed a knoll. These trees were mainly grey box, straight and tall, their bark tight and flaky. The old man leaned against one, caressing it with his hand.

'This fella grey box, he also tell us when the winter to come. When he flower they bin white it time to get ready for the cold weather.' Then he pointed to large burrows in the ground, two large ones and two smaller ones on the north facing side. 'This bin where Beewee camp. He use this as his site, he have several like this, see mound at the start here of the tunnel this where she come out.' He crouched beside the top entrance, running his hands over the smooth packed down earth. 'She sit here a while warming up, this Beewee fella he never do anything much before thinking long time about it, that why it be good if men be a bit like them. In dreamin that why them animals they pick this Beewee for talkin to Nooralie and them other spirit fellas. This one here she a big girl, maybe six feet, big as me. But when these Beewee make up their mind about something they go straight for it, run over all things to get their job done. He never stop till he be finished, he never make big noise or maken any fuss, he just do the job. She clever this girl, under here she have a tunnel that stop just near the surface. If she bin trapped she quickly dig out and get away.' Joseph walked over the site, every now and then stomping his foot. 'Look over here youngem. This one of her blind tunnel places. Bend down. Hear the differences in the sound.' The old man kept stomping his boots on the grey earth. 'Hear the differences in the sound, hollow, solid.'

'Yeh, she cunning, this Beewee, like you say, Ulwai.'

The old man looked at him. 'Thank you, Maiyarare, for that kind word. I hopen I can be good for it.'

Sean put his ear to the ground.

'She not here now, she come back this place in warmer dryer time. But when she does we know how to trap her and then eat her. Good tucker, this mam, the grease good for all sort of bite and sting. We make soup out of the bone, good for achy belly. Them old fella say if use grease in hair never lose it. It work for me.' He swept his hat off and ran his fingers through his hair and laughed. 'We get some for you this spring time, maybe I think your father he bin start lose his hair. Yeh, I have some in my oorla, I bin put some in a tin for your father when we get there. If we be as useful as this Beewee fella we bin done good'. The old man bent to the ground. 'Let's find this girl's eggs.'

They went down a slight slope, picking their way over fallen trees and the short grass of midwinter. The old man crouched low to the ground, stopping and looking, prodding the ground with his piece of wire. He felt the trunks as they passed. Finally about two hundred yards from the first burrows, he stopped at a small clearing.

'Ah, we bin find here this nest for Beewee.'

Sean looked. There was nothing out of the usual.

'Lookem, young fella. This place, see the tree here.' The old man pointed to some faint scratch marks on the trunk. 'Here that fella she bin climb here and watch, makem sure no stealer come to take her egg while her marks be fresh on the ground. After while she go away, never see young fella hatch. That where they bit different from us man fella, but maybe sometime I think it be good idea for us to copy Beewee in this also.' They smiled together.

They went over to the clearing and squatted down. The old man muttered, 'See here small indent in the ground under all this dead grass and stuff they drag in to cover nest. Here entrance they fill in with dirt. Maybe it be six or twelve feet long, it be full of grass.' Joseph prodded along the ground with the fencing wire, the first bit was hard to get in but then it became easy as the wire went through the cavity beneath. He prodded along every foot or so, six or seven times, following the burrow beneath. Then he said, 'See no more burrow we at the end, we go back to middle of tunnel dig down and then we finden them egg.'

They retraced their steps until they were about half way along the tunnel. Joseph gave him the shovel. 'Now, youngem, you dig carefully here down 'bout two feet and hit the burrow. Be careful. After that we find leaves and grass then them eggs.'

Sean slowly cleared away the covering debris and dug down slowly. The old man stood back and relit his pipe. Sean was soon down and into the burrow. The chamber was about three times as wide as the burrow itself and full of compacted grass, leaves and debris, just as the old man had said.

'Alright, young fella. We go careful now.' He bent down and slowly scooped out the debris. Soon he came across about thirty eggs lying in a bed of grass and leaves.

'Wow,' said Sean. 'They're beautiful.' The eggs were light green and about the size of turkey eggs.

'Now, youngem, we bin careful and remove about half, other half we leave for Beewee, so he not end.' As he said this the old man closed his eyes and muttered, 'an ungune Beewee yantel our ou an ungune Nooralie an ungune,' and he spread his hands and palms outwards.

Sean knelt with him and closed his eyes also, and said a prayer thanking god for this bounty. He felt he was lifted up and light as air for a fleeting second. Then he opened his eyes. The old man was looking at him and smiling.

Sean whispered, 'You said a prayer, grandfather.'

'Yes, say thank you to Beewee and Nooralie.'

'Me too.'

'Yeh, it bin good to say thank you always for great spirit gift to us.'

Joseph reached down and gathered the eggs, one by one. He wrapped them in cloth from the gunny bag. When they had removed about half of them, they returned all the debris carefully and Sean replaced the earth.

'We have feast tonight. The old ones say he who eat Beewee egg have strong way with women. Me too old to find out, you too young to know,' he laughed.

At the camp the old man put half a dozen of the eggs wrapped in newspaper into a biscuit tin. 'You takem home for your father, makem him strong for his job as man.' Going into the hut, he soon came out with an old vegemite jar. He showed Sean the cloudy grease inside. 'This here good for your father hair, maybe it still fall out but he feel better about it, if it does.' Then he gave Sean a little bundle of kangaroo hide, fastened with a rawhide strap. 'This here for your mother, and little sister girl, a gift from this old man. You bin said your mother bin strong on this Catholic religion same as Sister Louise.'

'Yes.'

'It bin for her to think about for that God Jesus fella.' He pressed the gift into Sean's hands.

'But, Ulwai, this is too much.'

'Worlba, worlba, you takem, it just a little thing. You bring me gift of young spirit self all time, these little thing is nothing to that.' The old man sat in front of his fire. Sean looked at him, he looked at the trees all around. Blue wrens were out for the evening pickings and the Tamba Tamba were circling to land.

'Thank you, grandfather, for today and the gifts.' Then he hugged him.

Joseph smiled and returned the hug gently. 'You head off now. I will seeya soon. Yant el ou ou, peace to you, Sean.'

Sean was home just before tea time. His father was out in the shed sharpening lawn mower blades.

'How was that Joseph bloke today?'

'Great, dad. We went on a goanna egg hunt over at Gunpowder Creek.' He pulled an egg out of the jam tin and unwrapped it.

'Beautiful,' his father said, dropping the file and taking one of the eggs. 'Did you have to dig it up?' He turned the egg over and over in his hands.

Sean told him about the search for the eggs.

'Well,' his dad finally said, 'that bugger knows his stuff. We probably walk over these nests all day long not even knowing they are there.'

Sean handed his father the vegemite jar. His father held it up to see it in the light of the kerosene lamp. 'You say this stuff helps your hair, and cures everything from scratches to ingrown toe nails? Well, between this and the eggs I should be the bloody most sought after man in Koonarook. It won't be safe for me to walk down the street,' he said. 'Probably best not to tell your mum these are goanna eggs. You know what she's like about such things.'

His mother and Katy were in the kitchen finishing off the icing on half a dozen sponges. His mother looked up as they came in.

'Ah, good, I was just about to call you in. Tea's ready. I'll just finish here. The CWL is having a cake stall tomorrow.'

'Sean brought home some eggs for you, Mary. From Joseph.' He put the egg tin on the bench beside the cakes and opened its lid.

'Wonderful, I've just about used up all the eggs on these sponges.'

Then she looked at the open tin and the green egg, out of its wrapping, on top. She picked it up. 'It's huge. And green. What sort of egg is this?'

His dad took it from her. 'Geese egg, Mary. Very good for cakes and omelettes. I'll have a couple in the morning.' He winked at Sean.

'Strange geese eggs,' his mother frowned. 'Anyway, they'll be handy.'

Sean picked up the hide bundle. His mum was taking off her apron. 'Mum,' he said, 'Joseph has sent you a gift.'

She stepped back. 'Oh, Sean, what is it? In that dead animal thing!' She backed further away, her face contorted.

His father looked around from where he was cleaning the dishes at the sink. 'Ah, Mary!' He grabbed the gift, 'It's just wrapped in some kangaroo hide. Do you want me to unwrap it for you?'

His mother kept backing away. Katy stopped sloshing her hands in the sink water and came to look. His father undid the hide thong and, laying the bundle on the table, he slowly unwrapped it. It revealed two little red gum statuettes of a mother holding a baby. His mother came back to the table. They crowded round to look at the little figures.

'Beautiful Madonnas and child,' his mother gasped. 'Joseph did these?'

'He's always carving and whittling things down at his camp. There's one for you and one for Katy.'

She picked up one of the little polished figures and looked at it carefully. 'Oh, Sean, these must have taken hours and hours. How can I ever repay him?'

'Joseph said they're a gift for you and Katy. You don't have to pay him. Dad got a jar of goanna oil.'

His mother looked at her husband, who did not return her gaze. She looked at the eggs on the bench, and smiled.

The Garden

Campbell's foreman Mr McCarthy was a medium-sized, bald-headed man with strong hands, big shoulders and a permanent stoop. His hat was battered but firm upon his head. When he took it off, his forehead showed a permanent border between the white above and the brown below. Tufts of hair on the side of his head were the only sign that he had once had had any hair. He wore a khaki shirt with a green tartan tie. His brown moleskins were held up by braces. On his feet were shiny brown Blundstones. Sean stood before him in the gardeners shed, which was an office, store, tool shed and tractor shed combined. It had once been a huge stable, and above it was a hay loft. Parked in a neat row facing the swing doors were two grey Massey Ferguson tractors and three Morris tray trucks. There was room for three or four other vehicles. Various mowers, trimmers and equipment were arranged along the far wall. Around the walls were pegs for tools. There were benches with lathes, grinders and anvils, all neat and orderly. Sean saw a worker in the green outfit filing a pick handle on a workbench. Mr McCarthy's office was portioned of from this complex by a wall which reached only part way to the high ceiling. His desk faced a large window, which afforded a good view. On the far wall hung a colour-coordinated map of the Caladonian estate. On his arrival at the shed, Sean had parked his bike outside in a bike rack, with four other bikes. Mr McCarthy had been talking to the worker at the bench. When he had seen Sean, he had gestured for him to follow him into the office.

Mr McCarthy's hat now resided on a peg behind the desk. His face was reflected in the office desk.

'Well, lad, your name would be Sean Buttenberg.' He had a smile on his face.

'Yes, sir.'

Mr McCarthy got up and shook his hand. 'Pleased to meet you.' He sat down. 'Mr Campbell has told me to employ and instruct you on Saturday mornings. You will work with Jack this morning.' He pointed to the man outside at the far bench. 'You will follow his instructions and do whatever he requires of you.' He looked down and opened a folder. 'Now, before you do that, you will be required to fill out and sign this form, take it home for your father to sign, and return it to us next week. Is that clear? Good. Now, are you able to read and write?'

'Yes, sir, I can.'

Mr McCarthy returned Sean's amused look. 'Sorry, lad, I have to ask that. Some of my fellas can't and I like to know beforehand, before it becomes an issue. Now, some instructions and rules. You will follow all instructions and orders given by me or Mr Johnson, my deputy. You will not do any wilful damage or show disrespect to any equipment.' Mr McCarthy was reciting well-known lines and Sean relaxed and let them flow over him. 'You will not remove any material, plant or equipment from this site. You will not speak to any of the household or any guests of the house unless approached by or specifically asked a question by them or asked for assistance by same.' The man looked up, pausing to study him. He made a note in the file. 'You will not divulge any information or knowledge of any household member or guest of this house gained while you are employed here to any person whatsoever. You will not enter into any of the private areas of the estate or garden unless you are instructed to by your superior. These areas include but are not confined to the following: the front promenade and garden directly in front of Culloden House, the back yard garden area designated by the picket fence at the rear of the house, and past the hawthorn hedges which bound both sides of the house. You will not walk or loiter on, or meander down, any road in this estate except if you are going to or from work, or are working on the path or road. You will not enter this property at any time except at your designated times of employment. You will wear the designated dress of your calling, in your case green overalls or shirt and trouser with appropriate identification. I will have a set of overalls for you next week, Sean. If any of these conditions of employment are not met, you will be instantly dismissed. Do you understand this, Sean?' He looked up with a wry smile.

'Yes, sir, I understand.'

'Good. I am led to believe that you have some knowledge of flora and fauna?'

'A little bit, sir. My dad is a supervisor for the Victorian Forestry Commission.'

'Yes. I know of your father. By all accounts a man who knows his work. Good. Let us go and introduce you to Jack.' He paused to put a log into the pot belly that was trying to keep the cold out of the office.

Jack was a thin man, about thirty, with big hands, long arms and a constant smile on his narrow face, which was split in half by a massive nose.

After introductions, Mr McCarthy said, 'Sean will be working with you today. Take care of him.' The head gardener gave him a wink and was off back to his office.

Jack looked at Sean. 'They normally don't employ 'em so young.

You out of nappies yet, boy?' he laughed.

'I'm here on Saturday mornings, sir, and I'm in grade six.'

Jack scratched his head. 'Cut the "sir" bits. Save that for the crust. Call me Jack, or Beak,' he laughed. 'Do you know anything about diggin' holes?'

'I've dug some with my dad.'

'Good. We'll be digging some for Mr Campbell so we can plant some more bloody trees. Fifty thousand trees here and he wants another forty. Let's go. We'll take one of the Fergies with a digger. You take this pick and grab a long-handled shovel off the wall over there.' He pointed to a wall where twenty or so shovels of all sizes and shapes hung on pegs.

Beak drove the Fergie out of the shed and waited, post-hole digger attached. He stopped and swung his arm. 'Get up, young fella.'

Sean climbed up beside him and put the shovel and pick in cradles welded onto the side of the wheel shield.

'Let's go and dig us some holes.'

Jack pressed down on the hand throttle. They swung left out of the shed and past a huge hot house and a stable nearly as big as the shed they had just left. The white, stone road soon gave way to a well-graded dirt track, which swung around behind the big house. A white picket fence marked its enclosure. A slim girl in a long grey dress was tending to a clothesline near the fence. The clothesline was hidden from the house by a high conifer hedge with beautiful rounded edges and dense foliage. An archway through it revealed a white, stone path leading to the back of the house. Beak waved at the girl as he went past. She waved back, showing an attractive face of light tan and long black hair. Beak had a smirk on his face. He shouted above the noise of the tractor.

'I'd like to get into her pants.' Sean went red. The man laughed and laughed. 'Sorry, mate, I forgot how old you are. That Nelly Ferguson would turn the bloody Pope himself from celibacy or whatever they call it. I'd like to be riding that Ferguson rather than this one any day.' He laughed again and the tractor swerved from side to side. Sean hung on tightly.

The English birches, oaks, beech and elders gave way to an American garden which swept around to the left of the big house. American ash, redwoods, chestnuts and maples were dominant. Through the trees a large and elaborate wrought iron lace pavilion stood out. The track turned and ran parallel with the river, and the landscape changed to open grey box eucalypt forest, then, as they descended to the river, they came onto a large open area. A substantial boathouse was set about one hundred feet from the water, and there was a concrete launching ramp on the bank of the river and a floating pier which jutted out. A narrow gauge railway line ran from the boathouse to the ramp.

Beak stopped the tractor and looked around. 'That boathouse has been rebuilt three times because of floods. The railway line we don't use anymore. In the old days they used to winch the boats into and outa the water on that, but nowadays we just use a tractor.' He pointed around the area. 'We gonna be planting claret ash all around this perimeter. The boss wants medium-sized shade trees that won't fall and kill someone like them bloody red gums. We took all them out last winter. Your job is to guide me to the planting holes marked there with lime by the boss. Then after I dig them, make sure the hole is clean.'

'Right,' said Sean. He hopped off the tractor and grabbed the shovel. He thought of the possums, galahs, pythons, squirrel gliders and parrots that he had seen in the Gunpowder red gum forest. Where had the ones here gone?

The corkscrew digger cut into the grey, loamy river soil. Beak whistled as he worked, cocking his hat back to keep an eye on things.

They worked for about two hours, then Beak announced, 'Let's go, young fella. Smoko's on at the shed. We'll bring the trees back after.' Sean climbed aboard the tractor. Beak shouted, 'Good work, young fella'.

When they got back to the work shed, seven or eight workers were standing around smoking and eating scones and drinking tea that had been laid out on a work bench. Beak introduced Sean to the group.

'Dig in, Sean,' Beak said. 'Help yourself.'

Sean helped himself to a mug of hot scolding black tea and a buttered scone with jam from a tarnished silver tray. He noted that most of the men were called by their nicknames, Bluey, Shorty, Ugly, Jock and Tiny. Mr McCarthy spoke to each man in turn, and there was a lot of good-natured banter and ribbing. After about fifteen minutes an alarm sounded and the men went off in various directions. Tractors and trucks parked outside started up.

Beak said, 'Come on, Sean, we'll get the plants from the nursery. Help me hitch up the trailer.' Sean was about to follow Beak when Mr McCarthy came over.

'Howyougoing, Sean?'

'Good, sir. I enjoyed it. I'll enjoy planting the ash.'

'Ah, yes, down at the landing. What do you know about ash trees, Sean?'

'They like a well-drained soil, sir, but don't like to completely dry out.'

'Very good, boy. Some of your father's learning, eh?'

'Yes, sir. He planted some at the bush office just last year.'

'Good, good. On you go.'

Sean went outside to where Beak was hooking a trailer onto the back of the Fergie. They went up the same road, turning to the left past the greenhouse and on to the front of a small, squat shed behind which was a huge covered area filled by rows and rows of trees in pots.

'Let me do the talking and don't worry about Paddy. He's a bit strange. Been here forever. Bark's worse than his bite.'

They went over to the small shed and knocked on the door. Beak sang out, 'Paddy, are you in?'

Smoke hung lazily in the cool, damp air. A rabbit grazed on the other side of the fence, no more than a hundred feet away. The harsh cries of a raven echoed above the trees, and the answer of its mate returned across the stillness.

Beak called again. 'Paddy, are ya in?'

The door on the little hut swung open. 'Stop ya bloody bawling, ya big-nosed twerp. Can't ya let a man have a little time to get out the bloody door?'

The voice was Irish and the man who carried it was small, but his shoulders were broad and his hands big. He was dressed in dirty leather trousers and off-white flannel. On his head was a greasy tweed hat, and sticking out of his mouth was a pipe. His face was craggy and wrinkled like a well-ridden saddle, but was twisted into a look of scorn.

Beak shifted on his feet, his hands defiantly on his hips. 'We've come to pick up the ash trees for the landing.'

The little man looked at them both and took a big suck on his pipe. 'What, are they bloody employing babies now?' He stared directly at Sean, tilting his hat to get a better look at him.

Sean felt his face colour. Drawing himself up, he uttered, 'No, sir, Mr Paddy. I'm Sean. I'm eleven and in grade six and working here Saturday mornings.'

'Bloody hell, boy! I don't want your whole life's bloody history! Now, cliff face, ya can only have ten at a time. I'm not having some bloody twerp crushing and destroying them. They've been nurturing here since last winter. Did McCarthy tell ya how to plant 'em? Has he delivered the right planting mix to the bloody landing?'

Beak laughed and started walking to the tractor. 'Yeh, mixed under his supervision, delivered yesterd'y. We'll only have time to plant about ten anyway. Tell me which ones to get. Come on, Sean,' he waved. 'Let's go.'

The old man shrugged his shoulders. 'Bloody amateurs,' he shouted. 'You get on your bloody tractor, nose, me and the baby will load 'em. Come on, junior.'

Sean helped Paddy gently load each plant. The old man was strong and lifted them easily. He cursed Sean and Beak each time he lifted one in. When they were all loaded, he tied them in and closed the tail gate. Beak looked on.

'What are you looking at, you bastard?' the Irishman snarled. 'You bloody don't plant them right by the almighty Jesus, Mary and Joseph, I'll have your balls.'

Beak smiled. 'Don't worry, Paddy. I'll take care of your babies.'

'Piss off,' he bellowed and walked back into his hut.

Sean climbed up onto the tractor. 'Sorry I upset him,' he whispered.

'Upset? Na, he wasn't upset. That was one of his better moods. Wait to ya see him really upset. That's somethin' to see. He thinks those seedlings are his bloody kids or somethin'. He raises them from seeds and cuttings. They say he can make a piece of wire grow. Been here forever. Worked for Campbell's old man. No kids, no family, nothin' except those bloody plants and his veggie patch. Let's go and plant these babies and get outa here.'

Later that day Sean walked with his dad to the football. He told him about Paddy.

'The blokes say he goes down to Kelly's every Friday night and sits in the same spot in the corner,' his dad said. 'Never talks to anyone. Just sits and drinks until he slumps onto the table, dead drunk.

Anyone tries to sit next to him or say anything to him, he tells them to piss off. Campbell's duty driver comes and picks him up and takes him home. That's the only time he comes into town. They say down at the RSL that he's a veteran. Somme, Passchendale, a few others. He was gassed and has a metal plate in his head. War affects us all in different ways. I hope you never have to go through one.'

The Laying Low

The Smythe gang at school was gone and Smyth was left with only a couple of mates to hang around with. His bravado was gone and he slunk around. He was often in trouble in class. He slammed desk tops, sprayed ink out of the ink wells and pulled other stunts. Sister Rose banned him from writing with nibs and ink. Often he picked fights with other kids or pulled the girls' pigtails, but he never came near Sean. He would be sent to Sister Hildegard's office, coming back chastened and hands tucked into his pockets. The King Brown had kissed again. Sean twice saw Smythe's mother going into the Head Sister's office. Her steps were small and hurried, her shoulders hunched and bowed, her face creased and worried.

Sean and Johnny often went to each other's places after school. They would race to Johnny's place. Johnny won most times. He was strong. Mrs McCarthy would have milk and biscuits on the table for them when they came in. Johnny's brothers, twins aged four, would be waiting for him to come in and would hang off his every word. His baby sister would be in the cradle by the big black stove. They would play with her, and then recant a few hurried lines about the day to Johnny's mother before going outside to play marbles, go down to the river or do chores. The same was repeated when Johnny came to his place. Sean had a bit of an advantage here in the race home as he was used to crossing the bridge and would often get a good lead on Johnny. Katy and his mother would be waiting for them in the kitchen when they arrived. Katy would join them for milk and biscuits, and then they were off outside, making the most of the short winter evenings. Often they even went down to the swamp on Saturdays and Sundays after their work. Johnny did deliveries for Muller's grocery shop in Caladonia on Saturday mornings. Johnny told Sean that Mr Muller was a big, tall German who spoke with an accent. He limped and only had two fingers on his left hand.

Sean asked his dad one night about Mr Muller.

'Do you know him?'

His father paused from his reading and cupped his pipe in his hand. 'Yes, his grocery shop is across the road from my office. We often meet around smoko time.'

Kris Muller smoked roll-your-owns and did not like to smoke in the shop because he said it gave the fruit and vegies a bad taste.

'Yeh, he's a German,' his dad said. 'Bavarian. Likes his food and beer. All Bavarians do. Likes a laugh as well. He married a local, Flo O'Rourke. I think her old man bankrolled the shop. He was working in the mill as a mechanic when he came here. He drops into Kelly's on Friday nights. Has a few beers. I think they have a few young 'uns. Is that right, Mary?'

His mother looked up from her sewing. 'Yes, Jim. The Mullers have three children, all under five. The oldest one starts at St Joseph's next year. I believe Flo is expecting again. She's on our roster for home visits.'

'Must be making up for lost time, that German,' his father said with a laugh.

'James, please!'

'Was he in the war, dad?'

'Yeh.' His father looked up at the ceiling and puffed on his pipe.

'I believe he was on the Russian front. Doesn't say much about it, just a few things he has said about frost bite, and places he has been. You put two and two together and it's pretty clear. I think he might have had something to do with Panzers. That was where he learned his mechanics from. Good bloke, though. Makes great German sausage and Strasburg.'

When Sean and Johnny went to the swamp together, they never saw Joseph. They played and fished in the graveyard and around the B17. Sean told Johnny about Joseph, but only that he was a friend he went walking, hunting and fishing with. He showed him the stump of the burned out tree and the jagged scar across his chest. He showed Johnny where the Smythe gang had attacked him and where Smythe had ended up in the mud.

Sean saw Joseph every other day and at least once every weekend. For one of these visits, his mother packed a battered old biscuit tin with a sponge and jam biscuits.

'Give that to Mr Wirrinum and thank him for the carvings. Tell him they are in a special place. And tell him if he ever needs anything to let me know.'

The carvings were on the family altar, her grandmother's sideboard in the lounge room. The family gathered round it at his mother's bidding every Friday night and feast days to say the rosary and prayers. There seemed to be a lot of feast days. Usually the saint in question had died some terrible death at the hands of the pagans after leading a life too good to be true. His mother read their lives out of a book called *The Lives of the Saints*.

Joseph took the tin with thanks. 'We'll have some with tea, eh?'

The tea ritual was carried out with more flourish than usual. Joseph went into the hut and bought out a gunny sack from which he produced items Sean had never seen before. The leaves of tea were grabbed with extra zeal. The billy was placed with extra care on its stand over the coals, and it was hit three times instead of the usual twice to sink the leaves. A large blue enamel plate appeared upon which the cream sponge was placed. It was sliced with a large bone-handled knife. The condensed milk was poured, tea added, the sugar stirred by spoons this time, not twigs, and a slice of his mother's cake was placed carefully on the enamel plates. When all was ready the old man give the signal to eat. Joseph savoured every bite, chewing carefully before following with a mouthful of the sweet tea.

'Ah, your mother has bin makin a good cake. When I bin in that mission learning with that Sister Hildegard, she bring me cake from that sisters' convent place, it like this one here, with cream and jam. It sweet like me mudder used to make me. She make seed cakes with honey and we eat till we can eat no more. She make them in the spring time, crush the seed and mix in the honey from the honey man and then she bake them on the hot rock around the fire. Ah they bin good, like this. Maybe them mother have magic in the makin of things.' The words trailed off in a sigh.

'Who was the honey man?'

The old man licked his fingers and looked at Sean. 'That honey man, Kurmoonah Wherto. He holy man or Gooweera man. Only he allowed to take the honey from Mingga tree where the bee, what we call warra nunna, make their home. Anyone else takes the honey he bin cursed and no longer allowed to live with Bindaree, he die. The Kurmoonah Wherto he go to holy place and find the white mud which sticks to you and he put this all over his body. He make holy fire near the Mingga tree and say Marmingatha, that mean prayer to Nooralie and to the warra nunna. When the warra nunna hear the Kurmoonah Wherto and smell and feel the smoke he no longer angry fella but calm and sleepy. The Kurmoonah Wherto put that warra nunna to sleep and then he bin able to climb up that tree and take the honey. The warra nunna, they know Kurmoonah Wherto he no take all their honey or hurt them. They know he protect them from other fellas and he their Koolkuna man, he take care of them.' The old man paused and poured himself some more tea and cut another slice of cake.

'How do they know the Kurmoonah Wherto will protect them?' Sean held his plate out for another slice of cake.

'Ah that bin some story. I tell you now, as we eat your mother's cake. When man and animals they talk and understand each other, Nooralie plan big Mai Mai to celebrate the coming of the warm time or spring and he ask all the animals to come, and he asks his wives to makem big fire and prepare big feast. All animals they come and sit and dance around the fire. They all wearing the flowers of spring around their neck and bodies. But, the Marmoo evil ones they bin around in the outside dark not daring to come into the circle of light. They whisper into warra nunna ear when he go to his wirra-way to fetch his music sticks. They telling him that he big fella and important, he should sit next to Nooralie at the fire not away on the other side. Warra nunna he bin made proud by this whispering of the Marmoo, he bin say to himself, I important fella, I will sit next to Nooralie and tell him all the things I can do and how good I have bin. Warra nunna he come back, all them fellas and animals they bin sitting around having their feast and laughin and singin, they all in good mood. Warra nunna he burst into the circle and moves up near Nooralie, he start pushing away those fella, he bin saying I bin make my place beside Nooralie, I important fella for him. He start big fight all them fella they wrestle and fight falling into the fire and makin lots of smoke and noise. It be a mighty fight. Nooralie he gets really angry. Finally all them fella they pin warra nunna down on the ground and gonna kill him. But Nooralie he stops them. He comes over to warra nunna and looks at him with pity and anger at the same time. "You want to be biggest and best? I will make you the smallest. You bin ruin all my feast here this special time. From now on you will provide sweet nectar for me, man and the animals, and because you wounded many it will heal their wounds. You make big fight here, from now you will only fight once, and then die. You will no longer live with the animals but in the trees, you bin stop my music, you will no longer talk and sing but hum all days from now on making music for all other animals but no longer with them. You bin scatter my fire, you will fall asleep and dozy all time from now when you near smoke and fire. You bin scatter all those flowers we wearing on the ground all trampled and broke, you will spend all your waken days servin the flowers and trees making them pretty and carrying their seed. For this I will give you wings to fly but not strong enough to carry you above the trees, just enough for you to get to them. You will no longer be multi-coloured and beautiful as now but black because you are black from the fire, and you listened to the Marmoo in the blackness. You will be cursed with anger if man or animal come upon you or your home and you will attack them and die." And all was done to warra nunna as Nooralie said. But, they bin producing beautiful golden nectar like it come from the hand of Nooralie, as it does, and this is why holy man he only to take this honey provided by Nooralie for man and the animals. Out of the bad pride of warra nunna and the evil of the Marmoo come a sweet nectar and food for our feasts and a great ointment also for our wounds and cuts.' The old man put his plate aside and swallowed the last of his tea. ' So even though bad come, Nooralie he able to turn it round and make good out of it. Warra nunna he small and away from all other fella but he important as he wanted to be and have a good life even though he work very hard all the time.' The old man stoked the fire and pulled out his pipe.

'Joseph, is there a story for everything?'

The old man laughed and lit his pipe. 'All things belong to

Nooralie, all thing part of him, everything spring from him, all thing have story even rock and water. Even if we do not know the story, they still gonna have one, even when all Bindaree gone the story or dreamin still live on, but maybe it change then, maybe the place be different and change when Tamba Tamba and Bindaree gone, he put us here to take care of his Billa place here.'

The old man sucked his pipe and said, 'Maybe it bin time for you to go home to your mother. It bin getting dark this place now.'

'I like it here so much, Joseph. It's like home here.'

'That maybe so, but even Dingarra fella like you have to go home to their mother and do as she want.'

Sean got up. 'Thanks for the story Wai.'

The old man looked at him intently. 'You smart fella pickin up the lingo from this old blackfella bloke. Thank your Gunee for the cakes and bikkies.'

The next Saturday Sean worked with Beak again. This time they were to rake the path, which led down to the small jetty. Beak threw a couple of rakes and a light wheelbarrow into the tray of a trailer and they were about to head off when Mr McCarthy gestured for Sean to come over to his office.

'Sean, your overalls. I hope they fit.' He handed him a green set of overalls – bib and brace style like all the others wore – with the roaring lions on the front. The overalls fitted well with a bit of room to spare. 'Ah, good. Mrs Brown made them especially for you, laddie. Good job, too.'

'Thank you, sir.'

'Make sure they are clean and in good order.'

'Yes, sir.'

'If you need any repairs, give them to me for Mrs Brown.'

Sean put the overalls on and ran to the tractor where Beak was waiting. They turned right out of the shed along the white gravelled road. It glistened in the weak sunshine and heavy dew of the morning. The trees hung listlessly. Beak whistled happily as he drove in front of the mansion. Sean saw it up close for the first time. It dwarfed everything around it. The windows were massive. The steps leading up to the huge red-gum doors must have numbered sixty. The tower reared above them, its flagpole bare and defiant, probing the sky. There were three tiers of windows looking out from the turret, each with its own balcony and landing. The gargle from the tractor rebounded from the walls and washed back over them. The fountain was still, the pond it resided in dark and calm. The lawn was patchy white from the retreating dew and the flower heads were bowed. The crisp cold air rushed into the crevices and seams of Sean's clothing, and in the sky above the eagle glided on the currents. Beak stopped the tractor directly opposite the mansion and adjacent to the fine white stone path that ran down to the river.

'Here, let's rake this path for the fine gentlemen and ladies.'

Beak jumped off the tractor and retrieved the wheelbarrow and a rake. Sean joined him as he started to rake the white pebbles of the path, making it smooth and collecting any twigs and foreign matter, which they deposited into the wheelbarrow. They took half the path each and worked backwards, moving the wheelbarrow along as they progressed. Superb scrub wrens darted in and out of the shadows and alongside them as they stirred up the insects. White-browed scrub wrens also came flitting in and out. Sean had never seen so many birds. Red wattle birds tended to the wattle trees growing just off the path. Yellow robins and little honeyeaters darted in and out. Faraway above the trees a raven gave a murderous cry, and Sean remembered the story of the rainbow snake. They worked steadily, moving their way towards the river.

Sean wheeled the barrow to the trailer. As he unloaded it, he watched the fountain, its lions and gargoyles now spraying water. Beyond, the mansion had come alive with lights. The curtains had been pulled back. On several of the balconies people were smoking and enjoying breakfast. Laughter and murmurs drifted over. The big doors opened and Mr Campbell and the little blond girl he had seen before came out. He heard her high-pitched giggle and the man's deeper voice. They looked over to where Sean was emptying the barrow, and started to walk towards him. He quickly scurried back to Beak and bent to his work. He heard the giggle and looked up. In front of him on the track was the girl and Mr Campbell. The man was surrounded by a cloud of cigar smoke, his spare frame covered by a three-quarter length dark green coat. The red and green tartan tie he wore stood out against a white shirt. The girl's hair was a sea of Shirley Temple curls that splashed down onto her shoulders and framed her pretty face. She wore a red, flared coat with black buttons down to her knees. Long thick socks and black, shiny, baby doll shoes covered her feet. Beak stood aside and doffed his hat. Sean did likewise and stood aside to let them pass.

'Good morning, sir. Good morning, miss,' he heard Beak say.

'Good morning,' Mr Campbell replied. He stopped and looked Sean up and down. It seemed like an eternity. Finally, he said, 'Good you could make it back here, Mr Buttenberg.'

Sean was struck again by the man's nasal twang. 'Yes, sir.'

'I hope you are learning something.'

'Yes, sir. I planted claret ash last week, and later we are to prune the roses.'

'Ah, yes, the landing. It is time for the roses.' He looked at Beak, who nodded. 'Good, Mr McCarthy will keep me informed of your progress. Come along, Meg, we will not hold these gentlemen up any longer.' They walked off at a brisk pace, a trail of blue grey smoke hanging in the morning air behind them.

'Well, that's a hang up,' said Beak as they bent over their rakes. 'Bloody Campbell doesn't stop and talk to anyone. First time he has ever acknowledged my presence, ever, and I've been here ten years. You must have impressed him?'

Sean stopped raking. 'Beak, I've only met the bloke once.' He bent once again into his task.

'Anyone would think you're rooting his daughter, but you're too young for that. Later, eh,' he laughed.

Sean looked down the path. Mr Campbell and his daughter were little figures on the jetty.

By the time they had finished the path it was time for smoko. The house was now bathed in the glow of the winter sun, and there was a bustle about the place, people coming and going, limousines pulling up. Women in mid-length coats and hats exited from them. The same stuffed shirt, who had met them on the Saturday morning a couple of weeks back, was greeting the people and directing them into the house. Other uniformed men parked the cars around the back of the house, sweeping past them slowly. Beak waved to a midnight blue Chevrolet.

'Bloody lucky bastards. Cushy job that, parkin' cars for the toffs.'

'What's on?'

'Oh, one of those high falutin' bloody morning teas Campbell's missus puts on every now and then. All the squats' and nobs' missus come and have a cuppa with the lady for a couple of hours and then they all take off again. Invitation only, of course.'

Sean looked over at a couple of ladies who were walking up the big stone staircase. They were beautiful. One wore a three-quarter length swagger coat with a fur collar. A dark hat sat rakishly on her head, the hair under it bobbed. She was in close conversation with her companion who held her coat over her arm and wore a close-fitting suit that showed a beautiful outline. She wore a little capo type hat atop beautiful bobbed blond hair. Both women wore dark high-heeled shoes, their legs slim and long. They walked slowly up the stairs. Their lilting voices and laughter carried over to Sean. He thought they were the most beautiful ladies he had ever seen.

Beak elbowed him in the ribs, startling him and making him catch his breath. 'Bit of a ladies' man, are we?' He jolted him again and laughed. 'Keep your eyes off 'em, boy. Those types are way outa your league.' He started up the tractor and eased out slowly onto the track. 'Only bloody arrowroot bikkies today. Bloody cooks will be too busy for scones.'

Sean rubbed his bruised ribs. Beak was right. There were arrowroot biscuits for morning tea, but the same scenario was followed as last week. The men stood around and gabbed and drank their tea. Sean followed the unwritten rule and spoke only when spoken to. He answered questions, if asked, and asked questions in reply but otherwise listened to their banter. They were full of stories about fishing, shooting, farming and football. There wasn't much talk on gardening. Mr McCarthy did the rounds. He asked what was happening and how the work was going. He stood beside Sean.

'How are you going, young fella? Jack tells me Mr Campbell said g'day on the path this morning.'

'Yes, sir.'

'Well, well,' the chief gardener said and scratched his chin. 'Take care and keep on going as you are now and we won't have any problems, eh, lad.'

Beak was full of talk as they swept behind the big mansion and around its western side to the rose garden. Beak explained that after ten in the morning or if something was on, no workers or tradesmen were allowed at the front of the house. They were soon at the rose garden. Its two acres were surrounded by a jewel-green cypress hedge and situated on a gently sloping piece of ground. Meandering black tracks wound through it. Where they intersected, brick-paved areas provided wrought iron garden seats. In the middle of all was a wrought iron pavilion with the lions crest as part of the iron work.

Beak showed Sean how he pruned the roses. 'You have to make them like wine glasses. Cut off all the dead and scraggly bits, give them air, give them space. The new roses will only appear on the new wood. The secateurs have to be sharp, can't crush the stems. A rose is like a sheila, Sean. She has to be dressed right to show off her best. If you treat her wrong they don't look too good. If you handle them wrong they bite ya with their thorns. But like a good sheila, a rose is tough underneath. It's hard to kill a rose, Sean, but if they run wild, they go scraggy. You look after them good, Sean, and they're the most beautiful thing in the world, just like a sheila.' Beak gazed affectionately at his work.

They worked on until eleven, by which time the trailer was full.

'Time to go, young fella', the gardener said. 'Loosin' good fishin' time.'

They drove on down behind the big house again. The place was quiet. Lazy grey smoke curled out of a couple of chimneys. When they got back to the shed, Mr McCarthy gave Sean an orange envelope.

'Pay, Sean.'

'Thank you, sir.' He held the envelope reverentially. He had never had a pay envelope before.

As Sean rode home, the envelope in his trouser pocket, he stopped his bike where the road intersected the circular drive. He looked along the front of the mansion. The ladies were coming out a procession of cars lined up. The ladies were ushered into their cars by the attendant houseman like chickens into their coup. Then the cars, one by one, swept around the drive. It was all so smooth and orderly, like a dance. Sean headed off. The big cars passed him, their wheels crunching on the gravel road.

At home Sean handed the orange pay envelope to his mum. She opened it with a flick of her nails.

'One pound eight! That's two shillings an hour. They must be very happy with you, Sean.'

'Mr Campbell said g'day as me and Beak were sweeping the path.'

'Really? Well, go and clean up for lunch and tell me about it over dinner. Dad is down at the RSL.'

His mother was particularly interested in the women at the morning tea. Did he recognise any? What were they wearing? What time did it start? Did he see Mrs Campbell? Sean answered as best he could.

'I'll talk to your father about your pay, Sean, but you'll get some to spend, some for the house and some for the bank. Now, clean up your room, and Dad asked if you could weed the cabbage bed before you go out.'

'Then can I go down and see Joseph?'

'Yes, but I want you back early this afternoon. We're going to the ball.'

'Arhh, mum, do we have to?'

'Sean! I'm on the committee and Father Riley will be there, as will the Bishop. We're going, that's the end of it.'

Sean went through his room like a tornado, dodging Katy's efforts to sabotage his work as she jumped on his bed and dragged her dolls in. She babbled away, asking him about his work and where he had been. Sean tackled her a few times on the bed and tickled her, and told her about the big house and the roses.

'Did you hurt the roses, Sean?'

'No, we use sharp cutters and they don't hurt.'

'Do they bleed?'

'No, they don't bleed.'

'Do they die?'

'No, they grow better.'

'Do they look sad when you cut them?'

'No, they look like a beautiful wine glass or lady.'

'Oh.' She ran off. He heard his mother telling Katy she had to have a sleep now, which was followed by howls of protest and then silence. After he was finished with the cabbages, he rushed to his mum.

'All finished. Can I go?'

'Make sure you are back at five so we can get ready for the ball, hear.'

He raced down to the swamp and burst through the small saplings and wattles to Joseph's clearing. The small hut was wrong. Sean stopped. He remembered his father's advice, 'Never rush in on the unknown, leave it alone until you know.' The kerosene can chimney was leaning. The slat wooden door was torn off and lying crookedly against the outside wall. The fire grate, ashes and utensils were spread over a wide area. One of the pokers had been speared into the wall of the hut. Pieces of clothing were scattered all over the clearing. There was a quietness which assaulted his ears, and a haze which clouded his eyes. Sean watched and waited for what seemed like an eternity. He approached the hut in a slow crouch. He felt bile in his throat and a pain in his stomach. He was sweating. He looked around. Where was Joseph?

Josephs' billy was crushed and broken, a piece of hessian caught in its handle. Enamelled cups and mugs lay scattered and broken. One of Joseph's chequered shirts was ripped and torn in front of the doorway. He stepped around it. His breathing was the only thing he could hear. His heart thumped. He realised he had never seen inside Joseph's hut. He peered through the doorway.

The walls were covered in hessian lining, which had been torn and ripped. An iron bed was broken and on its side, its springs hanging off and dangling. A red-gum bench was smashed and splintered bits of it were stuck in the fireplace, through which light pierced the gloom. Its grill and grate had been pulled out and flung on the floor. Pictures and papers were scatted everywhere. Flour, sugar canisters and cans of tucker spewed their contents into the chaos. But where was Joseph?

Sean backed out of the hut. Everything was still. No bird cried or whistled, no branch creaked, no wind rustled the undergrowth. He walked around the hut. The garden bed was broken up, its fence prone and smashed on the ground. The back of the hut was in shadow. Joseph's tools, fishing drums and nets, nestled under a lean-to against the main structure, seemed to be untouched and orderly. Sean stopped as his eyes adjusted to the gloom. A movement caught his eyes.

A boot stuck out from the midst of the pile of gear. It moved from side to side. Sean recognised the Blundstones, big size twelves. Sean remembered Joseph's laughter.

'I have a good grip on Australia, I bin have these boots for long, long time. I polish with grease from the Beewee they makem last longem time. But maybe I no longer run as fast as them Beewee fella.'

Sean went over to the boot. He saw the other foot now as he got closer, bare, with blood caked between the toes. Joseph never wore socks. The sole was bruised, cut and bleeding.

'Joseph, Joseph,' he whimpered. 'What have they have done to you?'

The tears welled in his eyes and spilled over and down his cheek and into the dirt. The legs disappeared into the blackness of the overhanging pile of tools, fishing nets and ropes. Sean pulled on the booted leg. The old man began moaning. Sean pulled but he couldn't move him.

Sean ran around to the front of the hut. Inside the gloom he found a torn blanket and a packet of Red Heads. He ran back to the lean-to. Lighting a match, he crawled into the hollow, following the legs up to the body of the man. In the light of the match he saw the broken face of his friend. The blood mingled with grime and vomit. The smell made him retch and the match went out and it was dark. He lit another and leaned over the Joseph's face. He felt the rasp of laboured breathing and the struggling rise and fall of the man chest. Joseph groaned again. Sean felt for his hand and held it. The tears came again and stung his eyes and made salt in his mouth.

'I'll come back for you, Joseph,' he whispered into the man's ear. 'You hold on.' Sean spread the blanket over the broken body and backed his way out of the dark cave. Muttering 'Hold on, Joseph. I'll come for back for you. I'll get dad!' He raced off up the path to Koonarook. He ran like he had never run before.

Illa Booker Mer Ley Urrie Urrie

Sean ran through the bush and into the sawmill, squeezing through a hole in the fence, running past the stacked logs, idle trucks and machinery, out the open gate and onto the river end of Manning Street, the railway turnstile a silent blur as he rushed past. Sean veered right to the RSL. The front door was open. The flags hanging limp along the walls made an archway of red, white and blue. Sean heard voices through the back door. He raced past the kitchen and burst into the back yard. His father and a group of men were gathered round a barbecue. The smell of meat and smoky wood were thick in the air. Sean raced up to his father.

'Dad, dad! Joseph's hurt and dying. We need to help!'

The men turned around as one. Their faces showed good will and cheer.

'Dad, dad!'

'Settle, Sean, settle.' His father said in a quiet deliberate tone, stepping towards him. 'Tell us what happened and where you have been.'

'I was down the swamp at Joseph's hut. The whole place is wrecked. Joseph's been beaten up. He's lying under the lean-to out the back. I couldn't move him. He's gonna die!'

'No one is going to die, Sean. He's a tough old bastard,' his father replied firmly.

His father spun on his heels and faced the men. The good cheer had vanished. 'Harry, go get Bill at the garage. Tell him we need the ambo. Make sure he's not pissed and can drive it. If he is, you drive it. Rexy, go to O'Shanassy's and phone the hospital. Tell them we have a bash victim coming in and tell them we want the doc there. Then give Shorty Malone a call and tell him what has happened. Bring your FJ down to swamp track. We'll need a ride to the hospital.'

'Righto!' The man was away.

His father continued with authority. 'Curly, grab the med kit in the kitchen and follow us. Let's go. Everyone knows where Joseph Wirrinum's place is? Let's go. Sean, lead the way.'

Sean led the group of six men out the way he had come. They walked with purpose but did not rush.

'You see anyone around Joseph's place, Sean?'

'No, it was all quiet when I got there. Just wrecked.'

'Okay,' his father replied. The look on his face was like thunder.

They were soon at the start of the track leading to Joseph's hut. Jim Buttenberg turned to a big red-headed man. 'Bluey, you wait here for Harry and Bill. Tell them to bring the stretcher when they come.'

'Right,' the big man muttered. Bluey pulled out a cigarette.

The track gently sloped down towards the hut through the dense undergrowth. Sean raced to the dark space where Joseph lay. He was still breathing. Sean's dad crawled in and had a look, striking a match.

Sean's father retreated out of the lean-to and gave his instructions. 'Alright, let's get him out, fellas. We just have room for one of us either side. Harry, you support his legs while Fred and I crawl in and ease him out. Joe and Blighty, make sure no one else is around, will ya, then come back here.'

Two of the men headed to the front of the hut. Fred and his father crawled in and gently eased the old man out. Sean helped

Harry support Joseph's legs. Curly arrived with the first-aid kit as they got Joseph clear. His father stood up stiffly.

'Curly, give me that kit.' He began cleaning away the debris and vomit from the old man's mouth. He checked Joseph's pulse and breathing. One of the men put another blanket around him. He turned his head and moaned.

'Broken collarbone left side,' said his dad, as he strapped the old man's arm to his body with two joined triangular bandages. 'If he vomits, fellas, we'll turn him on his stomach. Don't want him choking.' The men nodded. One of them put a bit of folded-up hessian under his head. 'Broken left leg. Here, Curly, give me that piece of board over there. We'll make a splint.'

Sean watched as the men did their work. They worked as a team. Must be their army training, Sean thought. Now and then Joseph turned his head and moaned. Sean edged between the men and reached out a hand to touch Joseph lightly.

Suddenly the old man lifted up his head and moaned and muttered incoherently' Blood flowed from his mouth.

'Settle down, old fella,' his dad said quietly. 'We'll get you in hospital soon.' He gently pushed him down.

Joe and Blighty returned from their wanderings around the hut and surrounds.

'No one else around,' Blighty said. 'The whole place has been given a work over though. Must have been a few of them.'

Sean's eyes welled up again. His friend lay crushed and broken on the ground. He remembered the strong man he had been just a little time ago. Why would anyone do this to an old man? Why? But he knew why. The tears flowed down his cheeks, leaving a trail like railway tracks on his dusty face. The men looked at him uncomfortably.

Bluey, red faced and sweat stained despite the coolness of the day, and another man arrived with a green and brown army stretcher.

Jim Buttenberg said, 'Lay it by him, boys. We'll lift him up and you slip it under him, Bill. Now, boys, we'll slide our hands under him and lift him up on the count of three.' The men took their position and, bending over the old man, carefully worked their hands and arms under him. They looked up at Jim Buttenberg. 'All ready? Now on three. One, two, three.' They lifted in unison. Joseph groaned and gasped. Bill slid the stretcher in where he had lain. The men let the broken man down, and he let out a sigh.

'Now, Bill, he's all yours,' said Jim Buttenberg. 'I'll follow up to the hospital with Sean a bit later. You blokes right to go? Bluey, you go with Bill in the ambo. I'll get a ride over with Rexy.'

'One bloke on each handle,' Bill said. He waited while four of the men got into position. 'Righto, you blokes lift steady on my command, bend your legs not your backs. One, two, three.' They lifted the man and stretcher to waist height. Bill was by their side as he commanded in a military voice, 'Step off on the inside foot. Small steps, mind you. Let's get this bloke there in one piece.'

Jim Buttenberg put his hand on Sean's shoulder. 'Old Bill was a medic in the first show. Knows his stuff. Joseph will be all right. We'll go and see him at the hospital. First I want to have a look around. You alright, Sean?'

Sean nodded. 'Yep, I'll be right dad.'

'Good, let's have a look around and see if we can find anything which Joseph might need protecting, or in hospital'. They walked around to the front of the hut. They looked at the ruins of the campsite and the hut, the poker driven into the wall, the door off its hinges, the broken utensils and torn clothing. 'These people were vindictive bastards. White fellas for sure. No black fella would be game to touch Joseph. Who do you think it could be, Sean?'

'There's only one bloke it could be, dad. It has to be that Smythe bastard.' Sean looked at the ruins of Joseph's life.

'Yeh, they certainly have reason not to like this blackfella, especially after your episode with his little pig arse son. Let's have a look inside. Tomorrow I'll come and seal the place up, so no bastard can get in.'

They went into the hut, picking over the debris. There was a trunk of clothes tipped over and half empty. The clothes left in it were folded neatly. There was a box full of carvings, mostly figures of animals and wood engravings, spilled out onto the floor. They carefully put them back. A picture of black kids dressed in white shirts and shorts with an elderly whitefella in tight suit and hat lay broken on the floor. The old breast plate, pocket knives, and medallions spilled over what had once been a bush bench. They put them in a hessian bag, along with about a dozen other photographs and a roll of notes they found under the remains of the bed.

They found some shaving gear and a spare set of clothes and stuffed them in a Gladstone bag. 'I'll get a work party in here and clean this up, Sean. The boys at the RSL won't mind coming down and giving this place the once over. We'll put it back together for the old fella.'

As they left they ran into Rexy and a huge lump of a man with a red face and the uniform of the Victorian Police.

'Shorty, how ya going?' his father said amicably.

'Good, Jim. How are you?'

'Yeh, good, Joseph Wirrinum got a makeover today. We've got him off to hossy.'

'I met the fellas on the track. Rexy was saying your young 'un here found him.'

Sean felt the big man's eyes going over him like a dog licking a bone.

'When did you find him?'

'About an hour ago, sir.'

'You by yourself?'

'Yes, sir.'

'You come down here often?'

'Three or four times a week.'

The big policeman looked at Sean's dad. He nodded assent.

'Anyone around when you came down here?'

'No, sir.'

'Where did you find him?'

'Round the back under the fishing gear and tools, sir.'

'You run and get your dad straight away?'

'Yes, sir. I couldn't pull him out from the place he was in.'

'Right, I'll have a look around.' The big man went to walk off, and then turned around. 'You were involved in a fight down here a few months ago? You beat up a whole gang?'

'I had a fight with a few fellas near the bomber, sir.'

'The Smythes from Cal made a complaint, as I remember. Something about a black ghost and you nearly killing their kid.' The sergeant looked at Sean intently then abruptly said, 'I'll get a statement off you Jim, later in the week.'

'No worries, Shorty. Tomorrow I'll get a few fellas together and make this place secure.'

'Appreciate that, Jim.'

'We've taken a few of his valuables for safekeeping and we'll take some of his personal stuff over to him at the hospital. I'll make a list for you, Shorty. You going to the Ball tonight?'

'Yeh, Irene's draggin me along.'

'I'll let you know how the old bloke is'

The peeler man went around to the back of the hut, his notebook out. The late afternoon sun was turning the leaves of the scrub motley green and yellow. Red-capped robins hopped among the overhanging trees as the men left the clearing. A flock of yellow rosellas flew straight and true over head, and above them the ibis were circling to come in for the night. Sean looked at the Tamba Tamba. Maybe the last of their human branch was going to end tonight. The tears welled in his eyes again. His father put his arm around his shoulders.

'I'll run ahead and start the car,' Rexy stuttered.

'Righto.' The older man turned to his son. 'Sean, Joseph will be okay I'm sure. As I said, he's a tough old bastard.'

'Yeh, I know, dad, but I wonder if things will change now, with the swamp and Joseph's place.'

'H'mm, let's get over this bit first. Tomorrow has enough worries on its own.'

'He's the last of his mob here. He's special. If he goes, maybe this will all change.'

'Perhaps, but nothing is forever. Even this old place.'

Dingarra Dingarra Resurrection

'Rexy, can you stop at my place for a minute? I'll tell Mary what's happening, and drop this stuff off.'

'No worries.' Rexy gunned the FJ around Koonarook, they were soon home. Jim Buttenberg ran inside. Sean waited in the car with Rexy. The car had the smell of newness. It even had a heater and a place for a radio to go. The chrome handles and dial surrounds shone brightly.

'Sean, sorry, we've not been introduced. I'm Rex O'Connor. I own the Holden dealership in Caladonia, but I live in Koonarook, not far from here.'

Sean looked at Rexy sitting behind the wheel. He was dressed in a light blue shirt, tweed jacket and brown trousers. He looked very confident.

'Hello, Mr O'Connor.'

Rexy continued. 'You know this blackfella well?'

'Joseph is my friend, like a grandfather.'

'Your mum and dad think that's alright?'

'Yes, Mr O'Connor. I go fishing with him and we share stories. Joseph is a great storyteller. He's a very fine man, my dad says.'

'Hmm, your father is one of the best blokes I have met. If he says he's alright, then he must be. But it is a bit peculiar.' Rex O'Connor looked straight ahead and gripped the steering wheel.

'Why is it a bit peculiar, Mr O'Connor?'

Rexy turned to look at him. 'Well, ah, ah, it's unusual for a young whitefella like you to be hanging around with an old blackfella,' he said uncertainly. 'It just doesn't happen much. Around here, around anywhere.'

'Joseph is a very good man, Mr O'Connor.'

'Sure, Sean, I've no doubt he is, but there are a lot of them running round causing trouble, drinking and fighting all over the place, like what happened today.'

Sean looked straight at the car salesman. 'But, Mr O'Connor, I've never seen Joseph fight anyone. He's a Gooweera man.'

'He's a what?'

'A Gooweera man, a holy man, like a priest or witch doctor.'

'Sounds like a lot of mumbo jumbo to me. I'd be careful if I was you, hanging around with people like that.'

Sean's mum and dad came out of the house. His mother rushed over to the car.

Rex lowered the window.

'Are you alright, Sean?'

'Yeh, Mum, I'm fine.'

'Hello, Rex. How is Margaret?'

'Fine, Mary. She's looking forward to the ball tonight,' he said cheerfully.

'It should be a wonderful affair. They tell me the girls look lovely and the set they are doing is very elegant.'

'Colleen Wells does a good job on preparing the deb girls.'

'Yes she does and your Margaret is a wonderful dressmaker, I hear half the girls are wearing her creations.'

'We better get going, Rex,' Sean's dad interrupted. 'We've only got a couple of hours until we have to be back.'

'Sean, here are some cakes for you and the men at the hospital.' His mother handed him a large brown paper bag.

Sean felt a stab of familiarity as he entered the hospital. The polished floorboards, the soft lime green walls and ceilings, the smell of antiseptic and starched linen all greeted him and took him back to his time here not so long ago. They walked into a large space off the front entrance. A big sign announced, 'Waiting area. Report to duty nurse.' The place was empty except for four rows of what looked like church pews filling its central cavity. A huge picture of the Queen graced one wall, smaller pictures of doctors and matrons faded and sepia coloured faced her. They were distinguished by elaborately carved picture frames, each one looked down on those who would fill the pews. The duty nurse was situated behind a huge red-gum panelled counter, behind which was a door with words in bold red type: 'Casualty Room.' On the desk was a bell with a sign, 'Ring bell and be seated'. At the desk was a small, wiry nurse. She was writing furiously.

'Good afternoon. Joseph Wirrinum was brought here to casualty a short while ago. Could we see him, please?' Sean's dad enquired.

The nurse indicated with a point of her head that he was in the casualty room. 'He is being treated by Dr O'Loughlin. Would you mind taking a seat?'

'Could we find out how he is doing, thanks, nurse?'

The young nurse looked annoyed. 'I will speak to Sister Louise. Are you related or have some relationship with Mr Wirrinum?'

'Family friends.'

The nurse screwed up her face. 'Only family or custodial officers are allowed in to see patients in casualty.'

'Nurse Simpson,' he said, peering at her name tag, 'would you mind telling Sister Louise that Mr Jim Buttenberg and Sean Buttenberg are here to see Joseph?'

'I will tell her, sir, when I have the time.'

Sean saw his dad's face harden. He leaned into the counter.

'Nurse Simpson, I suggest that time might be now!'

'Sir, I am very busy. Please take a seat.' She fiddled with the pen and the letter in front of her.

Jim Buttenberg looked around at the empty waiting room. Sean edged around the counter and looked at the door. He made a bolt for the door, just as the bustling frame of Sister Louise came through. Sean crashed into her at some speed. He felt the hardness of her flesh and sprawled backwards onto the polished boards. His father picked him up.

'Sean, laddie, are you all right? Why in such a rush?'

'Sorry, Sister. I was going in to see Joseph.'

'I thought you would be here soon. Mr Buttenberg, how are you?'

'Fine, Sister Louise. Just trying to find out from Nurse Simpson here how Joseph is getting along.'

Nurse Simpson hurriedly tried to hide the letter under the ink blotter on the desk. On Sister Louise's orders, she scurried off into the casualty ward.

Sister Louise turned her attention to Rex O'Connor.

'Well, Mr O'Connor,' she said with some enthusiasm. 'It is good to see you, sir. I haven't seen you for many a year. Not since Margaret had your last one. Barry, wasn't it?'

'Yes, Sister. I was going to come and see you about donating for next year's hospital fundraiser.'

'Now, gentleman and Sean, let us sit over here and we will see what is to be done with poor Mr Wirrinum.' She led them over to the bench seats, and sat down beside them. 'Dr O'Loughlin is seeing to him now. We will get some x-rays done presently and then see how he goes. At the moment he looks as though he has concussion, a broken leg, clavicle, possible rib fractures and chest injuries, with multiple contusions and abrasions, some requiring stitches. He is, of course, unconscious and mercifully is in no pain. We are starting him on a course of penicillin, pain relief and will clean him up, stitch, splint and plaster him as need be and then see what happens. It is in God's hands if he recovers, but he is of a sound constitution, with a lot of spirit. He's a stubborn old man. But having said that, he is still an old man and the ordeal he has been through will test his resolve to the limit. It might help us if the doctor knows how long he has been unconscious. Who found him?' She looked enquiringly at them.

'Sean did, Sister, at around four this afternoon. From the look of the camp and surrounds it probably happened around two or three this afternoon,' Sean's dad said.

'Hmm.' The nun looked at Sean. 'He unconscious when you found him?'

'Yes, Sister, he was lying at the back of his hut, on his back and unconscious. He was groaning and moaning a bit.'

'Did he react when you moved him Sean?'

'Yes, Sister, he mumbled a few words, and groaned when we moved him.'

'Well, that is a good sign, really. He hasn't been unconscious for too long and he reacts to stimuli.' She smiled professionally and stood up. 'Now I will go in and see how everything is going, then I will come back and let you see him. I will be not long, I will get Nurse Simpson to make you a cuppa.' She strode back through the swinging doors, her funny head piece swinging awkwardly.

'It's amazing that bloke is still alive,' Rexy said, shaking his head.

'We've both seen a lot worse in the war, Rexy'.

'True, but they were not old like that poor old bastard in there.'

Nurse Simpson brought out tea and biscuits and went back into the casualty room again. The group sat quietly, sipping their drinks.

Finally the door opened and Nurse Simpson ushered them in. She gave a shy smile and a nervous giggle as they went past. Jim Buttenberg looked at her sourly. She shrunk under his gaze. The casualty room was a six-bed room with large double doors at the far end. There was a raised nurses station cordoned off from the rest of the room by a wall of indented panelling and glass which reached to the ceiling. Nurse Simpson disappeared up its steps and only her head could be been seen as she sat down behind it. Curtains hung from wrought iron rails suspended from the ceiling surrounded each of the six beds, and medical equipment were parked in diverse modes around the perimeter of the room. The roof was split by six sky lights, one over each bed. All was white, the air was intense with carbolic acid and light. Big segmented cast-iron hydronic heaters were spaced around the walls, giving the place a close warmth which had been absent from the waiting room.

Only the middle bed was occupied, the curtains pulled back. The compact figure of Dr O'Loughlin was bent over the shape in the bed, and the unmistakable odour of cigars mingled with the hospital aromas. Sister Louise gestured for them to stand at the end of the bed. They gathered in a group and watched silently as the physician went about his tasks. Joseph's head stood out from the white sheets and surrounds and was swathed in bandages and tape. His face was expressionless and drawn, the character lines which normally gave expression to it were gone. His breathing was shallow and slow. A pulley system ran from his left side over a big iron wheel at the end of the cast-iron bed which held a weight. The doctor put his stethoscope in his ears and pulled back the sheet to reveal Joseph's chest. It, too, was swathed in crepe and dressings. The men and boy watched as the chest went up and down in a slow rhythm. Sister Louise joined them at the end of the bed. The only sound was the weak breathing of the black man. Sean eyes welled up as he looked at the wreck of his friend. The feelings of loss and grief were so great he could taste them. The bile rose to his mouth. He bit down and ground his teeth. The image of the old man sitting around his fire and his ready smile and strong words came to him. The tears welled over and ran down his face. Sister Louise put one arm around his shoulders and they all waited, nothing moved.

Finally the doctor was finished. He turned to the group at the end of the bed.

'Well, well, our friend Joseph here has been through a whirlpool. I believe Sister Louise has told you of Joseph's injuries. We have some traction on his leg.' The doctor pointed at the pulley system. 'He is comfortable and although unconscious is breathing lightly but with good rhythm, thankfully. I do not think there is any lung puncture or rupture of the major organs. His heart is strong and all is well there, but he has been beaten fairly consistently over most of his body. There are many contusions and abrasions. The big question will be,' the doctor turned and looked at his patient and sighed, 'if and when he wakes up and regains consciousness, what will be his state? Will he be the same?' He moved to the end of the bed. 'Sister Louise will keep an eye on him and we will do all we can.'

'Thank you, Doctor.'

'Quite all right, Jim. I'm happy you found him when you did. If he had been left outside in these cold conditions he would most certainly have died.'

'Sean found him.'

The doctor looked at Sean for the first time. 'Ah, Sean, yes. How have you been? Sister Louise tells me you and Joseph are friends? I hope he gets better for you.'

Sean moved to the top of the bed where the doctor had been. He looked at his friend, his mate, his Ulwai. The adults talked at the end of the bed in a low murmur. Sean put his hand in Joseph's hand and squeezed it tightly. Joseph's hand felt cold and limp. Despair gripped Sean and held him like a wet blanket.

Suddenly the old man's face became animated. He tried to get up. 'Dingarra, Dingarra onom kalian en el our Dingarra onom kalian en el our,' he cried out loudly.

Sean cried in return, 'Dingarra, Dingarra is here to help you, he will not let you die, Joseph.'

Joseph's eyes opened. He looked directly at Sean. His eyes rolled. The people at the end of the bed were startled into action. Sister Louise grasped Sean's shoulders and whispered urgently, 'Sean, Sean, let go, laddie, let go!' The doctor tried to keep Joseph still, but again the old man cried out.

'Dingarra, Dingarra, onom kalian en el our Dingarra onom kalian en el our.'

Sean cried back. 'Dingarra, Dingarra ngai el our Joseph. Dingarra ngai el our Joseph.'

All now was commotion. Sister Louise tried to prise Sean's hand out of Joseph's. His hand was hot now, burning against the flesh of Sean's hand. Sean could hear his father's voice far way, coming down a long tunnel.

'Sean, step back, step back, boy,' his father was saying.

He felt the Sister's bulk pressing against him, her hands trying to prise his hand from Joseph's. The doctor pleaded with Joseph to be still, his hands on Joseph's chest trying to restrain him. But all Sean felt was the hand of Joseph, warm and strong, the pressure so fierce it hurt. An intense brightness burned his eyes. It seared into his brain, the pressure in his head felt like it would burst. The scar on his chest burned. There was nothing but light and heat. He glided into nothingness, into blackness.

Hospital Again

Sean woke up. He was in one of the emergency beds. The light was gone and he was looking up into the blackness of a skylight. He felt the soft pressure of his mother's hand on his and smelled her beautiful fragrance. His head hurt and his scar burned, otherwise he felt light and airy. By God he was hungry! His mother laughed and hugged him. He felt her softness.

His father, on his other side, patted him on the shoulder. 'Thank God, thank God, you are back with us.' He was smiling.

Sean looked past him to the bed where Joseph had been. His stomach knotted. 'Where is he?' He tried to get up.

'Settle, lad. Joseph is much improved. He has been taken up to the ward. He is conscious and was asking for you,' his father said softly.

Sean sighed and eased back onto the pillow. 'Can we go home? We have to go to the ball.'

His parents looked at each other. His mum said, 'Sean, it's two in the morning. You have been asleep for nearly eight hours.'

'Arrhh,' he groaned. She'd kill him!

'Sean, Sean.' She stroked his forehead. 'You're much more important than any silly old ball.' She turned to the nurses station and signalled to the night nurse.

The nurse came over. She dismissed his parents. 'I need to examine

Sean. Would you mind, Mr and Mrs Buttenberg, waiting just outside the curtains?' She introduced herself but said little. She purred like a cat as she wrote down all the observations.

'Can I go home now, Sister.'

She eyed him intently. 'No, not until Dr O'Loughlin says you can go.' Sean strained to hear her wispy voice. She opened the curtains and ushered his parents back to the bedside. 'Mr and Mrs Buttenberg, all seems to be well with Sean. His observations are normal and I will feed him now. May I suggest you go home and get a good rest and come back in the morning?'

His parents nodded and turned to Sean together. 'Is that all right with you, Sean'?

'Yeh, dad, I'll be fine.'

'You get some sleep. We will be back soon.' His mother kissed him. 'Love you,' she whispered. 'We'll talk later on about what happened.'

Sean felt the crimson creep onto his face. His father gave him a playful cuff across the hair.

Sean woke up to a murmur of voices. It was the nurses' change over. He nudged down into the bed, pulling the covers over him. The scar on his chest was sore, his head dull.

'Well, laddie, you certainly gave us a scare last night,' the big voice of Sister Louise boomed. Sean pushed back the sheets. 'Ding Dong tells me you had an uneventful night.'

'Ding Dong?'

'Sister Bell, our night nurse.' She gave a faint laugh and checked his chart.

'How is Joseph? Can I go and see him?'

'Steady on. You cannot go anywhere until the doctor has seen you.'

'How is he, Sister?'

'Apparently a lot better, awake, aware and asking about you.'

'Can I see him after the doctor has been?'

'You are very good friends aren't you?' She was standing at the head of the bed.

'Yes, Sister. Besides mum and dad, he's the most important friend in the world for me.'

'And where does Katy come in, then?'

'Oh, she's all right for a girl.'

Sister Louise pulled up a chair and sat down. Her face was close to Sean's. 'Sean, what happened last night. Do you remember?'

Sean thought carefully. 'Sister, I went to hold Joseph's hand, and then it got very hot and bright, even though I had my eyes closed. It felt as though I was going to burst.'

'I couldn't pull you apart. It was like you were both held together with Tarzans Grip.'

'I remember you trying to pull us apart. And then I can't remember anything.'

'The words, Sean. You were shouting something in Joseph's language.'

'Joseph has taught me a few words, Sister.'

'You collapsed. That's the only reason I could get you apart, and then Joseph woke up. I have never in all my life seen anything like it.'

Breakfast arrived soon after. Mrs Cruddace, the lady who delivered it, fussed around.

'Back again so soon, Sean? My son Anthony is in grade four at St Joseph's.'

'Yes, I know him, Mrs Cruddace. He's a good runner.'

'Yes, that he is. He runs away from his homework pretty fast,' she cackled. 'I heard you had a bit of an experience with that Abo Wirrinum last night.'

Sean looked at her, a piece of toast halfway to his open mouth.

'I was at the Catholic ball last night. It was the talk of the night. Rex O'Connor seen it. Said it was like some sort of transfiguration, a miracle or something.'

Sean stared at his untouched porridge and tried to ignore her. She ploughed on.

'He said you and the old Abo were talking in weird lingo, like in a trance.'

'Mrs Cruddace! I'm sure you have more things to do then burn the ears of our patients with your prattle.'

'Yes, Sister. Yes, sister.' Mrs Cruddace scurried away her trolley of dishes rattling.

'I will see you later, laddie.'

'Thank you, Sister.' Sean spread vegemite on his toast. Why did he feel so tired?

When Sean's parents came in they were dressed for mass.

'How ya going, son?'

'I'm fine. I just want to get out of here.'

'I'm sure the doctor will let you go,' his dad said.

'I've brought you in some pancakes and golden syrup. I thought you may be hungry.' His mother produced a plate with two pancake sandwiches on it.

'Thanks, mum.' He ate the pancakes. He was still tired, but they were much better than the toast and porridge. 'Sister Louise said I could go and see Joseph after I get discharged. She said he is doing well.' He licked golden syrup from his fingers. Why was his mum looking at his dad like that?

'Great pancakes, mum'.

She smiled. His father smiled, too.

'Sean, do you remember what happened last night?'

His father leaned over the bed. 'It almost seemed that you were joined to Joseph. The language you were using, do you remember that?'

Sean felt like he was under siege. 'Joseph has taught me some of his language, dad. I've picked up some of his lingo. He's very good at telling stories.'

His mother took a seat where Sister Louise had been sitting.

'Yes, I know, Sean. But last night it was like you were joined not only by the hand but in your head as well. Did you feel it?'

Sean took a deep breath, and told them what he had told Sister Louise. His mother held his hand, her soft, gentle fingers felt warm and comforting.

'Well, it is good to see you hungry and ready to go. We will see what Dr O'Loughlin has to say,' his mother said.

A portly Sister came out from behind her desk. She introduced herself as Sister Mathews and asked his parents to wait outside. She did a thorough examination on Sean, gave terse instructions said, 'Thank you, Mr Buttenberg. The doctor and Sister Louise will be here shortly. I will send one of the nurses in to give you a wash.'

'Is Nurse Harradine here?' he asked, then shrank into the bed as the Sister glared at him.

'Young man, the nurse attached here today is Nurse Crawford. She will be here shortly.'

Nurse Crawford was a plain girl tending to plumpness and with an attitude that said she had seen it all. She made up a bowl of warm, soapy water in a high-sided enamel basin, and instructed Sean to clean every part of his body. 'Make sure you clean all your body well, under your arm pits, clean the private bits last, right.' Sean blushed. 'No need to get embarrassed. With the people you've been hanging around with, you could have all kinds of vermin and nasties on you.'

'Who do you mean?' he gasped.

'Why, that scrawny old blackfella in here last night. Dirty old bugger.'

Sean's next movements were instinctive. He leaned over the enamel bowl, propelling a rigid hand into it. It flipped up, its contents propelled over the front of Nurse Crawford. She screamed and jumped backwards. The water dripped down her front. Sean fell back into the pillows, satisfied.

'Sorry, Nurse Crawford, guess I slipped.'

'You did that on purpose, you little bastard,' she hissed through clenched teeth. She stepped forward, her face red and contorted.

The voice of Sister Mathews thrilled out. 'Nurse Crawford, what is going on over there?'

Nurse Crawford turned towards the oncoming Sister. 'Sister, we had an accident. Sean upset the wash bowl and it spilled over me.'

Sister Mathews was clearly not impressed. 'Nurse, I would have you be more careful with your patients. Go and clean yourself up and send Amy into fix this mess.'

'Yes, Sister,' she said meekly. She shot a spiteful glance at Sean and trudged off, still dripping.

Sister Mathews looked at Sean, and at the upturned bowl and sighed. 'What a mess.' She retreated to the nurses station.

Sean sat up in his bed. His parents returned, and soon Dr O'Loughlin was in attendance with Sister Louise.

'Hello to the Buttenbergs.' He took them all in a cursory gaze. 'Interesting name, that,' he said, looking at Sean's chart. 'Most variants I believe are Battenberg, with an "A".'

'Yes, doctor they are. The immigration clerk in Melbourne spelled the name wrong a hundred years ago and it's been that way ever since.'

'Yes, yes,' the doctor nodded. 'Happened a lot. German, eh.'

'Yes, a German name, doctor.'

The doctor grunted. 'Now, young Buttenberg, strange episode here last night.' His eyes pierced into Sean. He adjusted his glasses and looked at Sean's mother. 'Mrs Buttenberg, Sean's indicators are all very good. He seems to be a very normal, fit young boy.' He took his glasses off and glanced at Sister Louise. 'It's hard to make out what happened last night. I'm led to believe that this young fellow and Mr Wirrinum are very good friends, which seems unusual in itself. Some sort of symbolic empathy or association seems to have led this boy into a state of unconsciousness – fortunately, short lived. At the same time Mr Wirrinum came out of his state of unconsciousness and there was communication at a level we do not understand. There are many things about the mind and the realm of psychoanalysis that we do not understand. However, it seems that this young man has fully recovered.' He looked at Sean again. 'Do you feel well, Sean?'

'Yes, doctor, I feel fine.' Sean said shuffling in the bed.

'Good. Sister, please discharge Mr Buttenberg.' He turned his attention to Sean's parents. 'Any questions?'

'Will this happen again, doctor?'

'As I said, Mrs Buttenberg, this field is one where our knowledge is limited. However, it is fair to say that Sean and all involved were very wrought up over the events of yesterday, and also fair to say if you are close to someone your feelings and empathic cognitions could lead to a state of shock or over anxiety. Sean has a good family and a stable background, so I see no reason that it would happen to him again.'

When the discharge process was complete, Sean's mother produced a bag of neatly pressed clothes. Sean pulled out a new pair of long trousers. He looked at his mother.

'Your father and I thought it was time for you to wear trousers.'

She beamed at him. 'I know most boys do not get a pair until they are confirmed, but we thought it was time. There is a new belt also and socks.' The cream moleskins and the brown belt with a brass buckle were just like his father's. 'Now close the curtains and get changed, then we will go and see Joseph.'

Sean felt older and more grown up. The trousers were strange on his legs.

St Luke's Ward stretched out before them. It was a wide hall-like structure. Big, bright lights enclosed by large reflective domes hung from the high ceiling. The floors were highly polished red-gum boards. Nurse Harradine welcomed them as they entered, and Sean blushed at a flood of memories. Along each side of the ward were twelve high, brass beds, each separated by white curtains. The empty beds were perfectly made with cover sheets emblazoned with a red cross in a circle. One corner of the emblem was occupied by a curling snake, and the opposing corner by a leopard etched into the cotton. About half the beds were occupied, mostly by old men. Their bald or grey heads poked out from the blankets.

Nurse Harradine said, 'Mr Wirrinum is in the end bed on the right. Please follow me.'

'How is he?' his mother enquired.

'You will have to speak to the duty sister, Sister White.' She glanced at the nurses station as they passed, and pressed on towards the end of the ward. When they were well past the station, she said, 'Mr Wirrinum seems to be doing well. He's conscious and is eating and drinking. I think he will be all right.' She smiled at Sean. They came to the end of the ward. Big wooden doors with glass panes led out onto the wide verandahs of the hospital. 'Mr Wirrinum, you have visitors,' she sang.

Joseph sat propped up in bed. His left arm was in a sling and rested on a pillow placed to take its weight. His head was swathed in crepe bandages. His eyes were slits that peered out from the swollen and disfigured face. His upper body was covered in a blue-striped hospital pyjama top. The buttons were undone and revealed more crepe bandages. Joseph's black skin contrasted sharply with the dressings. His breathing was slow and deliberate. From beneath the blankets wires protruded and ran over a pulley and down to a steel bar with three round lead weights attached. The nurse pulled the curtains to enclose the bed and quietly retreated up the ward. Sean ran forward and around to the right side of the bed. He sat gently on the bed and rested his head against the injured chest.

'Joseph, Joseph, Ulwai, Ulwai, I see you,' he quietly intoned.

'Sean, Sean, Maiyarare, Maiyarare, I see you, though not as well as I would bin want to.' The old man stifled a laugh and groaned. He put his good arm slowly around the boy. James and Mary Buttenberg shifted uncomfortably.

After a quiet interval, Sean's dad coughed. 'Sean, perhaps Mr Wirrinum needs some space to breathe,' he whispered.

Sean removed his head from the old man's chest and looked around. 'Sorry, mum and dad,' he muttered. He stood up. 'Joseph, this is my mum. You've met dad.'

Joseph looked at Sean's parents. His smile looked like a grotesque grimace on the battered face. 'I bin happy to meet you, Mrs Buttenberg, and to see you again, Mr Jim.' His voice was weak and tired.

'Jim and Mary, please, Mr Wirrinum,' Sean's mother said.

'Mrs Mary, I bin a friend of your boy here, Sean. He bin a good boy and shared some fishin, tucker and story with me.'

'Sean has told us many times about you and the adventures you both get up to. We are so sorry to see you like this.'

The wounded man took in a small breath. 'Yeh, some troubles happen to me.'

'We will not stay to long, just enough to say hello.'

Joseph nodded slowly. 'Mrs Mary, I bin not too good today but I get better. I thank you for those cakes and scones you sent to me.'

Jim Buttenberg shifted on his feet and said quietly, 'Joseph, we have secured your valuables at our place. We will fix up your hut. It will be right for you when you get home.'

'You a good fella, Mr Jim.'

'It's the least we can do.'

'I'll come every day and see you, Joseph, until you are better,' Sean said.

'You bin better ask your mum and dad about that one, but it will be goodum to see you sometime. You bin in hospital too after you helped me last night?'

'Yeh, I got a bit excited and went out of it for a while. I'm really good now.'

Jim Buttenberg moved to the end of the bed. 'Time to go, Sean. We'll let Joseph rest.' Sean gave his friend a gentle hug. The old man put his arm around the boy again, and a single tear ran down each side of the battered face.

'Seeya, Joseph, Ulwai.'

'Seeya, Sean, Maiyarare.'

'Good morning, Joseph,' Sean's parents chorused together.

Gooweera Healing

Sean stepped out of the hospital into the brightness of a sunny winter's day. A pair of Queensland fig trees framed the entrance. The magnificent trees were more than one hundred feet high, with massive serrated trunks and huge canopies that joined to form a massive sky structure. Long tendrils dropped down vertically, giving them a primeval look. Sean knew from Bill Heanen, the gardener at the hospital, that they had been there for more than one hundred years, a gift from the first Campbell.

Under the trees sat a group of about twenty Aborigines, a mixed group of men and women. When the Buttenbergs saw Sean's family they rose as one. Mary Buttenberg moved closer to her husband. Sean looked at them curiously. An elderly man removed his Akubra and gingerly moved towards them. He wore blue faded jeans, check shirt and a Driza-Bone faded almost to white. His jet black face and crown was topped by wavy white hair neatly combed and lacquered down. He was tall, spare of frame and moved with the slow deliberate gait of the bushman.

Sean's dad stopped and waited for the man to approach him. Mary Buttenberg put her arm through her husband's crocked arm. The man reminded Sean of his Ulwai. He stopped at a respectful distance and looked with bright steady eyes at Jim Buttenberg.

'Hello. You bin Mr Jim Buttenberg?'

'How can I help?'

'My name be William Grimble. I bin belogem to same mob as Gooweera man Joseph Wirrinum. We bin travel longem way from Mathoura station to see this fella in there, this Wirrinum fella.'

Jim Buttenberg stepped forward and shook the man's hand.

'This is Mary, my wife, and this young fella is my son, Sean.'

'Uh, Dingarra fella. This Sean friend of the Gooweera.'

Sean felt many eyes upon him. He blushed.

'Yes, Sean is a friend of Joseph. They are quite good friends.'

'I bin ask you bin seein this Wirrinum fella. How he be?'

His father told William about Joseph's injuries. 'He'll be in hospital for some time, but they seem to think he will recover well and go back home. He is strong.'

'Thank you, Mr Jim, thank you.'

'I'm sure if you see Sister Louise the head sister she will allow you to see him.'

William thought about this for a moment. 'Ah, we will wait for Gooweera to see us, thank you, Mr Jim.' He turned to join his group.

'What's Gooweera mean?'

The old man stopped. He looked at Jim Buttenberg, then at Sean. A flicker crossed his face. He whispered quietly. Sean had to strain forward to hear. 'Ah, that bin old black man magic man or spirit man, that Wirrinum he be powerful fella. He big spirit man.'

'And Dungaree or Dingarra?' Sean's dad asked.

There was a pause, then the old man answered. 'It bin mean lightning spirit or spirit of the storm.'

'Thank you, William.'

The old man nodded shuffled away and rejoined the group.

Sean sat in the back of the big car as it chomped its way home. His parents were silent. Finally his mother broke it.

'Who would do such a thing to an old man, Jim?' She shook her head.

'I have a fair idea who it was and it was no blackfella. You saw how that fella Grimble was so respectful of Joseph. Remember when Sean was attacked down in the swamp by that gang of kids, and someone or somebody came to his aid. Well, that someone was Joseph. The kid who was beaten up and embarrassed by that affair was our friend, young Smythe.'

'But to take the law into their own hands!'

'They probably think they can get away with it. He's an old Abo living down on the river. He doesn't even count as a citizen. They're always in strife. What's one more bashing?'

His mother snorted. 'That's inhuman, Jim!'

'I know, Mary, but plenty of people think that way. I saw enough of that in the war.' His father grasped the steering wheel tightly. 'These people are bad, Mary. Remember they have been embarrassed and hold a grudge against Sean and the old fella.'

'Is Sean safe with these people around?' She looked over into the back of the car. Sean tried to smile.

His father's voice was calm. 'Yeh, I'm sure Sean will be all right. From what I hear young Smythe doesn't have many friends left at school and is kept on a fairly tight leash by Sister Hildegard. Isn't that right, Sean?'

'Yeh, he's pretty much on his own now.'

His parents nodded and they drove on. Soon they were pulling into the back yard.

'Sean, would you please go over and get Katy from the Hirds while I prepare lunch?'

'Yes Mum.'

'Tell Mrs Hird I'll come over and see her later on when we've all had a rest.'

'Yes Mum.'

Sean entered the Hird's property, directly opposite the Butten-berg's, through the back yard. There were bits and pieces of machin-ery and equipment here and there, half-finished garden beds and an incomplete redbrick path. Sean's dad said Mr Hird was a good fella but a mucker. Mr Hird worked at the timber mill as a machine operator and walked to work. The back of the high, timber house had been painted to about two-thirds of the way up. The outhouse looked like it was going to fall over.

Sean knocked. 'Mrs Hird, can I come in?' he called

'Come in, Sean.' Sean took his shoes off and placed them with the other shoes and boots just inside the door. He peered down the long hallway. Mr Hird might have been a mucker, but Sean's dad said that Mrs Hird was a goer and a fanatic in her house. From the polished Baltic pine floorboards and carpet run, down the hallway to the family portraits and side tables, all was neat and in order. Sean turned right into the large kitchen at the rear of the house.

The kitchen was spacious and consisted of a huge combustion stove nestled into a large fireplace and chimney, walls lined with cup-boards and a large sideboard opposite the stove. Light was admitted by a large three-pane window that faced the back yard. The deep steel sink and cast-iron taps were directly under the window. The ceiling was fifteen foot high and from its centre hung a large brass light fit-ting from which hung a pair of globes. They cast their light onto a magnificent but scarred red-gum table.

At this table were the three children. Andrew was three and Mar-tha four. Katy, his sister, was there also. They were engrossed in draw-ing and colouring with butchers paper and crayon. The other two Hird children, Charles, five, and Elizabeth, six, were not to be seen. Mrs Hird was at the stove stirring a pot. The rich, thick smell of chicken soup filled the air, warm and heavy from the heat and steam from the stove. Mrs Hird was a tall, thin lady with beautiful wavy hair and a face that was always creased with a smile. She wore a simple cotton house smock and a ribbon through her hair. Her feet and ankles were covered in thick woollen socks and knitted house slippers. Sean's mum said that Mrs Hird had cold feet since she had had the children. She also said that she didn't care what people thought, just because the Hirds weren't Catholics, didn't mean that she and Sally could not be friends.

'G'day, Mrs Hird. I've come to take Katy home.'

Mrs Hird turned around. Little beads of sweat stood at her brow. Sean noticed the perspiration that made the front of her dress cling to her. She had the wooden stirring spoon in her hand and a look of concentration, her face broke into a beautiful smile on seeing Sean.

'My, you do look grown up in your new trousers and shirt! Mary said she'd give them to you soon. You look like a real little man.'

Sean blushed and stuttered. 'Thank you, Mrs Hird.'

Mrs Hird spoke like a teacher, which she had been until she had to leave after she married. His dad had warned him once to be careful of Mrs Hird.

'She knows more about you then I do, Sean. She knows more about *me* then I do. She's your mother's best friend, and knows everything. She knows everything from the size of my undies to the way I proposed to you mother all those years ago and everything in between,' and he had laughed and laughed.

Sean did not quite get it, but it was true that Mrs Hird seemed to know most things that were going on with his family. Katy looked up and burst around the table as did Martha. She banged into Sean.

'Sean, look I drew you in 'ospital with needles and nurses and broken things. Do you have anything broken?'

'No, Katy, I just felt a bit sick last night, that's all. I'm good now.'

'Orrhh, that's what mum said. I want to be your nurse. Martha can help.'

'I can give you a needle to make you better,' Martha squealed.

Mrs Hird shook her head. 'Enough girls, enough. Poor Sean has had enough excitement without you jumping all over him. Now, Sean, I have made some scones for you to take home to your poor mother and father, worried sick they were.'

'Thank you, Mrs Hird.'

'And tell your mum old Mr Watkins had some boilers he was nearly giving away. I bought half a dozen and she can have three of them if she wants.' She began cleaning up the table. 'Katy, pack up and grab your coat. It's time for you to go.'

She stopped her cleaning and looked closely at Sean. 'Are you really all right, Sean?' She stepped close and put the back of her hand against his forehead. 'You look a little pale, Sean.'

'I'm fine, Mrs Hird,' he said quietly.

'Well, you go home and have a good rest. Emotional excitement and disturbance is as bad as a disease.

'Yes, Mrs Hird.'

'Here is some apricot jam to go with those scones. You tell your Mum I will see her for afternoon tea.'

Sean and Katy walked across the road to home. Katy babbled but held onto his hand tightly, which was unusual.

'Did you get stuck onto a black man, Sean?' she said as they entered their back yard.

Sean stopped and looked down at her. Her elf face peered back at him.

'No, Katy, I did not.'

'Mr Hird said you and a black man were stuck together last night and they couldn't get you apart. Is that what made you sick? Being stuck to a black man?' She ran through the back door and he heard her crying, 'Mum, Sean's alive. He's not sick anymore.'

Sean was reading a volume of *Birds of Australia* in front of the fire. His mother was putting Katy to bed. His father leaned out of his lounge chair.

'Now, about last night, do you know what happened?'

'Dad, I told you!'

'Are you sure it's as simple as that – holding hands then passing out? Those Abo words you used. They seemed to be a call from somewhere beyond.'

His father knew there was some other thing here, something beyond his understanding. His father liked to accumulate knowledge, sometimes over long periods, and then make a decision. He was thorough and did not act in haste.

Sean fidgeted. 'That night I nearly got killed by the lightning...'

'Yes, I remember it very well.'

'Well, Joseph thinks I was struck by Dingarra, the Spirit in the lightning and storm, and the scar on my chest is a sign.' Sean opened his pyjama top and ran his fingers along the raised scar, still tender from the night before. 'He thinks it is a mark from Dingarra, a sign that he has marked me for something. He thinks Dingarra was sent by Nooralie.' His father sat up straight

'Who the hell is Nooralie?

'Nooralie is the big spirit in the universe, in their Dreaming.' His father was listening carefully. 'The local people here were the Bindaree, and where Joseph lives now, they were called the Tamba Tamba clan.'

'Joseph told you all this?'

'He's told me lots of stories.'

'And Tamba Tamba, what does that mean?'

'It means the sacred ibis. You know, those birds that nest down near Joseph's place? They're the totem of the people who used to live here, and Joseph's special totem. If they go from this place the Bindaree believe the river will die.'

There was a long pause. 'You believe this?'

The book in front of Sean was open to the page about the ibis. He touched his fingers lightly to the lithograph. 'It's like a holy grotto in there, dad. Joseph is a great storyteller. It's hard not to believe it when he is telling his stories.'

'And last night was connected to all this?'

'I don't know! But it was like Dingarra came and took over. It was like a brightness. Like the night of the lightning. My scar hurt like hell. I couldn't see, I can't remember. But I did feel like I was joined to Joseph.'

'Joseph certainly came to life when you held his hand. It was like he was getting a charge of electricity or something. I never saw anything like it. I saw my share of wounded and dying men in the war, but never anything like that.' His father eased back into his lounge chair. 'Let's keep this to ourselves for a while and think about it. You can go and see Joseph a couple of times this week but only with either mum or me present. So it will be in the evening.'

Sean closed the book. He had hoped to go after school.

'It's not that bad, is it Sean?'

'I was thinking I might be able to...'

'No! Enough is enough. I'll see the fellas about organising some work on the old man's hut.'

Sean sat in the winter sun with Johnny McCarthy on the verandah step of the school. Their sandwiches lay half eaten between them.

'Swap you a cheese sandwich for a vegemite,' said Johnny.

'Have it. I'm not that hungry.' Sean handed his cheese sandwich to Johnny. 'For a little bloke, you sure eat a lot.'

'Mum says it's my constitution,' Johnny said as he took another bite. 'I don't even know what that means.'

'I think it's something to do with you running around with your arse hanging out.'

'You should talk!'

'What d'ya mean?'

'I heard tell that you were stuck to that Abo friend of yours like there was no tomorrow.'

'Who told you?'

'They were all talking about it at the ball. We were s'posed to meet there, remember? We were gonna explore under the hall. You were s'posed to bring your dad's torch. What happened anyway?'

How many times must he tell this story?

'They say you brought that old blackfella back to life, like bloody Jesus Christ or something.' Johnny looked around apprehensively.

'Joseph wasn't bloody well dead, he was only injured.' Sean put his head close to Johnny's. He could almost taste the cheese sandwich. 'You know we are friends and like, you look after your mates, right? Well, that's how it was. Joseph was in trouble. I held his hand. Just because he's an Abo and a bit bloody different people think it's strange. If it had been you Johnny, I would of felt the bloody same.'

'Why you didn't say that in the first place?'

'Well, I haven't had a chance, have I? What with getting to school and all them kids gawking at me as though I'm a freak or something.'

'Well, you did make quite an entrance this morning, like bloody Jesus Christ parting the waters or something.' They looked around again.

Sean said quietly, 'That was bloody Moses, you idiot.'

'Well, now, what have we got here?' Sister Hildegard chimed. 'Two boys in earnest conversation eating their lunch where they are not supposed to be? Shelter shed or under the big elm, you know the rules, laddies.'

Both boys stood up instinctively taking off their school caps. They faced the Head Sister like penitents.

'You two look like the cat who stole the milk. Do not let me catch you eating up here on the school steps again. I want to have a word with you, Mr Buttenberg. Run along with you, Mr McCarthy, and tuck your shirt in and clean your shoes when you get home.'

'Yes, Sister.'

Another bloody grilling, thought Sean. When would it end?

'Mr Buttenberg, I hear you have had an interesting weekend? I stopped in to see Mr Wirrinum this morning. He seems to be going as well as can be expected.'

Sean nodded. 'I hope he gets better soon, Sister. I'll see him tonight.' They walked along the school verandah and stopped in its shadow.

'And how are you, laddie? You have had a trying time.'

'I'm well, Sister. I'm feeling good.'

'Good, Sean, good. Now off you go and play.'

'Thank you, Sister.'

'And Sean,' she stopped him before he got far, 'if you need to talk about this, please see me.'

At the tea table his father announced that the RSL had organised a working bee for Sunday.

'I think it may be a good idea if you don't go down that way, Sean, for a little while, but you can come and help us on Sunday. Shorty Malone said he won't have to interview you about Joseph's bashing. He's taken a statement from me and a couple of the other fellas, and been over to the hospital to see Joseph.'

'Do they know any more about it, James. Who did it?'

'You know Shorty, pretty tight lipped about things. But he did seem pretty confident today. Sean, we'll see Joseph after we do these dishes, eh?'

Joseph was sitting straight up in bed looking at the ceiling when Sean and his father walked in. He saw them and his face opened into a big smile.

'Ah, me bin thinkin of you young fella, you bin in my dreamin a lot today. I bin have a lot to thank you for. Hello, Mr Jim.'

Sean's dad shook Joseph's good hand gently. 'Just "Jim," Joseph. We'll only stay five minutes. How have you been?'

'I bin getting better but it be some pain. They give me some tablet which makes it good and I float a bit away like I bin like a fluffy cloud. Then that Sister give me needle and that bin put me to sleep real well. She gonna give me one in the bum tonight.'

'You're getting the best treatment here.'

'Yeh but I bin get out of here real quick, I done miss my pipe, the wind on my face and the smoke from my fire.'

'I understand, Joseph. It's always hard being away from your own place. Need anything from home?'

'Just my pipe and chewin baccy.'

'Right, I'll go over and see Sister Walters there. Stay here, Sean. I'll be back in a minute.'

'That fella your dad he bin one nice fella.'

'Yeh, not bad.' Sean could see his father at the nurses station, engaged in conversation with the sister. She was giggling. Sean had heard his mum say to Sally Hird once that Jim Buttenberg was a ladies' man.

The Curse of the Yunbeai

Sean pulled a chair up to Joseph's bed. He looked at the old weathered face swathed in dressings, the bright eyes, the humour lines marked and prominent despite the pain they disguised.

'You know what happened on Saturday night Joseph?'

'What you thinkem, young fella?'

'I felt like there was a thing inside me, bright and warm, taking me over and drawing us together, like a magnet force or something.'

The old man stifled a laugh. 'It bin Dingarra, you his fella now. He bin gonna work through you. He powerful one that one, he come to help us when we bin laid low.'

'But...'

'The Dream Time fella, they know big time all time. This old fella, he bin around longem time, he bin see this dreamin fella, but me do not understand them full time.'

'Like the Immaculate Conception. I don't understand that either.'

'Something like that one. We bin not made to understand all these dreamin things.'

Sean's head ached, there were a lot of things he didn't understand.

'Who did this to you, Joseph?'

'I bin know this one but I not tell anyone, not even that peeler fella. I bin tell him I do not know, I not bin tellim him all the truth today.'

'Why not?' he uttered angrily.

The old man put his good hand on Sean's shoulder. 'Sean, some-time you get a bit citable,' and he laughed. He drew Sean in closer until their faces were nearly touching. 'This I let you know. Them fella do this to me, they will have the Coocoa Loora, the evil ones, after them forever, till they be sorry or die. It go for their close ones also if they bin not change. I bin dreamin with the Yunbeai. He bin say to me, them fella they bin gonna leave this place, but these Coo-coa Loora fella, they folla them and makem sad, even kill them.'

'You put a curse on them?'

'You bin readim them comic books too much. I bin dreamin on this and that which come to me. This curse can only come from Yun-beai spirit fella, it not come through this Joseph bloke or any fella even if he be Gooweera man. Like that fella Dingarra the other night. It not bin you who do it, it bin him spirit man, from the Dreamin. Same thing with this one, them spirit fella ask me in dreamin not bin tell any fella who they are, even Dingarra fella like you. But they give you Dingarra young fella a clue. All them bloke that hurt me or be knowin about this, they leave this place soon. Let them leave young fella, do not go after them or your father do not fight them, the evil ones will follow for longem time.'

Sean closed his eyes. It was an awful truth. Finally, he whispered, 'Ulwai, I hear you.'

'You be good one. You no tell anyone about this Gooweera dreamin.'

'You two telling tall stories?' Sean's dad rejoined them, his face creased with good humour. 'Time to go, Sean. Mary sends her regards, Joseph.'

Over the next week Sean returned to the hospital twice. Joseph, although in pain, was slowly getting better, but they had no chance to speak alone together. His dad took him and they stayed for short periods. His mum sent along knitted socks and hankies with little fish embroidered on them. Joseph looked at the fish hankies.

'Kooya nose rag, your mother bin good woman round a man's camp she bin makem a man happy I think.'

His father laughed. 'You keep your eyes of her, Joseph. She's taken.'

That was the way it was his father and the old man, joking, talking and exchanging stories, relaxed in each other's company. But his father never asked Joseph who had bashed him or what had happened. Sean asked him about it on one of their trips home.

'I figure if he wants to tell me, he will.'

Marbles and Other Mysteries

The September holidays were coming, Sean hoped Joseph would be out of the hospital by then. School was good, with Harry Smythe nowhere to be seen.

It was a cold day, a southerly wind swirled around the playground. Berty White was in a short-sleeved shirt and school cap, his shorts showing stubby legs. The tip of his nose and cheeks were scarlet, his nose was running, but he showed no discomfort other than rubbing his hands together before he had his shot at marbles. Johnny and Sean were decked out in long-sleeved, heavy woollen shirts, school jumpers and caps.

'Bloody hell, Berty, do you feel anything?' Johnny grumbled. He handed over one of his prized twisters.

'I guess I'm just good at marbles.'

'I mean, don't you feel the cold, its bloody freezing, brass monkey stuff. My fingers are gonna fall off, no wonder you're bloody beating me.'

'Berty beats us on warm days too.'

Johnny looked at Sean sourly. 'Yeh, I suppose your right, Butts.'

'My dad says that the Smythes are leaving town.' Berty was setting up the next game. 'You gonna play, Sean?'

The news snapped Sean to full attention.

'When are the Smythes leaving?'

'Dad says they've sold the business and are leaving for Melbourne in the next few days. It's bloody quick. He says they got an offer too good to refuse. Old man Smythe was in for a haircut and bragging about it. My dad calls him the fat slug bastard. He says he was cleaning up the back of the slug's neck after his haircut when he cut him. The fat slug wouldn't stop bleeding. Smythe started swearing and cursing, calling my dad a useless bloody bastard and more. There was blood all over his collar. My dad had some of that stuff they use for haemorrhoids. He dabbed some of that on, it always works, but the blood just wouldn't stop. Strangest thing, my dad said.'

Berty set up some prized marbles in a centre ring, Sean did the same.

'Who'd buy that produce store?' Johnny hesitated about putting his best marbles in the middle.

'Johnny, if you're gonna only put colours in the middle, you'll have to put four to one cat's eye at least.'

'You're a bloody bandit, Berty!' Johnny replied, hands on hips.

'You gotta play by the rules, Johnny.'

'We should have a bloody handicap when we play sharks like you.'

'I said who'd bloody wanna buy that broken down produce store of the Smythes?' Sean interjected. 'Most everyone goes to the Joneses.'

Berty studied one of his cat's eyes. 'Dad didn't say, but he did say if his bloody livelihood didn't depend on it he would have cut the bloody bastard's throat, after what he did to that poor old black bastard.'

'What d'ya mean, Berty? How's your dad know who done that to Joseph?'

'Everyone knows that Smythe and a few of his drinkin' mates fixed up the poor bastard. They even took young Harry, that's how stupid they are.'

Sean fumbled with his marbles, they dropped to the ground. 'But how does everyone know?'

Berty rubbed his hands and took aim. 'Those drinkin' mates of Smythe's aren't the smartest arseholes around. My dad always says if they drink, they talk. How do you think my dad gets his tips on the horses? It's only that your soul mate Joseph can't remember or is not game enough to tell the coppers.'

'My soul mate? Where d'ya get that from?'

Berty shrugged his shoulders.

'Are we playing marbles or bloody standing here like sheilas?' Johnny interrupted.

Berty bent over to place his shot marble on the large outer ring. Sean blocked his way.

'Listen, Berty.'

Berty braced up. Johnny stepped back. Then Sean laughed. He could not help smiling at the freckled red head.

Sean shook his head 'Just as well I like you, you bloody bastard.'

'I should be so lucky, having a friend like you, nothing but bloody trouble.'

'When you blokes have finished cuddling, can we get on with the bloody marbles?' Johnny grumbled.

'Anyway, my dad says you're a bloody saint, what you did for that blackfella.'

'My mum said the same,' Johnny said. 'It was like you almost lifted him off the bed, like Jesus or bloody Saint Patrick himself.'

'Bloody hell! Where'd this all come from? I told you what happened.'

Johnny bored on. 'My Dad said that you were speaking in strange languages like the apostles at Pentecost. My Mum said she is going to speak to Father Mc Duff about it.'

'Anyway, Berty, if everyone knows, why hasn't Shorty Malone got the New South Wales coppers onto Smythe?'

'Dad says if the old bloke doesn't talk or know who it is, it won't stand up before the magistrate. Even if he did, it's the black's word against theirs.'

'S'pose'

'It's the bloody truth,' Johnny agreed. 'For a smart fella you sure are dumb sometimes.'

He bent down and fired his shot marble on a beautiful curving trajectory that knocked one of Sean's prized flecks out of the circle.

'Christ, Johnny, where d'ya get a shot like that from?' Sean groaned.

Johnny puffed his chest out. 'You're not the only one who does miracles!'

Sean's mother put her right index finger under his chin and lifted his face up.

'Why so mournful?' When he didn't answer, she continued. 'Slip into the laundry Sean, and fire up the boiler and fill the copper.'

Sean was hanging clothes on the clothes hoist in front of the fire when his dad came home.

'How was school? No flack over that thing with Joseph?'

'A little.'

'Yeh, well, you have caused quite a stir. Rexy must have told everyone he met. I'm bloody fed up with telling people what happened. It's strange that the *Caladonian Times* didn't run a story. Normally they're right onto that sort of thing.' His father put his back to the fire, and indicated to Sean to do the same. He stood there arching and rubbing his back. 'That rag is owned by Campbell, like most everything else in Caladonia. Funny, not even a line on it. Shorty Malone came around today for a chat. Asked me about the whole matter again. The old bloke won't tell him anything. He reckons he's holding back. It's got him stumped. "I'd like to nail that Smythe bastard and his mates," those were his very words.'

'The cops know who did it!' Berty was right. Everyone knew.

'Yeh, they knew the next day. Big mouths from Morang can't keep their mouths shut. Everyone knows, but if the old man won't talk and those blokes back each other up, there's nothing the cops can do.'

'Why don't they question them?'

'They have. Smythe said he was out bush cutting firewood with his mates from Morang. They all tell the same bloody story, they even have the firewood to prove it. The cops had to take action against Smythe and his mates in Morang last night, anyway. They were all out drinkin' at the top pub, seems they disturbed the peace. One ended up in hospital and the others won't be doing too much for a couple of days. Seems likely the same thing may happen to Smythe tonight on his way home from Kelly's.'

'You mean Shorty is gonna go over there and bash him up?'

'No, not Shorty. His mates in New South Wales are just gonna make sure the peace is kept in Caladonia tonight. Seems the Chief Inspector from Morang is a bit pissed off with a disturbance of the peace in his district, race relations being jeopardised and everything. He knows Joseph from way back and thinks he's a top bloke. He's not gonna have any old bloke treated like that, even if he is a black-fella.'

'Isn't that against the law?' Sean was not sure that he understood what his father was telling him.

'Not if they're disturbing the peace. The peelers will have it worked out, don't you worry, not that I totally agree with it. Them blokes should have told the cops the bloody truth, it would have been easier for them. They'll be marked men around here, especially if the Chief Inspector has it in for them. Jesus, this is a good fire,' he rubbed his back again. 'Oh, another thing, I'd better tell you before you hear it from someone else. Shorty said those blokes had stacked paper and wood against the far end of the building. It had been lit but went out. They stacked it against the kerosene can chimney, the dickheads. They would have burned that poor old bastard to death. Shorty thinks they must have heard you or seen you coming, and ran off. There would've been nothing left. It would have looked as though the old man was smoking or the chimney had caught alight or something. It's lucky you came along, Sean, otherwise Joseph would be dead meat, and not much meat left at that.'

Sean felt sick. 'Berty told me the Smythes are leaving town pretty soon.'

'That's what I've heard. Strange anyone would buy that dump. The whole bloody thing is strange.'

Kutkuti Man

Sean and his dad went to the hospital that night. It was one of those clear wintry evenings that hurt your nose. The stars shimmered.

'Bloody beautiful, isn't it?' His father stopped halfway along the hospital path and looked up.

'Yeh, bloody beautiful,' Sean agreed. It was like the stars were drawing him to them. He stood on his tiptoes. He wanted to reach up and touch them.

'See there, the Southern Cross in the middle of the sky, and the two stars just to the left and slightly higher, they are called the pointers.' Sean nodded. He had studied the Southern Cross at school. 'The brightest one is Alpha Centauri, the closest star to us, only four-and-a-half light years away. The one to the left and slightly higher again, what do you think that is? I'll give you a clue. It's a nasty, big insect. Check your boots in the bush for these before putting them on.'

'A scorpion.'

'Right. Now follow the scorpion's tale down. What do you see? Your mum likes to make a brew in these with her girlfriends?' "A teapot.' By Jingo, you're right. It's the teapot.'

'Well, well, a couple of stargazers.' The soft lilt of Sister Louise's voice could not be mistaken. 'I like Hercules, don't you, Mr Buttenberg? Over there on the far left and very high.'

Jim Buttenberg looked once again into the sky. 'Yes, yes, you're right, it's a strong time of year. See the lion, Leo, on the right side directly opposite?'

'Surely it is a strong time of year,' the sister replied, 'in the sky anyway.' She looked at Sean. 'Well, young Sean, you look very well. No effects from the other night?'

'No, Sister, thank you.'

'I suspect you're going in to see Mr Wirrinum? Tell him I will be in a bit later. I have an unfortunate in casualty who I need to look at.'

As they entered through the front door a nurse burst through the casualty door. 'Oh, Sister, thank God you are here! We can't stop Mr Smythe's bleeding, we can't stop the bleeding!'

The Sister placed a hand on the nurse's arm and turned to Sean and his father. 'Good evening, gentlemen.'

'Good evening, Sister.'

Then she was gone in her slow purposeful way, the nurse trailing in her wake. Sean glanced at this dad.

They were surprised to find Joseph sitting in a big cane chair, the injured lower limb encased in plaster resting on a stool, the left arm held tightly in a sling. His head had a small dressing. He was in a pair of red and white chequered pyjamas. His good foot rested easily on the floor in a new red easy slipper. A throw rug lay haphazardly across his middle. He was breathing easily, his eyes bright. The smile lines filled out as he saw them.

'It bin good to see ya Mr Jim and Sean.'

'Good to see you looking so well, Joseph.' Sean's dad pulled up a couple of chairs.

'Well, Mr Jim, it bin good tucker in here and I bin started to eat like a horse. That Sister Louise, she bin bring me milk drink with all kind of stuff in it. It make me strong I bin thinkin.'

'You'll soon be up and around.'

'Sister Hildegard she bin say I stay in hut at end of the convent, that be when I get up to walkin.'

'Good stuff.'

'She and the nuns they give me the pyjamas. The Church of England ladies they come in today and they give me this blanket here.' He fingered the throw rug. 'Then Father Riley, you know that little priest fella, he comes in and asks me about slippers and he comes back later with these ones here. He bin say the CWL ladies wanted to buy me something. I bin lucky fella this day.'

'Yeh,' his father laughed, 'all you need is the Presbyterians and you'll have a clean sweep.'

Nurse Harradine bustled over from the nurses station. 'Good evening, Mr Buttenberg, Sean,' she whispered in her wispy, soft voice.

'Oh that bin why I bin lucky also,' Joseph croaked. 'This one here bin takin care of this old blackfella.' He looked at Sean and laughed.

Nurse Harradine blushed. 'Are you comfortable, Mr Wirrinum?'

'Yeh, I bin plenty comfortable, thank you missy, no pain.'

'Good.' She straightened the pillow behind him. 'Mr Buttenberg, would you like a cup of tea? Sean, a glass of milk?'

'Thank you, Nurse.' His father nodded appreciatory as she moved away to the nurses station.

'Good girl, that. You know she is going out with that young fella Duggan, runs his father's spread out on the Moulamein road. He occasionally does some work for me, good fella with the swing saw, strong as an ox.'

'Thank you,' Sean's dad said when Nurse Harradine returned with the drinks and biscuits. Sean wondered what had happened to her plans for travel and the big city, getting away from the country.

'Some fellas over there in Morang broke the peace the other night,' Sean's dad said to Joseph. 'Ended up they were severely dealt with by the peelers.'

'Yeh I bin hear that.'

'I've been told they are to leave the district.'

The old man nodded, and sipped his tea.

'I understand Smythe is in casualty.'

Joseph looked up at the ceiling, his face creased into a faint look of bemusement. 'When I was a youngun, like this one here, my grandfather he tell me the story of the Kutkuti. There was a man in the group he bin not too good around the place, he bin lazy fella and not keep his place too good, he not treat his women right, he not like to tell the truth too often, he not listen to the old fellas and the law too well. We bin camped at a waterhole up in the Gwai Gwai country, that mean red country in white fella lingo, long way from here near that river fella the Murrumbidgee.' The old man paused. Sean and his dad listened carefully. 'Old time the Bindaree fellas they sometime fight these Gwai Gwai, they fierce people they bin liken our land and our kore. That bin mean women, Mr Jim. We like theirs, too. We have lot of big time fight with these fellas, but when white bloke come, that stop. Anyhow, we not fightin this time, we bin camped with those fella, the men fella only, having good food and Korobra together. This Kutkuti, ah, sorry sometime I bin speak old Bindaree lingo...'

'Quite all right, Joseph,' Sean's dad assured him.

'Kutkuti, that mean crooked or bent, he hold bad feelin about one of them Gwai fella. He old this fella but he have a younger Bindaree women, and two older Gwai women, that how it be sometime in the old time. Maybe this Kutkuti he want this old Gwai man's women, but maybe I think he did not like Gwai people anyway. This Gwai fella he be a Gooweera, that mean holy or spirit man, Mr Jim. The Kutkuti fella he go there one time when all other fella out dancing and huntin. That old fella he stay in his camp doin his dreamin. That Kutkuti beat him up good time and steal his stones. When all the other fella they come back they bin very unhappy at what been going on. That Gooweera man he not bin able to say too much, but he tell them that Nooralie big spirit fella he will fix this Kutkuti man up good time and that they should maybe stay with the Korobra. They do not need to punish him too much, Nooralie will punish him plenty. That Kutkuti go away, but he not only bad he also not smart, he have to show one of the old man's stone to another fella. That other fella he tell the old men. They grab him and take him back to Korobra.'

'Go on,' Sean's dad said when Joseph hesitated.

'This bin short story tellin, not long one,' Joseph said. 'The old fella Gwai and Bindaree they have talk and bring this Kutkuti man out. They spear this man but the Gooweera man say only spear him in one leg. He bin have big shame, he have no pride in his backbone. He bin slink away like a stray dog, he bin go away and join another group far away, near where the white moth come from. But Nooralie he knows him even there, he cannot get away, he cannot hide from this spirit fella. He slowly get sick and thin and he just die little by little. All time he never happy.'

'Sure was a hell of a punishment for beating up an old man, even if he was, what did you say, a Gooweera?'

'Yeh, Gooweera, a spirit fella or one who has the dreamin.'

'Are you a Gooweera, Joseph?'

There was silence before the old man answered. 'Some of them blackfella they bin say it, but a fella have to have the dreamin every day for all time.' He laughed. 'This old man he speakem too much sometime.'

Sean's dad finished his tea and placed his cup on the tray. Sean placed his glass beside it. His dad was looking at Joseph, waiting for him to continue.

'That Kutkuti man, he cursed alright. Some fella say he bin cursed by the Gooweera man, but it bin him curse himself by breaking Nooralie law. It no matter if he beatem up Gooweera man or other fella, he bin cursed. But it him that curse himself.'

'Did the Gwai Gwai and the Bindaree fight after this Kutkuti thing?'

'Ah, the Bindaree they make gift to makem thing right for Gwai Gooweera. They give him pelts, bora stone and the blue stone from the mountain far away, they give him a young women, so that he bin end up with four. He bin must be mighty big Gooweera fella or maybe, that one, he do not sleep at night.' The men's laughter echoed around the near-empty ward. The nurses looked up. Joseph held his side and tried to stifle his mirth. 'They bin have their fight now and later, but not over Kutkuti, just over the normal thing what they always fight on, the land or the women.'

'That's the way of it. As Billy Shakespeare said, "we go to gain a little patch of ground that hath in it no profit but the name."'

The old man nodded in agreement. 'That bloke Billy Shakespeare he must have been a dreamin fella. A good bloke to have round the campfire.'

As they stepped out of the hospital, the night sky greeted them again but it was lessened by the arc lamps lighting up the casualty ambulance entry. In the beam Sean could see the Austin ambulance, its back doors open and the inside light on. The engine was running. Leaning against the ambulance, a man was smoking a cigarette. He called out.

'Jim Buts! Jim Buts!'

'Bill O'Grady? Is that you, Bill?'

'How ya going, Jim? G'day, Sean. You been to see the old fella?' The ambulance driver spoke in a slow, laconic drawl. 'How's he going?'

'Better than expected. He's sitting up, quite chirpy.'

'Tough old bloke.'

'He's been through a lot, that's for sure.'

'I've got a job on, a bleeder. Me and one of the blokes and a nurse from here, we gotta get him to Melbourne.' Bill took a long drag on his cigarette. 'Jim, can you give Angry Symons a call and tell him I can't do his Ford tomorrow. I'll be away till probably six or seven.'

'No worries, Bill.'

'Need anything down in the big smoke?'

Bottlebrush

The next day at school Johnny was felled in a marking contest. Sean and Berty dragged him over to the shelter shed. Sean noted the grazed nose, the blood on his shorts and a cut on his knee.

Johnny coughed and spat out blood. 'Bloody hell, what happened?'

'Ya tried to take a specky, bloody show pony.' Johnny looked at Sean with clouded eyes, and shook his head.

'Jesus, Sean, mum's gonna kill me,' he groaned.

Sean went over to the toilets and tore a long strip of toilet paper and dunked it under the water bubbler. He ran back to Johnny. His head was between his knees and there was blood on the bluemetal.

'Sit up, mate.' He dabbed the soft wet tissue on Johnny's nose.

Johnny nearly jumped off the bench. 'Take it easy!'

'Bloody hell! I felt like I got hit by a bloody train.'

'Well, you did back into a big pack.'

Johnny took a swig of water from the empty quart bottle that Sean had nicked from the verandah and filled with water. 'Yeh well maybe next time I'll be bloody more careful.' He touched his fingers lightly to his nose. 'You see your mate Joseph last night? My dad's going over to help them Koonarook fellas with the hut on Sunday. I'm going too. We can muck around.' 'Yeh, that'll be great' 'bloody beaudy, yeh, I'll bring my jacks over, we need to beat that little bastard Berty.'

'Right, hey?'

'You know Smythe's dad was in hospital last night? They took him to Melbourne.'

'Nah, but I heard that all the Smythes are gone, moved out of their house and everything. Harry's not comin back. My mum said Smythe's mother has family in Melbourne.'

'Hey, Johnny, talkin' bout family, is that bloke McCarthy, you know, the chief gardener at Campbell's, is he related to you? You know, the one I work for?'

Johnny looked at him and put his head between his knees again. 'He's my bloody great uncle, my dad's uncle.'

'So why don't you get a job there with me on Saturdays, we can work together?'

'No chance, them McCarthys don't speak to us. Same old bullshit, you know. My dad's dad married a Catholic, caused a helluva stink with all the bloody Presbyterians. If we see them down the street we pretend they're not there, same with them.'

At work the next day Sean took a lot of notice of Mr McCarthy as he doled out work and instructions. He did not look like a Presbyterian who hated Catholics. He was joking and talking to the workers. Many of them were Catholics. Sean could see the family resemblance.

'This morning you'll sweep the verandah around the house. Take a wheelbarrow and a soft broom and a straw broom, also a flat shovel for any rubbish.'

'Yes, sir.'

'And, Sean, I do not have to remind you to keep the noise down and stay out of people's way around the house? Good boy, you should have that done by morning tea.'

Sean gathered the tools together and headed up the path to the house. He looked up, its bulk reared before him. At the massive verandah, a set of steps led to a side door, where his father must have gone that first day when he had spoken to Mr Campbell. At the back was a ramp onto the verandah. He looked along the huge expanse of sandstone paving and again at the huge edifice, he felt small.

Sean started to sweep, cutting the verandah into sections. He swept about six feet then turned sideways, and swept towards the outside. He collected the debris as he went, and shovelled it into the barrow. His dad always said that if the job looks big, cut it into small sections. If you do each section one at a time, you'll soon knock it over.

'Hello,' a high-pitched girl's voice interrupted his thoughts. 'Would you like a glass of lemonade?'

Sean looked around. Standing on the verandah was one of the most beautiful girls he had ever seen. She was tall but well rounded, her face was long and angular with high cheek bones. Large white eyes with huge brown irises and long curving black lashes looked at him. Her skin was the colour of amber, hair black as coal but held in a tight coil beneath a small doily. She wore a white blouse held at the throat by a clasp, and embroidered on the left side with the lions crest. It contrasted starkly with the darker skin, and fell from the well rounded ample mounds of her breasts to a tiny waist, at which a belt held the dark green skirt that fell below her knees. Two dark stockinged legs emerged from the skirt and her feet were covered in stout, no nonsense, black shiny house shoes. In her outstretched hands was a metal tray with a gold-rimmed glass emblazoned with the house crest. A small, delicate plate with jam biscuits rested beside it.

Sean stared at her.

The girl tried again. She smiled widely, revealing two rows of pearl-like teeth. She took a step towards him. 'Would you like a glass of lemonade?'

Sean dropped his broom, which clattered on the verandah. He

took off his cap. 'Yes, ma'am, thank you, ma'am,' he stammered.

'Nelly. My name is Nelly,' she purred, and the smile broke over him again.

'Yes, ma'am, ah, Nelly,' he managed.

'Mrs Henderson sent me to give you lemonade after she saw you working so hard out here.'

'Mrs Henderson?' He took the proffered lemonade, and the biscuits. The girl was still smiling. Sean thought this must be what angels look like.

'Mrs Henderson, the head housekeeper. You are Sean Buttenberg?' she intoned in a musical voice. 'You have been helping in the garden here. You work with that man Jack, the one they call Beak. They say you are a very good worker and know a lot about everything, even though you are only eleven.' Sean blushed. 'They say you are friends with the old black devil man who lives over on the other side of the river . They say you saved his life and that it is all very strange what happened in the hospital.'

Sean was taken aback. He realised now that this was Nelly Ferguson, the girl they had passed on his first day here and of whom Beak had made the tractor joke. 'This lemonade is really good, Nelly. Thank you. I better get back to work.'

Nelly Ferguson was not finished. 'What is the name of your old black man friend? Is he a witchdoctor?'

'Joseph. He's a Gooweera, a holy man.'

'Can he put a curse on you, or point the bone?'

'You are Aboriginal, aren't you, Nelly?' he said. It was her turn to blush. The amber skin went a honey colour. Her face lost its smile, the eyes lost their joy. She took the glass from him, spun around and left. Sean cried out a belated 'thank you'. It was poetry the way she walked.

Sean picked up the broom. He finished the side of the mansion and turned onto the front, which was twice as wide. He did not slacken his pace or change his system. He emptied the barrow a couple of times in the rubbish heap at the back of the shed. The curtains of the huge bay windows on each side of the main entrance were drawn back, and as he worked his way along the verandah, out of the corner of his eyes he saw movement and the comings and goings of people. He heard the subdued murmur of voices and the clunk, clunk of a house awakening. He kept on with his task. The repetition of the job soothed him.

The smell of cigar hit his nostrils and he felt eyes upon him. He kept working. He was nearly finished.

'Hello, Sean.'

He looked up to see Mr Campbell leaning on his cane and looking directly at him. The man was as prim and proper as ever. The tie was red and blue striped this time, the suit with waistcoat a very dark blue, and the grey blue hat had a little red feather in it.

'Never seen a fellow work so hard.'

'Thank you, sir.'

'How is your father?'

'Very busy, sir.'

Mr Campbell moved closer. The cane upon which he leaned had a bright silver point and a silver lions handle.

'They tell me you saved that blackfella from a group of thugs last Saturday.' He took a drag on his cigar and blew into the air. Blue smoke gathered round him like mist on a pond. 'From what I hear tell of it, you saved that blackfella then, and you saved him again at the hospital.'

Sean shifted on his feet and looked down at the broom handle. 'It was just one of those things, sir. I am a friend of Joseph's.'

'You are far too modest, young Buttenberg,' Mr Campbell said humorously. 'Have you been friends with this Joseph for long? It is strange that a good boy like you has made friends with a dirty old blackfella.'

Sean clenched the broom tightly. 'My dad says it's not the colour of a man's skin that counts or the size of his wallet, sir, it's the size of his heart and the richness of his character that matters, sir!'

Mr Campbell nodded. 'Wise man, your father.'

Sean answered calmly, coolly. 'Yes, sir, he is. Joseph is a very wise man also. He's a spirit man, an elder.'

Mr Campbell laughed cruelly. 'And here I thought he was just a simple-minded stinking old no good black bastard, farting, pissed and out of it half the time, a burden like all the rest!'

Sean clenched his teeth. He brought the broom down hard on the verandah. Its thump echoed against the walls of the mansion.

'Settle down, young fellow,' Mr Campbell muttered, 'settle down.'

'Excuse me, sir. May I leave?'

'No,' he snarled. 'I wish to talk to you some more.'

'Sir, see that bush over there?' he pointed over to the Hawthorn hedge. The man squinted to see what he was pointing at. Sean continued harshly, 'It is a callistemon, sir, commonly called a bottlebrush. It has a lot of rough brushes on it.'

Mr Campbell gave Sean a puzzled look. 'Yes, yes, so what has this to do with...'

Sean interrupted. 'Sir, you go and pick one of them, and stick it up your ass, stick your job too!' Sean stormed off.

When he reached the shed he tore off his overalls roughly. He knocked on Mr McCarthy's door.

'Sean, you're early for morning tea.' He stopped as he saw Sean's expression and the overalls in his hand. He stood up and walked around the desk. 'What happened, laddie?'

'Sir, I told Mr Campbell to stick a bottlebrush up his ass!'

The man stopped. His pen clattered to the floor. 'Sean, laddie, why did you do that? I knew he wanted to speak to you. That is why I sent you up there, but...' The man sat down behind his desk again. His forehead beaded with sweat.

'Please say goodbye to Beak and the others. I really liked it here.'

The Race

Sean's mother was devastated. 'Oh, Sean! What are we to do with you and that temper of yours?'

Sean retreated to his room and read a book about King Richard and the third crusade, a tale of treachery, anger, blood and deceit. He heard the big Buick enter the back yard. What would his dad make of this? He wandered out as his dad emerged from the shed with the Gladstone bag in one hand and a small box balanced in the other. His dad's face broke into a broad smile as he saw his son, but then turned to concern.

'Sean, here, take this box, will you? What the hell is the matter?' Sean took the box and shook his head. 'Did you kill Campbell's favourite tree or run over his daughter?'

'Worse. I told him to stick a bottlebrush up his ass.'

'A bottlebrush! We better sit down.' His father led him to the wood heap. He placed their loads down carefully. His father undid his coat and reached for his pipe.

'Now, let's hear it, what happened?'

Sean went through the story. His father hummed and nodded, relit his pipe, adjusted the Akubra on his head.

'Did you tell your mother about this?'

'I told her I had a disagreement with Mr Campbell, not about why, or about the bottlebrush.' He felt better, lighter, having told his dad his story.

'Good boy, I'll fill her in on the details, maybe missing out on the bottlebrush placement. It's strange that Campbell would want to speak to you about Joseph. Why would he have an interest in that?' He paused for a while. 'Sean, I cannot really condone what you said to Campbell, being disrespectful to your employer and elder. But then I do not think he should have used those terms about Joseph. Even if they were true, and they are certainly not, he knew you were friends and his words would be distasteful. But, I don't think he thought he would get the reaction that he got. Maybe he was trying to cower you. People like him never say or do anything without thinking about it, that's the nature of the beast. But why his interest in you and Joseph?' He opened his Gladstone bag and pulled out a newspaper. 'I picked up the *Times* today. Remember they didn't have anything on the assault?' Sean nodded. 'This week they have a big article on police brutality and bullying, asking for an investigation after a number of incidents in the district. Strange, normally the *Times* is all about increasing police powers and cracking down on the lawless element in society. Very strange, the whole business, very strange, indeed. Let's go and have lunch and think on it for a while.'

The next day, Sunday, Sean helped his dad serve the girls breakfast in bed. His mum was having a sleep in, Katy had joined her.

His father gave Sean the plan for the day. 'After Mass we go down to Joseph's place. The fellas are meeting at ten. I have to pick up the trailer. Rexy and a few of the fellas loaded it up during the week. Sean, put my tool belt, good saw and nail box in the boot after we get home from mass. Some of the blokes are doing a sausage sizzle and we'll have a few longnecks when we're finished. God, this coffee is good. Let's get these dishes done.'

His mum and Katy got up to dress for Mass. Sean put on his long trousers and white shirt with school tie and a jumper. He gave his shoes a polish, so his mother would not send him back to clean them or line up a chore for him to do after Mass. His father was dressed in white shirt, dark wide tie, sleeveless pullover and tweed jacket with matching corduroy trousers and highly polished brown boots. He sat at the table drinking coffee and reading the papers. Sean sat beside him reading a book on river animals and fishes.

His mum came out in a close fitting two-piece woollen skirt and top with matching coat and hat. His dad gave a wolf whistle. 'Old father Riley will want to give up his vows when he sees you, Mary.'

'James, stop it. Don't be so disrespectful, and the children.' But she was smiling as she swept into the lounge.

Katy ran in. 'Daddy, look at my new shoes!' She jumped on his knee and bent her leg to show him patent leather red shoes.

'Wow, Katy they look great.' He gave her a hug and a kiss, then stood her up and smoothed down her flared red woollen coat. 'They match your coat.'

'They are only for best, dad. Next year when I go to school, mum is going to buy me some black sandals, like Sean.'

'Where did you buy them, honey?'

'Mrs Hird and mum took me and Martha to Crawford's and we had to try them on. Martha got the same and Andrew got some slippers.' She paused in her banter, suddenly serious. 'Mum said that Martha cannot go to school with me next year, she cannot go to St Joseph's. It's not fair dad, me and Martha are best friends, it's not fair dad!' She cried quietly.

'Katy, Martha is not a Catholic. Only Catholics can go to St Joseph's.'

'It's not fair! If we take Martha to Mass every Sunday, will she be allowed to go to St Joseph's?'

Sean's mum re-entered the kitchen with her missal and rosary beads.

'No, Katy, Martha goes to the Church of England each Sunday, Sunday school.'

'Can I go to her school?' Katy said turning around to face her mother.

'Yes, you could, but Catholic children go to Catholic schools if they can, and the others go to state or private schools. Katy, we cannot change that. That's how it is and always has been, Katy. We want you to be a good Catholic girl.'

'Are the Hirds not good?'

'Yes, of course, they are good people,' Sean's mother sighed. 'They follow their ways and we follow ours, but we can still be friends.'

After mass and morning tea Sean changed and went out to the shed to load up his dad's tools and work belt and then they were off. Koonarook was in its Sunday slumber. Going out of it about a half a mile, they turned onto a gravel road and pulled up in front of a neat workers cottage. A small man came out dressed in tattered blue overalls and an old battered slouch hat. His face was as brown as chewing tobacco and lined like an old horse blanket. It was broken by a ready grin, which showed dark gaps where teeth had once been. The black eyebrows met in the middle and overhung large luminous brown eyes, which picked up the light of the day and threw it back at the onlooker. He moved with a grace that reminded Sean of a cat, and seemed to cover the ground in an amble that was neither walking nor running but something in between. His arms were long and animated, and he wore scuffed old Blundstone boots. His father stepped out of the car and went over to meet him. Sean lowered the window so he could hear them talk.

'Joey, how are you? Long time no see.'

Joey's grin widened. 'Yeh, been shearin. Got home a couple of weeks ago, they bin bloody got their pound of flesh outa me. Walked out of the last shed, up near Gunnedah. The bloody cook was no bloody good, some wog bastard from Sydney. We damn well nearly killed him. He was poisoning us, I reckin. A few of the blokes took him out the back and gave him a workin over, then we walked off, bloody last time I work for Higgins.'

Sean's dad laughed. 'I heard Marty Higgins was a decent enough contractor but a bit skimpy on a few things.'

Joe grimaced. 'Yeh? Well, he won't get anyone to work for him if he doesn't pick up. We'll bloody blackball him, and that's that. We've got the union onto him and he'll be out of business if he doesn't fix it up.'

'You blokes are away for a long time, you need good tucker. Hey, listen. I'm here to pick up the trailer, we're gonna fix up that old man Joseph's hut.'

'I bin hear about that one.' The luminous eyes shifted to Sean. 'That bin your son over there? They say he saved his life.'

'Sean, come over and say hello to Mr Milo.'

Sean got out of the car and offered his hand to the small wiry man. 'Hello, Mr Milo.' The hand he grasped was small, bony and incredibly strong. Its grip was painful.

'You call me Joey, young fella. Any friend of Joseph Wirrinum is a friend of mine, and your father he been my friend ever since he bin come here. He got me in the RSL and helps me with that bloody repat bloody department.'

'We better get moving,' his father said. 'You gonna come down with us Joey?'

'No, I gonna come down a bit later on. I gotta drop a parcel off with the kids. I won't be long. You tell them fellas to save some work for me.'

'Right. The blokes are putting on a barbie, so don't worry about tucker. We'll have a beer after we finish. The mill pub has given us a few longnecks.'

'Righto. Let's get this trailer hooked up.'

The trailer was full of timber, glass, a couple of chairs, work benches and other bits and pieces. They drove in towards town.

'Bloody good bloke, that Joey Milo. He's the gun shearer in this town. Poor bastard was wounded in the shoulder a few miles outa Milne Bay and he gets fevers from the malaria. His ears are a mess. He earned Sergeant stripes and an MM and those repatriation bastards give him the run-around. We'll bloody fix their little red wagon, by bloody jingo we will.'

Someone had fixed up the door of the hut and nailed it shut. The surrounds had been cleaned up as well. Sean and his dad began by opening the door again and moving the red gum logs around the fire back into position. As they worked more men arrived, most with tools and gear, some wheeling barrows. A quick 'g'day' and a few instructions by his dad and they went to it. Someone collected wood and started the fire. Some of the men got to work in the hut, others fixed the bed and the bush furniture. A couple of fellas wheeled in a cedar cupboard. A trio of blokes straightened the chimney and others raked and cleaned up the clearing. Sean saw Joe Milo arrive and start cooking the sausages with Rexy. Through it all there was a constant banter and good natured ribbing.

Johnny McCarthy arrived. 'Sorry, Sean, we were held up. Bloody Aunt Liz from Melbourne arrived yesterd'y and we had to have morning tea with her after mass. Bloody boring, hearing about all the cousins and stuff.'

Sean smiled. 'Still all right for you to stay the night?'

'Yeh, nearly stuffed it, though. Bloody pulled Monica Nuttall's pig tail in Mass. Mum went right off. Anyway what's going on? We got a job to do for the old black bastard?'

'Grab that bag of nails there and help me nail the bark back on.'

They worked on for another hour or so, until the smell of the grilling sausages got too much and they all congregated around the fire, eating the sausages and bread, covered in tomato sauce and topped with onion. The fire surrounds were better than before, with metal rods and stakes supporting the various hooks and plates of a bushman's kitchen. There was a new camp oven and some rough-honed timber chairs placed around it.

Sean and Johnny started a game of marbles. They played chase. Johnny was good at it and was well ahead when their fathers came over.

'How's it going, fellas?'

'Caladonia is well ahead, dad,' said Johnny.

Sean's dad gave them their job for the afternoon. 'You boys do a clean up around the clearing after the fellas are back at work. Collect any rubbish and put it in the trailer. Anything that will burn, throw it on the fire. After that you're free, don't get in the way.'

They picked up scraps and pieces of wood and debris from the work areas. They moved inside the hut, which was neat and orderly. The photos were back in place and some had new frames. In one, a young nun and a group of Aboriginals stood before a tin hut. Sean called out to Johnny.

'Look, who d'ya think that is?'

'Bloody hell! It's Sister Hildegard. A young version, no wrinkles.'

'And Joseph looks like he just got off his horse, get the outfit.'

'Righto boys, out you get. We gotta get this bed back in.'

A group of men brought in the repaired wrought iron bed and placed it back in position. The boys had soon finished their job. Gradually the men finished also, and again gathered around the fire. The longnecks came out, someone produced a box of glasses and the stories flowed as quickly as the beer. Sean and Johnny played marbles in the gathering twilight.

The next morning Sean and Johnny woke up early. They pulled the blankets up to their chins as they talked. Johnny was in a swag beside Sean's bed. Vaporous clouds were produced as their words hit the cold air. They talked about the hut and Joseph. Sean said he would take him down to meet Joseph after he came back from hospital and maybe they could go fishing and hunting.

They were soon up and making the fire. Then out to the chooks, feeding them and collecting the eggs. Sean sent Johnny on to get the milk, which had been dropped off by the milky.

'Bags the cream,' Sean said.

In the kitchen his dad was fully dressed, shaved and cooking eggs and bacon. Sean had expected porridge and toast.

'You boys did a good job yesterday so I'm getting you some decent tucker. Sean, can you make some toast? I've sliced the bread.'

The boys spent the next ten minutes with the long toasting forks in front of the open door of the fire box, turning the thick slices of bread until they were crispy brown and hot. Sean heard the sounds of his mother rising.

'Dad, can I go and see Joseph after school and tell him about his hut?'

'Don't spend too long with him. He'll still be tired. Also, make sure you get permission from the nuns. I'll write you a note to give to Sister Hildegard.'

Johnny and Sean had the compulsory inspection by his mother. She gave them both special lunches, corn beef and pickle sandwiches and cake. After the kiss goodbye for her and Katy they had set off down Kane's Way at a sedate pace.

They pulled up at the edge of the highway that led to the bridge.

Sean Buttenberg cuffed his mate on the shoulder. 'Righto, carrot head, race you to school...'

Kiss from a King Brown

Sean and Johnny sat by themselves. Sean remembering all that had gone on over the last year. What a year and it was not nearly finished yet, now this bloody race from home with Johnny. He thought of Joseph, broken and injured. As he did the Dingarra scar pained and he rubbed it absent mindedly. He looked at his mate and smiled Johnny gave a weak smile back.

They were not to talk or be spoken to. Sean was on one side at the back of the classroom and Johnny on the other. Sean's hands stung and he held his pencil and chalk with difficulty. Sister Rose was cool and detached. She ignored them, except for the essential directions.

Some of the Victorian kids made it to the school at around eleven o'clock but most did not arrive. At play time Sean and Johnny were each given a sheet of spelling to complete. At lunchtime they were instructed to eat their lunches on stools at opposite ends of the verandah. They were then to go on duty. Johnny was to clean up the classroom, Sean to rake and clean the shelter shed. Sean took a rake and moved around the shelter shed, making it smooth and neat. He put rubbish in a hessian bag. His hands could not grasp the rake properly. They seemed paralysed. But other than butterflies in his stomach, he felt good.

He looked up and saw Mrs McCarthy entering the Head Sister's office. She wore her Sunday best, a two-piece light green suite, belted at the waist, an open three-quarter coat to match, pale green gloves and a wide-brimmed hat. She walked hurriedly, her movements quick and jerky. She was a small woman with pale skin and light auburn hair. She knocked on the Head Sister's door, and then entered. Sean was not surprised to see Johnny saunter along and position himself outside the door. Sean watched as his mate stood on one leg, the other balanced against the back wall, his expression one of complete indifference. Bloody cool bugger. Johnny looked at Sean and gave a small underhand wave and a big cheeky grin. The door opened and Sister Hildegard stood there, looking directly at Sean, thunder crossed her face. Sean quickly went about his duties. When he looked up Johnny was gone and the door was closed. Soon Johnny reappeared and retraced his steps along the verandah. He looked neither right nor left but walked quickly back to the classroom. Sean raked the shelter shed again. After five minutes Mrs McCarthy reappeared and also quickly walked away, in the opposite direction, dabbing a hanky to her nose and looking down. Sean kept on working. The other school children kept a wide berth.

Sean saw his mother arrive and walk onto the verandah. She was also dressed as if for Mass. She wore a tidy, navy check dress, the skirt flaring sharply from her waist. Her golden locks bobbed and were partly hidden by a little white and blue hat. She carried a matching bag and pair of white gloves. Before knocking on the door, she turned and scanned the playground. Her eyes locked onto him. He felt the blood rush to his face, and a feeling – was it shame? He gave a subdued wave. She did not return it. Instead, her left knuckle went to her mouth in the familiar gesture. Her face was strained and drawn. She turned, knocked and was swallowed up by the office. Sean kept on raking, going over the same ground again and again.

The Head Sister's door opened again and the Head Sister summoned to him. The door was left open as she retreated inside. Sean made his way over to the verandah. The feeling of dread he had felt before was returning. He entered the office and closed the door slowly. His eyes took a little while to adjust to the light.

'Please sit down, Mr Buttenberg,' Sister Hildegard said sternly.

'Yes, Sister. Hello, mum,' he said looking at his mother's distraught face.

'Hello, Sean,' his mother said wearily, without looking at him.

Sean's eyes adjusted. His mother was seated stiffly in the adjacent seat, her back ramrod straight. Her feet were tucked neatly under the chair, bag perched tidily on her lap, slender fingers clutching its top. She looked straight at the Sister behind the big table. Sean also sat up straight. His back did not touch the chair.

'Mr Buttenberg, I have given your mother a brief description of what has happened here today, including the punishment you have received thus far. You are not expected to say anything at this meeting. I am sure that your mother and father will have plenty to say to you on your return home. You will have a chance then to tell your story to them, and I hope that you are a bit more forthcoming then what I heard this morning. Your mother is aware that you are to be interviewed by the New South Wales police and has given permission for this. I will be present at this meeting. She is aware that you are not to ride home and she has indicated to me that your father will be picking you up this afternoon. You are to wait at the school, is that understood? Mrs Buttenberg, do you have anything to say?'

His mother shifted in her seat. For the first time she looked at Sean. Sean noted that she had been crying. Even the careful application of makeup could not hide that fact. The blue irises of her eyes stood out like beacons, her nose was flaring, and he could see the pulsing of the raised veins on her neck. She looked back at the sister as she began to speak quietly.

'I am very grateful to you, Sister Hildegard, for everything you have done in disciplining Sean. Please be assured that Sean's father and I will also be taking measures to make it known to Sean the seriousness of this matter.' Her gaze turned back to Sean, her face was grave and she continued to speak in measured tones. 'Sean, your father and I are very disappointed in what you did this morning. I have spoken to him and he is very concerned. He indicated to me that he will deal with you this afternoon. He also said that you are to tell the police the whole and complete story of what happened. I want you to know, Sean, that you have inflicted great heartache and pain to me and your father. You have also inconvenienced many people on both sides of the river. Please do not do anything to shame us further. Furthermore, it was a very dangerous and silly act you and Johnny performed. It could have resulted in death and injury to yourselves or other people.' She reached into her bag and pulled out a tiny hanky and dabbed her nose, then turned back to the sister. 'Thank you, Sister Hildegard, that is all I have to say.'

Sister Hildegard nodded, and then looked at Sean. 'You may go, Mr Buttenberg, and please tell Sister Rose to call me.'

'Yes, Sister.' Sean rose. He hesitated, then he whispered, 'I'm sorry, mum, I...'

The Sister cut him off. 'You may go, Mr Buttenberg!'

Sean looked at the Sister, then at his mum. She turned her head away from him. 'Goodbye, mum.'

'Goodbye, Sean,' his mother said sadly without looking at him.

The New South Wales police were two burly fellows in dark blue trousers and coats, peaked military-style hats and wary looks. Sean and Johnny were interviewed in Sister Hildegard's office. The police sat in two extra chairs that had been placed at right angles in front of the big desk. Sister Hildegard sat in her usual spot. The policemen introduced themselves as Senior Sergeant O'Grady, and Senior Constable Riley. Senior Constable Riley took notes in a large loose-leaf notebook. To Sean, it felt like an interrogation rather than an interview. They fired question after question and the boys answered with short, sharp replies. If they tried to say too much the police cut them off. Each boy was expected to answer in turn.

'Did you ride your bikes recklessly from Kane's Way in Koona-rook this morning?'

'We had a race. Sir.'

'Was it reckless?'

'Yes, sir, I guess.'

'Did you nearly run into Mr Filo, the manager of the co-op?'

'He nearly ran into us.'

'Did you nearly hit his car with your bikes?'

'Yes, sir.'

The questioning continued for more than an hour. At the end of it Sean felt numb. He felt tired. He limped back to the classroom with Johnny. Thank God the school day was almost over. By the time they got back to class the kids were tidying and packing up to go home.

'Mr Buttenberg and Mr McCarthy, please wait behind for a moment,' Sister Rose said as the class was leaving. As Mary Addison passed his desk she smiled and pressed a note onto the desk. Sean rapidly dragged it into his pocket. Sister Rose waited for all to leave, then closed the door carefully, after checking that no one was in the outside corridor. She asked them to sit together in one desk. She sat in the desk directly in front of them. Leaning back, she addressed them quietly.

'I know you boys have had a big day and I will not keep you long. You have done a reckless thing, something young boys like you are prone to do. You have been and are going to be punished for some time yet. Be that as it may, you need to think carefully about what has happened, and make some proper conclusions. If during this time I can be of some help, please come and speak to me. It will be just be between you and me.' She looked at them each in turn and smiled. She adjusted her veil and leaned back again. 'Alright, be off with you and, please, not too much haste now.' She laughed. Sean gave a tired smile in return. 'Oh, before you go, Sister Hildegard has given me a sheet of road safety questions for you to answer and hand in tomorrow.'

Sean thought of Joseph but he knew that it would be useless to even ask his father about seeing him tonight. Everything was buggered, and all for a bloody race. It was a great bloody race though.

Sean's father and Mr McCarthy were waiting just outside the main gate. They were lounging against the Buick and talking easily, sharing a joke. The look on their faces and the way they were shaking, the guffaws coming from them, indicated it was a good one. When they saw Sean and Johnny they stopped laughing and stood up straight, the humour lines gave way to ones of concern. Or was it retribution?

'How you blokes going?' Sean's father said good naturedly, stepping forward.

'Not too bad,' Sean replied cautiously.

'Alright, Mr Buttenberg,' Johnny mumbled. He stood beside his father, who patted his shoulder.

'Better get these malcontents home, eh,' Johnny's father said. He was a larger version of Johnny, red hair and white alpine skin with multiple freckles, a small but wiry stature.

'Seeya. Jim. Sean, take care, will be in touch.'

'No worries, Dick. Say hello to Helen for me.'

Mr McCarthy drove off in his shiny, dark blue Ford. Its rounded shape and neat lines were tidy. The tyres were white walled.

Sean got into their car. His father was about to start it, when he hesitated. He turned to Sean, looking at him with interest across the wide bench seat.

'Tell me, Sean, what happened to make you and Johnny greater pariahs in this town then foxes in a hen house?'

'What's a pariah, dad?'

'An outsider or somebody not wanted, like lepers in the old days.'

'Like Aboriginals today or Jews in Germany during the war?'

'Yeh, something like that. Anyway, back to today.'

Sean started slowly and deliberately. He told his dad the whole saga, piece by piece, as he remembered it. His father nodded and at some points asked for more details

Sean's dad rubbed the stubble on his chin. 'Bloody hell!'

Sean smiled in spite of the situation.

'What's that bit about you not crying when you got the cuts from Sister Hildegard? I hear her straps are like kisses from a King Brown.'

'Well, when I was getting the strap it was like I was in a trance, like I was connected but not. It was really scary. It was like that Dingarra bloke, the lightning, filled my brain and took over.'

'The lightning character Joseph told you about, who makes the lightning and the storm?' His dad looked through the windscreen of the big car and into the distance. Sean finally said, 'I still felt the pain, dad. It was terrible and my hands and arms are still sore, but it was like I was somewhere else.'

'Mmm,' his father murmured. 'I've heard similar tales from the war, men who get taken over by some outside force or their mind. It often led to remarkable feats of bravery and self-sacrifice. We could talk on that forever, but right now we will get you home. Wonder what's for tea.'

As they approached the bridge, all was quiet. His father drove very slowly and stopped on the approach. He glanced in the rear vision mirror.

'Where was Jimmy Owen's Blitz when you passed it?'

'Nearly half way across. Mr Willis was waiting on the other side. We passed him and went onto the bridge. I was in front.' Sean sat up and leaned forward to see over the bonnet of the big car.

'Couldn't have been much bloody room,' his father surmised.

'There wasn't. A few feet either way.'

'Bloody hell! It's a wonder you buggers weren't crushed like bloody meat ants on a Sunday picnic.'

They drove slowly across the bridge. There were tremendous gashes and scour marks on its surface, and numerous tyre marks. Part of the side rail facing the pedestrian walkway on their left had been dismantled, replaced by white ribbon and temporary fencing.

'They had to call in a lifter from the mill to move the logs, and a work gang to dismantle some of the railing. Bloody big job,' his father observed dryly.

Sean sunk down in the seat. They drove towards home. The swamp on the left looked inviting. If he could only hide out there for a few weeks.

'Anyway, the councils on both sides have been asking for an upgrade on that bridge for years. I think this may spur them on. If it wasn't you, Sean, it would have been someone else, some other incident. I think you've had enough physical punishment, but mum is pretty upset. I'll speak to her tonight about it and see what she thinks. It's fairly hard to control recklessness and foolishness in eleven-year-old fellas. It's a learning process, I suppose. I'm just happy no one was killed. Bloody silly, it was, Sean. Bloody stupid, actually.'

Bloody Idiot

As they pulled into the back yard, Katy raced out to meet them. His father quietened Katy's excited questions and took her inside. His mother stood at the back door in her waisted cotton print dress, house cardigan and apron. He dragged himself to her, and looked up apprehensively. She opened her arms and crushed him into her. Her tears stung his neck and face. Her sobs shook his body, his tears came stinging his cheeks, mingled with hers wetting her dress. He looked up at her. She brushed his dishevelled hair back with the softness of her hand, and she hugged him again.

'I'm sorry, mum,' he whispered.

'Sean, you could have been killed!'

'I was an idiot.'

'Yes, you were, Sean. Yes you were.'

Later on she lathered his bruised, red and swollen hands with Rawleighs Balm. He thought he was lucky to have his mum and dad, lucky to be alive, lucky to have that Dingarra fella in his brain. He shook his head. What in the hell was going on with him? He had got off lightly. Any other parents would have killed him. He wondered what had happened to Johnny, getting him into all this shit. His mother agreed that he'd had enough physical punishment and was being punished adequately at school, but they had imposed some further conditions. He ticked them off in his mind: no sweets, no bike for a month, no stopovers, no grand finale, which was on next week between Koonarook and Morang. That hurt. His Dad and a few of his mates were all heading to Morang for the day. Extra chores, like an extra line of stove wood to be stacked along the fence. And he was to paint the shed over the school holidays. Yes, he had got off lightly.

The next day at school was a long one. Sean had to walk to school. He tried to keep a low profile but everyone saw him. Mr Filo blinked his lights at him as he drove past. He walked on. The school bus came trundling past and all the kids hung out and waved and shouted at him. Brian McPhee leaned out the window.

'How bout blocking the bridge again, Sean?' he shouted. 'We could do with another day off.'

Sean ignored him and kept trudging on. People and kids from school passed him on their bikes and in their cars. They all looked at him. He knew they were talking about him. He crossed to the other side of the road. The remnants of the black stump were there. He touched its jagged curves. When he took his hands away, they were black, against the red welts. They certainly were like the kiss of a King Brown. The track wound seductively into the swamp. His mother had given him strict instructions to walk straight to school. No deviating off course for any reason. He was given permission to visit Joseph after school, but only for fifteen minutes and only if he asked permission of the nuns. Then he was to walk straight home.

He climbed the approach to the big suspension bridge. Its grey form was sharp against the bright blue of the morning sky. He noticed a collection of people on the pedestrian footway of the bridge, leaning against the temporary railing. There was animated discussion and much pointing and gesturing. Sean pulled his school cap over his eyes and increased his pace. He needed to make his way through and around them. But they noticed him and there was a hush. As a group, they looked at him as he went by. He kept his eyes down and quickly made his way past. As he drew away from them he noted the hum of voices start up again. He reached the end of the bridge. Senior Constable Riley was surveying the scene. When he saw Sean he started to swing the truncheon in his hand. Sean put his head down again and kept on walking. He could feel the peeler's eyes boring into him.

He strove down into Church Street, looking right. High Street was coming alive. The pub bars on each corner were silent of course, but their kitchens and dining rooms were full and their back stables and garages were busy as people packed up and moved on to their day's business. The merchants were out sweeping the streets, chatting, loading goods in or having a smoke before the day's work began. Drays and trucks were pulling into Sadler's Lane on the high side and Rivers Lane on the river side. The colour and intensity always amazed him. He stood and watched the ebb and flow.

Then he saw Berty White coming toward him. The little round figure was the most untidy person in the whole street. His shirt hung out, his cap was marked and sitting sideways, and his shorts were torn and ragged. His school jumper had holes in it and was too big. He had a smile on his face and it got bigger when he saw Sean.

'How ya going mate?'

'Yeh, good.'

'Town is back to normal today,' Berty observed, looking back down High Street.

'Yeh,' Sean replied sourly. They began walking.

'Hey, Sean, remember I was telling you about the swamp? They are gonna clear it and make it into one of those new caravan park things. My dad reckons Campbell is behind it. He wants to turn this place into a recreational paradise that was the very words his bookkeeper used when he told my dad.'

Sean felt uneasy. 'They can't do that. Joseph and the Aboriginals own that land. It's theirs. Why would anyone want to drive around with a caravan behind them? Doesn't make sense.'

'I dunno about that, but the bookkeeper reckons it's the coming thing for holidays, what with all these new cars.'

They were coming up to the school. Sean remembered the note from Mary Addison. He pulled it out. On it, scrawled neatly, were the words, 'Bad luck for what happened. All the best Mary A.' He smiled. He looked up and saw Johnny and hastily stuffed it back into his pocket.

Separation, no play, work and more homework were the order of the day again, but during lunch hour Johnny managed to sneak back into the classroom that Sean was sweeping. He was supposed to be cleaning the toilets. Johnny told him his home punishments. He had had a similar experience to Sean, except his mother had given him a couple of whacks across the backside. He had extra jobs, no playing with Sean, no comics, no movies at the Lyric during the holidays. The rest of the day dragged on. Sean dropped Mary Addison's note back on her desk, with a big 'thank you' on the back of it during a break in class when Sister Rose wasn't watching and the other students were distracted by Blighty Roberts getting into trouble again for drawing rude pictures. Mary turned from the front seat and gave him a smile.

During the day Sean asked Sister Rose if he could visit Joseph. He had been discharged from the hospital and was now staying in the cottage at the convent. Sister Rose said she would speak to Sister Hildegard. Well, that's the end of that, Sean thought. But just as they were about to leave for afternoon play time Sister Rose pulled him aside and said Sister Hildegard said it would be alright to see Joseph, but only for ten minutes.

Ponde Ponderings

After school Sean wandered out onto the playground and watched as it emptied, then he turned left instead of right and headed up along the school and then down its other side and onto O'Connor Street. This street formed a corner with Church Street and upon this corner sat the school. Right next door was St Bartholomew's Church, a big imposing redbrick edifice raised its massive bulwark into the sky. Sean always thought that its square turreted belltower made it look unbalanced. The bell it housed called the faithful to the Angelus and Mass daily. He looked at the massive red-gum double doors, open to the world, and the big brick steps leading up to them. People were making their way in and out. Sean hurried past not, wanting to waste any time. Next to the church was the presbytery, a sprawling weatherboard Federation-style building with verandahs all around and set in a massive Australian garden. It looked as though it belonged out on a station, not in the middle of town. Sean noticed Jack O'Dea trimming the bushes along the fence. He had six children, four of them at Saint Josephs. Sean raised his hat.

'G'day, Mr O'Dea.'

The man straightened up slowly and recognised Sean. 'G'day, Sean. How is your father?'

'Well, sir.'

Sean hurried on. Next to the presbytery was the convent. It was a long, neat single-story building. It was painted white with light tan trim. Its iron lattice work showed the symbol of the order, the heart of Mary with a cross and sword imbedded in it. The convent was surrounded by simple gardens of lawn and shrubs and large well-established deciduous trees. This place was out of bounds to all, including the parish priest, unless there was an invite from the nuns, but it was not the practice of the nuns to host events here. Visitors did not get past the front atrium.

It was surprising, then, that Joseph should be here. He was staying in a simple two-room timber slab and red-gum shingle cottage that stood by itself in the far corner of the large block. Sean knew from repeated religious instruction and history lessons, that more than fifty years before, on the request of the local bishop, the order had sent two nuns from Ireland to establish a school. They had started their school in the simple timber building that had served as the church, school and assembly hall for the growing community of Catholic workers and their families who were coming to the district as timber workers, farmers and labourers. This building had since been replaced by the redbrick church.

Sean went through the front gate and angled off over the soft turf towards the cottage. He trod slowly. He was on hallowed ground. He looked around. It felt as though someone was watching him. Joseph was sitting outside the little cottage in a large cane chair, basking in the afternoon sun. His injured leg rested on a timber milk crate, and a pipe drooped from his mouth. His left arm was in a simple triangular sling, glaringly white against the grey flannel shirt and the dark trousers. The left leg of the trousers was split to allow for the plaster. The red braces Sean noted were new, their chrome keepers bright in the sunlight, but the felt hat was the same battered Akubra. Joseph was dozing. Sean stood off and gently uttered, 'I see you, Ulwai.' His face creased in a smile, and the lips parted to show the starkly white teeth. He moved in his seat. Sean saw that his right hand held a walking cane, gnarled and scarred. It moved up and tapped Sean's leg.

'Ah, Maiyarare, Maiyarare, I see you, and it be good.' Sean went up to the old man and hugged him gently. 'You bin catch me in a doze. This place be a good place to sleep when the sun warm me and fill me with dreamin.'

'It's a nice place for you, grandfather.'

'Them nuns they bin feed me all the time, bringem me cake and scone, biscuits and fruitcake. I stay here this place much longer it make me like that Ponde fella fish fat and lazy after the spring time rain.'

Sean nodded as he settled himself on a small cane chair. 'How long are you staying here, Ulwai?'

'I bin here maybe this week and then I bin go home, to my place, next week, if that Sister Louise let me go. She a strong women that one, what she say go, it no matter what the doctor bin say. She make the law with me, where I go, to what I bin do at this time.' The old man smiled.

'She's a strong lady, Ulwai.'

'Yeh, maybe it be good she a nun lady, no marry, she bin hard on a fella maybe he run away to another place if she boss him. Ah, but she good to this old fella here. Maybe it bin good she marry that dead fella Jesus that got killed on that cross. He maybe cannot run away from her,' Joseph laughed. Sean smiled, but looked around warily. He could still sense someone watching him. 'That Sister Hildegard, the boss nun at the school, she bin come over and talk. She tell me you bin plenty of trouble yesterday with the bridge.'

Sean grimaced. 'Ah, yeh me and Johnny McCarthy were racing to school from my place, and we were like going a bit too fast and acting like idiots and a timber jinker had to stop suddenly and dropped its load on the bridge.'

'It always seem to me that the young fella he lucky to make it to be an old fella sometimes. You bin look around them animals like even that Ponde fella, your totem. He bin start off with many brothers and sisters but not many reach it to be like him, all big fat and round. But then he must reach it by taking his chance but maybe he not take chance, he do not need to.'

Sean nodded. 'I know, Joseph. It was a bit reckless.'

The man looked at the boy softly. 'You know we speak of this Ponde fella a lot today, he bin in my dreamin. Well he may be well fed and not need a feed, he just have to float there under his log in that water, he no need to move into the danger. But them white fellas, the smart ones, they bin know this big Ponde he have a weakness that will let them have him for their pan. He know that this Ponde fish he sometimes not think before he act. They know if they put a lure bait in his space that big Ponde he lose his temper and chase that lure bait, then he be hooked up and end up in their pan. Sometime that Ponde should wait before he chases that pretend lure fella. He plenty smart most time, but sometime he act a bit quick.'

Sean could almost feel the pain of the hook. 'You're right, grand-father. I sometimes act with haste, just like that Ponde.'

Joseph laughed. 'We all that way sometime. We have to be brave some days no matter what it cost, even up to your life, that the man way, the Wundara way. But, most time it much better to think about what you may gonna die for, see if it worth it. If so, then alright, do it.'

'What would it be worth dying for, Ulwai?'

'That another thing about getting this old fella way, it bin make you see that there not many things that bin worth the dyin for, maybe your people, your land, your dreamin, that all, not much else in this place.' He looked around the grounds of the nunnery and faraway. Across the grass a squadron of Willy Wagtails were swooping and gathering up the afternoon harvest. The old man studied them closely and smiled. 'Yep, we all bin have to be do what we made to do, like them Gumalkoolin there. They have to get them insect, they bin no other choice. That sometime with us, we have no choice in it, we do what we do and the Wundara way take us into that place where the death maybe gonna be.'

'I am not a Wundara.'

'Ah, you gonna be sometime, I bin dreamin it. Hey, it bin getting too serious here, all this talken about death and fightin. It will come soon enough. Let us have one of them nun cakes, they makem good stuff them nuns. Maybe they put all their time into the food as they havem no man.' He laughed again. 'On that table there.' He pointed to a table against the wall. 'You have one young fella, it give you strength before you move on.'

Sean went over to the table and lifted an embroidered cover with a little blue stitching of Mary on it. It covered half a dozen cupcakes which sat daintily on a crisp white doily. They were filled with cream and made into butterfly shapes with red jelly, and looked too good to eat. Sean gave one to Joseph and ate one himself.

'These are bloody good, Joseph,' Sean said with appreciation. 'Joseph, I have to go, otherwise mum will kill me. Ulwai, thank you for being my friend.'

Dying Race

When he got home Sean was busy with chores and making a start on the firewood stack. His dad was late also. They both went into the house together at nightfall. Sean washed up for tea and went to the kitchen. Katy was helping her mother make a rice pudding. She was stirring the milk and flour into the rice as Sean watched. His little sister was growing up, going to school next year. She joked and babbled away as she stirred. It was comforting for Sean to see her and his mum together. It made him think about what Joseph had said about what was worth dying for.

Sean sat at the table, his head cupped in one hand, his eyes half closed. Suddenly, his dad slapped him gently on the back.

'You falling asleep, Sean? We haven't had tea yet.'

'I'm a bit sleepy, dad. I saw Joseph. He looks really well and the nuns are spoiling him rotten.'

'So I heard,' his dad said sitting down beside him. His mum turned around.

'There's a delegation from the ladies of the parish going to see Sister Hildegard tomorrow about Joseph. They think it is a disgrace and a moral outrage to have a man and a blackfella staying there. They asked me to go along but I told them Joseph was a friend of ours and a real gentleman.'

'What did they say to that, Mary?'

'Some of them gave me a real look. I think I have gone down in their estimation. I do not think I will be chairwoman of the CWL any time soon. The meeting broke up soon after and quite a few of the ladies I normally speak to, ignored me.'

'There are a lot of small-minded people around, Mary.'

'Well, with what happened with Sean at the hospital and all that, and the bridge thing, I think they are starting to wonder about me.' Sean's mother wiped her hands with agitation on her apron.

'Maybe now we will find out who our real friends are,' Sean's dad replied. There was a pause as his mother got her thoughts together.

'Yes, maybe. They do have a point though, Jim. As they told me, no male, white or black, has ever been allowed to stay in the nun's grounds.'

'Yeh, but Joseph is nearly crippled. He's got no family close, and the blackfellas' places are out of town and crowded to the hilt. Plus I get the feeling that most of the blackfellas are uncomfortable having a man like him around. Anyway, he and Sister Hildegard have known each other for years. Did I tell you we saw a picture of them together when they were young? It was in his hut.'

His mother shook her head. 'No, you didn't tell me.'

'Well, Sister Hildegard must have given it to him. It's nice.'

'Having met Joseph now, I think it is quite all right. He is a wonderful man,' his mother said sincerely.

'That's the trouble with bigots. Most of them speak from a position of complete ignorance.'

His mother served the tea and they ate in silence for some time.

'Anyway,' his mother said, 'Maria Jolly said that they are a dying race, these Aboriginals, and all would be soon gone or integrated into society. What do you think about that, James?'

Sean's dad pushed a carrot around his plate with his fork, then looked up. 'I think she should keep her opinions to herself. But it's a common enough view. With the breakdown of their traditional ways and the intermarriage that has occurred, it may have some truth in it. But it's a culture worth preserving. Why, even the stuff that Sean has learned from Joseph and that I've gleaned by speaking to him a few times is so unique and valuable it would be sad if it was lost. A tragedy, I think. Just think if we lost our culture, our rich heritage which snakes back to the ancient Greeks and beyond. Just think if we lost that, what kind of world it would be. Just think if you had no knowledge of God or where you came from, Mary.'

'Yes, yes, I understand. Most people only see the bad side of the black people, the ones lying in the gutter and making a nuisance of themselves. They do not see their attachment to the land, their culture or the spiritual side.'

Sean's dad was animated now. 'It's like most Protestants only see idol worshipping papists instead of fellow Christians when they think of Catholics, and we hold similar views about them in reverse, sinners who have left the one true faith etcetera, all based on ignorance.'

'This is very deep, James, for the tea table.' She got up, the sweet smell of rice pudding filled the air as she took it from the stove.

'Well, that's Maria Jolly for you. She knows how to stir things up.'

The smell of the rice pudding made Sean's mouth water. His dad was sipping his tea. He turned to Sean.

'How you like walking to school, Sean?'

'I hate it, dad.' 'Everyone saw me, even Mr Willis, though he pretended not to.'

'Those who play must pay, Sean.' He laughed.

'Yeh, I know. That cop Riley saw me also. I thought he was going to arrest me if I cracked a smile.'

'You did cause them a hell of a lot of work, according to Shorty

Malone. They can't charge you but they're going to issue a warning. Shorty said they also have to write a report for the Roads Board and the councils. There's going to be action on this.'

'Dad, Berty White was telling me Mr Campbell has bought the mill here from Mr Hughes.'

His father nodded. 'He's right. The place is in a mess. Ever since he lost his son a few years ago, old Hughes has let the place slide. The other son in Melbourne is useless apparently.'

His mum placed the sweets on the table. The crusty top was smothered in cream and milk. Sean sprinkled sugar on his, as did the rest of the family.

'This is great, mum.'

'Thank you Sean, but you should thank Katy also. She helped me.'

'Thank you, Katy.'

Katy giggled. Sean's mother played with her sweets, she moved it around the bowl and finally tasted it. 'Why would Mr Campbell buy the mill, Jim?'

'Great pudding, Katy.' His huge pile of rice pudding was rapidly disappearing. 'To answer your question, Mary, Campbell owns nearly everything in the district now. This will near complete his monopoly. I've heard he has eyes on the swamp next.' Sean's dad looked at him as he said this.

'What on earth would he do with that? It's just a swamp,' she said, then hastily added, 'except, of course, for Joseph's place.'

'From what I'm led to believe and from what I can deduce, he wants to turn it into a park for caravans and campers, and he'll use the portion up near the mill to expand it for bigger loads and jinkers. The timber industry is getting bigger and bigger, Mary, only the big mechanised ones will survive, those that put through volume.'

Sean interjected. The uneasy feeling he had felt when Berty first told him about this had returned. 'But dad...'

'Sean, hear me out before you speak. The other factor is that once he has control of the mill, he controls Koonarook. Old Hughsey was easy going and didn't worry. But this bloke is all about power and monopolies. Half of the blokes in this town work at the mill. A lot of contractors cart to it, and most of the businesses in this place depend on it. By owning the mill he controls both sides of the Murray. Now, Sean what did you have to say?'

'The Bindaree, Joseph's people, they own the swamp. It's sacred. It's where the Tamba Tamba are.'

Sean's dad answered slowly, carefully. 'Sean, these people are barely recognised, they're not on the rolls or anything. How can they own anything?'

'But there's a paper given to Joseph's grandfather by the first Campbell. It gives them that land forever. It was in their truce or treaty, so they'd stop attacking the Campbells.'

'Be that as it may Sean, it's probably long gone. As of right now, that land is Crown land managed on behalf of the government by the council. They can do what they like with it. Like it or not, that's how it is.'

'It's not fair, dad! How can we save a dying race if they take away their bloody holy places?'

Sean's mother bristled. 'Sean Buttenberg, you may have a point but it is no use making it with profanity at my table.'

'Sorry, mum. Sorry, dad,' Sean mumbled. His dad smiled, and nodded his head knowingly.

His mother saw the look. 'James, no need to encourage the boy.'

Katy broke the tension by squealing at her baby doll lying over by the doorway.

'You can go now Katy. Go and get you pyjamas. Sean, you may start the dishes.'

'I thought I might have some more sweets,' Sean said hopefully.

'A mouth that swears at my table does not deserve any more sweets.'

'Yes, mum.' Sean dragged himself up. His dad cleared the table and his mother went off to help Katy change.

'The other thing,' his dad said as he picked up a tea towel, 'is they plan to put a weir downstream to make the water level even all year round. They also need it for a new water treatment plant.'

'But that will kill all the fish and change how they breed and everything.'

'I know, Sean, I know, but that is progress.'

'Joseph said if the Tamba go the river will die. That's what he believes.'

'I don't know about that, but I know these black people have a special relationship to this place. But for the river to die? That's a bit extreme.'

'But Joseph has been right about a lot of bloody things.' Sean looked around quickly. His father laughed and swished him over the head with the tea towel.

'You live dangerously, Sean.'

Just then his mother called out. 'Get changed for bed, please, Sean.'

After he had changed they sat by the fire. His mother was knitting and his father was reading a report. Katy was playing with her dolls and telling his mother about their ailments. Sean was happy she was not trying to fix him. He was trying to get his jack moves right. The scatters move had him. If he could master it, he would give Berty White a run for his money.

'You'll wear those jacks out, Sean.' His father's report had slumped to his knee.

Sean stopped his playing. 'I want to beat Berty. He's a freak.'

'His dad is a bit the same. Great on the figures for the SP, no one can beat him. He has it all worked out in his head. He's a bit of a freak too. They reckon a bloke can go in there and ask about a race or a horse and he can quote him a price off his head and all the other runners as well. He's incredible.'

'How's he on haircuts, dad?'

'Pretty good, I think.'

'Dad, you know how Joseph was bashed? Do you think that has anything to do with Mr Campbell buying the mill and wanting the swamp?'

His father thought for a while. 'It does seem curious, the whole business. It's a very serious accusation, Sean, one I wouldn't repeat to anyone else.'

'The blokes who did it, they meant to kill him. They wanted to get rid of his hut. It was only that they probably saw or heard me coming that they stopped.'

'And then the way Mr Campbell acted toward you that last day at his place was odd.'

Sean's jacks lay idle. This new idea eased his mind in one way. Perhaps it was not his fight with Harry Smythe at the swamp, and Joseph's frightening appearance, that had led to the attack on Joseph. However, an attack on an old man was one thing, bad as it was, but this was an attack on his whole way of life, his culture, on thousands of years of history and against his future.

Yerta Yerta

The week went quickly. The isolation from Johnny was not watertight, and they worked out a courier system with Berty. It was confirmed that they would meet at the B17 on Saturday afternoon at about two o'clock. It was also confirmed that if that failed they would get in contact through Berty. Sean was not allowed to go and see Joseph again until the last day of term. His mother said it was not good for Joseph to be getting excited over his antics, and he needed his rest. The last day of school couldn't go fast enough. It was the usual cleaning up, finishing up stuff. Sister Hildegard, at the end of term school assembly, gave the usual speech about being good boys, girls and Catholics with their prayers and Mass attendance. Then they were all herded into St Bartholomew's for an end of term Mass and Father O'Loughlin, the older of the two priests in Caladonia, gave the same sermon as Sister Hildegard. Sean struggled to stay awake as he droned on and on.

Sean found Joseph in the same chair as three days before. He was carving a message stick with his pocket knife. There were pictures of men and fish on it, but he knew not to ask what it was about. The old man would tell him if he needed to. Joseph's face changed from concentration into a big smile.

'Ah, you bin comin to see this old dry stick another time.'

'Yes, Ulwai. You are looking better.'

'Maiyarare, I am feeling better. It makes me better to see you also.' Sean blushed at the compliment. The old man continued. 'You bin feel like a walk around these grounds here? That Sister Louise she say I have to walk sometime, otherwise I be too stiff and seize up.'

He put the message stick aside and grabbed his walking stick. He struggled to get up, and waved Sean away when he tried to help him. 'I bin gotta get myself up here, otherwise that sister she won't let me home.'

Joseph pushed the chair from under him and, although crooked, he was standing. His left foot was off the ground and the stick supported him. With a gaited motion he headed off. Sean followed.

'It bin good to walk among the grass and air again. It bin good to feel the sun on my back. It bin good to be alive for a little while longer.'

'When were you born, Joseph?'

The old man stopped. He rested his two hands on his stick and looked up to the sky. 'That gonna be a long time, longem time, not much around here then, just the white fella Campbell station and a few huts.'

'Ulwai, I meant which year?'

'Ah, what year it now?'

'It's 1955.'

'1955,' Joseph repeated, deep in thought. 'It not be nineteen something, it be eighteen something when I be born. Yeh, longem time this fella be on this place. Government fella he ask me same question. I do not know. He tell me I born 1880, first of January, but he bin just makin up those numbers. How he know when I born? He not there, he not that smart that government fella.'

'Was he filling out a form?'

The old man nodded, 'Yeh, he have paper he bin fillin out.'

'What do you remember happening around here when you were young? Was there something going on you remember?'

Joseph looked up at the sky again. 'Yeh, they bin buildin that bridge there, that one go cross river, no more have to swim across, punt across, boat across. I only a young fella, like to wander a lot them days. It be after big flood sometime.'

They started to walk again. Sean knew from history lessons at school that the Murray had flooded in 1890 and 1917, amongst other times, but the bridge had been opened in 1905, so he must mean between 1890 and1905. So around 1880 would probably be right, making Joseph about seventy-five. Bloody old.

They walked slowly across the lawn. The old man was a bit straighter now. 'Those times the Warde Yallock he a different fella. He bin very low in the hot times then he get big in the cold time. It seem to be that these white fella bin change this. They clever fella, it make it good for growin things, but Warde Yallock, he not as good as them time, then big fish, plenty tucker. The water be a lot clearer then. You could see the fish and spear them. Not so clear now.'

Sean closed his eyes, he could see the Ponde, his totem, clearly in the deep water of the river. What would happen to the Ponde if the mill was expanded and a new weir built? He would die and the river would never be the same.'Ulwai, I've been told that they might try and take the swamp and make it into some kind of caravan park and add some land to the mill.'

The old man stopped. 'I bin wondering when you gonna hear that.'

Sean gasped. 'You know already?'

'I bin hearing some story about this. It very strange what some fella bin tell me. That be my place, where my people do their dreamin long time. That a special place for us.'

'What can we do about it?'

'This is a new place for me to stand. I only little fella in this big place, but I bin dreamin. If Bindaree no longer have Tamba Tamba place, then Nooralie very angry. This place be punished and then it is death for this place. Nooralie, he let the Marmoo loose and devils will come. I bin dreamin this.' The old man's face was creased in a sadness Sean had never seen before. They continued walking and reached a seat under a big flowering gum. The old man sat and looked to where he had come from. The cottage was about fifty yards away. 'One time I bin do that in quick time. Now, even if not crook, I take long time. It that way with men, animal fella, all live things. They same, grow old and lay down in Yerilla, our mother. From it we come and in the end all thing goem back. You know, Maiyarare, in my lingo the place where we get our drink, likem Billabong or waterhole, it be called namma. It also same for woman's breasts, they called namma kore. We live only because Yerilla our mother provide for us. When we no longer take care of her we gonna die. That the law and no one, white fella, blackfella, can change that law. I dunno how to do it, to stop it. I old but this place, this Yerta Yerta place, it always bin here, it be here longem time, it mean little what we do. It will be Nooralie and the Yerta Yerta and the law that will be here, they bin gonna be here all-time after all we fella all be gone.' The old man's face glowed, his hands on the walking stick were clasped, one over the other, firmly.

They sat in silence. Joseph seemed almost as resigned as Sean's parents to the inevitability of progress, but at least he had faith that Nooralie was in charge. But surely something could be done. Something had to be done! Mr Campbell couldn't just sweep away Joseph and the Tamba Tamba.

Sean changed the subject. 'Grandfather, will you be home next week, for the holidays?'

'Yeh, I think maybe it be Monday, Tuesday, if Sister Louise let me.

Sister Hildegard she drive me home. She bin sayin they gonna look after me well, them sisters.'

'I'll see you there. I have a lot of jobs on but I have some time to spend in the swamp.'

'It will be good to be warmed by my own fire, and to share tea with you, Maiyarare.'

'Maybe we can go fishing again.'

The old man smiled. 'You makem me like young fella agin, fishin, huntin and walkin in the bush, ah I bin like that. Maiyarare, you walk this fella backem to hut here.'

'Yes, Ulwai.'

Ralphs Fall

Sean walked back along O'Connor Street and past the nun's quarters it was quiet. He noted the blinds were up on some of the windows now and the chimneys billowing smoke. Next door the church was still open but it was also quiet. The school, when he passed it, was locked up and deserted. He turned left into Church Street and ambled down towards the bridge. On his left High Street was doing its usual Friday evening trade. The pubs were full, Kelly's on the left, the river pub on the right, men spilling out into the street. There was a good-natured hum, punctuated every now and then by a shout, loud laugh or guffaw. The rapid rise and fall of glasses was the one constant. The men were dressed in in working clothes; overalls, moleskins, and flannels intersperced by business suits and sports jackets. Being Friday this was the biggest swill of the week and the most raucous. Sean kept a wide birth. He had seen the effects of rapid drinking before and knew it was something to be avoided.

Further down the road, about six shops from the river pub, Sean saw Nick the Greek's fish and chip shop, as usual doing a roaring trade. People were crowded into its small space and out onto the street, where they waited for their order. Nick's fat little wife or one of his four shapely daughters, with white skin and black hair, could occasionally be seen bringing out orders wrapped in newspapers. His dad said that Nick's place was one of the best businesses in town, with cash money and constant turnover. Cars were parked here and there, but Sean knew that most of the blokes from the swill would walk home. It was not uncommon to see men staggering home, singing or talking animatedly. The constabulary from both sides of the river made patrols at about six or seven on foot and by vehicle, making sure the pubs closed and the stragglers and inebriated got home. Troublemakers normally ended up with a warning or biff over the ears. Repeat offenders were locked up for the night.

Sean was about to cross High Street and head up to the bridge when he heard his name being called coarsely.

'Hey you, Buttenberg, gonna close the bridge down tonight!'

Sean looked around. He saw a group of truck drivers standing on the edge of the swill. They were all young, with blue singlets and big black belts holding up grey or green baggy trousers. They were laughing and spilling beer. One of his dad's favourite sayings resounded in his head. 'You cannot deal with a mad dog. Walk away if you can, but if you can't, hit him with the biggest stick you can find.' Sean knew very well to walk away. He turned his back to the throng. But the voice bellowed again.

'Hey, you little shit, aren't you gonna answer me? I lost a morning's work over you and your mate closing that bridge.'

Sean spun around as a big bullock of a man stepped towards him. One of his mates grabbed his arm.

'Hey, Ralph, leave the kid.'

Ralph shook him off snarling. 'Someone should give this kid a kick up the arse, and maybe I'm the man to do it.'

His mates had stopped grinning now. 'Leave it Ralph. The kid was only doin' what we've all done,' a wiry, dark man in the group shouted, but Ralph shook his head.

'Nah. I'm gonna give this kid a hiding. He's a bloody nuisance.'

Ralph swayed on his feet, his face going redder. Some of the truck drivers turned away, which emboldened Ralph further. He yelled ferociously at Sean. 'Come here you little bastard!'

The swill went quiet, an unnatural silence, a menacing silence. Sean was bewildered, undecided as to what to do. He hoped one of Ralph's mates would stop him. He knew he would have to move fast if Ralph came at him.

'I am sorry, sir, for any problems I caused you, but I must get home.'

Ralph took another step toward him. His breathing was heavy, his fists clenched, his mouth dribbling. Suddenly there was a stir in the swill. The truck drivers parted for a group of older men. Sean recognised his father and some of the other faces were familiar; Rex, Mr O'Dea, Mr McCarthy and others. His father nodded to Sean.

'Stay where you are, Sean,' he said quietly as he faced the big truck driver. 'Got a problem Ralph?' he asked the drunken man serenely.

The big brute looked at his mates. They had faded into the swill. His eyes narrowed and he spat at the ground. 'He's a fuckin little cunt!' He directed a lightning round arm punch at the head of Jim Buttenberg.

His fist found only space. Sean's dad had ducked. He pivoted on his left foot, throwing his right one forward and catching the meat of Ralph's lower leg. The man lost his balance as Jim Buttenberg swung his leg viciously back pulling the big man off his feet. Ralph lost control. His feet flew forwards into the air, his arms flailed, he landed on his backside. Sean's dad stood over him, poised in a semi-crouched, combat position, his arms cocked like pistons, his legs slightly bent as he slowly rocked backwards and forwards, poised to deliver another strike. He did not have to. Ralph's mates manhandled the shocked and dishevelled man to his feet. Jim Buttenberg's mates came and stood around and behind him.

'Sorry, Jim. Ralph's a bit pissed,' his wiry, dark friend offered.

'No worries, Golly. Get him home, will ya, before he gets into any more bloody trouble.'

The young truckies dragged the humbled man away. Sean's dad lowered his arms and looked around at his son.

'How ya going mate, I'll buy you a raspberry. I'm nearly finished here but always time for one more.'

Sean joined his father's group as they stood around talking about tomorrow's game between Morang and Koonarook. Most of the town was going to cheer on the boys. Sean was bitterly disappointed that he wasn't going. He would be cutting wood and painting the shed. His father's group did not dwell on the encounter with Ralph. It was just one of those things.

'Don't worry about mum, Sean,' his father turned to him. 'I've asked Shirley to phone and tell her you're with me. After you finish your drink you can run down and order some fish and chips at Nick's. Wait down there for me. I'll be there shortly.' His dad gave him an envelope. On the outside was written 'Four fish, two bobs worth of chips, four potato cakes'. Inside the envelope Sean could feel the money.

He made his way through the swill and along the top end of High Street under the verandahs. He crossed over to Nick's. The crowd was still there. He knew a lot of them from church, school and around. 'G'days' were exchanged as he edged through the crowd. People waited patiently and in a queue to place their order. Finally he made it to the counter. He could barely see over it. Big Nick had his back to the throng. The sweat made his white shirt stick to his back. The four bays of hot oil bubbled franticly with frying fish and chips. Beside him, also with her back to him, was one of his daughters, flipping and browning hamburgers and toasted sandwiches on a huge grill plate. The smell of the cooking was overwhelming. He handed his envelope to another daughter at the cash register. She read it out to him and asked his name.

'Ah, Sean,' she repeated in haltingly Greek English. She was beautiful. Her black hair was swept back into a neat bun and a little dolly cap posed upon her head. Her skin was crystal white, her eyes black and lively. High cheekbones and vivid red lips provided a contrast. She wore a white lace shirt, and through its light sheen Sean saw the outlines of a bra enclosing very big namma. Sean missed his cue. She was talking to him from far away.

'Sean, we will call you in about fifteen minutes. My mama or sister will bring it out for you.' She touched his hand to gain his attention.

Her touch was like a lightning bolt.

'Sean, we will call you in about fifteen minutes. My mama or sister will bring it out for you all right.'

'Sorry, yeh, alright.'

She smiled at him. He stumbled away and made his way out of the shop.

Sean leaned against the bike rack and looked at the picture of the mermaid painted on the window of Nick's. Golden locks covered her strategically, she had the aspect of a playful child swimming through the ocean. Her shape contrasted markedly with Nick's outline, bent over his work on the other side of the glass. The proper name of the shop was The Mermaid, but everyone called it Nick's.

'Sean, how ya going?' It was his dad. His face slightly flushed and relaxed as he sat next to Sean on the bike rack and followed Sean's gaze to the mermaid and Nick, his wife and daughters. 'Dunno how a man so ugly can have such daughters, it's bloody got me beat.'

Sean looked at his father. His father looked at him.

'Dad, I didn't say anything to that Ralph bloke.'

'Yeh, I know. Ralph Harris is bloody hopeless when he gets a few drinks in him. All the Harrises are the same. He'll wake up in the morning and not remember a thing. Golly will take care of him.'

'Golly, the short dark bloke?'

'Yeh, good bloke. He and Ralph are partners, jinker drivers for the mill.'

'Is he Aboriginal?'

'Nah, they say his grandfather was an Afghan came over to drive the camels in South Australia somewhere. He drifted here after the war. No one can pronounce his name, Ali something, so they call him Golly. Bloody hard worker.'

'Where d'ya learn to put a bloke down like that, dad?'

His father smiled. 'Learned a few tricks in the war, Sean. They come in handy sometimes. Mind you do not say a word to your mother. She'll just worry, nothing like a worried woman to cramp a man. Anyway, it only takes a feather to knock a drunk down.'

'Mr Sean, Mr Sean!' Nick's wife bellowed. Sean put up his hand, and she delivered the fish and chips.

'Let's go home, Sean. Enough bloody excitement for one night.'

Dreaming Desolation

The first Saturday of the holidays started wistfully for Sean, he got up early when he heard his dad. He was cooking eggs, sausages and bacon.

'Sorry you're not coming with us, should be a cracker of a game.'

Sean nodded. The only thing ahead was painting the shed, but at least he should be able to swing the meeting with Johnny in the swamp.

'It's amazing Caladonia didn't make the grand final this year. The amount of money they spent, it's bloody incredible. I don't think they ever got over losing to us. That was a grand game. I'll never forget that kick by Noah Midjeeri, scoring the point after the siren.'

'Yeh, what a beauty,' Sean agreed. He slowly chewed his bacon.

'Sean, I have been asking around about the swamp and what's going on.' Sean stopped eating. 'The long and the short of it is the council has been asked by the mill for a slice of the swamp along its back so they can expand. It's also been asked by another company for the long-term lease of the remainder. Both companies are owned by Campbell. The veiled threat is if he doesn't get his way, he'll close the mill and throw sixty men out of work. On past performances, it would not be past him. The council will ask the New South Wales State Rivers to put in a weir to keep the river at a constant level.'

Sean poked at the scrambled eggs on his plate. 'It's bad, dad?'

'Yeh, you could say that. The whole bloody council is pro-development, as is probably right in an area like this. It goes with the territory. The next council meeting is a couple of weeks after the holidays. They're going to debate it then. If they get a majority they'll go with it.'

'Can't we do anything?'

His dad stood up from the table taking his plate to the sink. 'I'll think about it. You say Joseph said his grandfather was given a letter by the government giving him or his group this ground forever?'

'Yeh, that was the story he told me.'

'Well, it must be somewhere, probably in government archives. I have an ex-army mate in government records in Melbourne. I'll give him a call, see what comes up. It's our only hope, though I don't think it will do any good.'

Painting must be the worst job in the world, thought Sean. Up and down, up and down, clean and scrape, clean and scrape. He worked all morning, stopping only for morning tea when his mother brought out milk and scones with his favourite apricot jam. His mum and Katy then went to the Hird's. After a while, Sean got into the swing of it, up and down, up and down. The sun beat down and the monotony of the job took him back. It had been extraordinary, the attack, the coming of Dingarra , Joseph , the danger to the swamp, the race and its aftermath. Up and down, up and down. What was to come? Up and down, up and down. He saw lightning and flood, the river blood red, dryness and death, dying cattle and kangaroos, birds and fish, lifeless trees and crops, people with deep hollows under their eyes and the look of skeletons. He heard someone calling, calling, calling his name.

'Sean, Sean, are you alright?'

He turned around. It was hard to focus. It was his mum, and Katy. His sister had her hand in his mothers. They were looking up at him. His mother's face creased with concern.

'Sean, are you alright? I have been calling you for ages.'

Sean looked at them. He had been somewhere else, somewhere frightening. He felt a chill still on him. A power held him.

'Sean, come down from the ladder.'

He slowly moved down the ladder. He put the paint bucket down and the brush on its top. He looked at his mother again. She looked at him closely. Katy was swinging her left leg backwards and forwards.

'I was daydreaming, mum. This painting sure is boring.'

She nodded as she looked at the shed. 'Well, I must say, it seems to be a good job. You are nearly finished. Time for lunch, and then you go and have a play.'

Sean made it to the swamp at around two. The bomber lay in the early afternoon sunshine. Its defiance against the surrounding bush always impressed him, clean, symmetrical lines clashing against the raggedness and jumble of the bush. He climbed up through its belly and into the pilot's seat. He felt again the thrill of imagination that had grabbed him that first time. Two little drop tails were sunning themselves on the canopy directly in front of him. The little blue wren was hustling his hens on the edge of the clearing, out on the river swallows were picking up insects. Suddenly the vision came back. The river was a trickle, dead and dying animals were every-where, locusts filled the air. Fish lay against the banks, their bodies swollen and eaten out. Red gums stood gaunt like sticks against the sky. The lightning crashed, babies cried. The sun baked the land so hard it cracked. Huge fires filled the sky. It was horrible, horrible. A terrible sadness rolled through him.

'Sean, are you a bloody asleep up there?'

It was Johnny. Why was he here, in this thing, this terrible thing?
'Sean, don't play games, you bastard.'

Sean looked down. Johnny picked up a rock and threw it at the cockpit. It landed with a thud near Sean. The drop tails scurried away. Sean leaned over the cockpit and blasted his mate with an imaginary machine gun. 'Nun na nat, nun na nat.'

Johnny pretended to be shot. He bounded into the air, wounded in his gut. He staggered, cried and crashed. Sean burst out laughing.

'Come on up, Johnny, come on up.'

Johnny made a miraculous recovery and scampered up. He scrambled in beside Sean in the co-pilot's seat. Sean put his arm around his shoulders. Johnny responded by giving Sean a mock punch in his stomach. Sean flinched at the pulled blow.

'Mum is giving me hell since the race. My ass is dragging on the ground, all these jobs she has found, lawn mowing, cleaning, sweeping, washing. You name it, I do it. I only got here because I'm supposed to be at my cousin's place. You know, the O'Callaghans. They don't have a phone, so mum can't check. I can only stay an hour or so. I'm not supposed to meet with a crim.'

Sean laughed. 'Yeh, I know how you feel.'

Then they were away, flying the big bomber into a world of bombs, aeroplanes and machine gun fire. They took it in turns to be pilot and co-pilot, bombardier and navigator. The time flew by. Suddenly Johnny interrupted their sortie.

'I gotta go, mate.'

'I'll try and get here on Monday. Tomorrow is a write off with Mass and family stuff.'

It was quiet again. The drop tails came back, as did the blue wren and his hens. Sean left the bomber and followed the track towards Joseph's. As he got nearer he heard voices. He stopped just short of the clearing, crouching behind some saplings. Sister Rose's tall form was not to be mistaken. The brown working habit was covered by a light tan apron, her sleeves rolled up, her veil pulled back. She was sweeping the packed ground around the campfire. From inside the hut Sean saw the occasional swish of a nun's habit. Sister Hildegard appeared from behind the hut, carrying a potted flower. She disappeared into the hut and then reappeared. She seemed to be appraising the area, then she hitched up her skirts and stepped over the low stick and chicken wire fence of the little garden. She bent over and pulled weeds. Sean backed up. He had had enough of nuns, the past week or so. It was a strange world, a world where all was not as it seemed. He went back to attack the meat ants near the bomber.

Sunday was a write off as expected, except for getting up with his dad and helping him clean the Buick. His dad was a bit the worse for wear. The grand finale had been a triumph for Koonarook. The team had come home with a wet sail and from eighteen points down at half time had triumphed by eleven. What a game! What a day! His father had been expansive, in a good mood. Sean had heard the blaring of horns and the roar of cars past their place during the night.

Mass was unusual. Many of the faithful were pale. Father Riley gave his sermon on victory through adversity, 'Like our footy team', and so on and so on. His father was happy to leave promptly after church. He did not have the fortitude to carry on. At home his dad collapsed into his big armchair and slept for three hours, missing Sunday roast.

On Monday Sean continued with painting the shed, cleaning out the chook pen and weeding the veggie garden. Before leaving for work, his father congratulated him on his paint job, and after lunch he headed down to the swamp and the bomber. He waited by the river for Johnny but he didn't show. A superb parrot chewed on twigs in the tree above his head.

The lightning and the picture of despair came to him again. It scared him. He consciously pulled himself away from it. He got up and walked along the river. It had risen overnight even though there had been no rain for a while. They must be letting water down. Sean walked toward Joseph's place. He approached cautiously. He surveyed the hut from the same spot from where he had watched the nuns. To his surprise the old man was there, prodding the fire. He was seated in the same cane chair that had been at the convent. Sean was very still and watched him for a minute or so. The old man's head slowly swivelled in his direction. His dark eyes stared through him. Sean felt discomfited. He stood up and strode over.

'Sorry, grandfather, I was watching you. The last few times I have been here have been interesting.'

The old man nodded and picked up his pipe. 'The sisters were here yesterday,' he laughed. 'Them girls they bin cleanin and plantin vegies. This place it never bin so clean. That Sister Louise she bring me back this morning early before she startem at the hospital. If they feed me any more I bin as wide as that hut there.'

Sean sat down. 'Can I make you a mug of tea, Ulwai?'

'Ah, that would be good, young fella.' Joseph shifted in his seat and moved his injured left leg onto a log. Sean followed the routine.

'This be dam good tea, best I have had in some time.'

'As you said, Ulwai, the brew around your own fire is always the best.'

The old man nodded. 'It bin all depend who make that brew.'

'Grandfather?'

'Yes, Maiyarare?'

'I've been having bad dreams, like during the day, quiet times. Always Dingarra comes with lightning and rain, than drought and fire, but most of all death. It makes me really sad and scared, really sad.'

The old man did not turn his gaze from the fire. He said quietly, 'I bin having the same dreamin. It no look well for this place.'

'You mean, this is going to happen?'

Joseph looked at Sean intently. The lines and creases deep in his face. 'Nothin for sure. We can bin change things, but if the law be broken, the Gunee Yerilla be not taken care of, then maybe it gonna be bad. My fella, the Bindaree, they bin be here long, long time, they not be good all that time, sometime they bin not follow the law. Then Nooralie, he punish us, our mother this earth place, it not feed us or take care of us, we bin gonna die, we turn back to the law. That the only way.'

'But Joseph, my people, the Amerjig, they do not know the law?'

'Ah, the law is very simple mostly, for all fella, not only blackfella. It bin like you take care of other fella like you like him to take care of you. This Gunee Yerilla, she must be treated like you gonna treat your mother, that because she is our mother. That all the law is, it be same one for all fella, no matter what you are. Bindaree havem no church likem white fella. This place here bin like our church, lot of places, trees, hill, river, rocks and sand, they all have some meaning. Our dreamin come from them, our people's spirits live in them. If we no longer be here then we die. If we no longem respect them, we die.'

Sean nodded. They sat in silence. Sean walked over to the pile of logs and carefully put one on the fire. The fire greedily accepted its new member. Sean sat down and Joseph spoke again.

'If the law be broken, grief will come. That go for all fella, white or black. You young fella and your friend, you find this out last week you bin break white fella road law, you have lot of grief.'

'Yeh, that's all it's been since then, bloody grief.'

Beewee Song

When he got home his mother enquired of Joseph, he told her he was doing fine.

'Sister Hildegard told the CWL ladies in no uncertain terms that Joseph could stay as long as it took for him to heal. She said she had never heard of such unchristian things. The CWL ladies, shame on them, have informed her they will be writing to the Bishop and the Mother General of the order. Sister Hildegard told them that was their prerogative and to go right ahead. Sean, if you go down tomorrow, I will make some scones for you to take.'

That night during tea his father said, 'Sean, I have contacted Sam Peters in Melbourne, that bloke I told you about. He's going to do some digging around for me in the government archives. He knows an old friend who works at the Melbourne Museum, an expert on Aboriginal affairs. He's going to get back to me. If there's anything in the records they should be able to find it.'

'If they find anything, what can we do?'

'We might be able to table it at the council meeting, though I don't know really. I'll think about it.'

Sean's mother entered the debate. 'Jim, is this wise? You know you might be standing on a few toes. This development is getting widespread support.'

'I know, Mary, but Joseph's people, if they have a right to that land and they have an agreement, well, we may be able to work in with them. According to what Sean has told me, it is a special place.'

'Mum, it's the heart of the whole land, like Saint Patrick's Cathedral in Melbourne.'

'Well, I think we should be very careful about what we do and how we do it, James.'

'I know, Mary. Most people here have a lot riding on this, but I think we could have something for everybody. We could do the development and preserve significant areas. The ibis rookery could be a drawcard. Anyway, we'll see if Sam can dig up anything.'

Sean's next two weeks were wonderful. He finished his jobs in the morning and was at the swamp by the afternoon. Johnny often made it down and they mounted sorties for bomber command, killed ants, wrestled, played jacks and marbles, went fishing, and chased sleepy goannas and lizards, sneaking up on them as they sunned themselves, and then throwing rocks or trying to catch them. They chased wallabies and kangaroos like Banjees through the bush. They ranged over the swamp and onto Gunpowder Island, and painted themselves like red Indians. Johnny stole some of his sister's paints, and Sean took one of his mother's old lipsticks.

They took fish and goanna to Joseph, who cooked it on the fire. He told them how to cook it and the law to follow. Each animal had its own ritual. The first time they killed a goanna they had taken it to Joseph, sitting by his fire. He was overjoyed to see them bringing in the goanna, which was about three feet long.

'Beewee, Beewee!' he exclaimed and jumped out of his chair, forgetting his injury. The sudden movement caught him as he rose, he flinched, then hobbled over to them. 'Ah, Beewee, you are nunkeri, nunkeri.' He stroked its flanks and looked at it with admiration.

'We brought it for you, grandfather,' Sean said. The old man looked at Sean and then at Johnny. 'This is my mate, Johnny. He was the one who killed it. He can throw a yonnie real good and we made shanghais.'

The old man held out his hand. Johnny grabbed it with enthusiasm.

'Pleased to meet you, Mr Wirrinum.'

'Ah, you bin gotta call me Joseph. If you Sean's mate, you be mate of mine. You share my fire anytime.'

'Ulwai, Johnny hit it and I cut its throat and bled it as you told me. I hung it for a while in a tree and let it bleed.'

'Good fella, Sean, good fella. We cook it now, we have a feast. It bin right time for this Beewee fella to make us strong. He give us his strength, his spirit make you strong.' He stroked its side again. 'We put it in coals, make place for this bloke in fire, need bed of hot coal on bottom and we put some on top. I make damper too.'

Sean and Johnny helped. They ran back and forth to the hut to fetch things he needed.

'Time for a tea, we bin workin so hard we thirsty,' the old man said as they sat back to wait for their feast to cook. 'You fellas bein runnin wild out there on that Gunpowder Island?

'How did you know?'

'Ah, it pretty easy. You have that black mud on your sandal. And that fella Beewee is from that Allue Island, that what we call it. I recognise his markin under his leg, they only come from that place.'

'Wow!' Johnny exclaimed.

Joseph smiled. 'You young fella must always take notice of what is around you. Those little thing they tell you a lot, the seed in the fur, the short nail on a paw, the heavy foot, all animal they same as man, they all different. All things different, no one ever the same. If you see my brother Tamba there in the middle of this place when they flyin they all look the same but they not, they all have different feather, different mark, different colour maybe. Nooralie make us all different, he never make anything bad or rubbish, all he make is good, it all be different. If you remember that you always lookin, you always are findin things.

'We saw snakes to Joseph.'

'You remember Sean no killin King Brown, he our brother.'

Johnny looked at Sean uncomprehending. 'Yeh we left them alone grandfather.'

'Why do they call it Gunpowder Island?' Johnny asked.

'That was in the olden day. They clear the land round here and have to move the big tree root and all that. They store the gunpowder somewhere away from the people. They build a dry store over there. It safe then if it blow up. But Bindaree they call it Allure because that our word for liver and that place, it same shape as a liver, a man liver. It has little rivers and creeks in it like liver.'

Sean watched the lazy tendrils of smoke curling up through the air. Soon the damper was ready and Sean showed Johnny how to drag the camp oven out from the fire and open the lid. The aroma washed over them.

'God that smells good,' cried Johnny.

'Now, Sean, you remove that Beewee, it bin ready now.'

Sean carefully scraped away the hot coals with the fire shovel and gently lifted the reptile out and away from the heat.

'Let it cool bit, then scrape off the coals bit more with those metal spoons over there.'

Under the careful instruction of the old man he and Johnny scraped and exposed the blackened leathery skin of the Beewee. Then Sean took a knife and cut down one side of the spine and then the other. He peeled the hide back, revealing the white, thick flesh. He scooped it up onto three enamel plates and Johnny cut big slices of damper and spread lashings of butter on them. It was delicious, and soon gone. Only the cloudy white fat around the stomach was left. Joseph pointed at the fat with a twig.

'That fat there it be good for lot of things, good for sore joint, it good job for pain, rub it on your hair you never lose it. Sean, you scoop out that fat. Johnny, you grab that tin over there. I keep it for later.'

Sean scooped the fat out from the carcass and put it in the tin. He handed it to Joseph.

'This like gold, it bring me joy.' He scooped a dollop out and rubbed it on his hands and wrists, then through his hair, singing as he did so. '*Beewee, Beewee, murna, murna, matong, matong, mooroop, mooroop, yallambee, yallambee, al, al guana, guana, ngruwar, ngruwar, gora, gora, arr-reedy.* I sing a song in praise of that Beewee fella spirit, he with us now, he never leave us all our lives, he make us strong Wundara.'

Sean and Johnny joined in singing.

'How can you say it never makes you lose hair?' Sean asked when the singing had finished.

'Maiyarare, you bin ever see a bald blackman round here?' Laughter filled the swamp. Then the old man became serious. 'Sean, you must gather up this fella remains. We no longer need him. You put in that bag, you and Johnny must bury him under a tree, you know that Bora Bora tree over on Gunpowder, you know that one? We keep his spirit happy and he no come and makem trouble for us. These Beewee, they special spirit fella for us Bindaree. They part of creation story. We take care of them even if we eat them, they keep us strong.'

Measuring Stick and Council Meeting

By the end of the holidays, Joseph was better. He was walking around with the aid of his stick and even went down to the river sometimes. He would watch Sean and Johnny play in the bomber and helped them fish. The dreaming desolation came and went, but infrequently, not every day.

School began again. Sean still had to walk. The bridge had been fixed and, except for the presence of police around it in the morning, was the same. Sean sat in his place beside Mary Addison. One day when no one was looking she had squeezed his hand as if by accident, but Sean knew it was no accident. Bloody girls, he thought. He could not work them out.

One night his father took him aside and told him something of what was going on. They sat in the lounge, his father looked worried. 'Sean, the council meeting is this Wednesday. I've spoken to our local councillor, Angus McNeil, a cocky. I asked him if the council would consider a joint tourist and mill development with the ibis rookery as centrepiece, and to consider Joseph's position. Angus heard me out and said he'd present any evidence of Aboriginal claims. But it's a done deal. No one in his right mind would oppose this development. We have our work cut out.' His father started to assemble his pipe. He continued. 'Sam Peters phoned from Melbourne. He's sent an extract from the first Lachlan Campbell's journal. Get this Sean, it was donated to the State Library of Victoria by the Campbells. Anyway, in it he discusses a treaty with the local Aborigines. He mentions giving them rations, blankets and even guns. It also details the awarding of a breastplate to a King Joseph. But the most important part mentioned is the fact that they granted them land over the river directly opposite their station. In the journal he calls it Tamba Bindaree and mentions that an ibis rookery stands there.' Sean's father paused and lit his pipe, sucking in the aromatic smoke and letting it loose toward the ceiling.

Sean considered what his dad had said. 'Wow that's great dad!' Sean stood up excited.

'That is as exactly as Joseph told me.'

'Yeh, well, no other paper work can be found at this moment. But he said he'll keep on looking. The parcel with the copy of the extract in it should arrive tomorrow, and then I'll square up with Angus and get him to take it on Wednesday night. I'll be there in the gallery, but I don't hold up much hope. I've been asking around and getting a lot of flak.'

'Sorry, dad.'

'No need to be, Sean. I can't see why they can't have their development and maintain the heritage of the place at the same time, but it's as if I'm speaking a foreign language.'

Sean went to the swamp the next day after school. He walked through the thick undergrowth. The scurry of animals in its lower stories gave away the presence of birds, lizards and little marsupials. He looked at the bomber. It was sad to think that it would all be gone. The little blue wren was doing his never ending round of hens. One of the resident kookaburras watched from a tree branch overhead. The swallows dipped and dived on the river. Sean felt the presence of his totem, the Ponde, deep under the waters. A great sadness washed through him. Their home was going. Their life was coming to an end.

From the corner of his eye he caught sight of a stake with a red ribbon located at the high water mark. Sean walked over to it noting the boot marks around it. He looked up and down the river and saw a line of similar pegs. They were pegging out the land already. Bloody arrogant bastards. Sean pulled out the peg. He walked on up towards Joseph's place.

The old man was in his garden. He looked up when he heard Sean. Sean marvelled at the old man's acute hearing and intuitive knowledge of his presence. He looked at the immaculate garden.

'Garden's looking good, grandfather.'

'Yes, Maiyarare. I happy those nuns and the RSL fella fix up my place and they plant some veggie plants. It keep me busy and I like to watch them grow.' The old man stood up slowly, using his stick to elevate his body to the vertical. 'Ah, Sean, it is good to make it to be old but it hard when ya can't move, when your head want you to move.' Sean helped the old man over the fence, they settled by the fire. 'I see you have a markin stick.' Joseph indicated the peg Sean still held in his hand. 'Them fella they come yesterd'y and this morning, they move round like a sick horse, they makem a lot of noise, but they no come over to this place.'

Sean threw the peg onto the fire and watched as it licked and destroyed it. 'You know, this means they are going to tear this whole place down, Ulwai. They're bloody gonna kill everything, all my friends, the birds, the Beewee, all the trees. Even the ants will be gone. We can't let them. We can't let them!' Tears stung his eyes.

Joseph put a hand on Sean's shoulder. 'Sometime we do only what we can do. A lot change around here since I bin a birra-li. No make a lot of sense for this fella. One time the Bindaree Tamba

Tamba be many, we walk around our county no worry. Now Binda-ree all gone, all scattered. They do not know their country, they do not know their law. All this place it change, plenty white fella, plenty change.'

'I'm sorry, Ulwai.'

'Ah, you not be sorry for this fella. I bin try hard to follow my law to takem care of country, I bin havem a good longem time here. But sometime it the way it be. Nooralie and the spirit fella, they have some other way for this place, if they think it be time for Bindaree to no longer be here, this place, then that how it gonna be. But it not mean we do not try change them spirit fella mind. We try and change Amerjig mind too. We bin always gonna fight for this place.'

'I'll fight with you.'

'I know you a brave Wundara,' Joseph said gently. 'We try and talk first. Most fella fight first, talk later, that not the way. I bin ask that Sister Hildegard to write a letter for me in proper English, one for the council and one for the government. That Aboriginal protector bloke and some local bloke who goem to Melbourne. She write it for me and I make my name. She gonna take it to the meeting place tomorrow night, where Koonarook council fellas meet.'

Sean nodded. 'Dad is going. He has a copy of a journal the first Campbell wrote about that early time and about your grandfather, saying how they gave you this place and that breast plate.'

'That be good. We havem strong words to give them Koonarook council fella to think about. It bin good to have strong friends to help me.'

'I'll try my best Sean, but I have a bad feeling about this,' Sean's dad said as he left for the meeting. 'Sister Hildegard and Sister Louise are going to be there to present a letter from Joseph, I'm told. There are a lot of people going. Most have told me to pull my head in. I've been getting phone calls and people dropping by the office all bloody day. Even Rexy phoned me up and told me to get off the case.'

His mother was anxious. Her tension transferred to him in the subdued hug and kiss when he went to bed. He went into a fitful sleep with the vision of desolation playing in his mind.

Sean woke in the morning, his bed sheets and blankets twisted and strewn about. He could hear the morning noises of his father. He hurried out to bring in the morning's wood and light the stove. His father was washing and shaving.

'Good morning, Sean,' he yelled out as Sean hurried past with an armful of kindling. There were soon two plates of scrambled eggs and toast on the table.

'I suppose you want to hear how the council meeting went last night, Sean? It was a bloody sham, the whole thing. It was all cut and dried, but we have managed to delay them for a month. A big crowd there. They had to move the meeting into the town hall. When the swamp matter came up it was called, believe it or not, the reclamation of Koonarook foreshore and adjacent marshland, Government Crown Land Allotments 35, 34, 33 and 32, Parish of Koonarook motion. All the councillors supported the motion. There was cheering and clapping for every councillor who spoke for the motion. There were submissions from the mill, Campbell and letters of support from all over the place. Angus McNeil, to give him his due, read out the excerpts from the diary. That set the council back a bit and the mayor, that bloody conservative Frank Meadows, has sent it off to the council's legal eagles for review. It caused quite a storm and there was a lot of booing and clamour, some of it not very pleasant.' His father added some HP sauce to his eggs. 'Ah, this is why we saved the poms in the war, bloody HP sauce, it's to bloody die for.'

Sean added some to his own plate. 'Yeh, dad, not too good about the meeting though.'

'A lot of people have a big stake in this, from the workers to the local shopkeepers. They probably think, quite rightly in some respects, that it's alright for Jim Buttenberg to be spouting off but he'll get paid by the government come what may, but their livelihoods depend on it.' His father ate his eggs slowly, deliberately, and said slowly, 'Then the Shire Secretary Fred McCaughey tabled a letter from me outlining another way to do the development while retaining Joseph's property and the rookery. Then one from Sister Louise about the welfare of the local Aboriginals and Joseph. There was more booing and racial slurs which was only silenced when Sister Louise stood up and faced them down. She told them off by name. She put the wind up them.'

'Yeh, I saw her in operation in the hospital. She's the boss.'

'Bloody Fred had to call the place to order and ask her to sit down. I thought they might have to call on Shorty Malone there at one stage. Poor old Fred had to table a letter written by Sister Hildegard for Joseph, and you know what was in that. No one made a boo about that. I suppose they didn't want another Sister on the warpath. Sister Hildegard had also written asking for permission to address the council. That was refused on a vote. But they did allow a letter she had written to be read out. She wrote about the strong ties to the land the local Aboriginals have, that it was a holy piece of land to them, and the fact that Joseph actually occupied a portion of the land in question. She basically asked for a balanced approach with all parties to be considered. It was a very fine letter. The booing started again. This time Shorty did get up when Fred couldn't control them.'

'What happened next?'

'Oh, after some more waffle and procedural stuff, the council deferred the decision, pending a legal opinion next month. It will most certainly be passed then. I spoke to a few of them afterwards and they all said it was only a matter of protocol.'

'So it will go ahead?'

'Yep, those bastards cannot see past their bloody noses. It's all over red rover.'

'Dad, will you go and speak to Joseph?'

'Yeh, but Sister Louise and Sister Hildegard are going down to see him today, and it has been muted by a couple of the councillors that they'll put up a motion to provide Joseph with housing when the swamp is reclaimed.'

'He won't accept it.'

'I had the same feeling.'

Sean's mum walked into the kitchen. 'What are my two men so serious about?'

They looked up in unison. There was a long pause.

'We're just trying to decide what to get you for Christmas, Mary,' Sean's dad said.

She smiled and mockingly wagged her finger at him. 'Jim Buttenberg, you are not. You are talking about the council meeting.'

'True, Mary. I was just telling Sean what I told you last night. It doesn't look good, not good at all.'

She sat down and faced him square on. She spoke in a quavering voice. 'Jim, I am concerned for Joseph and his place, of course, but I am also concerned for us. All our friends and neighbours are for this.'

'I know, Mary, I know.'

She held his attention with her steady gaze and serious voice. 'Even the other day, Sally Hird was talking to me about how it was so good for the town and how Eddy would get a pay rise and promotion when the mill expanded. There is a lot of feeling in the town about this, Jim. If you go on against it, I do not know what could happen. Mr Campbell is a powerful man with influential friends.'

He replied painfully. 'Yes, I know, Mary, but the town could have their Aboriginal heritage and their development too. It's just a matter of planning, instead of knocking everything over.'

'Jim, I do not think it is a wise course you are following.' She stood up and whisked his plate away. There was still toast on it.

'Mary, do you want me to go back on my principles and our friend, Joseph?'

'James Buttenberg, you and your principles.'

Sean felt uncomfortable. He expected his dad to laugh or to say something witty, but he didn't. He shifted on his seat. Finally he said, 'Nice eggs, dad. I'll go and muck out the chooks.'

Unusual Happenings

Joseph was slowly regaining his strength and was not so bent over now. He regaled Sean and Johnny with stories from his boyhood and droving days. He promised to take them on a hunting trip with spears over on Gunpowder Island when he was able. The days were lengthening, tea was not until six o'clock, so Sean had more time to be out. It should have been a golden time, but it was not. The impending vote of the council and the near certainty of the swamp and Joseph's place being destroyed were never far from his mind. The continuing of the desolation dreaming reminded him of impending disaster and clouded his thoughts. Joseph seemed to be resigned to the outcome. He confided to Sean that he was happy that the nuns and his dad were trying to help him, but he did not want them to get into trouble. There was a sadness and weariness in his voice when he spoke. Sean could almost feel the loss, the lament, the powerlessness. It enfolded them both in its cloud.

At home the tension between his mum and dad grew. Where before they would have laughed something off, now it was an occasion for antagonism. Sean spent a lot more time in his room then he had before. Although his mum and dad would not tell him everything, from overheard conversations and what he gathered, the way they were being treated in town had altered.

First they stopped being greeted friendly in the streets and in the neighbourhood by most of their friends and neighbours. Some even ignored them. His mum said the CWL ladies had knocked her back on being secretary, a job she had been earmarked for earlier in the year. She could not get a satisfactory answer to why this had happened. They received phone calls from people they knew, asking them to change their mind about backing this Aboriginal stuff and trying to block the redevelopment. His dad said they were driving him mad at work, all harping on about it.

The biggest blow to his mother, though, was the row she had with Sally Hird when she had tried to put Joseph's side of the story to her. It had apparently erupted into a full-scale argument. His mum had not been back to her house since and neither had Sally been to their place.

Tea time, on the day of the argument, was particularly painful. The plate of mince and potato pie was tasteless and underdone. His mother was deathly quiet and pale. Her makeup, normally perfect, was smudged and her eyes red rimmed and raw. Sean felt the tension and remained quiet. Even Katy seemed to feel it. Finally Sean's dad had had enough of the silence.

'Mary, what the heck is wrong?'

His mum shook and withered before his eyes. Her face collapsed in on itself, she burst into tears, as she stood up from the table.

'I have no friends left, and now Sally Hird and I have had a fight over that silly swamp,' she cried tearfully in barely intelligible English as she left the room. Her quailing voice tailed off down to the bedroom. Sean's dad ran after her. Katy also rose and ran crying into her bedroom. Sean was alone.

Then as the family was still recovering from this argument, his father had left for work one morning only to come back in with a face like thunder.

'Some bastard has let my tyres down and thrown bloody mud all over the Buick.'

Sean raced out to the shed. The Buick was covered in blotchy, clotted grey mud. Its four tyres were flat. His father came out in a pair of overalls. Sean's mum and Katy stood behind him, their faces miserable.

'Bloody hell, I'd like to get the bastards who did this,' he snarled. 'Sean, get the pump will ya.'

The tool shed was at the end of the car shed. Sean went through the door and stopped. The place was ransacked and more grey mud was all over the place. Sean noted that the tyre pump, which usually resided on the wall directly to the right, was not there.

'Bloody mongrels!' His father was soon standing behind him. He shook his head in disbelief. 'Bloody hell. Bloody hell!' his father muttered over and over again.

After that his father locked the shed and closed the gate with a padlock chain. Other things were happening also to his father of which Sean could only get a partial gist. He never passed it on directly. Sean picked up on conversations between his mum and dad and also from his mate Berty White.

'How about a game of marbles?' Berty asked as usual one day. What was unusual though, was that Sean was winning. Berty was missing shots he would normally make easily.

'How's ya dad?' Berty asked casually.

'He's alright.'

'My dad was shaving a bloke from one of your father's gangs.'

'What of it?'

'He was saying that that Mr Caruthers from Melbourne has been up to see your dad and warned him to stay out of the mill affair.'

Sean faced his friend. 'How did that bloke know anything anyway?'

'He heard it from Merle in your dad's office.'

'Bloody hell. It's my fault, it's my bloody fault! If I wasn't involved with Joseph, if I hadn't gone down to the bloody swamp, had not been such an idiot. It's my bloody fault.'

Berty moved closer. His moon shaped face full of remorse. 'Sorry, Sean, I shouldn't have told you,' he whispered.

Sean looked at Berty and smiled weakly. 'Ah, it's not your fault, Berty, just everything seems to be turning to shit at the moment.'

Berty moved even closer to Sean and spoke very quietly. 'My dad says if you cross the Campbells in this town you are dead meat. My dad also says your dad is not very popular, trying to stop that development and being an Abo lover. They expect the nuns to be do-gooders but not one of them, like your dad.'

That night Sean sat at the kitchen table doing some maths homework. He asked his dad for a hand. His father looked at the multiplication sums.

'You've never had trouble with these in the past, Sean.'

'I know dad,' Sean spoke quietly. 'Berty White told me today you are in trouble with that Mr Caruthers.'

His father looked at him in surprise. 'Did he now?' He sat down beside Sean.

'He also said anyone who crosses the Campbells in this town is dead meat.'

'Well, I'll tell you, Sean, it has been a bit tough, with all this pressure going on and Mr Caruthers making a special trip up to see me.'

Sean put his head in his hands. 'I'm sorry, dad. It's my fault,' he mumbled.

'Nonsense! You're just helpin' a mate. Same as me, I'm just helpin' a mate. The fact that he is black shouldn't have anything to do with it.'

'But you could lose your job.'

'Well, if I do it's a bloody job not worth keeping.'

Sean stared at the multiplication tables. He sighed.

'Look, Sean. I've been in the army through a bloody war, seen what bastards people can be, and done some things I would rather not have. What they are throwing at me here is nothing, I'm not saying it's easy, but we're into it now. Even if we wanted to we couldn't change what has happened. I'd rather sleep well at night then let down a mate.'

Sean looked at his father's determined face. 'What if we have to leave?'

'So be it. Good riddance to the bastards.'

'But what about mum and her friends and Katy starting school?'

There was a pause. 'Yeh, I know Sean. Anything that is worthwhile comes at a price, I know that much. Most people are not prepared to pay the price. Don't you worry about it. You only did what came natural. You made a friend and he happened to be old and black. I'm proud of you, Sean, and your mum is too. You're a good kid and a good son. Come what may, we will always love you and be with you. Now, do you still need a hand with those tables?'

His mother stopped going to the CWL. She went down the street early to avoid people. She had not seen Sally Hird. If they were both outside, they ignored each other. Katy was upset she could not go and play with her friends. After a while his mum did not answer the telephone. She clung to his father closely, but at the same time they were still snappy and tension prevailed. One night as they ate tea there was a firm knock on the front door. His father went to answer it. Sean heard the voice of Shorty Malone and his father speaking in subdued tones. After a short time his father came back, his face drawn and pale.

'What is it, Jim?' Sean's mum's face took on the shade of her husband's.

'That was Shorty Malone. He apologised for coming around late but he wanted to speak to me about a matter.'

Tears rolled from his mother's eyes. Her hands went to her face, as if it had become too heavy to hold up. 'It's about this swamp business and all that, isn't it?'

Sean's dad said nothing, but his slumping shoulders and downcast eyes were enough. She was weeping now. He moved around to her, knelt and put his arm around her.

'Take your sister into the lounge, Sean. I'll be in a moment.'

Sean had started to read 'Hansel and Gretel' to Katy from the volume of Grimms' fairy tales.

Finally Katy said in a whisper, 'Why is mum crying, Sean?'

'The policeman, Mr Malone, he brought some bad news about a man they know. It made her sad.'

'Who?'

'I don't know, Katy.'

'Are they going to move your friend Joseph from his house?'

'I don't know, Katy.'

'Why won't anyone speak to us anymore, Sean?'

'They just don't understand us, I think.'

'I miss Andrew and Martha.'

'Yeh, I know, Katy, but it can't be helped.'

Suddenly Katy was cuddling into Sean, her eyes welling with tears. Sean put his arms around her. In a little whimper, she cried, 'You will always be my friend, won't you, Sean?'

'Yes, Katy, I will always be your friend.'

She pressed into Sean harder, putting her arms around him. 'I love you, Sean.'

Later, Sean was in bed when his father came into his room. He was reading *The Last of the Mohicans*. His dad sat down on the end of the bed.

'I loved that book too. Very sad, do you know, Sean, the American

Constitution is part based on the Iroquois Federation?'

'No, I didn't. They were powerful and well organised.'

'They certainly were. Like the Americans we could learn a lot from our native peoples.'

'Yeh,' Sean replied sadly.

'I suppose you're wondering why Shorty Malone was here.'

'I thought it might be something to do with Joseph.'

'Not really, in a roundabout way, yes. The police are checking on you, Sean. The Child Welfare Board is sending an officer up from Morang to interview us and to interview your teachers. They have asked for a report from Shorty Malone on the bridge incident, and they want to know why you missed so much school. They've been led to believe that you've been loitering around with undesirable people, and been mentioned by the police.' His father paused. Sean could see that he was struggling to get the words out. 'Your mother is taking it very hard, Sean. She thinks it's an embarrassment to be investigated by Child Welfare and a blight on us.'

Sean slumped back in the bed and shook his head. It was a nightmare but he was not even asleep. 'Dad, I didn't mean for us to get into trouble.'

'Look, Sean, it will be all right. You were injured by the lightning the first time. You had a legitimate right to be away from school. Sister Hildegard will give you a good report, I'm sure. And Shorty Malone is going to give them a good report about you and us. He told me himself. He told me that kids have been playing chicken on that bridge for years. You and Johnny were just plain unlucky, stupid, but unlucky. He's also going to give them a good report about Joseph. I'm sure that's who they are referring to when they say "undesirable persons", the bastards.'

'Dad, this is too much.'

'Sean, don't you worry, we'll sort it out.' He took the book from

Sean and placed it on the bedside table. Sean snuggled down into the sheets. 'It's another trick of the powers that be. Campbell has set his minions loose. We can't let them beat us, and in the end they won't. Even if we lose this one, in the long run we'll have the victory. It might only be a morale one but that is the most important.' His father gave him a hug. 'We'll be alright, Sean.' Then he kissed Sean on the forehead.

The Man from the Child Welfare Board

The next day Sean was called up to the Head Sister's office. He knocked and waited outside. Sister Hildegard ushered him in and directed him to the usual chair. The office was unchanged. The framed couple outside the thatched hut almost looked like family, thought Sean. In the seat beside his a young man sat stiffly. His back did not touch the chair. His suit looked tight even though he was thin. His face was angular and gaunt, and he had a very thin moustache.

Sister Hildegard said, 'Sean, this is Mr Flynn from the Child Welfare Board. He is here to see to your welfare and to ask you a few questions.'

'Hello, Mr Flynn,' Sean said cheerily. He looked directly at the welfare man.

The man did not look at him. He ignored Sean's greeting and launched into a prepared statement. 'It has come to our attention that you, Mr Buttenberg, have not attended school for a large part of this year, have been mentioned in two police reports, one involving a brawl and the other a traffic matter. Also, it has been mentioned by persons of good standing that you have been in the company of people of low repute. What do you have to say about these matters?' He spoke in a funny way, like a pom. His pen was poised over a large yellow note pad with double binding. On the man's lap, Sean could see a manila file with his name on it and forms jutting out at odd angles.

Sean took a deep breath and tried to look the welfare man in the eye. His hands were suddenly sweaty. He remembered what had happened the last time he sat in this office. He looked at the snake lamp and caressed his hands. The welfare man gazed at the ceiling.

'Sean,' Sister Hildegard butted in. She leaned across the table earnestly. 'I have informed Mr Flynn that you are an excellent student and have had a few unavoidable issues through the year.'

'Thank you, Sister. I think Mr Buttenberg should explain what has occurred, if you do not mind.' The welfare man moved irritably in his seat.

Sister Hildegard glowed with indignation but her voice was calm as she spoke again to Sean, ignoring Mr Flynn. 'Take your time, Sean, and tell it in your own language slowly and carefully. Everything will be all right.'

For the first time the welfare man took his eyes off the ceiling and stared angrily at the Head Sister. She smiled back at him.

Sean took heart from Sister Hildegard's encouragement. 'Mr Flynn, earlier in the year I was hit by lightning. I had to go into hospital, but I continued my school work from home. Another time I was playing down in the swamp and Harry Smythe and a number of other fellas came down and tried to make a fight, but it ended up bad for them and Harry Smyth fell in the mud. The traffic thing was that I challenged my mate Johnny to a race from home to school. It was my fault and we nearly had a collision with Mr Owens on the bridge and he lost his load, which blocked the bridge. Sister Hildegard gave me the cuts and other punishments and I was punished at home as well, Mr Flynn. The low repute people I do not know. Do you mean people who are not honest or treat you badly, Mr Flynn?'

Mr Flynn answered with a sneer. 'Yes, so to speak, people of low morals and repute, Mr Buttenberg.'

Sean looked at Sister Hildegard. She nodded encouragement and smiled at him. 'I do not know, Mr Flynn.'

'Mr Buttenberg, I am conducting an investigation into your welfare for the Child Welfare Board. Please can you give me the names of the people of low repute who you have been associating with?' The man was very annoyed. He was now sitting on the edge of his chair and writing furiously.

'The only people I can think of, who have no repute, especially to me, Mr Flynn, are Harry Smythe – he certainly has no repute, he was a bully, but he has left school – and Mr Campbell, who was racist and insulted one of my friends.'

The welfare man's pen stopped. For the first time he looked at Sean. The man was shaking. His eyes seemed about to pop out of his head. He wagged his pen at Sean as he broke off eye contact. Sean did not like this man. Sean turned to Sister Hildegard, who gave him another encouraging smile.

Mr Flynn angrily asserted. 'Mr Buttenberg, I do not know of Mr Smythe but I do know of Mr Campbell. He is a gentleman and one of the most highly respected members of this community. How dare you call him a racist? I can see you have an undesirable attitude.'

Sister Hildegard interrupted again, her eyes fiery. 'Mr Flynn, you have asked Sean for his opinion on people of low repute. You gave him a definition and he has replied to the best of his ability. Please remember he is only eleven. He does not have the benefit of your age or training, Mr Flynn.'

'Sister Hildegard, may I say...'

'Mr Flynn, I know for a fact that Mr Campbell employed Sean for a short time and I also know for a fact that Sean left his employment after a disagreement. I am led to believe by certain people whom I trust that Sean left because of a matter of principle not because of any work-related matter. As a matter of fact, these same people tell me that Sean was an excellent worker for one his age.'

The Child Welfare man chewed on his pen. Sean suppressed a grin. It was strangely satisfying to think that Sister Hildegard should be his ally. The man squirmed under her gaze.

He continued. 'Mr Buttenberg, it has come to our attention that you spend a great deal of your time down in the place you call the swamp with a, with a...' he was struggling to find a word. He looked at the Sister, then at the ceiling again. His voice had lost some of its pommy overtones. 'With a person who may not be the best possible company, for a young, impressionable person such as yourself.' The pen slipped from his hand and clattered to the floor. Sean retrieved it and handed it to the man.

'Yes, sir. I do spend some time down in the swamp after all my chores and jobs are finished. The only person I meet there regularly, beside my mate Johnny, is Mr Wirrinum, sir. He is a very good man, a very holy man. He is very old, sir, and he knows all the plants and animals and all their stories. His family and people have always lived there, sir.'

The child welfare man's sallow complexion completely drained. He spat out the next statement with venom. 'Mr Buttenberg, is that man a stinking black man?'

The accusation and the sudden silence thumped into Sean's ears. The blood rushed to his face and he was suddenly aware that his fists were clenched as tightly as his teeth. He looked at the lamp the snake coiling , he turned to Mr Flynn.

'You have no right Mr Flynn to say that about Mr Wirrinum he is wise, honest and good, just because he is black does not mean he is not. You do not even know him you you..!

'Sean please.' Sister Hildegard cut in suddenly 'Mr Flynn I believe you have probably asked enough questions for now. May I have the name of your superior? I believe you are in the Morang office.' Sister Hildegard picked up her pen and looked directly at Mr Flynn. Then she bent her head and started to write on a note pad.

The child welfare man now looked at the floor. 'What do you need that information for, Sister?'

'I will, of course, want to comment on your interview with Sean,' she said coldly and with venom, the words escaping through clenched teeth. 'I will need to speak to your supervisor.'

'There is no need for that sister.' He fumbled with the manila folder, trying to push the loose sheets back into place.

Sister Hildegard ignored him and continued writing. 'Are you finished with Sean, Mr Flynn?'

'Yes, yes, of course, thank you, thank you, Mr Buttenberg,' he stammered.

Sean stood up. In his most courteous voice, he said, 'Good bye, Mr Flynn. Good morning, Sister.'

The child welfare man murmured unintelligibly.

The Head Sister cheerily replied, 'Good morning, Sean.'

Sean walked straight back to the classroom. He saw a butcher bird collecting twigs for its nest. Must be a repair job, thought Sean.

At tea he told his parents about his interview with the man from the Child Welfare Board, about how mean and stiff he was, and how he had called Joseph a stinking blackfella. Sean's mum also related her experience with him. She had met him just before lunch, not long after Sean, in the Sister's office also. He had been very polite, over polite. In fact, sickly sweet. He had made only good comments about the school and about Sean. He had even commented on how well Sean was doing and had said that the report was obviously a misunderstanding. Sister Hildegard had said she looked forward to the man's report and thanked him very much. There had been no mention of his comment about Joseph. But Sister Hildegard had said something that she thought odd at the time. She had said, 'Misunderstandings do sometimes happen, even to the best of us. Sometimes words are said that, in the heat of the moment, could be misconstrued by those in authority.'

Sean's dad had reached across the table and enclosed his mother's hand in his. It remained there throughout her story. When she had finished, she looked from Sean to his dad. Sean saw them smile at each other for the first time in ages. Then his dad squeezed his mum's hand.

Dingo Churinga

On his next visit to Joseph on a late afternoon, Sean found the old man polishing another Churinga. It was a bit like Sean's but this one was a lighter grain of wood and the carvings were of a dingo, standing defiant and proud. The old man smiled with satisfaction at Sean's admiration.

'It be for your friend Johnny. It have Purnung, that be dingo. He be a good friend to you, brave and loyal, like Purnung to his pack. He a warrior also, I put spear and shield on other side. I have dreamin about him when I make it.' Joseph turned it over. The spear and shield lay side by side. 'You bin test it for me, Sean. I no able to fly it, too hard on this old man now.' Joseph tied a string to the bullroarer and gave it to Sean. 'You remember how I fly your one first time, Maiyarare?'

Sean played out about a foot of line. He moved over into the clear and closed his eyes. Johnny would be so proud to own this. He opened his eyes and looked across at the old man leaning back in his chair, watching him intently. He closed his eyes again and began to swing the bullroarer around, gradually playing out line and starting the chant.

'*Illa booker mer ley urrie urrie, illa booker mer ley urrie urrie, Dingarra,*

337

Dingarra. Illa booker mer ley urrie urrie, illa booker mer ley urrie urrie, Dingarra, Dingarra.'

The swinging of the churinga melded into a rhythmic motion. All else was blotted out. Then a vision came to him of lightning and rain, explosions and gunfire, fire and smoke. The dingo was running through it all, on and on, until it fell. The greenness of the bush startled his mind. The savagery of the images made him sweat. On and on he swung until he could swing no more, the image faded. He looked at Joseph. His eyes were closed and he was leaning back in his chair. He watched as the Churinga came to ground, and closed his eyes again. His mind also came to rest. He opened his eyes at the same time as Joseph opened his. Their eyes locked. Sean felt the understanding that passed between them like a flash of lightning.

The old man spoke quietly. 'You be good bullroarer man. Come sit down have tea.'

Sean handed him the Churinga. The old man wrapped it in the oily cloth and gave it back to Sean. 'I had a vision, Maiyarare.'

Sean whispered, 'Yes, Ulwai, I had the same one, about the dingo and the green place, fire and guns.'

'Me think it be something to do with Johnny later on in his years, not for longem time yet. It come to me as I make that and it been come to you also. I think it be good not to tell that fella about that dreamin.' The old man started on his tea ritual.

'Yes, grandfather, I think so.'

Sean gave the gift to Johnny. He asked Sean for all the details. He was impressed by the old man's carvings of the dingo, spear and shield. He turned it over and over, feeling it, caressing it with his fingers, noting every groove and indentation. He was anxious to try it.

The met that afternoon at the B17. Johnny bought along his own string, which he carefully tied to the Churinga. Johnny was a natural. The sound and vibration was almost earth changing. The sound reverberated through the bush and came back. Sean watched in fascination as his mate spun it around and danced to its tune, taking little steps and bending his knees up and down. He smiled at Johnny's obvious joy and innate skill.

'Beautiful, Johnny, almost magic,' Sean yelled as Johnny let the bullroarer down.

'It feels so good! It's like I was about to take off. It's like I was the centre of the world.'

The boys played with the bullroarer for the next half an hour, giving it a real working over, trying out different patterns and speeds. Johnny was keen to visit the old man before they had to go home. Joseph was sitting in front of his hut, smoking a pipe. His face lit up when he saw them.

'Ah, Johnny, you are welcome to this place. The sound of your Churinga filled my heart with joy. It brought me some thinkin about my own time as a worlba ah boy, it bin good.'

'Thank you, Joseph,' Johnny said. 'It flies really well and makes a great sound.'

'Yeh, I bin think it be good right away when I bin pick that piece of wood up. It feel that it always wanted to be a bullroarer. It that way sometime with wood, same with men. When they do what suit them and what right, it always work the best. You boys want some biscuits?'

'Better not, better get home,' said Sean. Then he looked at the old battered enamel tray that Joseph thrust at him. 'Well, maybe one.'

Return to Tamba Tamba Dreaming

The next time Sean saw the old man it was a Saturday afternoon. He took with him a plate of his mum's vanilla slices. Joseph was out the back repairing fishing nets. He turned.

'Ah, Sean, next time we go fishing we drag that creek at Gunpowder Island, we get some yabby.'

'Ulwai, mum asked me to give you these.' They settled down to their brew and each took a slice.

The old man drew himself up. 'A fella from the Board, he bin come here and tell me I have to leave this place. It bin council place, not my place. He tell me they gunna fix me up with much bigger better place in Caladonia'

'What did you say?'

'I not sayem too much. I tell him my people all ways bin here. We have this place forever and it bin agreed. Then I tell him if he do not get off my land then I have to shoot him.'

'You what!'

'I went and got my shotgun, it inside there, behind board in the hut, it have no shell in it, but he not know that.'

'What did he do?

'He get mighty scared that fella, he start to run away quickly. Me thinks he done gonna wet himself.' They both laughed and then fell silent. 'I sorry I get angry with that fella, but he no listen, he just keep talkin and pushin me this way and that.'

'I'm sorry, Joseph. It looks as though we may be losing this battle. It's not looking good.' Sean poked at the fire, the old man's eyes were watery and cheerless.

'It very sad that you and your family be hurtin over this fella,' Joseph said wistfully.

Sean shook his head. 'Joseph, you are my best friend. We wouldn't abandon you to those bastards.'

'Let us visit that Tamba Tamba place. May be not much time left before this place be no longer with us. Maybe Nooralie he give us dreamin time answer.'

The clearing was as Sean remembered, but not as silent as the last time. From the tree tops came the raucous cries of young ibises. Sean looked at the old man.

Joseph smiled. 'This bin a good year for them Tamba Tamba fella, they have lot of food. So they bin busy layin eggs, and feedin young ones. They make a noise them young ibis fella like the Bindaree used to do. The older Tamba they be back bit later on, and then those young ones they get a feed.'

They walked among the trees. Sean felt again the pervading majesty. He looked at the Bora Bora trees feeling the carvings on the trunks and limbs. He could almost see the people who had been here. It was dark and cool. The trees and nests crowded out the sky. They sat down in front of the tree they had marked.

'Ulwai, how does this place grow or make new trees? All the trees are dead.'

'Ah, that a good one to ask. The Tamba they kill the tree with their picking at them and stopping the light to them and their droppings. But after longem time some part of the tree, it fall down and then they no longer can make their nest there. It means the light comes there and new tree grow, until they big enough to be good for nest, but it takem a longem time for this. We Bindaree have ceremony here. Only initiated men fella be here. They make their mark like you, they fuse the tree, then them spirit fella tie and cut the tree, make them join and be together.' The old man got up stiffly and ran his hand over the carvings, reflectively. 'Sean, it be good we do this earlier on'

'Yes, Ulwai, it was good to do this.'

'It seem like long time we do this but it be only short time. We do a lot together, this old man and you.'

'Yes, Ulwai, a lot has happened.'

'Maiyarare, you carve another circle inside the first one here.' The old man drew a pocket knife out of his pocket. Sean hesitated.

'But, grandfather, I am not a Taldree fella yet.'

'Yeh, me know that one, but maybe you older than you think. You bin thinkin older then what you be in age, longem time. It maybe not much time here left for Bindaree,' he whispered sadly and handed the knife to Sean. 'You carve inside that first one, even if this place be not longem here, Nooralie he bin see your carvin, it be with him.'

Joseph squatted on the ground and watched Sean make his Bora mark inside the first circle. The old man closed his eyes and started to chant words that Sean could not make out, but which came in slow rhythmic pulses that enveloped him as he carved.

Sean was finally finished. He stepped back. 'How is that, Joseph?'

Joseph startled looked up. 'It bin good what you make.'

Sean stood further back to admire his circle within a circle. Joseph closed his eyes again and his breathing slowed. Sean squatted down also and closed his eyes. The dreaming came to him, all that had happened; the lightning Dingarra, the fights with the Smythe gang, Ponde, his totem, the Beewee, fishing, Johnny, school, Sister Hildegard, the kiss of the King Brown, Mary Addison, the race, hospital, his family, Joseph, the creator serpent, on and on in no order it flashed and crashed through his mind. Some made him laugh with joy and happiness, other stung hurting him and tears sprung to his eyes. Then the desolation dreaming came to him again and he struggled against it and shook himself loose from its grip with an effort.

He looked over at Joseph. His gaze was fixed on the carving.

Without turning, the Gooweera man said with satisfaction, 'Ah, it has been good you been here this year, you make this old fella days good.'

'It is good that Dingarra helped me to meet you.'

'Maybe we meet anyway, you always down in this swamp and playing around. But yeh he mark you big, we get on anyway. We what Sister Hildegard say, we kindred spirit, like we made to be together.'

'Sister Hildegard said that?'

The old man nodded his head and looked up to the top of the canopy. 'She full of ideas and know lot bout things when I bin talk to her. It the way she always bin, she a smart one, that one. Yeh, them Sister Lady, they just think and pray to that fella Jesus, and that Mary mother lady, no fella to bother them or porle. They read and think long time, they bin get smart about things.' But she no listen to me when I say her totem be the snake fella, she told me not to be saying those things. But it be true.'

Sean pondered on this for a while. Sister Hildegard a snake. Then he thought about her office dark and cool. The yellow light from the snake lamp. Her unpredictability, her quickness of movement and thought. And had'nt his dad even said her strap was like the kiss of a King Brown.

'Mmm, yeh I think you may be right about the snake bit grandfather."

"Yeh well as I tell you that King Brown he be special to us, maybe that why we get on most times.'

Sean nodded. 'She said we were kindred spirits?'

'Yeh, she bin say it a few times. Me thinkin, yeh, sometime I see it happen not only with people but with animal and human, they share your dreamin, your soul. They like your brother but more even.'

Sean followed Joseph's gaze to the tree tops. The young ibises grew louder.

'We bin go now, Sean. It nearly time for the Tamba Tamba to come back.'

The light was growing dim. He wondered how long he had been dreaming.

Bugger Them

That night after tea his dad was smoking his pipe in the lounge room. Sean was looking up a book on snakes. His mum and Katy were in the kitchen sewing a dress.

'I heard from Sam Peters today.'

'Good news, dad? Has he found anything?'

'No, but he did tell me that Lachlan Campbell has withdrawn his grandfather's diary and other memorabilia from the museum. Apparently they were on loan from the family trust. Sam has had to give good reason why he sent the extract to me. He said it's getting a bit nasty. He has to lay low for a bit.'

'That's terrible, dad.'

His father pulled at his pipe. 'He'll keep on trying. He has to be careful, though, and do it in his own time and with his own resources. He's contacted a few of his colleagues and they'll look also.'

'This means we have no more evidence.'

His father pulled his pipe apart viciously. 'I'm afraid that's right. No more evidence and the council meeting is next week.'

'And the Tamba Tamba rookery is full of young ibis.' Sean looked at a King Brown.

As Sean was riding to school and past the co-op some of the day labourers lounging around the front gate gave him a bit of stick.

'Tell your do-gooder father to mind his own fucking business.'

'Go back to the city, ya coon lover.'

'Gonna kamikaze the bridge today, ya little bastard?'

The men chorused other insults, sniggering and laughing. One picked up a rock and went through the motions of throwing it. Sean put his head down. He would ride on the other side from now on. When he got to school Johnny told him his family's name was mud. Johnny's dad said there was a lot of resentment and anger at the Buttenbergs. Berty said it was the major topic of discussion, and the general line was that city people come here thinking they know everything.

Sean watched as his father left for the council meeting. His hat perched at a jaunty angle, his boots shiny, a sheaf of papers in his hand. He wore a tan sports coat and his green country shirt was shaded by the red tartan of his fighting tie. Sean smiled. His father had told him this was the tartan of the Royal Stuarts, last of the Catholic kings. His father had told him he wore it when he needed courage.

Longem Time My People Have Lived Here

The next morning over bowls of steaming porridge, and before Katy and his mum were up, Sean's dad had told him the story of what had happened.

'The meeting went as I expected. There was a big crowd, they were standing down the sides of the hall. Every councillor spoke in favour of the motion to redevelop the swamp. People cheered as they spoke, same as last time. The legal ruling came back that the entry in old Campbell's diary was not a binding or legal document. No other proof of ownership exists, so the council controls the land as trustee on behalf of the government. They can basically develop, lease it or do with it as they like. The fact that there's a hut there, occupied by a person, is immaterial. I had arranged for a letter to be read from an ex-army mate, Red Smith-Haliston, who is a barrister and part-time constitutional expert in Melbourne, asking for a stay in proceedings while further searches are done on government records. This was dismissed.'

'Did you speak, dad?'

'The council didn't allow anyone from the floor to speak. But they did allow letters from the floor to be tabled. But there were too many in support of the proposal for all of them to be read out. They just gave a list of those for it – every prominent person and lots of ordinary people as well. Then they gave the list against the proposal, and it was the same four as last time – the two Sisters, Joseph and me. The crowd cheered the for list and booed the against list, same as last time. Then as the vote was about to be taken, Joseph walked in.'

'Bloody hell.'

'Bloody hell, alright. He walked into the hall, tall and straight. He went straight to the front and started speaking to the councillors. The crowd started to boo, but Shorty Malone stood up. He had two peeler boys down from Morang, one of them next to us. The booing stopped. Shorty moved over to where Joseph was speaking. No one could hear him, the din was so loud. Shorty was going to lead him away. But Angus McNeil asked the council to let him speak, and after some debate this was passed.' His father took a big swig of his coffee. Then he pulled a piece of paper from his shirt pocket and unfolded it. 'I took notes. Thought you'd want to know all the details of Joseph's speech.' He grinned at Sean. Then he coughed to clear his throat and started.'

"Me thankem you the elders of this place for letting me speak this day. For longem time my people the Bindaree have lived in this place along this Billa fella this river, we hunt, collect fish and net this place. From the time that Julungul the Serpent made this place, we have lived here, at this place you call the swamp. Kamballa our mother and the Tamba Tamba live here, it be part of us, it a holy place with many Bora Bora tree and it is a place where our elders meet and make ceremony. If our people are to live on and be strong we need this place. If it be destroyed then this Warde Yallock, this river, he be in for big trouble. In old time when white men first come here we fight for this place, but after some time we make agreement with that man Campbell and that government fella, we keep this place forever, and then more white fella come. Not so many Bindaree now and plenty of white fella. But I still make my place there at the

Tamba Tamba place, it my home. Please do not destroy this place, my friends, wise elders. We can save Tamba Tamba, we can save this river fella and live happy together."

'Then Joseph looked every councillor in the eye. There was an awkward silence. You could've heard a pin drop. Then the booing started again until Shorty Malone threatened arrests and expulsions. The council put the motion to the vote and it was carried unanimously. It sure was a fine speech, very firm and impassioned. One of the best I've heard. But the council would've been lynched if they had not passed it. The police escorted us out, and Joseph went off quietly. The Sisters were sad and resigned. The crowd was like they had won the grand final again. I'm not the most popular bloke around, but strangely I feel pretty relaxed about it. I did my best.' He leaned across and gave Sean a pat on his arm. 'We did our best.'

'Yeh, dad, you tried hard. What d'ya think will happen now?'

'I reckon they'll move pretty fast and rip into the place before anything else happens. You know it's all pegged out. They only have to move Joseph out, and then they'll be free to act. They'll get the police to do that, evict him, and then the bulldozers will move in.'

'Can I go and see Joseph this afternoon, after school?'

His father nodded. 'Should be alright, check with mum.'

Endota Quarra

The fire was burning and the billy hissed steam as Sean entered Joseph's clearing, a smoky haze hovered. The ground was freshly raked, the stumps and logs were neatly arranged around the fire. The waiting wood was stacked in order. It looked peaceful. Joseph came out of his hut, he smiled a sad smile, he looked tired.

'Ah, Sean, my young Maiyarare, it be good to see you.'

'Ulwai.' Sean put his arms around Joseph gently. He felt frail. The old man returned his hug. 'Dad told me about what happened last night.'

'Yeh, I try to talk to them fella, but they not listen. I try hard but it too difficult for Amerjig to understand Bindaree way.' The old man sat down and commenced his tea ceremony. Sean sat beside him.

'What are you going to do?'

'Them fella they bin say I gonna get a house, over there at Caladonia.' Joseph gazed into the fire and poked at it with a poker. He looked at Sean his face grim. 'I no go there, I die over there bit by bit. That would be the end for me, I cannot live in that place.'

'You're going away, aren't you, Ulwai?'

'I go away. That peeler man Malone, he gonna come and get me. I no go with him. He gonna come soon, but I no be here when he come.'

'It's not fair, it's not bloody fair!'

'Ah, Sean, that not good for you to feel this sadness. We have some good time this last little bit. It not be long, but we have good time together, it bin good time for this old fella. I learnin big time off you and maybe you be learnin something off me.' He handed Sean an Anzac biscuit. 'I tell you a story while we sit here this time, maybe it be last time.' The old man spread his legs in front of the fire comfortably.

'Long time back there be a Bindaree fella called Quarra. He be a bright young man about my size, he very powerful fella in this place, good hunter and big Wundara, he have much respect. He could have any woman he choose, as long as it not wrong wertun.'

'What is wrong wertun, grandfather?'

'Ah, that a hard one for Amerjig and sometime hard for black-fella, but it mean that he cannot marry girl who may be related, even sometime if it be distant related. All these blackfella they have skin, each group a bit different but it make you into group or skin. Same skin cannot marry another same skin, and some different skin not be allowed to be together.'

'Like we are not allowed to marry our first cousin and that sort of thing.'

'That right, Maiyarare. Anyway this Quarra fella he out huntin and across the river he see a beautiful lubra. She standing by the river washing and her beauty made Quarra heart start to race and run like he chasing a Beewee. He stands behind a tree and watch her as she wash, then she go away and he feels sad. He comes back to that spot every day and sometime he sees her again, sometime alone and sometime with other lubra. He mad for her. He find out that that group over there they be Bindaree but other clan, not Tamba Tamba. He ask elders if he can go there and visit with them. He tell them he trade spear, they say this be alright. He go over on his korong and he visit with them and trade with them. Those fella make good trade with Quarra, his mind not on tradin. While he there that lubra, her name Endota, she see this big tall handsome Wundara and she fall in love with him straight away. Her body quiver with the excitement of being near him.'

'But they were cousins or skins. They could not marry, right, Joseph?'

'Yeh, that bin right. He find out that she the wrong skin, they cannot be married, he have to find someone else. They offer a lot of other girls but Quarra no want them. He so sad he go home and fall into deep worry. He goes to that place on the river every day and one day she there. He call to her, she call back, they call out their love for each other and they say lovin things to each other. They meet there every day. That place, it still be there just up from Gunpowder Island, it called Endota place after her, it a beautiful place, but only women allowed to be there.' Joseph threw a handful of tea leaves into the small billy and used a forked stick to pick up the larger billy. He poured the boiling water into the small billy. 'Quarra no longer hunts or fights so good. He begin fallin down in eye of Bindaree. Bindaree wonder what happen to this bloke. They follow him down to river one day and they see him callin out there. The Bindaree they tell fella across the river that they wrong skins and they stop Endota from going to that place. Quarra get more lonely and more sad. The old fella they tell him to stop being sad and not to see this Endota again.'

'This is a sad story, grandfather.' Sean took the mug of tea that Joseph offered.

'Yeh, it be sad this life sometime. Well this Quarra he get sadder and sadder. He no longer great man in the Tamba Tamba, he become outsider. He bin get all his things together, spear and woomera, jilly bag and possum coat. He go over river and steal this Endota away from her clan and run away. They only on run for short time, the Bindaree chase them, they cannot have this fella break the law. But while they on the run they have beautiful time together, they seem to be made to be together, even though they wrong skin. But them Bindaree fella they catch up with them and they tell them to come quietly to be punished. But Quarra he says, "No, I would rather be dead then to be apart from this Endota girl". She screams out that she would rather be dead also than live away from her man, Quarra. The Bindaree attack them. Quarra, he fight them, but there many of them Bindaree fella, and they spear him many time, but he keep on fighting till he die. They have to spear him. They sad to do this but it happen like that. They go to take Endota back but she race over to her man, lying in his blood on the ground, and she fall on his body and they cannot get her off him. They pull and pull, then she give one last breath and her spirit be gone and she dies, her heart be broken. The Bindaree clans are very sad now and they all cry and make big moaning and groaning. You can still see that place up there near Morang, it all salty there from their tears, it still no good that place. Nooralie he lookem down and see them young people dying and them Bindaree they all crying and he have great pity. He says, Quarra you will no longer be grey, that what his name mean, but bright, and Endota, you who covered your man in death, you will be beautiful forever. He say to the Bindaree they breakem the law but they have great love, a love which drew me to them. Now I hear you crying and making my land sad, I will put their spirit together and you will see them but only for a short time. They will be the there in the morning very bright. That star what you Amerjig call Morning Star, Bindaree call it Endota Quarra because it have the brightness of two stars, they be together so close and for all time, but we only see em short time in the mornin.'

They sat quietly for some time. Finally Sean said, 'That is sad, so sad. Does it teach us to value our time together, even though it may be short?'

'Yeh, I bin thinkin on it. It teach us Bindaree about the skins. It also teach us that our time together even though it be only short, can be strong. Some time we not supposed to be together, but it teach us that although the law be strong, it cannot be stronger then love. Sometime it be a strong pull between people that draw them together no matter what, like kindred spirits. Sean, later on you look at that morning star Endota Quarra and you think of us. Old Blackman and young Amerjig, we not supposed to be friend but we joined together by Dingarra, our friendship never be killed or end, it be bright and live like Endota Quarra. That what we Bindaree say of those who are strong together, we call them Endota Quarra. No matter it be woman or man, or man and man, it not a sex thing, it be somethin much stronger. No matter one of us go, our friendship last for all time. Nooralie, he make it be.'

Tears stung Sean's eyes. 'Thank you, grandfather,' he whispered. 'I will always remember the story. This last year with you has been the best.'

'It bin pretty good for this old fella too.'

They sat quietly for a long time. Joseph's eyes filled, and Sean's tears fell and both mingled with the grey earth of Warde Yallock.

After Katy had gone to bed, Sean told his mum and dad that Joseph was going away. His parents were instantly alert.

'Will he be alright out in the bush, James?'

'Mary, Joseph has been living in the bush all his years. He'll be fine. They'll never find him.'

'Dad, Joseph asked if you would collect his stuff. He said he'd like to give some things to me, and some to Sister Hildegard and Sister Louise and some to his cousins. He's marked it all, but there's not much really. Just some old photos and carvings and a few tools.'

'No worries. I'll go on Saturday. You can come with me, Sean.'

Sean's voice started to waver. 'He said he'd leave a note for Shorty Malone on the door of the hut, to say it's okay for you to pick up his stuff.'

'That man thinks of everything.'

I Cannot Be Going With You

On Saturday they went down to Joseph's. The trailer was hitched to the Buick, piano trolley tied on. Joseph's place was quiet. The air was hazy and little dust devils danced in the air. The fire was dead. The cooking stake stood like a skeleton among the ashes. The trees hung heavy and languid in the dank morning air, even the birds were missing. Drop tails lazed in the morning sun on the door post. On the door was a note written in indelible blue ink.

> *'Sergeant Malone I cannot be going with you.*
> *Jim Butts and Sean they comin to pick up my gear*
> *Joseph Wirrinum.'*

Sean's dad looked at the note. He pulled it off and stuffed it in his pocket. 'Straight to the point, no mucking around with that bloke. I'll drop this off at the station on the way back.'

They went into the gloom of the hut, stalling at its entrance as their eyes adjusted. The shelves and trays were bare. An old metal bucket sat upside on the furthest bench. Alongside it were some old metal pots, pans and a blackened grill. In another tray were cleaning scrubbers and a jex. The fireplace was stacked with kindling and small logs, ready to light. A flimsy fireguard stood at an angle. The bed had a brown army blanket with two dark green stripes running down it. The single pillow had a green pillowcase. The hessian walls were light brown, new hessian. An old, battered metal luggage case sat on the hard, packed floor; and next to it was a tea box, sealed and lidded, inscribed in faded blue stencil writing were the words 'Koonarook Fruit Cooperative'.

Overhead, Sean could hear the Tamba Tamba crying as they made their way out of the sacred grove.

The modest but solid redbrick police station stood in the main street, behind it was a federation-style house. Children's trikes, a bike and a baby's playpen sheltered under its wide veranda. A black Austin police motor car waited in the drive. Shorty Malone was in long baggy army shorts and blue singlet, cleaning the car. He waved to them and came over to the Buick.

'G'day, Shorty.'

'G'day, Jim, Sean, you're out early Jim.'

'Yeh, I've been up to Joseph's. He asked us to pick up some of his things. There was a note on the door.' Sean's dad retrieved the note and passed it to the policeman. His brow furrowed as he read it.

'"I cannot be going with you",' he read aloud. 'The hut was empty?'

'All packed up. The old fella's gone.'

'When did you last see him?'

'Not since the council meeting, but Sean saw him Thursday evening.'

The policeman shifted on his feet uncomfortably. 'Mmm, I saw him on Thursday afternoon, after I got the eviction notice.'

'He told Sean it would kill him moving to Caladonia.'

The policeman looked at the boy. 'You're close to Joseph, aren't you, Sean?'

'Yes, sir, we're good friends.'

'Did he tell you where he was going?'

'No sir. He just said he had to go away, he could not go to Caladonia.'

Shorty Malone wiped his forehead. He shrugged. 'Can't say I blame him, poor old bastard.' He turned back to the Austin, then hesitated.

'Oh, Jim, the bulldozers are moving in on Saturday. The mayor, Frank Meadows, is going to cut a ribbon. They're making it an event, Campbell is paying for it.' The policeman said this with barely concealed contempt.

'Well, I won't be there!'

'Probably a good idea.' He sounded relieved. 'Campbell won't be there either. Apparently he's pretty crook. He hasn't been back here for a while. He's staying in Melbourne, I hear.'

'See ya, Shorty.'

'Goodbye, Sergeant Malone.'

The Sergeant looked closely at Sean. 'You will let me know if you see or hear of Joseph?'

'Yes, Sergeant.'

'Good boy.'

'Bloody Campbell, the bastard!' his father muttered on the way home.

'He's cursed, dad.'

'He's what?'

'He's cursed.'

'What do ya mean, he's cursed?'

They parked in the shed. 'Remember when Joseph was beaten up? He said whoever was involved would leave the town and get sick.'

'Did Joseph tell you that he cursed them?'

'No dad.'

'Well, how do ya know then?'

'He told me that it would happen and it did. Smythe, them blokes in Morang and Campbell, they all left town, and got sick or beaten up.'

'Bloody hell, Sean, do ya know what you're saying?'

'I know it's strange, but it did happen.'

His father shrugged. 'Well it couldn't have happened to a nicer bloke. Many a time I've cursed that bastard myself.'

We Have To Do Something

The decision of the council seemed to make it easier on Sean and his family. His parents were still ignored or cold shouldered but they were not actively pursued or harassed. On Monday after play lunch Sean was summoned to the Head Sister's office. Sister Hildegard was writing with a big black fountain pen at her desk. She smiled as Sean walked in and indicated for him to sit down. She capped her pen and leaned back. Sean waited, he thought about what Joseph had said about her totem being a snake. He looked at the cobra lamp, now so familiar. Joseph was bloody right. She coughed.

'Mr Buttenberg, I understand you saw Mr Wirrinum last week and he told you he was leaving.'

'Yes, Sister,' he said quietly.

'Did he tell you where he was going?'

'No, Sister.'

'Did he seem in good health and spirits?'

'Yes, Sister, but he was sad.' He saw the anxiety in her frown and quickly added, 'But he was healthy. We picked up his things on Saturday.'

She nodded. 'I believe you and he are kindred spirits,' she mused. 'Mr Buttenberg, I want to thank you for being such a good friend to Mr Wirrinum, and for your family's concern for him and his people's land. I will be writing a letter to your family in due course expressing my full support. Your father is a very fine man, very courageous, as is your family.'

'Thank you, Sister.'

'How can they destroy it?' he asked Johnny at lunch time on Friday. He just couldn't get it out of his mind. 'How can they do that? Don't they know how many birds and animals live there, besides it being the bloody special place for the local Abos?'

They were playing knuckles with Berty. The game was close. 'You sure have improved,' Berty said.

'Had a good teacher.' Sean slapped him on the back.

'Hey, just as well the council passed that thing on the swamp, otherwise your dad would have been really in for it.'

Sean snatched up his knuckles. 'Yeh, how do you know?'

'Some of the locals let loose in my dad's shop. My dad calls them the great unwashed, but they pay their two bob. Some of them were out to get him, and they say ya dad's boss, Mr Caruthers, has been on the blower.'

'Yeh, he got flak over it alright.'

'Yeh, well, as they say, that's progress.'

Sean threw his jacks on the ground and faced up to Berty. 'It's bloody murder! Everything's gonna bloody die. The trees, birds, lizards, even Joseph! Ya call that bloody progress, Berty?'

He felt a hand on his arm. 'Calm down, mate, calm down.' It was Johnny.'

Berty squinted at Sean and Johnny through narrowed eyes.

'Sorry Berty sometimes I get a bit agitated, bloody like a big cod after a lure.'

Saturday introduced itself with a blood red sky. Sean looked out the window of his bedroom window. The dawn light was pink, the back shed effervescent, its edges blushing in the light. He looked at the back of his hand, it was as though he could see through it. Blood vessels stood out like highways. He dressed, washed and went into the kitchen. The air was humid and oppressive, the fire was hard to start. He put the kettle on and went out to the chook house. The chickens were quiet, normally they were out and picking around by now. All over the back yard sugar ants had built mounds. The sky was turning a steely grey blue, but there was not a sign of a cloud or storm. His shirt clung to him, he felt clammy. He collected the eggs while the chickens cowered in a corner. He spoke to them reassuringly.

'Come on girls, it's time to get moving.'

He delivered the eggs to the kitchen. He heard his father in the bathroom. Out the kitchen window he saw Robby Watson, the paper boy, go past on his bike. He must ask his dad if he could deliver papers next year. He walked out the door into the front garden. The funny light hit him again, everything seemed to have pink edges. He picked the paper from the fence and took it in and put it on the table. The kettle was nearly boiling. He took his father's coffee gear out. He went to the ice box and got out a knob of smoked bacon. He carved two thick slices and put them aside. Then he cut four slices of bread from the high tin loaf and started to toast them in front of the open fire box. His father came in shaven and dressed.

'Good boy, Sean,' he said cheerily. 'Funny sky out there, must be a storm coming. Red sky at dawn, shepherd be warned and all that, humid too.'

Sean buttered the toast with thick swathes and put them on top of the stove.

'You want to fry the eggs and bacon, Sean?'

'Yeh, sure, chooks are acting funny, dad.'

'The Harringtons lost all their chickens the other night to a fox.

Took one and bit the others heads off for fun. What you doing today, Sean?'

'I have to weed under the fruit trees and clean the outhouse, then my room. I thought I might go and see what Johnny is up to.'

'Can you collect the rubbish? I'm going to clean the gutters. Put the leaves and rubbish on the compost heap, will ya?'

'No worries, dad.' Sean put the toast on plates and arranged the bacon and eggs on top. 'Eggs are up.' They settled at the table.

'Bloody good eggs,' his father said. 'Sad day today. That bastard Meadows is gonna cut the ribbon down at Joseph's place and the ibis rookery.' Sean bowed his head. 'Bloody strange looking day, alright, better get them gutters cleaned out before it rains. No news on Joseph?'

Sean blinked his eyes misty. 'No.'

'I don't blame him for staying away, you'll keep out of trouble, won't you?' His dad peered at him over his cup. Then he slammed it on the table, spilling its contents.

'It's so bloody short sighted, how'd they like it if I put a bulldozer through St Mary's? I feel like bloody throttling some of the bastards around here.'

Churinga's Roar

Sean made his way down the highway, past the Dingarra stump and onto the track. It was unusually quiet, the birds he normally encountered, swallows, ducks, honey eaters, were missing. He strode on through the grass and reeds, a snake slithered away just feet from where he trod, he froze. A bloody King Brown! Bloody better be careful. He noted the bats hanging in their trees; he looked up at them and shook his head.

He moved on cautiously, the bomber lay there glowing and beautiful. Beyond it the river ran slick and smooth, in the sullen stillness, which clung to him like a heavy coat.

'What took ya so long?' Johnny stepped out from behind the bomber, Berty behind him.

Berty blurted out, 'Hey Sean.'

Sean looked at them. 'Thanks for coming fellas.'

Johnny and Berty fell in behind Sean as he walked on. They stopped in the bush just before Joseph's place. They looked at the hut, lonely and squat, shimmering in the strange light. The boys made their way into the clearing, warily checking out the surrounds, moving quietly, stealthily.

The boys set up, taking their churingas out of their pockets. Sean unwrapping his from its kangaroo pouch, Johnny from its oil skin.

'Give it a good go Johnny, for Joseph.'

Johnny smiled back. 'Yeh no worries Sean,' then he laughed. 'Berty make sure no one comes along, keep watch, thanks mate.'

They swung the churingas into life, building up momentum, letting out string. The churingas began to hum, then suddenly they burst into life with a deep throaty roar covering them in sound. The boys put everything they had into it.

Sean began to chant.

'Tamba Tamba nindah yallambee,
Bindaree, Bindaree kodkuna nindah,
Booula naweenda angk barloona.'

On and on the two churingas flew. The air vibrating and the bush mesmerised by the sound.

'Tamba Tamba nindah yallambee,
Bindaree, Bindaree kodkuna nindah,
Booula naweenda angk barloona.'

Sean saw the past year flash by: The school, Sister Hildegard, football, the Smythes, the fight, the Campbells, Beak, Koonarook, Johnny, Berty, Sister Rose, Mary Addison, Caladonia, The King Brown hissed, the eagle flew high over the Bora Bora trees and the river where his Totem the Ponde exploded though the shallows... the dreaming went through him and around him.

Then his dad, mum and Katy were there. His love for them and their love for him overwhelmed him. The Churinga flew harder. Then Joseph came, smiling. The Tamba flew and Dingaree struck. Joseph and the Tamba faded away. Julungul the serpent emerged from his cave.

'Tamba Tamba nindah yallambee,
Bindaree, Bindaree kodkuna nindah,
Booula naweenda angk barloona.'

Then it was still. He felt rather then heard Johnny stopping his churinga. A great peace come over him, a calmness and quietness that invaded his dreaming and being, it felt good. He opened his eyes, the boys were looking at him intently.

'Thanks fellas, that's the best. Joseph and this place have had a great send off.'

He went over and shook each of their hands, clapping them on the shoulders. They laughed.

'Let's go and see what's happening at the mill, it starts in a little while. Might as well eat Campbell's food while we can, it's the only thing he'll be handing out for free.'

Frank Meadows' Speech

The mill's rear fence had been taken down and tarp pavilions set up. Women were handing out tea, coffee, soft drinks, cakes and sandwiches, there was a large gathering. A big plan of the development was pinned to a board. The ladies were dressed in their summer frocks, colourful, bright and light. The men were mostly in belted trousers and white shirts, the sleeves rolled up.

The central attraction was two huge bulldozers that had been brought in on low loaders from Morang. Sean had never seen machinery as big as these monsters. International Harvesters, orange and black. Their blades, huge and curved, were already cutting into the grey river soil as they rested, one behind the other, in the clearing just before the track to Joseph's hut. Beyond them, across the track, a red ribbon was strung between two saplings. The two drivers were busy answering queries about the bulldozers from the locals and keeping the kids off. Their blue singlets and shorts contrasted with the Sunday best of the locals.

Sean was downing a glass of lemonade, when Sergeant Maloney sidled up to him.

'G'day Sean.'

'Hello Sergeant Malone'

'Sean, you blokes play the bull roarers before?' The big policeman inclined his head to where Johnny and Berty were loading up on cakes at another pavilion.

'Yes Sergeant.'

Shorty Malone looked over the crowd. I was here setting up, nice it was young fella. Sean nodded waiting for the punch line.

'You down at Joseph's place?'

'Yes Sir, we were saying goodbye with the bullroarers, he made them'.

'Mmm, so you haven't seen him then?'

'No, Sergeant Maloney" The policeman nodded and looked over the crowd again. Sean continued.

'I do not think we will see him again, he cannot live anywhere but here.'

The Policeman looked at Sean intently, took off his hat, wiping the sweat off his brow with a service handkerchief, then inside the hat band.

'Yeh I think your right young fella, I think your right. Bloody shame the whole business. Take care of yourself and pass on my regards to your dad and mum.'

'Yes, thank you Mr Maloney I will, thank you.' The policeman smiled, and turned to move away, but then turned back.

'That child welfare fellow, Mr Flynn, you will not be hearing from him anymore. All a misunderstanding I am led to believe.' He smiled again, put his hat on and moved off through the crowd working, his way through them to the lectern, the mill workers had constructed earlier.

Frank Meadows adjusted his tie, and mounted the lectern, pulling out some notes. He looked out over the crowd, and then signalled to one of the dozer drivers. The driver climbed into his rig. A large honking sound came out of the beast, the crowd turned, silenced.

Frank Meadows looked over the crowd. Most of Koonarook and

the surrounding district were crowding around. From Sean's vantage point at the lemonade stand, he could see the satisfied smile on his face. Dad had said next year's election was looking good for Fred Meadows, with the new development and expansion of the mill. Yes, it was a winner for the mayor alright, his dad had said.

Frank Meadows began. 'Friends, ladies and gentlemen, please step forward. A few words before we set this great project in motion.' The crowd edged around and up to the speaker. He cleared his throat.

'Distinguished guests, fellow councillors, ladies and gentlemen, it is with great pleasure that I...'

Suddenly there was a scream, a woman's scream penetrating, piercing and filled with terror.

'Ah, Ah...A snake, a snake!'

The crowd gave out a collective gasp. Instinctively families moved closer together, children huddled and mothers looked for young ones.

Then Sean saw the big policeman moving beside the lectern, clearing a path through the throng. His movement seemed to have Moses intensity. Several men were drawn in behind him. Sean was drawn forward too, and made his way through the stilled crowd.

A bulldozer driver was writhing in agony on the beaten ground, clutching at his exposed thigh. His blue singlet was grey, coated by fine river dust. His face was a mask of agony, deadly white and sweat stained. He groaned and flecks of foam were at his lips.

'Mulga, Mulga' he cried.

Shorty Maloney tried to restrain him.

'Ando, Chrissy, Fergy!' he yelled. 'Give me a hand here.'

'Spike grab the first aid kit from the mill shed. Longy run and get Bill, tell him we've got a snake bite. Probably King Brown.'

He took of his belt and applied a tourniquet. As the man was held down someone produced a water bag, he doused the wound area. Then he wrapped the leg downwards in a spiral bandage from the first aid kit, splinting it against the good leg.

All the while the crowd watched in fascination, largely silent. The bulldozer driver, became calmer, not requiring restraining as he slipped out of consciousness. Sean had been joined at the front of the crowd by Berty and Johnny, they watched in awe as the policeman and helpers went about their business.

After the man had been taken away by Bill O'Grady and a team on a stretcher to the waiting ambulance. The boys retreated to the lemonade stand moving through the subdued, hesitant and diminishing crowd easily.

'Bloody hell, he got a good one, that's for sure!' exclaimed Johnny.

'A Mulga-King Brown. He'll be lucky to get out of it alive,' whispered Berty.

Sean nodded, looking up and over to where the policeman had just come off a fruitless search in the surrounding bush with a few blokes. He was conferring with Frank Meadows. He turned back to his mates.

'Yeh sure is strange, I saw one this morning before we sounded the bullroarers, they reckon they stay away from people if they can.'

They nodded and downed another glass of lemonade.

'Bloody hot,' Johnny muttered.

Frank Meadows was mounting the lectern again. He rapped it with a stick, the crowd turned in his direction. The air was thick the clouds were billowing up into mountainous mounds filling the whole northern sky.

'Ladies and Gentlemen without further ado, and with hopes for a full recovery for Mr Garnish. I will open this wonderful project...'

Suddenly the raucous braying of Ibis filled the air and the sky was full of circling, wheeling loud aggressive birds. Around and around they flew big white and majestic, swirling and then swooping down over the swamp.

All stopped, looking skywards, except the mayor who head was bowed, his head shaking. Some were standing mute like statues perplexed by this sudden happening. The birds kept up an incessant raucous baying and came down hard, just above the heads of the crowd. Sean looked up in wonder and joy as the big birds did their routine. It reminded him of Joseph, the bora boras trees and the sacred rookery. After a short while the birds started to settle into the middle of the swamp.

Sean's reverie was stopped by big drops of rain hitting his head, arms and legs as hard as hail. The sky was black and ominous. People were cowering under the pavilions, the great bulldozers, abandoned. Great peels of thunder rent the air almost knocking him over, the earth shook, lightning split and broke the sky. The land took on a luminescent glow. Sean looked up at the onrushing storm.

'Ah Dingarra, Dingarra and Ulwai, ngai, mina, ngune! Dingarra, Dingarra and Ulwai, ngai, mina, ngune!'

He cried then he turned to his mates cowering under the lemonade marquee. Time to go fellas, time to go home, they laughed and ran out into the storm with him.

At home his dad was waiting for him on the back porch.

'Sean I was getting worried, this storm is a beauty, just like when you were hit that night. I was just about to drive out and get you.' He put his arms protectively around Sean's shoulders.

'You betta get changed out of those wet clothes.'

'Thanks dad.' Sean gave his dad a brief rundown on the day's events as he changed.

His dad pondered on Sean's story for a moment.

'Bloody good news about The Child Welfare thing, that was all bullshit anyway. Bad luck about that bloke getting bitten, a Mulga a

King Brown you say?'

'Yeh that's what Shorty said, dad'

'He would know, bloody unusual though. The opening day is cursed that's for sure. Oh by the way that reminds me. Mr Campbell is home and seems to be on the mend they say he had been very unwell but started to improve a week or so ago. About the time Joseph left.'

Sean nodded looking wistful. His dad gave him a thoughtful look. At that moment His mother came down the passage, took one look at him and said.

'Straight into the bath young fella.'

Murray River Dreaming

The next day Sean woke early, he lay in his bed looking out his window into the pale grey of dawn. Yhi had not arisen Bahloo was slipping away. They would only glimpse each other today. I wonder when they will be together? He sat up Endota Quarra! Enndota Quarra was there, shining brightly, their light shone into him. The lovers were strong today. Suddenly he was carried away and high above. Joseph and he stood in the sky looking down on this wonderful land. The mighty Murray-Warde Yallock flowed where Julungull had snaked his way across the great plains and bushlands. The Ibis soared high flying in great arcs, seeming to greet him. He knew then that Joseph would always be with him. All that he had learnt and been taught would stay with him and be a part of him, giving him strength. The desolation dreaming would not be back, he knew that then. The great Ponde in the river, his totem would be his strength and guide. Like him he would be strong against all the things that came against him. He would always love this place, this strange and wonderful place. Joseph had shown him how to be a part of it, and now he was, for always. The lightning crashed through him. Joseph faded and was gone, Sean was back on his bed. He could hear his father's morning noises. He rose, changed and ran out to do his chores.

Over brekkie his dad said, 'Sean do you want to check Joseph's stuff and repack properly? I am going to store it in the ceiling, it is dry up there. Shorty said to keep it here until he can find next of kin or anyone who may claim it.'

Sean sat in the shed beside the tea box, sorting and repacking. Suddenly the breast plate looked up at him- King Joseph. He paused looking at it wondering at its beauty and what it meant. Was the time of the Bindaree Tamba Tamba over? He hoped not, but times were changing. For good or bad who knew. But he was stronger now, Joseph had made him so. He picked up the breast plate shining it with a cloth, wrapping it in an oil cloth. Keeping it safe for those who would need it in the future. He came upon the little jar of Beewee fat. He smiled and opened the lid. The aroma of Beewee and the memories of the day out finding the Beewee nest overtook him. He remembered Joseph's words:

'He never stop till he be finished, he never make big noise or maken any fuss, he just do the job.'

He smiled at the memory that's how he would be. He felt his Dingarra scar twinge. Undoing his shirt he massaged some of the fat into it. It felt better; the scar would always be with him. He knew in his heart that Joseph was gone. The Bora Bora penny swung free he rubbed it reflectively. He heard Joseph in the sacred Ibis grove.

'You gonna be mighty big fella I think maybe, by the size of that Bora Bora circle you carved,'

I will be my best for you Joseph. I will try and be a good Ponde-Wundara for you Joseph and Dingarra. I will never forget you. He buttoned his shirt, packed and closed the tea case carefully and went inside.

Postscript

Two days later Sean walked along the highway. He stopped by the Dingarra Stump, it leaned on a crazy angle, nearly horizontal to the ground. He bent down looking into the hollow. Tears welled into his eyes, standing up he looked over at the river. He could see it now, sullen and grey in the oppressive humid heat. The bush and the swamp were gone, piled into great smouldering heaps. The swamp was a smooth contour sweeping down to the river. The two monster bulldozers were going backwards and forwards crushing, ripping, and tearing. Mr Garnish was recovering in hospital and another fella had come up from Morang his dad had told him. An army of men were using axes, picks and shovels. The bomber was lying where it had been pushed, crumpled and flattened, by the water's edge. Tip trucks were lining up to take away the debris. A low loader was unloading a scoop; a flat barge on the river was winching up grave yard skeletons. Not a tree, bush or blade of grass was standing. Josephs hut was gone, it was as though it had never existed. Mill workers were extending the fences out to where it had stood. There was nothing left, nothing. Sean shook his head and walked home.

Notes

- In 1956 the year after this story is set, the Murray River system recorded its highest ever and most disastrous flood in recorded European settlement history.
- The Murray River system recently experienced its severest drought in recorded history. Prompting a series of reviews by government and authorities.
- The River Murray is regulated by weirs and locks and the normal flow has been reversed – flowing high in summer, low in winter – to support irrigation and towns.
- The Murray River system is now regarded by many experts and leading authorities to be a system in crisis. Over-allocation of water, deforestation, farming practices and population pressures has had very significant impacts.
- Indigenous Australians have, since the Mabo case in 1988, been able to lay claim to native title over places they have been associated with or to which they make special claim.
- The slang and wording in some parts of this story is racist (Blackman, Abo, etc). No offence is intended, but it reflects the speech of the day.
- The Bindaree Tamba Tamba people in this story are completely imaginary. If people want to read or find out more

on the Victorian Aboriginals they should read a book such as *Aboriginal Victorians: A History since 1800* by Richard Broome (Allen & Unwin, Sydney, 2005).

- The Indigenous language in this novel is manufactured. However, it is amalgam of real Indigenous words from a fantastic book by A.W. Reed, *Aboriginal Words of Australia* (Reed Books Pty Ltd, Sydney, 1991).
- All events and persons in this novel are fictional; any resemblance to persons living or dead is not intended.
- The Aboriginal Dreaming stories in this story are fictional and the creation of the author.
- Aboriginal law is complex and varied – only the initiated have the right to full knowledge of the law. Law in this story is the work of the author and is shown as through the eyes of a child (Sean).
- The Second Seventh Battalion (mud on blood) was a very real Second World War battalion of mostly Victorian country fellows (including the author's father). It was a part of the famous Sixth Division and the Anzac Corps of the Second World War (The Forgotten Anzacs).
- Hetra akameri Dingarra worlba Itterra Yelga = get going you dogs Dingarra will get you.
- Illa booker mer ley urrie urrie = the soul will not die.
- Nooralie Nooralie kulpernatoma, kulpernatoma = Nooralie I speak to you.
- Dingarra onom kalian en el our = Dingarra you must be here.
- Tamba Tamba nindah yallambee, Bindaree, Bindaree kodkuna nindah, Booula naweenda angk barloona = Tamba Tamba you stay, Bindaree will protect you, it be a good day to die.
- Maiyarare, Maiyarare, Dingarra, taiyin angk guana, Ah, ngune tumbetin Bindaree wal wal = grandchild, grandchild Dingarra

send you to me, you save Bindaree place.

- Tamba Tamba, Ah, adloo tumbetin Bindaree wal wal = Tamba, Tamba we save Bindaree place.
- Dingarra Dingarra, Ulwai, ngai, mina, ngune = Dingarra, and Grandfather, I see you.

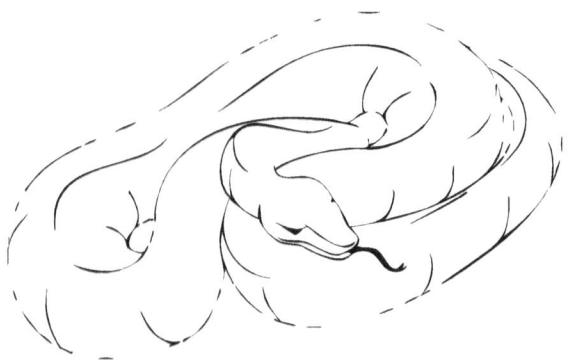

About the Author

John Condliffe 1952–

John Condliffe is a fourth-generation Australian of English and Irish Stock. He was born in Echuca on the Murray River and spent the first part of his life in the riverland and then Bendigo in Central Victoria. John has had a multi-faceted life and career with stints as a paper boy, milk bar attendant, sheet metal worker, lay missionary in an Aboriginal hostel, soldier, medic, nurse, handyman, manager owner of his own business and radiographer. John's interests include family, music, community work, writing, gardening, cooking, camping and fly-fishing. He lives in Kyneton Victoria with his wife Maureen; nearby live his four daughters, their partners and seven grandchildren.

Read about the writing of this book at the blog: *Diary of a Failed Author* (www.kissofthekingbrown.blogspot.com).

www.ingramcontent.com/pod-product-compliance
Lightning Source LLC
Chambersburg PA
CBHW032144010726
47494CB00002B/348